Praise for *My Champion*

"Ms. Campbell's debut novel propels readers into the four-teenth century with vivid descriptions and details of the life of the commoner. The nonstop action, strong plot, and fascinating characters draw you deeply into the story. As the first in a trilogy about the de Ware brothers, *My Champion* will have readers clamoring for more."

—*Romantic Times*

"Well-written, with a fine sense of detail, *My Champion* is a sexy, lighthearted romp of a story."

—Rexanne Becnel

"*My Champion* is a breathtaking story!"

—Tanya Anne Crosby

Jove Titles by Glynnis Campbell

MY CHAMPION
MY WARRIOR

MY WARRIOR

GLYNNIS CAMPBELL

JOVE BOOKS, NEW YORK

This is a work of fiction. Names, characters, places, and incidents are either the product of the author's imagination or are used fictitiously, and any resemblance to actual persons, living or dead, business establishments, events, or locales is entirely coincidental.

MY WARRIOR

A Jove Book / published by arrangement with
the author

PRINTING HISTORY
Jove edition / October 2001

All rights reserved.
Copyright © 2001 by Glynnis Campbell.
Cover art by One by Two
Cover design by George Long
This book, or parts thereof, may not be
reproduced in any form without permission.
For information address: The Berkley Publishing Group,
a division of Penguin Putnam Inc.,
375 Hudson Street, New York, New York 10014.

Visit our website at
www.penguinputnam.com

ISBN: 0-515-13153-9

A JOVE BOOK®
Jove Books are published by The Berkley Publishing Group,
a division of Penguin Putnam Inc.,
375 Hudson Street, New York, New York 10014.
JOVE and the "J" design
are trademarks belonging to Penguin Putnam Inc.

PRINTED IN THE UNITED STATES OF AMERICA

10   9   8   7   6   5   4   3   2   1

For my father,
who raised me on
King Arthur and Zorro,
Robin Hood and Black Bart,
and taught me how to
buckle a swash

With special thanks to
Helen and Cindy,
my sisters at OCC/RWA,
and women warriors everywhere

prologue

MARCH 1333

HOLDEN DE WARE STRETCHED HIS LONG LEGS OUT TOWARD the dying fire, stared up at the clear night sky salted with brilliant stars, and shook his head sadly. "We've lost him then?"

His half brother Garth nodded from his makeshift seat on a pine stump, gazing silently into his foamy cup of ale.

"Poor Duncan," Holden continued. "'Tis a wretched thing when a man falls to such a foe, to be cut down in his youth before he's—"

"Oh, for the love of . . ." Sir Guy grumbled, spitting onto the coals so they crackled and hissed. "Your brother's not dead. He's only taken himself a wife, for God's sake."

Holden watched as Guy continued to mutter into his black beard before he irritably hied himself off to bed in one of the several pavilions of the encampment, leaving the two brothers alone.

"It's easy for him to make little of it," Holden confided. "He's not a de Ware." He picked up a long stick and poked distractedly at the embers. "A de Ware lives for the feel of a fine blade in his hand, a trusty steed between his legs, and the wind of adventure blowing through his hair."

Garth had his own opinions about that, but said nothing, only sipping from his cup of ale.

"But a wife," Holden said on a heavy sigh.

The brothers sat in silence while an owl hooted from the wood and one of Holden's retinue coughed in his sleep.

"*You* know what I mean, don't you?" Holden said, turning toward his younger brother with new respect. "The holy orders have it aright. You've managed to avoid entanglements of the heart altogether, what with your priestly pursuits. You've stayed chaste and true, and look what you've achieved."

Garth paused with his cup halfway to his lips and looked over at Holden as if questioning that himself.

Holden cuffed him companionably on the shoulder, sloshing ale over the lip of the cup. "Come now, brother. You are indisputably the most learned lad in our father's household. Do you honestly think you could have attained half as much if your heart were enslaved to a woman?"

Garth lowered his cup and dropped his gaze, staring into the glow of the fire. The boy's eyes were uncharacteristically moody tonight, much like their father's.

"Then why am I not content?"

Holden leaned forward in surprise. Garth was a man of few words. When he spoke, it was usually significant. "You are not content?"

Garth frowned, gathering his thoughts. "Not as content as I think I should be."

Holden stroked his chin, rough now with a day's growth of beard. "How so?"

Garth set his cup on the ground and rested his elbows on his spread knees. "There was . . ." He clasped his hands before him as if to pray, a gesture that was habit with him now. "At Duncan's wedding feast, when his bride sat beside him, there was something in his eyes—a light, a calmness, joy, I'm not certain. But it transformed him. And I knew in that moment that no matter how many rousing sermons I delivered, no matter how many psalms I copied or how many souls I shrived, I would never feel that joy."

Holden whistled out a weighty breath. He'd had no idea

Garth felt thus. Garth had always been so solemn, so busy with his studies, so reluctant to join his older brothers in their battle sport. It was as if he had none of the de Warc blood flowing through his veins, as if he were cut of different cloth than Duncan and him, who would sooner strut about without their hose than without their swords. But now, what he was hearing . . .

Holden ran his fingers through his mussed hair and glanced at Garth from the corner of his eye, entertaining a daring possibility. He'd lost Duncan. But perhaps it wasn't too late for his little brother. Perhaps he could rescue him from his saintly doom and introduce him to the heady pleasures of life and freedom and an open road.

"Garth!" he said, clapping the lad on the knee and nearly startling him from his perch. "Travel with me."

"What?"

"Join my retinue. Edward can use another sword arm, if yours hasn't gone to rust." He rubbed his hands together. The more he thought about it, the better it sounded. "Travel on campaign with me. Taste life. See the countryside." He laughed. "Tame wenches and slay dragons."

"But my studies . . ."

"Pah! Do you think they'll add a new book to the Bible while you're away?"

Garth's brow looked troubled, but there was a spark in his eyes now, a spark that wasn't there a moment ago, a spark of hope.

"It's your last chance, lad," Holden coaxed.

Garth chewed his lip in indecision.

"If I don't have your blood coursing and fire in your eye after this campaign," Holden promised, "you can go back home to your books." He stood and extended his right arm toward Garth. "So what do you say, Garth? Aye or nay?"

Garth hesitantly came to his feet. After a long moment, he reluctantly returned the gesture, and they clasped forearms. "Aye."

"Good. I'll teach you everything I know," Holden promised, wrapping an arm around Garth's shoulders as they ambled toward the serge tents. "How to conquer fear, how to inspire loyalty, how to rule men with an iron hand and a just heart, how to seduce wenches, how to lay siege to castles. . . ."

Garth stopped in his tracks and looked dubiously up at Holden.

"Aye, even that," he vowed. "'Tis not so difficult as you'd imagine, lad. The lesser ones are more than willing to surrender. One knock at their barbican and the drawbridge comes winding down. They change masters as often as the moon changes its face, and they're easily won." He gazed dreamily off into the night. "Others are untouchable, flawlessly constructed. They'll never be possessed. Such perfection you must be content to gaze upon from afar." He thumped Garth on the chest. "Nay, the most challenging and most rewarding conquest is the one that puts up a good fight. You win, of course. De Wares always win. But the taste of victory is so much sweeter when . . . what?"

Garth was staring at him as if he were addled in the head. "This is to be my first campaign. I don't think I'll be laying siege to many castles."

"Castles?" Holden said, chuckling. "Who's talking about laying siege to castles?" He hauled Garth off with him toward the pavilions. "I'm speaking of seducing women."

1

A BRINDLED RABBIT SAT UP SUDDENLY ON ITS HAUNCHES, sniffing warily at the cold, crisp air. The sun caressed a leaf here and there, steaming the moisture from the mossy trees. The sparrows had yet to rise, and an owl flew home on soundless wings. For a moment, the irresistible scent of tender, green shoots beckoned from a nearby meadow. But then a faint, unfamiliar odor wafted by. The rabbit froze.

The silence of the morning was broken abruptly by the sharp whisper of an arrow slicing neatly through the mist to embed itself in the damp earth. In a flurry of leaves, the rabbit scampered away into the brake, more startled by the sudden loud oath that rent the air than by the wayward shaft.

"Damn him! Damn that brainless ox of a fletcher!"

The hunter's azure eyes, as bright as a Highland stream, narrowed in disgust as the rabbit made its escape.

The ash longbow, flung in anger, bounced upon the ground, followed by the quiver of ill-fletched arrows that spilled out over well-worn leather boots. In a sweep of russet brown, the hunter's cloak swirled like a storm cloud. The hood fell back, spilling out long chestnut hair burnished red-gold by the early sunlight.

Nearby, Laird Angus Gavin chuckled, his voice both rough and warm, like strong mulled wine. "Temper, lass, temper."

Cambria expelled a foggy puff of air and glared at her father over an indignant shoulder. He was a fine one to talk. She certainly hadn't inherited her temperament from her timid deer of a mother, God rest her soul.

"I told that bloody addlepate to check the balance of the shafts this time before he gave them to me," she fumed, swatting her hair back from her face. "These are utterly *useless!*"

Her father nodded and wrapped a consoling arm around her. "I'll speak to him, lass."

"I'd have skewered that one," she muttered, vengefully kicking over a toadstool.

She knew she was right. Although Malcolm the Steward oft complained about her distasteful penchant for what the old boar referred to as hunting, hawking, and hacking, even *he* had to admit she possessed considerable skill with the longbow. At least till now.

She scooped up the faulty arrows with a swipe of her hand and flung the quiver over her shoulder. 'Twasn't just the unbalanced shafts. And 'twasn't her temper. She'd hardly been able to concentrate on anything since . . .

Laird Gavin took her hands between his own meaty paws and studied her face. " 'Tis the clan troubling you, and this inevitable war," he guessed.

She gazed solemnly into his wise old eyes, and the anger drained out of her. Her father could always sense her worries. In sooth, she swore sometimes he could divine a person's soul.

The trouble had begun a fortnight ago. Her cousin Robbie had been at the heart of it. Robbie, with his mischief-bright blue eyes and the unruly thatch of red hair that made him recognizable clear across the glen. The boy who'd waded with her in summer ponds and battled against her with the wooden swords of childhood, who'd lent her his shoulder to cry on when her mother died a dozen years past. It seemed only days ago that she and Robbie had been laughing over a cutthroat game of chess.

Everything was changed now.

"You're not pining over that upstart cousin, are you?" the laird grumbled.

She poked at the wet carpet of last year's leaves with the toe of her boot. "Robbie was right, you know. We owe a debt to the memory of Robert the Bruce. 'Tis up to us to continue his fight for the Scots cause."

"Faugh!" Laird Gavin barked. "What that young whelp Robbie knows about the Scots cause would fit in a thimble. He'd get himself and half the clan slaughtered, and for what? He has nae home now, nae land, and," he added pointedly, "nae clan."

She tried to ignore the hollow ache in her heart. Damn that fool Robbie. If *she* were laird, she'd forgive him, take him back into the clan, even if her father was too proud to do it. Robbie had only made a stupid mistake, after all, trying to convince her to join their cause, forgetting that her place was beside her father, who put clan before country.

She picked at a ragged fingernail. "The English *are* our enemy," she muttered.

"Aye, at times," he agreed, bending stiffly to retrieve Cambria's bow, "and so are the Highlanders."

'Twas true. The Highlanders generally mistrusted the Border clans like the Gavins, with good cause. Loyalties along the Borders shifted as frequently as the tides of the North Sea, rallying to whomever commanded the superior power.

But there was no question in Cambria's mind who wielded the mightier sword. She'd been raised alongside the great knights of Gavin. Surely there wasn't an Englishman alive who could match her magnificent clan warriors in strength, courage, and loyalty. Scotland would eventually triumph, and a Scots king would occupy the throne.

"There's simply no unity among the clans," Laird Angus said, "and there never will be."

"But Robert the Bruce . . ."

"Tried and failed."

The wind swept out of Cambria's sails. "Will you side against them then—Robbie and Graham and Jamie and all the others? If it comes to war, will you raise your sword against a Gavin?"

"Robbie and the others betrayed their clan," the laird snarled, his eyes trained on the path ahead. "They are nae longer Gavins. They abandoned their home, they abandoned their family . . . for God's sake, they abandoned you, Cambria."

Her chin quivered once before she could clamp it still. He was right, and the sting of that betrayal was yet as painful as a thistle in her heart.

Silently she padded homeward beside her father, along the winding path they'd trod together from the time she'd taken her first steps. Any other day, she would have delighted in the songs of the wakening thrushes and sparrows and breathed deep the pungent fragrance of the towering pines.

But today, all she felt was a tight knot of pain in her chest. The canopy overhead was a green blur. She clenched her hands into tight fists. She wouldn't let her father see her cry, wouldn't let him doubt for a moment that she was strong enough to inherit the lairdship. 'Twas only the bright sunlight, dappling her face, making her eyes water. That was all.

Laird Gavin cleared his throat several times along the way, but she didn't encourage him to speak. She had a feeling she wouldn't like what he intended to say.

At long last he stopped, leisurely uncorking the wineskin at his hip and taking a long pull at it, then staring off into the wood. He offered her a drink, but she waved it away.

"Cambria," he said, stuffing the cork back into the bag, "I am far too old to be fighting battles I have little chance to win. Nae, do not shake your head at me. We both know 'tis true."

She hated it when he spoke this way. He wasn't growing old. He couldn't grow old. He was all she had.

Laird Gavin pressed his thumb into the palm of his hand, rubbing out of habit the stiffness that had plagued him for the past several years. "I don't intend to spend the last moments of my life engaged in war."

She frowned. Wasn't that what every warrior wanted? Surely, these weren't the words of the man who'd taught her to fight, sword, dagger, and fists, with her last breath, for every inch of Gavin land.

The laird continued more vehemently, but he'd not meet

her eyes. "I wish to have grandchildren. I wish to know my family will continue, and I wish for them to live in peace."

She only stared at him, struck dumb. Was the laird becoming soft with the advancing years? Not only did he suggest betrayal of his mother country, but he was hinting rather broadly, again, that he might like Cambria to start a family. She groaned inwardly. 'Twas a point they'd argued interminably.

She was ill-suited to be any man's wife. Everyone knew it. She was the laird's only child, and she'd been raised by her father and Malcolm the Steward to enjoy leadership, trained to inherit the Gavin clan and its responsibilities. There had been no time for courting, even if she'd had any inclination toward it, which she didn't, and even if anyone had shown any interest in her whatsoever, which they hadn't.

'Twasn't that she was uncomely. She'd seen her face often enough in steel mirrors to know that she bore no ugly marks or scars. 'Twas just that the men who knew her looked upon her as the future laird of the Gavin—the land and the people—a woman of power, proud and unbiddable, qualities most undesirable in a wife.

Robbie had understood her best. He'd respected her strengths and her intellect, and he'd shared her fascination with politics. But even he had never regarded her with anything save brotherly affection. The truth be told, Cambria herself rarely glanced twice at a man, except to admire his prowess on the battlefield or to assess his loyalty to the clan.

Aye, her father had brought up marriage in the past, but their altercations had always flared quickly and subsided, like pine needles on the fire. Now as she looked into his suddenly weary eyes, she felt a queer misgiving in the pit of her stomach.

"What is this about, Father?"

He said something foul under his breath, then jutted out his gray-whiskered chin and spoke decisively. "Tomorrow a company of English knights will come to meet with me and our men, seeking my oath of allegiance to Balliol as king of Scotland."

She sucked in her breath. She couldn't have been more

surprised if he'd admitted to possessing two heads. 'Twasn't marriage he was bullying her into after all. 'Twas far worse.

"Balliol?" she whispered in shock. "King Edward's puppet?"

Angus closed his lips firmly in legendary Gavin stubbornness.

"Of course you'll refuse," she said, trying to convince herself that the laird hadn't lost his wits. The twinge in her stomach told her otherwise. "Father?"

The laird wouldn't meet her eyes. The pain increased.

"Father," she bit out, trying to reason calmly with him, "you're tired. Once you've slept on it, had a chance—"

"Cambria," he chided.

Her temper snapped faster than a kindling twig. "But Balliol is not even Scots!"

"He was born in Scotland."

She spat on the ground. "A pig born in a mews does not make it a dove."

"Cambria," he warned.

"Edward thinks to placate the Scots by putting that . . ."

"Cambria."

"That fawning runt of a . . ."

"Cambria!"

"What!"

"Listen to me," he said with an uncharacteristic patience that worried her even more. "Accepting Balliol as king is our only hope to hold onto what lands we have. 'Tis true I have agreed to swear this oath, but only as long as the English guarantee that the Gavin property will remain in our name . . . mine and *yours*," he added, poking her in the chest with a blunt finger. "You know what will happen to those who oppose the English . . . and lose."

"The Gavins will win!"

"The Gavins could not fight them even if we wished it," Laird Gavin muttered. "Our forces have been irreparably diminished because of the deserters."

"They did not . . . d-desert us," she retorted, stumbling over the very words she'd used herself when she found Robbie had gone. "They fight for Scotland now! *You* mean to desert us!"

"Do you nae understand?" The laird reddened and tensed his hands as if he fought the urge to throttle her. "Should battle ensue, we will lose . . . everything—our land, our people, our way of life."

She shook her head. The Gavins were invincible. Malcolm the Steward had said so countless times. "We will not lose, Father," she insisted, placing her palm square on his thick chest. "The Scots army will come to our aid."

"Bah!" he scoffed, shaking off her hand. "They could nae agree on the proper way to extinguish a kitchen fire. Nae, they will not rescue us from the English."

Cambria's ire rose at this insult. " 'Tis because they have no support from the likes of us. That's the only reason they seem . . ."

"Inept?" her father supplied with caustic humor.

She exhaled sharply in frustration. "Father, you ask me to put down my sword in the midst of battle. I cannot do it."

"Cambria," Laird Gavin reasoned, "I know you think to uphold your principles, but *you* should well know the price of recklessness and poor timing. Have you not learned that lesson countless times from my own blade?"

His hand on her shoulder suddenly felt unbearably heavy.

"One way or another," he continued, "England will conquer Scotland and crown whom they will. 'Tis my intent to keep as much as possible of the Gavin clan and property intact. Now is nae the time for battle. The enemy's sword is already at our throat, and the storm is upon us. Now is the time to gather what we'll need to weather it." He squeezed her shoulder, then released her. "I've agreed to meet with one of King Edward's knights, Lord Holden de Ware. 'Tis said he is a just man, one who can be trusted."

"Trusted?" She wheeled away from the laird so he wouldn't see the despair gathering in her eyes. "*No* Englishman can be trusted," she whispered. "Father, we are Scots. How can you do this?"

" 'Tis already done, daughter," he answered harshly. "Lord Holden's men will be here on the morrow. I expect your full cooperation in making our English guests feel welcome."

English guests? The twinge in her stomach blossomed into a full-blown ache. She followed her father in stunned silence over slippery, moss-covered stones, through leaves that might be the last to fall on Scots soil, and thought about the approaching invaders. If the English were indeed already making their way north, then it *was* too late. There was no choice to be made.

How had they come to this pass? In the space of a morning, her entire world had been turned upside down, and life would never be the same again. The wall she'd spent years building against the enemy shuddered dangerously with Laird Gavin's shocking pronouncement.

Cambria knew in her heart she couldn't deny her father anything. The laird came first. 'Twas what had been ingrained in her from the time she was old enough to gurgle out the words. The laird came first. And for the laird, the clan came first. There was no question about it. He was doing what he thought best for the clan.

Aye, she'd stand by him in this decision, which must have been as difficult for him to make as it was for her to accept. But, she decided, kicking a pebble from her path, she'd not go down without a fight.

"I trust they'll not stay overlong," she muttered, frowning at the spongy ground.

"Several knights will no doubt remain to secure the castle."

She sniffed. "Our winter provisions didn't take into account extra guests."

"Then 'tis well the deserters have so kindly left their portions behind," he countered dryly.

"Well," she said, flicking a beetle from her cloak, "I'll not *kneel* to this . . . de Warren. I don't care if he *is* a lord."

"De Ware," he corrected, "Lord Holden de Ware. He's renowned for his swordsmanship and his ferocity. Some call him the Wolf. 'Tis said he's never known defeat in battle."

She bristled at this piece of nonsense. The man had obviously never fought a Scotsman.

They stopped on the grassy mound before Castle Black-haugh, the ancient seat of the Gavin clan, and stood for a moment, looking up reverently at the worn, blue-gray stones.

"I'll put the matter before the clan in the hall tonight," the laird said. "'Twould ease the way had I your support."

She stiffened.

"I know 'tis a difficult thing I ask of you," he said, "but please, for the sake of the Gavin, for the sake of your dear departed mother, and for an old man's dreams, make no trouble for this English lord. He will be our only defender, and I've faith he'll defend us well."

She couldn't help but wonder who would defend them against *him*, but she swallowed her pride and the urge to rail against the powerlessness that gripped her.

"It seems I have lodging arrangements to attend to for our English . . . guests," she bit out.

Laird Gavin kissed her on the forehead. Then she turned and fled toward the gates of Blackhaugh.

Katie, the steward's wife, turned into the kitchen and gasped at the chaos before her.

Fine white flour dusted everything like the first light snow of winter—the flagstone floor, the iron pot swinging perilously on its hook over the fire, even the quivering black beard of the enraged cook. Broken bits of crockery littered the tables, and an ugly brown substance oozed down one wall where it had splattered.

Cambria Gavin paced through the midst of the maelstrom, sending up tiny clouds of flour. She barked out demands to the cowering scullion lads, her stormy eyes flashing in an ill temper. Then she cornered the cook, haranguing the man with impossible requests. When the cook's hand began to tighten around the handle of the enormous knife he held, Katie decided 'twas time to step in. She took her charge's elbow and tugged her out of range.

"Come, lass," she soothed, clucking her tongue. "'Tis too small a space for battle. Besides, it's as hot as Hades in here." She lifted the corner of her surcoat and dabbed at the dusting of flour across Cambria's nose.

Katie supposed she was as near a mother to Cambria as anyone. She knew the lass's quicksilver moods and the volatile temper that could be the dread of many a servant. But she'd also seen the girl cry when she thought no one was watching, sobbing soundlessly into her sleeve as if her heart would break.

"What does he mean, he can't make more cheese for tomorrow?" Cambria demanded, scowling at the cook.

"Lass," Katie tried to explain gently, steering her away from the red-faced man, "cheese must be aged."

"Will it be ready the following day?"

"No, lass."

"How old must it be?" Cambria ground out.

"It won't be ready till winter, milady." She chuckled.

Katie wondered at times what Cambria would do without her. For all her ability to read and write, to wield sword and longbow, the lass was useless when it came to household affairs. Cambria had once told her that preparing the household for guests was more painful for her than taking a lance blow in the stomach.

If the present state of the castle were proof, Katie could well believe it. More than a dozen pallets had had to be tossed out, having become a haven for rats and fleas, and they lay like dead cattle in the courtyard. Chambers unused for weeks had proved a nightmare of cobwebs. Fresh rushes had been mistakenly spread atop the old in the great hall, and so all had to be swept out. Cambria had completely tangled the needlework crest she'd meant to repair on her father's finest tabard and, in a fit of anger, had run her dagger through the cloth. Consequently, the poor white hawk of the Gavin appeared to have been mortally wounded. Already this morning the cook looked ready to spit and roast his young mistress.

Katie sighed. She'd be up half the night repairing the fruits of Cambria's labor. And now the lass was glaring coldly at her, as if she were to blame for the physical properties of cheese.

Her look was wasted. Katie never let Cambria's nasty

temper bother her. The lass's rages usually blew over quicker than an April storm.

Tucking Cambria into a relatively safe corner of the kitchen, she bubbled merrily about, shooing some of the grateful scullery lads out.

"Milady," she sang, dipping a huge wooden spoon into a pot of thick stock, "there's no shortage of good food. We've fowl and hare aplenty and even fresh trout today."

"I see no reason to deplete our stores of meat for visitors when pottage and cheese will do," Cambria snapped.

Katie laughed and blew on the spoonful of broth. "Why, lass, what grudge would you be holdin' against visitors? Your father wishes to show 'em every courtesy. Pottage and cheese indeed!" She ignored Cambria's scowl and sipped at the spoon.

"Mm, you've outdone yourself, Hamish," she crooned.

The cook grunted, pacified for the moment.

Katie glanced at Cambria. The poor girl's fingers were worrying her surcoat to rags. She'd never seen her quite so distraught.

All at once, the reason thumped her on the head like an iron pot.

"You know, your father is bein' all mysterious about these visitors," she confided. "Is it possible, do you think, he's arranged a match for you?"

All the color drained from Cambria's face. Horror shadowed her eyes. "Not that," she choked out. "Never that."

Then Cambria fled, leaving behind the relieved cook, a handful of bewildered kitchen-boys, and one foolish old woman who wrung her hands, wishing she could take back her careless words.

Cambria pulled at the neck of her dark madder surcoat. The heavy wool was stifling in the crowded great hall. The greasy smell of the mutton stew congealing in its doughy trencher turned her stomach, and so she only picked at it, which left plenty for Malcolm the Steward, who was more than willing to eat the better part of the meal they shared. The familiar sounds and smells of supper had taken on a sharper cast somehow, making her strangely sensitive to every taste, every word, almost as if 'twere her last meal.

Her father spoke quietly with Malcolm about the size of the brook trout. Two ladies further down the table discussed remedies for aches of the head. The chatter at the lower tables was raucous and indiscernible. Hounds growled at her father's feet as he tossed them bones to gnaw on. The pungent smells of robust wine, onions, peppery mutton, and mustard assailed her nostrils.

Today, Cambria felt the hard, worn oak bench beneath the cushion, smelled the delicate meadowsweet strewn among the rushes, heard every smack of lips, every swallow of wine. Her nerves stretched taut in anticipation. Each dagger that clattered on the wooden table made her flinch. As she let her gaze wander around the room, she wondered how many enemies her father was about to make.

Finally, rising and banging on his pewter cup with the haft of his knife, the laird commanded the attention of all within the great hall.

The sudden silence was deafening to Cambria's ears. Her heart thumped in her throat. It seemed as if all the faded shields of the conquered, hung along the length of the hall, were somehow watching her. She prayed for the strength to lend convincing support to her father.

"We are all Gavins," he began, his voice as strong and comforting as honey mead on a winter night, "those of you sprung from the loins of the clan and those of you who've chosen to abide within these walls, under the clan's protection. There is nothing"—he banged his fist on the table for emphasis, and Cambria's heart leaped into her throat—"nothing more important than the survival of the clan and its claim to this land."

A few isolated cheers arose at his words, but most waited breathlessly for the crux of his speech.

"I'm a man of little politic. I freely admit I care not who is by rights the king, only that he who rules is just and fair."

"And distant!" someone cried out.

Chuckles circled the room. The laird smiled. Then he held up his hand for quiet.

"War is imminent between Scotland and England. Those of us in the Borders must choose who we will support." He cleared his throat and stroked his grizzled chin. "A fortnight ago we lost many fine lads to a battle cry their foolish hearts could not resist. They chose their lot. I bear them no ill will."

Cambria knew otherwise, but was silent.

"I have chosen as well," he continued, resting his fingertips on the table before him. "I have done so not from the leanings of my heart, but from the dictates of my head." He paused a long while, studying the faces of every clan member. "I've chosen to ally with the English and Balliol."

A collective gasp filled the hall, and a low rumbling of exchanges began, which seemed to Cambria like the thunder before a summer storm. The laird needed her now. Glancing nervously about, she rose on quaking legs, acknowledging her father with a formal nod.

"Good folk," she began tentatively.

No one heard her.

"Good folk!" she bellowed, the sound this time like a chapel bell ringing in a garderobe. The murmuring ceased instantly. Cambria folded her hands before her and tried not to fidget. "Like most of you, I do not wish to see Balliol take the throne."

Several people nodded in agreement, and she continued in a surer tone. "But neither do I wish to see our clan destroyed and our land divided. The English . . . will win," she bit out painfully. "They have greater strength and number, and they have unity, which the Scots have not. Because of the . . . deserters, our own forces have been diminished. We do not have the option of resistance. They are already upon us, and there is no Scots army to deliver us from siege."

The voices rose again, some contemplative, some indignant.

"Our only hope," the laird added, his eyes glowing with pride as he glanced at Cambria, "is to ally with the English. But on our terms. I've agreed to the alliance only on the contingency that our holdings remain in the name of the Gavin." He paused and winked at Cambria. "And they've accepted my demand. They wish only to use our fortress and our knights. When they've quelled the rebellion, they will go home." He added with a grin, "They will have to go home. Their lily-white English skin could not endure our winter."

Everyone in the hall chuckled at his jest. Even Cambria felt the tension ease as a grin stole across her face. She stared in wonder at the twinkle-eyed, gruff-voiced bear of a man who willingly bore the weight of his clan's troubles on his sturdy shoulders. She was truly proud of her father, and the light that shone back from his eyes proved that he felt the same way about her. Her vision grew watery, and joy swelled her heart. Suddenly inspired, she raised her goblet.

"To the Gavin!" she cheered, and all about her lifted their cups. "May the clan forever endure, and may it be the fault of the English that we do so!"

Good humor rang out in the hall long into the night. 'Twas with relief and hope that Cambria ascended the winding steps to her chamber much later to go to bed. She snuggled under the furs to sleep soundly by the crackling fire Katie had laid, alas too soundly to prevent the tragedy that lurked but a few dark hours hence.

2

SIR ROGER FITZROI MASSAGED THE STUBBLE ON HIS CHEEK AS he squinted through the pines toward the distant slumbering castle. He'd not slept well, unlike the other knights of his company, who snored comfortably on the sod around him in the chill light before dawn. His bitterness toward his new overlord, Holden de Ware, festered like an untended wound.

King Edward had turned his favor not upon Roger, but upon the Wolf, despite the fact that, for all purposes, Roger was the king's own uncle. Once again the king had ignored the blood tie, slighting his grandsire's bastard and giving Holden de Ware command over the forces in the north. Then he'd let the Wolf lay siege to the best, most formidable keep, granting him lordship of it.

The siege on Castle Bowden, if one could rightly call it that, had lasted no more than three days, and the newly made Lord Holden de Ware settled into his grand accommodations with relative ease. It had been with great zeal, then, that Roger embraced the opportunity to claim his own similar victory at nearby Castle Blackhaugh.

That was until he learned there was a special provision for this keep. Apparently, the Border laird had willingly agreed to its use by the English and pledged to sign support for Balliol so long as the castle and its property remained in its present owner's name. And that damned Holden de Ware had approved the conditions.

He spit on the ground in disgust at this ridiculous coddling of the enemy. Roger would sooner sell his own mother as a whore than let a Scotsman hold property while he remained landless. Curse the Wolf! Edward had promised the victors the spoils. He'd be damned if he'd be cheated of his.

Suddenly eager for the fight in spite of the early hour, he nudged his half brothers with his boot.

"Hugh. Owen. Arise," he grunted, ignoring their drowsy protests. "We go to take a castle."

The great hall of Blackhaugh had likely never seen so impressive a display of knights, Roger thought with satisfaction as he slowly removed his gauntlets. Nearly twoscore of them strutted in full mail with tabards in a rainbow of colors and proud English crests. Even his own, branded with the bar sinister that proclaimed him bastard, was finer than any of the threadbare rags he saw on the Border knights.

Servants only recently jostled awake rushed hither and thither, lighting wall sconces, heating porridge, trying in vain to keep the knights' tankards filled. Though he towered above them all like a golden god, it amused him to play at humility. He graciously accepted the silver chalice of ale his host, Laird Angus Gavin, pressed into his hands.

Pushing back his steel coif, Roger tipped back the brew and sipped politely when he would have preferred to guzzle. He was playing the role of Holden de Ware's reluctant mediator to perfection, and he knew it. But a small flaw to his plans niggled at the back of his mind.

Roger had been misinformed about the number of knights in residence at Blackhaugh. He'd asked three different maidservants if all their men were present, and they'd told him aye, but the dearth of defenders still disturbed him. His entire plan, after all, hinged on his ability to make it look as if the Scots had put up a fight. Their lack of armed men would almost certainly cast a shadow on his credibility.

Hugh and Owen were being difficult, as usual. Roger wished he didn't have to bring his stupid brothers with him everywhere he went. But their mother would have it no other way. One did as one was told, or the royal stipend would be cut off. Roger grimaced, praying they'd keep their mouths shut and let him handle things his own way.

Impatient to begin, Roger shoved his empty cup into Owen's hands.

"Laird Gavin," he announced, "my brothers and I . . ."

The laird looked dubiously back and forth between the three men. Roger was used to that. The three brothers looked no more similar than whelps born of a promiscuous bitch, and so they were. Owen was small and dark like their mother. Hugh was tall and thin, with stringy blond hair. Only Roger could boast the stature and golden good looks of his noble sire.

"My brothers and I would prefer to discuss the terms of your surrender privately," he explained with exaggerated courtesy. For what they would say and do he wanted no witnesses.

Laird Angus felt the hairs stiffen at the back of his neck. He didn't like the Englishman's use of the word *surrender.* He glowered at Roger Fitzroi a long while, until the man's smile grew stale. Then he let out a sigh. He supposed a bit of bent pride was a small price to pay for the survival of the clan.

He sent a wordless message to Malcolm the Steward, directing him to keep an eye on the rest of the company, then motioned the brothers toward the adjoining chamber. The door closed behind them with a hollow thud.

He gestured toward the benches at the table in the midst of the room, but the Englishmen remained standing. Fitzroi leaned almost insolently against the door.

It was just as well, Angus decided. The quicker this business was over with, the better. He offered his hand.

"You have the document then?"

Fitzroi patted his chest, then withdrew a piece of parchment, feigning astonishment to find it there. "This?" His brothers snickered. He grinned.

Angus resisted the urge to make that grin toothless. Instead, he thought of the clan and rubbed his hands together. "I'll have to call for a quill and—"

The slow tear of parchment violated the air like lightning. The two halves of the document drifted to the rushes. The grin never left Fitzroi's face.

Misgiving slithered its way up Angus's spine.

"We don't need this," Fitzroi said with a shrug. He nodded once to his dark brother.

There was a flash of silver.

And then it was too late.

Before Angus could draw breath to cry out an alarm, the cold length of a sword burned impossibly deep into his chest.

Then Fitzroi was beside him, clutching the front of his tabard, so close he could see the golden stubble on his chin going in and out of focus, so close he could see the spittle at the corners of the man's mouth.

"De Ware will believe you refused the alliance," Fitzroi bit out, "that your clan met us with swords."

Angus's body was curiously numb, but his mind suffered an agony of hopelessness and disbelief. The English had betrayed him. He had failed his clan. Horrible images assailed him—images of Gavins starving in the hills, of brave knights executed like traitors, of Cambria . . .

"Cam— . . ." he wheezed.

"Blackhaugh will be mine," the devil sneered, "and your precious clan will be no more."

Roger saw his taunts were wasted. The light of life had already flickered and faded in the old man's eyes. He released his grip. The laird slumped to the floor. Roger dusted off his hands.

"Well done, Owen," he said. "Hugh?"

Hugh gingerly reached over the top of the dead body with one skinny arm and wiggled the laird's sword free from its sheath. Then he turned toward Owen. Without warning, he drew the blade viciously across his brother's ribs.

Owen gasped in pain and disbelief, clutching his chest. Blood from the shallow wound dripped between his dark-haired knuckles.

"It has to appear you were provoked, dear brother," Roger explained without a shred of pity.

Hugh sniffed delicately, then shrugged his bony shoulders. He tossed the sword to the floor, dappling the rushes with flecks of Owen's blood.

Roger watched, amused, as Owen glared at Hugh through the oily brown strands of his hair, like a mangy dog about to turn on its owner. Then Hugh made the mistake of laughing, tittering like a court whore, pushing Owen over the edge.

Roger's eyes glittered as he realized that mayhem was about to take place. He could have stopped it, but there was something fascinating about watching Owen attack their sibling like a rabid mongrel. Owen was the smaller of the two, but he was wiry and stronger than he looked. Even wounded, it was easy for him to bowl over their lance-thin brother.

Perhaps if Roger had noticed the drawn dagger in Owen's hand, he might have stopped the fight. Or perhaps not. But by the time he saw the candlelight reflected dully in the steel blade, it was too late.

Hugh was pinned through the heart, his heels drumming on the stone floor like the erratic beating of a moth's wings.

After Hugh gurgled out his last feeble words, Owen viciously wrenched the dagger free and dropped it to the floor. Then he looked up, wiping his sleeve across his mouth.

Roger narrowed his eyes at his little murdering brother. Even *he* wasn't certain if the smile he gave Owen was one of disbelief or approval.

But time was a-wasting. With a nod of mutual understanding, he and Owen put their shoulders to the heavy oak table and heaved it over with a loud thud. Then, hauling open the door, Roger called his startled knights to arms.

Cambria saw her father in the dream, walking toward her with his arms outstretched. She smiled as he crossed the sunny meadow toward her. But suddenly a great gray wolf appeared between them, its paws massive, its eyes penetrating. The beast opened his jaws in a mournful howl, and a great black shadow fell across the laird.

She woke with a scream stuck in her throat. Her heart

raced like a sparrow's as she tried to break the threads of the
nightmare. She rested her damp head in trembling hands.
They came more frequently now, the dreams that haunted her
sleep, that seemed to show her a glimpse of the future. This
one was a warning, she was certain. The Wolf boded ill for
her father.

Shaken, she rose on wobbly legs, dragging the fur coverlet with her, and peered out the window. Damn! The sun was
in the sky already. Katie had let her oversleep, probably out
of kindness—Cambria had been up past midnight polishing
armor—but she couldn't afford to be late, not today. She let
out a string of curses and tossed the fur back onto the pallet.

A loud crash echoed through the stone corridors and
shook the oak floor, bringing her instantly alert.

The clan! she thought at once.

The shouting of unfamiliar voices rumbled up from be-
lowstairs, and then she heard the frenzied barking of the
hounds. Her heart began to pound in her chest like an armorer's mallet. She scrambled over the bed, snatching her
broadsword from the wall. With frantic haste, she struggled
into her shift, cursing as her tangled hair caught in the sleeve.
The crash of hurled crockery and women's terrified shrieks
pierced the air as Cambria finally pulled open her chamber
door and rushed out.

She was fairly flying down the long hallway when she
heard the unmistakable clang of blades colliding. She hurtled
forward, descending the spiraling steps that opened onto the
gallery above the great hall.

At the top of the landing, she froze.

The scene before her took shape as a series of gruesome
paintings, none of which she could connect to make any
sense: brightly colored tabards flecked with gore; servants
huddled in the corners, sobbing and holding each other in terror; hounds yapping and scrambling on the rush-covered
stone floor; lifeless, twisted bodies of Gavin knights
sprawled in puddles of their own blood; Malcolm and the rest
of the men chained together like animals. For a moment, a
numbing cold seemed to enclose her heart like a great helm
warding off the attack of a blade.

But as her eyes moved from the overturned trestle tables to the slaughtered knights and cowering servants, trying to make reason out of the confusion before her, that armor shattered into a million fragments.

The laird. Where was the laird?

Panic began to clutch at her with desperate claws. She shifted her death grip on the pommel of her sword, her eyes frantically seeking out her father. If she could only find him, she thought, everything would be all right. The laird would explain everything. He always took care of the clan.

She ran trembling fingers over her lips. Dear God, where was the laird?

As if she'd willed it, two lads came forth from the side chamber, struggling with the weight of the grisly burden they carried between them.

Dear God, no! Cambria silently screamed as she recognized the tabard of her father. Not the laird!

Even as her heart clenched in her breast, she dared to hope he yet lived. But his body was limp, drenched with blood, far too much blood, and when his head flopped back, the glazed eyes stared sightlessly toward the heavens, where, 'twas clear, his spirit already resided.

The shrill keening initiated in her soul pierced through her heart and escaped her lips. "Nay!" she screamed, hurtling down the steps, her gown floating behind her like a wraith. "Nay!"

No one made a move to stop her, neither friend nor foe, and the young boys bearing her father set him gently upon the stones and stepped aside.

Cambria dropped her sword and shook the pale body, unwilling to accept the laird's impossible stillness. He had to wake up. The clan needed him.

She stroked his forehead, but there was no response. She took his big hand in hers, but 'twas as heavy and slack as a slain rabbit. Blood soaked her linen gown, smearing across her breast as she embraced his silent form.

"Nay," she whispered, "nay."

He couldn't be dead. He couldn't. He wouldn't have left

her alone. She'd already lost her mother. He wouldn't have made her endure that pain again.

And yet there he lay, as silent as stone.

A wretched sob tore from her throat, choking her. Dagger-sharp pain lanced through the empty place in her chest.

The laird was lost to her forever.

Hot tears spilled down her cheeks onto her father, mingling with the blood of the Gavin who was no more. She wept as all around her the nameless invaders murmured on, calmly wiping the blood from their blades, blood of the brave Gavin men who'd not live to fight again. She peered at them through the wild strands of her hair, the obscene enemy who had massacred her people.

Who were they? Who were these bastards who had in one bloody moment destroyed the Gavins?

The pain in her heart twisted into a bitter knot of hatred. Nay. She refused to believe it. These strangers hadn't destroyed the Gavins. No one could destroy the Gavins. Gavins had lived for hundreds of years. They would never die. They lived in her. She was the life's blood of the clan now.

Wiping the tears from her face with the back of one hand, she reached down to clasp the pommel of her fallen sword with the other. She kicked her gown out of her ankles' way and tossed her hair over her shoulder. Whirling, she came up with the blade and faced her foe. Several of the servants crossed themselves as she turned toward the knights with all the fury of a madwoman.

"You bastards!" she shouted. "You have slain my father!"

Malcolm the Steward could bear it no longer. Cambria was going to get herself killed. "Nay, lass!" he bellowed from the corner of the room.

His shout earned him a cuff from one of the knights that held him, but that didn't stop him from wrenching at the chains binding his wrists. He watched helplessly as his dearest friend's daughter began a battle she was sure to lose. The muscles of his throat worked painfully. Ah, God, he'd already lost his laird. He couldn't watch Cambria die, too.

But she was beyond hearing. He could see that. The lust for vengeance was in her eyes. Like an avenging angel, she raised her sword high with both hands. With a battle cry, she charged at the enemy, swinging the blade in a wide arc like a crofter harvesting grain.

The knights scattered, dodging her slashing broadsword, and her steel flashed wildly as Cambria attempted to take on the entire company. To Malcolm's satisfaction, the Englishmen were dumbfounded for a moment by the mere slip of a girl who faced them boldly, watching for advances and striking with a deliberate arm. His chin quivered with pride. He and her father had trained her well, the little lioness.

She slashed forward and back, using both hands on the pommel to strengthen her blows. Two men who underestimated her sincerity received serious wounds, wounds he feared she'd likely pay for later.

But the element of surprise couldn't remain long on her side. Though Cambria kept them at bay briefly, using what skills he'd taught her, the enemy far outnumbered her. Two of the knights finally caught her from behind, squeezing her wrists till she dropped the sword, which clattered heavily to the floor.

At least, Malcolm thought with relief, the English didn't slay *women* in cold blood.

Half-crazed with fury, Cambria struggled to get free, swearing, straining from the men's grasp on her arms and tossing her head violently.

Malcolm bit out a curse. Why hadn't the lass stayed abed?

A dark-bearded knight yanked her head back by the hair. She bared her teeth, and her eyes narrowed like a cornered animal's.

Suddenly the unguarded doors of the great hall burst open. An enormous black destrier galloped like thunder across the hard floor, bearing a helmed knight. He was flanked by several other riders, who hauled their horses to a skidding stop on the stones. Rushes scattered everywhere, and the knights fought to control their mounts in the close quarters.

Cambria was forced to her knees by the hulking dark captor beside her, and she squinted against the rising dust.

"My l-lord," the golden knight stammered in surprise, inclining his head toward the newcomer.

Tension hung in the air as he awaited a reply, but the silence was only broached by the snorting of the horses, the squeak of leather tack, and the sniffling of maidservants.

Cambria sucked in great gulps of air through her open mouth and tried to center her mind. She could feel her body drifting toward unconsciousness, toward the place where nothing could harm her, but she resisted its lure, clinging desperately to reality by reminding herself over and over that she was the Gavin. She clenched her nails into the palms of her hands to keep from fainting and focused intently on the rider at the fore, who was nudging his mount closer.

The knight set his huge destrier into motion, Cambria noted, using only the slightest pressure of one of his armor-plated knees. The steed tossed its head proudly and ambled forward. Man and beast no doubt made a formidable foe in battle, their carriage that of champions.

With bullying arrogance, the rider let the steed come to within a foot of the golden knight till it huffed its breath into the man's eyes.

Cambria scowled up at the helmed rider. This had to be the monster responsible for the laird's murder. She swayed momentarily with nausea, recalling too clearly her father's bloody surcoat and his dead, glassy eyes. She swallowed to control her rising gorge. She prayed God would give her the strength to hold out until help came, until de Ware's knights arrived. The English lord was bound by his word, after all, to protect Blackhaugh from enemies such as these. He'd be obliged to capture and punish these murderers. She hoped the Wolf would tear them limb from limb.

She watched, unable to move, unable to speak, as the knight before her removed his helm, eased the mail coif from his head, and ran a hand through his dark curls.

Then her heart stilled as well.

A heavy weight seemed to press on her chest, making it nigh impossible to breathe as she looked upon his face.

He wasn't at all the villain she'd expected. In fact, he was the most striking man she'd ever beheld. His face was evenly chiseled, so perfect it might have been pretty were it not for his furrowed brow and the scars that told of many seasons of battle. His hair, damp with sweat, reminded her of the rich shade of roasted walnuts, and it fell recklessly about his corded neck. His jaw was firm, resolute, but something about the generous curve of his lips marked him as far from heartless.

Most startling, however, were his eyes. They were the color of the pines in a Highland forest, deep and almost sad, eyes that had seen violence and suffering, and had endured. Those eyes caused her heart to beat unsteadily, and she wasn't entirely certain 'twas from fear.

He angled his mount with another nudge of his knee and cocked a brow at the golden knight. "Have you finished here, Roger?" His voice was low, powerful, and laced with irony.

The golden knight regarded him with ill-concealed hostility. "Aye, my lord. They resisted, as you see, but . . ." He shrugged.

The man shifted in his saddle, tossed his helm to his squire, and blew out a long breath.

The carnage before him was inexcusable. As he'd suspected when he set out this morning to intercept Roger's advance, something here was amiss. He should never have trusted Roger Fitzroi. The man obviously didn't understand the proper use of violence. Judging by the age of the shields of the conquered lining the great hall and the frayed edges of the Gavin knights' garments, this poor clan could hardly have posed a threat. Good Lord, there weren't even that many of them, he thought as he let his gaze roam over the broken bodies.

And then he saw her, kneeling at his knights' feet, in the midst of all the slaughter. The breath caught in his throat. For a moment he forgot where he was.

It was an angel. Nay, he corrected as he continued to stare at the eyes that were too fierce, the jaw too square, the hair too dark. Not an angel. Something more fey—a sprite. Accustomed to the fleshy, languorous women at court, this lass's exotic looks were as refreshing as the dip he'd had yesterday in the cool loch.

He couldn't take his eyes from her. She looked the way he'd made women look many a time in his bed—hair spilled carelessly, lips a-quiver, cheeks flushed—and all at once, he wished to caress that fine-boned cheek, run his fingers through those too dark, tangled tresses, kiss that spot on her neck where her pulse visibly raced.

The wench was glaring at him with those cut-crystal eyes, and he was amazed to see her defiance falter only infinitesimally beneath his regard, a thorough scrutiny that usually made his foes tremble.

She reminded him of a wildcat he'd seen once on his travels through the moors, one caught in an abandoned snare. Before he'd cut the animal free, it had looked at him just this way—frightened, hateful, suspicious. He suddenly had an absurd longing to remove the pain from the liquid pools of her eyes as he'd done for the wildcat.

Ariel nickered softly beneath him and stamped an impatient hoof, jarring him back to reality. Damn, he thought, shaking off his insipid dreaming with a toss of his head. This new life of lordly leisure was making him soft.

He frowned into the girl's face. Then his gaze dropped lower. Her body strained against the thin linen of her gown, and he could clearly see a perverse crimson streak across her fair breast.

Desire fled. He grew instantly livid. "Have we taken to wounding innocents?" he demanded.

Roger answered belligerently. "'Tis not her blood, my lord. 'Tis that of her traitor father, Laird Gavin. Though this 'innocent' wounded two of my men!"

He snorted in disbelief. A wee Border lass was hardly capable of fighting off the formidable de Ware knights. He looked dubiously down at her again to see if he'd overlooked something. He was sorry it was the sprite's father who had died, but if the laird was indeed a traitor, it would only have been a matter of time before he was executed for his treachery. Perhaps it was better he'd died nobly, with a sword in his hand.

"Who is your father's successor, lass?" he asked her quietly.

The girl lifted her chin bravely and replied, "I am."

He should have guessed. "And your husband?"

"I have no husband."

"Your betrothed?"

"I have no betrothed. I am ... the Gavin." Her voice broke as she said it. He could see she was fighting back tears.

Several of his countrymen smirked at the idea of a young woman claiming a castle, but he knew there was nothing odd about it for the Scots. He stared at the girl with a mixture of pity and disgust at the laird's foolishness in leaving his daughter unmarried and, therefore, unprotected. He swore he'd never understand the Scots' ways.

"I'll spare your life if you swear fealty to me."

To his amazement, the girl fixed him with a jewel-hard stare and shook her head firmly once. "Even now the castle is being surrounded by an army of the king," she proclaimed. "You'll not escape alive."

"Lass ..." a burly old Gavin man called from the corner, but his captor jerked his chain, ordering him to silence.

He scowled down at the girl and held up a hand to quiet his men's snickering. "The king ... Edward's army?"

"Aye!" she hissed, her eyes sparking like sapphires. "Lord Holden de Ware will slay you for the murder you've committed! He is a powerful warrior, known to all as the Wolf for his savagery, and he has sworn to protect this keep!"

He stared at her, stunned. Her eyes gleamed with victory, and the thrust of her chin was confident and proud. He almost hated to dash her hopes.

But he had to.

He held her gaze with his own and explained softly, "I am the Wolf. I am Lord Holden de Ware."

3

THE GIRL'S GAZE DROPPED TO THE FIGURE OF THE WOLF EM-
blazoned on his tabard, and she turned as white as her
linen shift. By the saints, he thought in alarm, the wench was
going to faint.

Her eyes rolled in her head. He reached his hand forward
futilely as if he could cushion her fall. But it was too late. She
collapsed in a heap on the rushes.

Holden turned his scowl upon Roger. "You say Gavin refused the alliance?"

Roger sneered. "You can never trust a Scot." He spat on
the ground. "The devil slew my own brother before my
eyes." His glance slid over to Owen.

"My sympathies," Holden said, although the two brothers
hardly seemed grief-ridden. "In sooth, it's difficult to believe
they preferred to fight with so small a force."

"You know these Scots and their stubborn loyalty. Even
the wench fought," Roger smirked, nodding at the bundle on
the floor.

Holden glanced at the girl again. She certainly couldn't
have been much of a threat. She was, after all, but a young
woman, one apparently prone to fainting.

He looked around the hall at the cowering servants, the
whimpering hounds, the Gavin men chained together in the

corner. What had really happened here? Perhaps the daughter knew.

He would have liked to question her, to question all of them, but the unfortunate truth was that he had other urgent matters to attend to. He was a lord in his own right now, and much obligation came with the position.

Besides, he couldn't bring the laird back to life. Whatever brutal mistakes Roger had made, he was the king's kin, and the deed was done. Blackhaugh was secure, and the bloodshed was over. Their work here was finished.

"Let her be," he instructed, more reluctant than he cared to admit about leaving the intriguing Border lass behind. It had been too long since he'd had a woman. Perhaps he'd summon some eager maidservant to his bed when he returned to his keep.

"Roger, Owen, you'll come with me to Bowden." Then he turned to his brother Garth. The lad had learned much in their weeks together, and Holden felt it was time to test that knowledge. "Garth, you'll serve as steward here and hold Blackhaugh. Obtain their fealty," he said, nodding to the Gavin survivors, "and they may be released."

Garth visibly paled. It was a great responsibility. But he drew himself up proudly and accepted the command.

Holden ignored Fitzroi's scowl of outrage at the obvious slight. Roger no doubt expected to be handed the castle on a platter. He was, after all, half-uncle to the king. But Garth was the better man for the task. Despite Roger's fostering at Castle de Ware, Roger had never quite learned the true meaning of chivalry, and Holden trusted the man about as much as he did his mistresses. Garth, on the other hand, though only nineteen, possessed an innate sense of decency, justice, and loyalty that would serve him well as steward.

At Holden's order, Garth immediately dismounted and came forward. Holden knew his little brother would do well in inspiring trust in the remaining castle folk, trust that Roger had probably weakened with his vicious tactics.

"The rest of us must go," Holden commanded. "We came to borrow provisions from Blackhaugh." If any remain, he thought. Looking about the hall at the shabby tapestries and threadbare surcoats, he wondered if all the Border holdings were similarly impoverished. "As fate would have it, Bowden's larder was nearly empty. 'Tis doubtless why the castle surrendered so readily."

There was a stirring in the rushes as he spoke. The girl was rousing from her faint, lifting herself on shaky arms and blinking the cobwebs from her bewildered eyes.

He should have been moved to pity. The poor wench had in one blow lost her father and her title. But pity was not at all what he felt as she abruptly met and matched his stare, her teeth clenched, her sapphire gaze smoldering. As if she transmitted it to him with those eyes, he felt her power, power he'd never sensed from a woman before, and with it came a wave of lust, pure and strong and immediate. Every fiber of his being felt drawn to her, like iron to a lodestone.

He swallowed hard. It was absurd. He was on a mission, and she was the enemy. He would leave her behind, just as he always had the victims of war. Such were the sacrifices of his profession. He'd earned his considerable fortune with his sword and his allegiance, and he could ill afford to let a comely face distract him from his duties.

Quickly, before he could lose his resolve, he turned his steed briskly and galloped out of the hall.

Cambria watched Lord Holden de Ware go, hate burning white-hot in her heart. She swore she'd kill the Englishman, destroy the bastard who had betrayed her father.

While she made that silent oath, a rat of a man with dark, stringy hair hobbled close. He swept up her father's broadsword, turning it over in his hands.

"A fine blade," he whispered, leering at her with evil ocher eyes. "A pity your father didn't know how to use it. When I am lord of Blackhaugh, I shall do better."

Before she could spit in his face, he set the point of the blade at her throat, chuckling at her instant silence. Then he slid the sword into his own scabbard and marched from the hall after the others.

Squires removed the horses from the great hall, but when the last of the departing hooves had soiled Blackhaugh's rushes, there were still a score of English knights left. They murmured amongst themselves in the sudden silence like shy cousins awaiting introduction.

Finally, the new steward cautiously crept near. He was a young man, tall, brown-haired, and fair of face, with a strong jaw and gray-green eyes that marked him plainly as Lord Holden's brother, even if the Wolf's ruthlessness was missing from his countenance.

"My lady," he said in a low, gentle voice, "I am training for a position in the church. If you have no priest available, I'd be happy to bless the bodies and—"

"Do not dare to touch them! Do not dare to utter a single word over them, English pig, or 'twill be your last!"

The youth looked stricken by her remarks, but there was no room in Cambria's grieving heart for remorse. She wanted English hands on as little as possible of Blackhaugh, including its dead.

The wind rose in a mood that warned of a spring squall, whipping Cambria's shift around her ankles like the foam of the surf and deftly tangling her hair. She paused in her labors, shoving the spade hard into the soil and leaning upon it. By the look of the gray gathering clouds, the storm would start before the veiled sun sank below the hills. But she'd be finished by nightfall. She'd rather dig the grave herself than let those English dogs desecrate the burial with their presence.

'Twas a travesty. The laird deserved a tomb in the chapel and an effigy with the hawk of the Gavin carved at its feet. He deserved a month of mourning and visits from the lairds of the neighboring clans. He had died a warrior's death, and he deserved at least to be buried with his sword.

As if her bitterness could be heard in the heavens, the sky flashed and cracked with current, and all around the grass-swept knoll, the clouds darkened like a flock of ravens come to feed. A gale lifted her hair and fluttered the woolen plaid covering the laird's body. Then fine drops of rain began to fall, slowly at first, staining the sod like tears.

She wiped her brow on a muddy sleeve, then resumed digging. She paid no heed to the blisters on her hands or the wind flaying her legs or the rain soaking her shift. The storm rose around her, but she continued gouging away at the soil until the hole was deep enough that no animal would disturb it. Then she gently dragged her father to the edge, tipping his body into the grave.

She gave him all the benedictions she knew, falling to her knees and calling on saints and ancient gods alike, pleading with the angry heavens to take and keep the laird of Gavin well. Then she stood, with the storm raging all about her, while the lightning wounded the purple clouds and thunder shook the earth, and she raised her hands to the sky.

"Father," she whispered fervently, though the sound was lost in the maelstrom, "I swear upon the clan of Gavin, I will avenge your death."

The wind roared through the trees, carrying her oath of vengeance across the land that was no longer Gavin's.

By April, the Border hills burst forth torrents of water like tears from the earth, but the spring bulbs paid no heed to their sorrow. They blossomed joyfully with their heady perfume. The land was new and green once again, its old wounds forgotten and life reborn.

Garth de Ware had tamed the denizens of Blackhaugh to his rule like a falconer gentling a tiercel, with patience and persistence. The maidservants had begun to gaze longingly at the tall, comely knight, and even old Malcolm seemed to have attached himself to the young Englishman, conferring with him on matters of the castle's defense and provisions.

Only Cambria remained steadfast in her hatred of the invaders, a hatred that consumed every moment of every day. It seemed only she remembered the treachery the enemy had dealt. She had cuts that had mended badly and scarred, and until her vengeance was fulfilled, she'd carry the volatile seeds of abhorrence with her.

The naive Englishman left in command hadn't an inkling of the dark purpose in her heart, of course. He presumed that she was like most of the other women of his acquaintance, docile and sweet, and so he'd given her completely free run of the castle and its lands. He assumed she was collecting herbs and gossip.

In truth, she spent every waking moment orchestrating the revenge for her kinsmen's betrayal.

The sun bid a lingering farewell over the hills, turning the sky the colors of a ripening peach. She watched, as usual, from the haven of her bedchamber, where she'd just set aside the half-eaten trencher of pottage.

She pounded her fist on the embrasure in frustration. Another day gone, and still she'd found no champion to do battle with Lord Holden de Ware. The Wolf was evidently renowned for his skill at arms, for everyone seemed to have heard of his matchless swordsmanship.

She hung her head. She'd tried pleading, cajoling, flattering, and shaming them, but thus far none of the seasoned knights of her own or neighboring castles would undertake her mission of retribution. They believed her father had indeed succumbed to the hotheaded pride for which he was famed, that he had turned on the enemy at the last moment and made a rash mistake in underestimating the power of the English. Cambria, however, couldn't accept that. She'd glimpsed the dream of peace in her father's eyes. He'd had no fighting left in him.

What was she to do? She'd promised her father revenge, sworn it upon his grave. Now it seemed a Herculean feat. Sweet Mary, was there no one to take up her cause? No champion for her vengeance? No man of courage and honor and chivalry in all of Scotland?

Lord Holden de Ware casually sipped at his mead as the sun peeked through the elms and between the merlons of the wall walk at Bowden. He sighed heavily and watched with indifference as two sparrows made chase in the air. It should prove a glorious day, he tried to persuade himself, breathing in a deep lungful of crisp air. The Border forces had been defused weeks ago. Rested now from that ordeal, he knew he should be happily enjoying the comforts due the lord of the manor. But in truth he was unaccustomed to peace. His spirit was restless.

He set his flagon down on a crenel of the battlement, yawning and stretching his stiff muscles. Perhaps it was time, he thought, to leave Bowden in the hands of a steward and make a visit to his other prize, Blackhaugh. He wished to see how his little brother fared.

When he thought of Blackhaugh Castle, however, it wasn't Garth's face that came to mind. He was haunted once again by the image of that fascinating Scotswoman, the elfish lass who'd rendered him unable to even *think* of dallying with the many perfectly willing wenches at Bowden. She'd worked a charm on him—that had to be the answer—and it was ruining his hard-earned reputation as a virile lover.

Perhaps he'd just swive the wench while he was at Blackhaugh and be done with it. He closed his eyes, picturing once again her tempting mouth, that luxurious mane of chestnut hair, her creamy bosom. Just as he began to imagine what he'd like to do with her, a glint of metal from across the field below flashed, catching his eye.

A single knight on horseback galloped through the meadow. Holden watched silently for a moment, unable to discern whether the rider was friend or foe, and waited until the distance between them closed.

"Ho, fellow knight," he called down at last, "what are you about this morning?"

The knight made no response. Holden raised a brow at his lack of courtesy and studied the rider carefully. He'd come alone, as far as Holden could ascertain, indicating he was local, as only a fool would travel without escort along the Borders. But the knight bore no crest upon his plain blue tabard, and his helm was likewise unadorned.

Once again Holden called down. "Hola, Sir Knight, by what name are you known?"

There was no reply. Holden wrinkled his brow. This game was growing rather tedious, unless . . . unless it was a jest planned by one of his men, played perhaps to relieve his obvious boredom. Yes, that was it, he supposed.

"You are in battle dress!" he remarked, picking up his cup and swirling the mead around the rim. "Is it then your intent to joust one of my knights?"

The rider abruptly lifted his long ash lance, and Holden cocked his head at this unexpected gesture. Ah, it must be his cousin Myles, he decided. Myles, a newly made knight, had probably been goaded into this challenge by Holden's uncles.

"Whom do you come to battle, sirrah?"

Slowly, the knight lowered the tip of the lance till it pointed directly at him.

Pleased with the thought of his men's comeuppance, Holden smiled. "Me?" he murmured. "What a surprise."

He waved. Then he called out, "I shall arm myself and be down presently, sirrah, to uncover your identity!"

Several moments later, when Holden's squire had fully armed him, he rode out to meet the challenger. His suspicions about the knight's identity were confirmed as he noted the small frame and youthful posture. Nonetheless, he'd humor the bold lad.

"You have no design upon your tabard, sir. Will you not at least do me the honor of telling me with whom I joust before I trounce you?"

There was no answer, of course. Holden would have recognized the voice. Bemused, he chuckled to himself as the horse and rider stormed to one end of the field.

Scarcely had he placed his helm on his head when the young knight surged toward him with lance forward. Angered at the boy's rude haste, he lowered his lance and prepared to unhorse the whelp.

Ariel bolted forward without prompting, flinging up chunks of sod. When they met with a thunderous crash, the small rider was carried easily from the saddle to the earth with a thud.

Holden allowed the dazed lad to rise laboriously. They drew swords, and he gave the young knight many sound punishing buffets upon the helm.

The boy was quick, but haphazard, spinning and slashing with a recklessness Holden hadn't noticed in Myles before. He was an agile opponent, Holden admitted, but hardly a match for his own sheer power, which he tempered for the sake of a fair fight.

Noting how quickly the lad tired, Holden offered aid.

"Hold your shield higher, man! Your fighting grows careless!"

This made the knight's attack all the more brash.

After nearly a quarter of an hour, bored of the battle, which had become sluggish, Holden decided to make an end of it. He swung a powerful blow with the flat of his sword across the knight's chest. His victim went sprawling in the grass, dropping both sword and shield on the way.

Holden shook his head, then leisurely set his own shield, helm, and sword on the ground, offering his hand to aid the foolish novice.

Unexpectedly, the fallen knight reached for his own blade and swung it in a swift, wide path, forcing Holden to block the blow with his arm. He winced as the blade caught him painfully on the shoulder and fell just short of penetrating the mail.

His arm throbbing from the impact, he fiercely swept up his sword and knocked his kneeling opponent's weapon away.

This varlet was not his cousin. No de Ware would fight so unchivalrously. He caught the knight's helm, tore it off, and flung it to the ground. Blinded by rage, he yanked the dark hair back violently, exposing the fiend's vulnerable throat, and raised his sword to slay the traitorous knight.

Then the very breath was sucked from him.

Nay, he thought. It wasn't possible.

"You!" he choked.

Cambria gasped, despite her brave intentions. That last blow had been unworthy of her, and she knew it. Lord Holden should by rights slay her for it.

Clenching her hair in his fist, the Wolf gazed at her bared neck and hesitated. Indecision warred in his steely eyes as his blade hung over her. She forced herself to stare at him, even if she couldn't draw air into her lungs. She'd be damned if she'd die wincing from her foe. His expression wavered between anger and disbelief and something resembling fear, and then it evolved into a mask of pure fury.

With a bellow of rage, he brought the sword down violently. She screamed as he jammed its point into the ground beside her.

Her heart knifed painfully within her chest, though she was out of immediate peril. Then she gasped in great sobs of air. For a long while, naught but their turbulent breathing rent the silence. Hers was born of shuddering relief, his of barely suppressed savagery.

His eyes flashed green fire when he was at last able to speak. "You little fool!" he snapped hoarsely. "Are you mad?" He plowed his mailed hand through his hair and began to pace like a cornered destrier. "What game do you . . . How could . . . Jesu, I almost kil— . . ."

If she thought she glimpsed a speck of self-reproach in his eyes, it vanished in the next instant, the moment he realized her scheme. He wheeled on her, incredulous. His words fell like blows, and she flinched from the sheer power of his voice.

"By God! You thought to avenge your father by murdering me!" He swore, then kicked the sod with so much force that a chunk of it came loose. He wrenched his sword from the earth, sheathing it so violently the hilt rang against its bronze catch. Then he came to stand over her, clenching and unclenching his mailed fists, his breath ragged, his jaw set. Though he brandished no weapon other than his iron gaze, 'twas enough to pin her there.

He almost broke her with his unnerving silence, which seemed to stretch into torturous eternity. But at last he sank to a crouch beside her, so close she could feel the moisture of his breath on her cheek. And the harsh intimacy of his measured whisper inspired more terror than either his shouting or his silence.

"I will not strike you down," he growled, "as you are by some strange providence a lady. But, by God, you shall be chastised."

She bit back a startled shriek as he muscled her up and nudged her roughly toward the castle, pinioning her arm. Dear God, he could probably snap her bones like twigs in his great hand. He pushed her through the main gate, ignoring the curious stares of the guards. He snarled at a groom to fetch their grazing mounts, then hauled her across the courtyard as if she were no more unwieldy than a sack of chain mail.

She balked when he pushed open the doors of the great hall, but he prodded her forward, kneeing her with the sharp poleyn of his armor. Her face burned with shame as he forced her through the crowded hall. Even with her eyes lowered, she could see men and women stepping out of the Wolf's path, hear them gasp in shock at the spectacle.

They came to a stairwell at the far side of the hall, and he half-dragged her up the winding stone steps. Her heart began to beat against her ribs like a caged falcon as she imagined what horrible punishments he intended, and suddenly she longed to be in the great hall again among witnesses. She struggled against him, despite the wrenching pain it caused her shoulder, but he only cursed and drew her other arm behind her as well.

At the top of the steps, he kicked open a thick oak door, revealing a dismal little room with a thin straw pallet and a barred window. There, he shoved her in and followed after, slamming the door behind them. Before she could even whirl to face him, he pressed her back against the wall with his immense body, leaving her breathless. He pinned her to the rough stones as easily as if she were a rabbit for skinning, holding her wrists immobile on each side of her head.

She shuddered. She'd thought about her confrontation with the Wolf for days now—rehearsed her attack, practiced her blows, imagined his defense—but nothing she'd envisioned had prepared her for this. At this proximity, the beads of sweat on his face were too real, his body intimate, his anger palpable. She felt like a moth trapped in a fist to be crushed at his whim. De Ware's eyes seared her with their intensity, yet his voice remained dangerously quiet.

"What have you done with my brother?"

Cambria was momentarily dazed. What kind of a question was that?

The human manacles on her wrists tightened the merest fraction. She swallowed convulsively. Lord, he was strong.

"Garth?" she gasped.

"Of course Garth," he said between his teeth.

She saw now. It made perfect sense. Lord Holden had concluded that her escape from Blackhaugh meant that some ill had befallen Garth. Leave it to an Englishman to consider his kin infallible to the simple wiles of a Scotswoman.

"What have you done?" the Wolf hissed, the cold fire in his eyes burning far more than his grasp on her wrists.

For a moment, she thought her voice had deserted her. Then she managed to choke out, "He is well."

"You are certain?" he demanded, pressing so close that she could have counted his eyelashes.

She closed her eyes and nodded.

"Look at me," he ordered. "Where are the others you brought with you?"

"There are no others."

He snarled at her, making her flinch. "You're lying!"

"Nay!" she insisted. "I came alone, of my own choosing. No one knows."

This last bit wasn't exactly true. She hadn't wanted Malcolm the Steward to worry. The squire who had armed her for the journey had been given a message to deliver to him after she was long gone. 'Twould inform Malcolm that she was safe, that she would return shortly, and that he wasn't to interfere.

Apparently convinced, the lord inspected her at greater leisure now and more thoroughly, as if she were a palfrey he might purchase, letting his gaze move over her hair, her lips, her throat. She shivered. This silent interrogation was far more intimidating than what he asked aloud.

"But your kinsmen will find out soon enough, will they not?" he murmured, almost to himself. "Such a precious jewel could not go missing for long."

She blinked, startled. No one had called her a precious jewel before, certainly not an Englishman. Surely he only mocked her.

His gaze lingered on her mouth, and his voice came out on a mere breath. "What if you had slain me, little sprite? Did you intend to fight the whole English army?"

She swallowed. She had no answer for him. In sooth, she'd not thought that far ahead.

His next words were so soft, she had to watch his lips to decipher them. "And what . . . what if I had slain you?"

He caught her gaze then, trapping her in the smoldering depths of his eyes, and some strange current passed through them, as fleeting as lightning, as ephemeral as mist. For one brief instant, she saw him not as the enemy, but as a man— troubled, vulnerable, human—and molten fire surged inexplicably through her veins.

But in the next moment, his eyes hardened like green glass. He became the warrior once more. He released her arms and stepped away.

"I'll send a squire to disarm you," he said gruffly, nodding at her in dismissal.

Then he took a key from the hook on the wall and left without another word, locking the oak door behind him.

Cambria pounded on the door, demanding freedom, but her captor's heavy footsteps faded resolutely away.

She sank down wearily upon the musty straw pallet in the corner, breathless and aching from the battle. Tears blurred her eyes, but she refused to shed them.

She had failed—both her father and her clan. She'd come for revenge, and she'd earned only shame. She'd lost the temper her father had always warned her about, and it had cost her the field. Lord, it had almost cost her her life.

She could still see vividly the fierce countenance of Lord Holden towering over her, and she understood now why he was called the Wolf. His teeth bared, his eyes glittering with malice at the moment he intended to strike her down, he'd resembled some unleashed beast.

Though her sex had saved her from death, Cambria dreaded the punishment Lord Holden would mete out for her. She'd felt his iron grip on her wrist, the solid wall of his chest, the powerful blow of his sword, and she knew she could never endure his strength should he decide to beat her.

She did deserve a beating. She knew that. She'd completely lost control. So caught up was she in her passion for vengeance that she'd forgotten every rule of warfare her fa-

ther had painstakingly taught her. Perhaps, she thought ruefully, if she'd kept her mind alert and her temper bridled, she
might have won the battle.

She rolled onto her side and idly picked at a crack in the
stone wall, thoroughly miserable.

Holden paced his chamber restlessly, shaken by the fact he'd
almost slain a woman. Her countenance was etched into his
brain now—the silky hair bunched in his fist, the crystalline
blue eyes bright with fear, the delicate nose glazed with the
sweat of battle, lips trembling as he held her life in his hands.
She'd been even more beautiful than he remembered, beautiful and dangerous, like the wildcat. He saw now what Roger
had meant about the savage Scots. Mother of God, even their
women were warriors. He tried to rub the headache from his
temples, completely at a loss as to what to do with the lass.

He had to believe she'd come alone. No knight worth his
armor would have stood by while a mere girl battled a seasoned warrior. But her clansmen would come for her eventually, he knew. She was their laird. What would he do when
they demanded her? He had to maintain peace between the
English and the Border Scots, but he couldn't simply release
the wench.

By all rights, he could claim her life—she'd attempted to
slay him underhandedly—but it was impossible for him to
imagine raising a fist against her. She was a woman, for the
love of God. They were gentle creatures. They were to be
protected. Even now, despite her crime, a wave of guilt
washed over him as he thought about the wisp of a girl he'd
imprisoned in a cold, dank tower cell by his own cruel hand.

He fingered the hilt of his sword. For the first time in his
life, his trusty blade felt like just a useless piece of steel, and
he realized he had no idea what weapon to use against this
perplexing foe.

Burdened by frustration and anxiety, he cursed and left for
the practice field, where his men were astounded by the rigorous bouts he made them endure the rest of the afternoon.

• • •

Cambria leaned against the iron bars of her prison and counted the stars as they emerged gradually from the darkening heavens. She'd stopped dwelling on her failure now and begun to use her clever Gavin brain.

Escape was a possibility. Just like his foolish little brother, Holden de Ware had made the mistake of underestimating her desperation and resourcefulness. Not only did he provide ample bread and pottage for her supper, but he generously sent the squire he'd promised to help her remove her armor, knowing she couldn't very well sleep in it. This last kindness would cost him his prisoner.

Without the heavy mail, she was sure she could squeeze through the bars at the window. Wearing only her linen undergarment, she tore her tabard into long strips, which she tied together. 'Twas a simple matter to secure the ladder of rags to the bars, letting it fall to the ground below.

Taking a few deep breaths, she expelled all her air and squeezed painfully through the grille. The faint light of the crescent moon afforded her cover, mercifully dimming her downward view. Nonetheless, her belly tightened as she teetered on the narrow ledge and gazed down the long wall of the tower.

She gave a testing tug on the rags, then, clamping her eyes shut, swung out over the empty darkness. The rope twisted at once, and she banged into the wall, bruising her shoulder, but the fabric held. She clung to the rags with trembling limbs and lowered herself inch by slow inch, not daring to look down into what seemed a bottomless black pit. Several times, she scraped her knees on the rough gray stone of the castle wall.

Then, after what seemed an eternity, she thankfully felt cold, damp earth beneath her bare feet. She edged cautiously from the shadow of the castle wall to the open field, then from the field to the forest. When she at last reached the haven of the trees, she cast aside stealth and ran as swiftly as she could in the thick black.

All night she ran, to the hooting of owls and the skittering of mice, shivering in her thin garment. The cold mist wrapped cruel fingers around her body, slowing her blood and making her muscles cramp. Her heart pounded in her ears as she scrambled through the brush, scratching her arms and legs. But always she thought of the Gavin, of her ancestors who had run naked through this savage land and survived. If any one of them could do it, she could do it.

She was the Gavin.

Hours passed, and dawn at last began to lighten the sky. Her knifelike breaths dulled to a steady throb, and she found herself in unfamiliar country. She could see no castles, no roads, only rolling meadows and oaks.

She kept up her spirits, denying the hopelessness of her situation by imagining her rescue. If she could only find Robbie and his band of Scots in this foreign landscape, they'd help her. She'd be safe. Robbie would protect her from the Englishman.

She paused for a moment at the crest of a grassy hillock, weary and hungry and in need of sleep, but she realized with a shiver that she must continue. She must make certain the Wolf would not find her.

"What?" Holden exploded, slamming his fist on the oak table. The impact startled the skittish servant and made his own watered wine splash up over the lip of its chalice. "Christ's bones!"

He ran his fingers through his uncombed mane in frustration and came to his feet, raking his chair across the rush-covered stones. He had to curse his own stupidity as much as the fey wench herself for the ease with which she'd escaped.

In truth, her ingenuity and determination intrigued him, but there was no room for intrigue when one was about the king's business. This was his first major coup for Edward. He couldn't afford to let one vengeful Scots lass undermine his plans.

"Trouble?" Roger Fitzroi ambled into the hall, looking annoyingly smug as he munched on his breakfast of oat bread.

"Nothing I cannot handle."

"The Gavin lass escaped?"

News evidently traveled fast in the castle. Holden took a swig of wine.

Roger nodded in empathy. Then he set aside his bread, lowered his eyes, and clasped his hands before him.

"My lord, I know you were displeased with the way Blackhaugh was managed. In sooth, I fear my brother's murder left me blind to reason. Perhaps I can make amends. It would be my honor to fetch the girl for you. I can leave within the hour."

Holden almost choked on his wine. Was Roger courting humility for the first time? Or had he at last realized that his rash actions might cost him his royal stipend? Holden stroked his chin. While Roger's motives might be less than pure, he *was* the best man on the hunt. If Holden sent along a few of his trusted men as well . . .

"Very well," he replied. "Take Myles and Guy with you."

"My lord." Roger inclined his head and turned to go.

"And Roger?"

The knight paused.

"I want her alive and unharmed, or I'll have your head, king's kin or no."

In spite of what she'd done, Holden admired the spirit of the girl, and he didn't want that spirit broken.

That spirit and what few berries and nuts she could scrounge in the forest kept Cambria alive. For two days she ran, her body weak with hunger, sleeping only briefly in nests of twigs and leaves. Her feet were blistered, her fair skin chapped by the harsh wind, her linen garment in rags from the underbrush.

Though the likelihood of her capture grew slimmer by the hour, so did the probability of meeting up with her clansmen. Avoiding the main road, she wasn't entirely sure she was headed in the right direction. She wondered if Robbie would recognize her in her disheveled state. She had no coin, no clothing, no proof of her birthright, and she was alone.

Another woman would have courted despair, but with each mile she traveled, Cambria grew more and more filled with hate and anger. No single person had caused so much destruction in her life as this demon, Holden de Ware. With one cruel stroke, he'd taken her father, her land, her rank, and reduced her to this, a half-naked fugitive foraging for berries. By God, she'd survive, if only to scratch out those devilish eyes that haunted her.

Inspired by the thought and certain she'd eluded the cursed English, she finally stopped to rest. Surely Holden's men would have given up or lost track of her by now. She'd chosen a strange, wandering path to deceive any followers. Comforted, she nestled against a gnarled oak, covering herself with its fallen mulch, and slipped into a heavy sleep.

The sun had moved halfway through the sky when she first heard the sound, the faraway baying of a hound. Swiftly she arose, shook off the leaves, and climbed up onto an oak branch to get a better view of the surrounding countryside.

Nay.

Her heart sank into a mire of despair as she peered at the meadow below. The hours of running, the lack of sleep, the pain and hunger, all had been for naught. The two knights restraining the wildly lunging hound wore the crest of de Ware.

4

"NAY!" SHE WHISPERED, CHOKING BACK A SOB.

They'd hunted her down like an animal. And now she was trapped, helpless. Terror clutched at her chest. Her breath grew short and shallow.

Dear God, how could she escape? The hound sounded half-starved. In another moment, it would catch her scent. Sweet Jesu, if it attacked . . .

She swallowed hard and tried not to think about it. She had to calm herself. Panic was a poor master. They were only two men, she reasoned, and they hadn't seen her yet. There was still time. There was still hope.

The baying intensified, threatening her determination. Quietly, she slipped from the tree and darted into the woods. It might be impossible to outdistance her pursuers, but the forest would at least provide a screen. And if she could find a stream to follow, she might throw the hound off her scent.

Her hopes withered quickly.

Tearing through a grove of oaks, she nearly collided with another pair of mounted knights, more of Holden's men. These two she remembered all too well from the Blackhaugh massacre—the big golden knight, Roger, and the rat of a man who'd stolen her father's sword.

Roger guffawed, clearly surprised. "So, you've made my

duties easier; *you* have come looking for *me*!" He whistled a loud signal and galloped toward her.

Her heart pounding, she whirled and bolted for the thick brush, all too aware she was only delaying the inevitable. She stumbled clumsily, aimlessly through the dense foliage, whimpers of panic rising in her throat.

Then she heard the command to unleash the hound. Jesu, it would flush her out like a rabbit! Her lungs ached, but when she heard the dog's crazed yelp, she forced her legs to pump harder, unable to quell her instincts to survive, despite all reason.

Clearing the edge of the wood, she glimpsed freedom. But the only escape was into an open field of thistles. She hesitated. The weeds were thick and sharp.

The hound bayed again.

Out of options, she loped forward, ignoring the thistles catching at her shift, gasping as the spines cut her bare feet.

The mongrel caught up to her in no time, snapping at her heels, and she stumbled to the earth. Wincing in pain, she tried to scramble away from the eager jaws. By the devil's bones, would they allow the beast to devour her?

Just as she felt the hound's dank breath on her skin, the black-bearded man spoke sharply to the animal, calling it back. He tethered it with a heavy chain, then tossed it a scrap of meat. The hound tore into its supper ravenously.

Cambria swallowed dryly, frozen with terror on the ground, her cheek pressed against the weeds, her breath coming in short, burning gulps.

"Take her, Myles," Roger ordered smugly.

A young knight dismounted and bent to pull her to her feet. Her strength nearly spent, she still struggled against his kindness. His was, after all, the charity of an Englishman. Undaunted by her resistance, he gallantly removed his cloak and wrapped it about her naked shoulders, regarding her with sympathetic gray eyes.

'Twas more than her weakened spirit could stand. To her horror, her eyes welled with moisture. Dear God, she couldn't cry now, not before her enemy! She twisted out of the young knight's grasp and turned on him, casting the cloak from her.

"Your garment stinks of England!" she cried. "I'd rather die from the Scottish cold!"

Displeasure flitted across the man's face as he retrieved his cloak. Stiffly, he lifted her onto his steed, then mounted up behind her. The four horses turned back through the trees.

At first she sat bolt upright, vigilant lest any part of her come into contact with her captor. But as they rode mile upon mile, her exhausted body betrayed her. Slouching wearily in the saddle, she faded in and out of sleep until she finally slumped against the broad chest of her guard.

Hours later, she awoke to the rude pawing of her bare thigh. 'Twas Roger. She jerked away in surprise, reaching for the dagger she always carried in her belt and nearly unhorsing both herself and Myles, who reined his steed away in irritation.

Roger only chuckled at her empty hand and gave her a mocking bow. Then he gestured toward a moss-grown thatched inn tucked into the shadowy wood. A reed-thin old man emerged from the dark doorway, followed by a wrinkled crone fidgeting with her dirty surcoat. Disoriented, it took Cambria a moment to realize that this was to be their lodging for the night.

The old man came forward to collect coin from Roger. His stooped wife muttered nervously, motioning for Cambria to come with her. The woman, apparently wary of the knights and thankful to have Cambria to tend to, left her husband to see to the comforts of the men.

Cambria dismounted with Myles's help, her numb legs nearly crumpling beneath her. She gripped the saddle until feeling returned. The woman clucked her tongue sympathetically and helped her into the cottage.

The inn's warmth and the comfortable smells of mutton and bitter ale almost brought tears to Cambria's eyes. The woman guided her to a rough-hewn trestle table. She sank gratefully down onto the worn bench, ignoring the curious stares of the other few patrons in the room.

The flickering fire felt like a balm upon her face, warming her through to her bones. When the woman returned with a trencher of pottage and a tankard of ale, she feasted ravenously, unmindful that the greasy fare might turn her stomach later.

No sooner had she gulped down the last morsel of her meal than Roger directed the woman to have a hot bath prepared for Cambria upstairs, grumbling all the while about the cost of Lord Holden's whims.

For once, Cambria didn't mind complying with the Englishman's instructions. Slipping out of her ragged, filthy shift and into the soothing water of the wooden tub, she relaxed for the first time in days. She soaked the myriad cuts on her body and scrubbed her head vigorously with the scraps of scented soap until her hair shone like a silk robe.

But eventually the water cooled. And as her sweet languor faded, she plotted her escape.

"Have you finished then?" the innkeeper's wife demanded, startling her from her thoughts.

"Oh! Aye." Cambria took the coarse linen towel from the woman and stepped from the tub. As she briskly rubbed herself dry, she glanced sideways at the old crone.

Mimicking her mother's timidity, she whispered, "They hold me against my will, you know."

The woman dried her hands anxiously on her grubby apron. "'Tis no business o' mine, mistress."

"But they killed my father!" Cambria snapped, then continued more softly, "And they may kill me as well."

"Oh, miss." The woman shook her head. "I'd like to help you, but I'd be puttin' a rope around me own neck, that I would."

"Please," Cambria pleaded. "You wouldn't have to help me. You could but leave a door open, a shutter ajar. . . ."

The withered old beldame was firm. "Nay. I cannot." She dug in her pouch and pulled out a tiny jar. "I'll give you balm for your hurts, and I'll give you a kirtle to wear, but I'll not call on the wrath o' those swordsmen below."

Cambria pursed her lips in frustration, then forced herself to smile at the woman. She accepted the balm and the rough kirtle with thanks.

After the woman had the tub taken away, Cambria hastily dressed, then plaited her wet hair into a thick braid. She scanned the room, reviewing the possibilities for escape. She studied the shutters of the room. They were nailed closed, probably to prevent unwelcome guests.

As she rose to investigate, her stomach churned in protest, reluctant to digest the heavy stew she'd eaten earlier. She cursed under her breath, as much at her poor judgment in wolfing down her meal as at the fact the shutters were nailed tight. She needed something to pry them open. Lord, she decided as a wave of nausea swelled in her, she needed a concoction for her stomach first or she wouldn't be able to think clearly.

Of course! she thought, clutching her belly—she could go to the kitchen to ask the innkeeper's wife for an elixir and possibly pilfer a tool of some kind to use on the shutters.

She eased the door open. The four de Ware knights were now the sole occupants of the common room, seated around the table close to the fire, swapping boasts and dares. They were obviously well steeped in ale and past all reason. Young Myles swayed on the bench, and Roger pushed at him belligerently every time he chanced to lean too far. Roger and the other one—the rat—cuffed each other, more out of habit than malice, it appeared. The black-haired giant snored loudly into his black beard atop the table, and beneath it, his hound crunched contentedly on a bone. Cambria held her breath as she descended the steps, trying to slip past unnoticed.

But Roger spied her at the bottom of the stairs.

"Well, look here, will you, Owen? There *was* a wench beneath that filth."

"And a right fair wench, too," his companion added with a leer. "Seems a waste all that sweet flesh lying alone up there in that cold chamber."

"Aye, it's weeks since I had me a clean-smelling woman."

She felt as if her legs were caught in a sticky bog, that no matter how she struggled, she was only going to sink deeper. Unaccustomed to this kind of warfare, she shrank back from the attention, up against the dingy wall. Suddenly, her stomach was the least of her worries.

"Are you surprised, wench?" Owen asked, his dark, greasy hair and crooked teeth garish in the firelight. "Do you not know it is the right of the victorious to all goods won in battle?"

Befuddled with drink, boyish Sir Myles nonetheless stepped forward hesitantly in her defense. "Sir Roger, Lord Holden gave orders she was to be unharmed."

Roger snickered and pushed the boy back onto his bench. "I'll not harm her! I'll just break her in like a good palfrey. Holden will be grateful for the service."

Her eyes widened in disbelief. She coiled her muscles to spring, but before she could move, Roger signaled to Owen, who caught her easily by the arms. She fought in earnest, heaving her body against his grasp, but he was as tenacious as a ferret. The two men laughed at her efforts, enjoying the sport.

From the corner of her eye, she glimpsed the innkeeper's wife emerging from the kitchen, but she knew no help would come from that quarter.

"What are you called, fiery maid?" Roger asked, stepping close to her. He reeked of ale.

She thought of her clan and clenched her teeth, refusing to answer.

"Your name, wench!" he repeated with a snarl.

She spat derisively at his feet.

Cold steel was his reply, sharp and immediate against her bosom, the dagger drawn rather quickly for a drunk man. But Cambria refused to flinch.

The wretched old crone crossed herself and scurried from the room.

"If you don't remember your name, wench," Roger drawled, "I shall inscribe a new one here for you where you won't forget it."

Myles took a faltering step toward her, but Roger blocked him with his arm.

She glanced down at the threatening blade and reluctantly complied, still struggling against Owen's grasp. "Cambria."

"Cambria? Cambria," he tried the name. "Ah now, that title does sing on the lips. But not as pretty as you do, I warrant. Shall I try, brother?"

Oh, God, not this, she thought—a cuff, a kick, but not this. Would no one stop him? From the corner of her eye, she saw Myles shift nervously from foot to foot, but knew he couldn't possibly lend her assistance, not with the brothers cheering their drunken encouragements to one another.

Roger sheathed his dagger, nodding at Owen for her release. Then, before she could twist free, he brought her up roughly against him, placed a meaty hand upon her face, and pressed his lips hard against hers. She battled to escape and tried to bite his lip, but he was too powerful. He opened her mouth with his, his beard scratching her skin like a whetstone, and she fought off the nausea of his sour breath and probing tongue.

When at last he released her to Owen's applause, she scrubbed at her mouth with the back of her hand. "You bastard!" she choked out. Her stomach was roiling again.

"Ah!" Roger swooned playfully, "now there's a song for your liking, lively and spirited! I think I shall enjoy learning to play this instrument!"

Myles had evidently seen enough. He took a step forward in her defense. But a sharp command from Roger set the hound of the still-slumbering knight upon Myles, growling and snapping at her young champion every time he moved a muscle. With rising desperation, Cambria cast about the room for an escape.

"Move not, wench!" Roger roared. "You are mine!"

"Never!" she cried, racing to the stairs.

The hulking knight followed at her heels and caught her about the legs. She stumbled and fell heavily on the stair, wincing as she bruised her knee and rent her kirtle. She clawed at the steps, kicking him as hard as she could, dragging herself slowly upward. But escape eluded her. He coiled his fist around her damp braid and lifted her up by the waist with one thick-muscled arm.

"Be not so anxious for my bed!" he laughed. "We'll be there soon enough!"

She felt like a jester's flopping puppet as he carried her ungracefully up the stairs and kicked open the bedchamber door. She beat at him with her fists, but her voice shook as she threatened him.

"If you lay a hand on me, you motherless cur, I shall kill you, I swear it!"

She cursed him, mostly to hide her very tangible fear. This was one battle she'd never been trained to fight. She didn't even know what weapon to use against a man's lust.

Roger slammed the door shut with his body, shoving the bolt home. Then he heaved her onto the crude pallet in the midst of the chamber. She scrambled to her knees, wishing to God she had her dagger.

"You will not touch me!" she announced, trying to regain some dignity by smoothing her garments.

He giggled and winked drunkenly at her.

She bit her lip. Her demands were not working. Perhaps she could shame him. "Is this the chivalry of an English knight?"

He ignored her and began to undress, humming to himself.

"Look, you bastard," she hissed, "I'm not some harlot. I'm a virgin." Surely he would leave her alone now.

"Are you?" he snorted carelessly. "Well, then, fortune's found you. You'll have the best teacher, you will." With that, he pulled off his gambeson to bare a wide, hairy chest.

She searched wildly for a weapon, anything. There was a clay chamberpot beside the bed. 'Twas heavy. 'Twas hard. She reached for it, flung it with all her might. But as soon as it left her hands, she sensed 'twould miss the target.

It shattered against the far wall.

Instantly, the massive knight was upon her. "Woman!" he shouted, pressing her against the plaster wall and spitting in his rage. "Make me not angry, or you shall suffer much in the losing of your maidenhead!"

She blanched.

He released his hold and pulled off the rest of his garments, leaving his huge body naked in the shadowy room.

His golden face was fierce and his size frightening. She swallowed hard. He couldn't mean to . . .

He weaved toward her. She clambered across the bed, heaving a bolster at him. He laughed and tossed it away. She picked up an empty wooden candle sconce and hurled it. It struck him on the shoulder.

"Damned bitch!" he swore. In one lunge, he flattened her, crushing the very breath from her. She tried to worm away from him as he covered her face with sloppy, ale-soaked kisses. His body was clammy and so impossibly heavy that her ribs could barely expand to allow her air. When he finally eased his weight off of her, it was only to yank her kirtle all the way up under her arms. He pressed his wet lips to her bared breast, and she fought to wake from the nightmare of his touch.

"You whoreson!" she screamed.

He bit her, and she shrieked.

"Hold your tongue, wench, I warn you!" he yelled through clenched teeth.

She shuddered as his knee forcefully spread her legs. In a final effort, she brought her knee up hard against him, but it had no effect upon him in his drunken state. He mumbled something as his weight fell upon her again, as heavy as a dozen mail hauberks. She couldn't move. Closing her eyes, she braced herself for the worst.

Within a few moments, she realized the worst had already happened. The lummox had passed out and was snoring loudly in her ear. She fought the desire to giggle hysterically. Fortune had found her indeed.

Struggling out from under the dozing hulk, she pulled her kirtle back down and ran shaky fingers through her tousled hair. Casting a wary eye toward her attacker, she crept to the door and lifted the bolt. She peered out.

Owen was still drinking and carrying on downstairs. She would never escape unnoticed.

Resignedly, she closed the door. She glanced at the huge golden knight and shuddered. She'd sleep sounder closeted with a bear. But she couldn't leave just yet, not until time was her ally. Afraid to move him for fear he'd awaken, she left

Roger where he was, taking a dark corner of the room for herself. She huddled against the cracked plaster and wrapped her arms around her knees. She had to think.

The windows were sealed shut. The men below were yet sober enough to be vigilant. The innkeeper's wife wasn't going to help her. And yet, she sighed, what did it matter? Even if she could escape, what would prevent the knights from finding her again? Lord Holden did not strike her as the sort of man who would give up easily. In fact, she thought with a shiver, he seemed the sort of man who would search the ends of the earth for what he wanted, if need be. It would avail her nothing to run.

Still, she couldn't bear the thought of facing the Wolf once more. The man was too dangerous, too powerful. His storm-green eyes seemed wont to invade the very fabric of her thoughts and wreak havoc there. Nay, she'd no desire to see him in the flesh again. She shuddered, pulling her kirtle tighter about her legs. She supposed she'd just have to run to the ends of the earth.

She never intended to fall asleep, propped against the sooty wall. She only meant to rest her eyes for a moment. But exhaustion overtook her, and she dozed off, mumbling a prayer that Roger would not awaken in the night.

Sir Roger did not awaken that night, nor any other night.

Cambria roused with a start an hour before dawn, dismayed that she'd slept so long. The knight yet lay where she'd left him. But when she saw his condition, the breath was ripped from her in a rough gasp.

A jagged blade protruded from Roger's breast. His blood, already drying in rivulets down his pale chest, spattered the furs and white walls and flecked his golden beard with scarlet-brown.

All her senses told her to run, but she stood frozen in morbid fascination. Dear God, even as she lay sleeping, soundlessly and in the space of a heartbeat, a man had been murdered. 'Twas as if the devil himself had done the deed.

Finally she broke free of her paralysis. Crossing herself superstitiously, she took a faltering step backward. She slipped out the door as quietly as she could. Fortunately, the knights and the hound below slept heavily after their evening of carousing. She carefully descended the complaining wooden stairs and inched to the front door of the inn, picking her way in the dark through the dozing bodies.

Suddenly the candled shadow of the innkeeper's wife fell across her. The woman was carrying a huge pot of water. Both froze for only an instant, but the look they exchanged spoke volumes. The woman nodded knowingly and continued about her labors as if she'd not seen Cambria.

Had the old woman murdered the knight? It didn't seem possible, and yet there was no other explanation.

Cambria sighed gratefully, then opened the door with painful stealth and edged through the crack. Shivering with the morning frost, she clutched the kirtle tightly about her and stole into the shadowy forest. The moss was still damp beneath her bare feet, and her breath came out in moist plumes.

She'd not traveled fifty paces from the inn when a twig snapped behind her. She spun in time to see a dark figure looming up. Wasting no time as the follower's footfalls closed the distance in the leaves behind her, she turned and fled through the mist-shrouded trees. The cold air knifed through her lungs, but still she ran desperately, aimlessly, into the thickening gorse, cursing the fact she had no weapon.

All at once, her luck and the narrowing path ran out. She was trapped in dense underbrush, like a boar cornered for the kill. She wheeled to find a dark knight brandishing a sword, her father's sword.

Owen.

As he came grimly forward to claim his prey, she searched the thicket for any way out. He swept his blade up to touch her vulnerable throat. She gasped once involuntarily and began to retreat. He followed her with the cold blade and colder eyes until she was pressed against the brambles and there was nowhere for her to go.

"You'll not escape this time, you murdering bitch," he growled.

The point of the sword nicked at her chin. Jesu, she realized, he could spill her life's blood at any moment.

"Murder? But I didn't . . ." she began.

The heel of his hand caught her temple hard, knocking her sideways. Branches clawed at her face like the bony fingers of ghouls, and black flecks danced before her eyes.

"Spare me your lying tongue!" he cried. "My brother lies dead, murdered in his sleep."

He snagged her arm then, pinioning her roughly before him. She staggered, and he shoved her forward, back toward the inn.

"You are a stupid wench," he snarled. "Roger was the son of a king. You'll swing from the gallows within a sennight."

She gulped. Was it true? Would she be blamed for Roger's murder? The devil take her temper, she *had* threatened to slay the man only last night. But she'd never have done it. Did they not know that? How could anyone believe the laird of Gavin would stab a man as he slept?

Still, she couldn't tell them the innkeeper's wife was responsible for Roger's death. The old woman had done Cambria a favor. She couldn't betray that kindness.

And yet, if she didn't, she was doomed. Owen was one of de Ware's knights. And Cambria was only a Scotswoman who'd already attempted to kill their lord. Sweet Mary, she thought in despair, she *was* going to the gallows.

Or perchance, she dared to hope, Lord Holden couldn't afford to execute her. After all, he might need her alive for the sake of the new alliance. Perhaps he wouldn't hang her immediately. Perhaps time was on her side. Still she swallowed in spite of herself, already feeling the noose around her tender neck.

By the time they returned to the inn, 'twas nearly dawn. Her arm ached from being gripped so cruelly. Sir Owen roused the entire inn with his bellowing until, groggy and only half-dressed, the de Ware knights came out to hear him.

"We have a murderer!" he shouted, his voice breaking in lament. "My brother lies dead in his chamber! This witch slew him while he slept, then tried to escape!"

A cry of pain was wrung from her as Owen viciously twisted her arm.

The knights looked amazed. The black-haired giant seethed with outrage. He bolted forward and seized her by the throat with one large hand. Already towering over her, he moved just inches from her face, so close that she could see the two gray hairs in his black beard. He spoke as if he chewed upon tough meat, clenching his fist before him and branding her with his coal black eyes.

"You cursed wench, it's a pity my cousin wishes you alive, or I'd slay you with my own hand! Be watchful once you are safely returned, for I'll not be far away."

He closed his hand tightly about her throat. Black spots swam before her, and she felt her heart struggling to pump blood through her veins. Her fingers clawed frantically at his. Then he released her abruptly, and she fell to the ground, coughing.

When she dared to look up, Myles was staring down at her, his gray eyes filled with disappointment and pity.

"She's dangerous! She must be bound!" Owen snapped, running his fingers through his greasy hair.

She was still quaking when the black-bearded ogre wrapped cords around her wrists and ankles, carried her out, and draped her, belly down, over Roger's horse, in the custom of a dishonored knight. She swallowed back rising bile as the knights placed Roger's cloaked dead body beside her on the steed.

In disgrace, Cambria returned to Castle Bowden.

Holden was already in a foul temper. He tossed his helm to the ground and jabbed the toe of his boot into the dust of the tiltyard. His efforts at training these Scots to fight were futile. They stubbornly resisted any attempts on his part to refine their wild technique and insisted on aimless hacking with their weapons rather than precise blows.

His frustration was only compounded by the fact that he'd been outwitted by one of them, a mere child. Nay, a woman, he corrected, as he remembered vividly the soft curves of her body. He was doubly incensed that she should have such an effect on him, and he'd spent long hours in the tiltyard the last few days, taking his anger out on his knights.

He pressed his weary eyes with the heels of his hands.

Damn Roger! The hound should have caught the girl's scent by now. What was taking so long? Perhaps he should have hunted her down himself.

Thus far, none of the Gavin clan had come for their laird, but it was certain they would. How would he explain to them that he'd . . . lost her?

Distracted by his thoughts and the artless display of combat taking place before him, Holden only stared blankly at the messenger who came to him until the words finally registered.

"What?" he exploded, bringing the farcical battle to a halt.

The page began to repeat the memorized message yet again. "Sir Owen, Sir Guy, and Sir Myles return. They have the Gavin girl, but Sir Roger is dead by her hand, and—"

Livid with rage, he interrupted the boy. "Have her brought to me at once in the hall!"

Within moments, Owen, dogged by Myles and Guy, dragged their captive before the dais of the great hall. Holden, still sweaty and disheveled from the practice field, stopped pacing when they entered. Owen threw the girl viciously to her knees. Holden saw her bite back a cry as she struck the stone floor, but he clenched his teeth against the mercy that came naturally to him. After all, the woman before him was now a full-fledged murderess. Not only that, but she'd murdered the king's issue. It was just fortunate that King Edward had little affection for his grandsire's bastard. Still, royal blood had been spilled.

"What happened?" he demanded.

They all began speaking at once. He held up his hand for silence. "Owen?"

"The Scots bitch slew my brother, my lord, as he slept."

"That's a lie!" the girl cried out. "I'd never—"

"Silence!" Holden was sure his face registered only half of the outrage he felt. "All of you would concur with this?"

He looked carefully from one to another. Owen thrust out his chin in challenge. Sir Guy scowled and nodded with the certainty of an executioner. Myles glanced down at the girl and opened his mouth as if to say something, then looked away quickly, nodding his assent.

Holden turned his back. He pinched the bridge of his nose between his fingers. Dear God, what was he going to do now? "My condolences, Sir Owen. You are welcome to send one of my servants to your mother with the news."

Owen murmured an acknowledgment.

"Now go, all of you . . . except the girl."

The knights vacated the hall, closing the heavy door with a hollow thud.

Holden paced for a long while before he could trust himself to speak civilly. Finally, he wheeled, looked down his nose at the bloodthirsty wench, and bit out, "You have slain one of my knights—a king's son, no less." His voice grew louder, harsher. "You have attempted to slay *me,* a lord." His vehement words rang out in the hall. "And you return unharmed after escaping from my prison!" Now he was shouting in a voice he usually reserved for the most unruly of his men, a voice he'd never used on a woman before. "You are fortunate to be living! Tell me this. What revenge could be so sweet that it would cost you your life three times over?"

She said nothing, but her defiant glare wavered. Perhaps she realized at last how precarious her life was.

Frustrated beyond his limits, he wiped the dust from his brow with both hands and paced heatedly. If only she were a man, he thought in irritation, they could simply draw swords and be done with it.

"When I was but a lad," he muttered, "I was told my mother died giving birth to me. On that day, I made a solemn vow never to harm another woman as long as I lived. But you—you are trying that promise." He cursed again and punched his fist into his hand. "Roger's kin will want your blood. King Edward may even require it. Are you aware of that?" he pressed.

The girl stared steadily past him. "I didn't slay him."

He threw up his hands. "Spare me your denial. You insult my intelligence."

"But I didn't slay him."

God, the woman was stubborn. He shoved his hand through his hair. "Three of my men have lent witness to your guilt."

She raised her chin. "I don't care if all of England lends witness to my guilt. I didn't slay your man."

He squeezed his eyes shut in frustration and cursed under his breath. Then he looked at her, hard.

She was still gazing off into the distance, well past him, as if their conversation was of no consequence to her. But he could see on closer inspection that her body trembled. Her false bravery was a mask for the fear in her eyes. And yet there was something achingly familiar about her expression, something that took him back to his own youth.

He himself had once worn that brave face, awaiting the whip for killing one of his uncle's hunting hounds. It had been an accident. He'd been training the dog to fetch a stick, rewarding him with scraps of meat from the kitchen. How could a young boy have known the hound would choke on a chicken bone? Still he'd been punished, and he'd accepted his punishment stoically, even though it wasn't in him to slay an innocent creature. . . .

Just as it wasn't in *her* to commit murder.

Despite the others' confirmation of Owen's charge, despite an obvious motive and an apparent opportunity for her to accomplish the crime, he was certain she hadn't done it. The trembling of her upraised chin and the flicker of uncertainty in her moist gaze told him the truth. Aye, the reckless wench had a penchant for violence, and she'd probably challenge anything on two legs to battle. Indeed, she might have slain Sir Roger in defense. But she was incapable of cold-blooded killing.

His men, however, were sure she'd done the deed, and until he could sort out what had really happened, he'd have to take them at their word. He needed time, both to dredge up the truth and to let his men's heads cool. And then there was the whole Gavin clan, waiting with bated breath for news of their laird.

"Listen well, my lady," he sighed. "For the moment I'll

spare your life, but you must yield to me and renounce your quest for revenge, once and for all."

The girl straightened her back and focused on a point over his head. "Never could I yield to my father's murderers. I, too . . . made a vow."

His blood froze in his veins. Was she completely addled? Pride was one thing, but this . . . He was handing the wench her life on a silver tray. How dare she throw it back in his face? His voice grew perilously soft. "Then you may live to regret your vow as I regret mine."

She tried to resist him as he stepped from the dais and hauled her to her feet, but in truth she was no more trouble for him than a spitting kitten. He tossed her over one shoulder, ignoring her shrieks, then mounted the stairs at the corner of the hall.

Damn the wench, he wished she'd stop squirming. He could feel vividly the points of her delicate hipbones against his shoulder and her soft breasts upon his back. Besides, all her thrashing could do naught but add to the numerous bruises she already bore as her heels bumped against the narrow stone walls.

He struggled up the last winding steps to the tower cell. Kicking open the thick door, he set her on her feet with a bone-jarring bang.

"You will not escape again." He jabbed a finger at the air before her as if speaking to a child. "I will post a guard below the window to prevent the temptation."

"What do you intend to do with me?" she demanded venomously.

He gave her his most diabolical smile. "I'll let you think on that. I am a just man. I assure you, the punishment shall befit the crime."

"But I've done nothing," she insisted, her eyes flashing like the devil's own.

"Lady," he replied, disbelief clouding his brow, "you've done more to destroy any hope of peace in the last week than your father ever did in his lifetime to assure it."

He could see his words were like a dagger twisted in her heart, but he was infuriated by the girl's stubbornness and the perilous position she'd put him in. If nothing else, she should suffer for *that.*

The fire deserted the wench's eyes. She sank down dejectedly onto the straw pallet.

Damn her, he almost felt a pang of remorse for his harsh words. But he couldn't let his pity interfere with his sense of justice. He was going to have to somehow placate both Roger's family and the Gavins without damaging the fragile harmony between their people. He raked a hand wearily through his hair. He wondered if such a thing would be possible.

"You will be safer for the moment here in confinement," he informed her, "and I want you where I won't need to constantly watch my back. Our time of reckoning will come later."

Before she could completely melt his resolve with her beautiful, watery eyes, he turned and left her, cursing his weakness for women's tears. Why did this have to happen now, he wondered, just as he was beginning to gain real favor with the king?

Cambria rose and walked to the locked door. She dashed away her tears and rested her forehead against the rough wood. Beyond that door dwelled men who believed her capable of cold-blooded murder, men who longed to mete out their own justice for her imagined crimes.

De Ware was right. She was safer here. Of course, that didn't mean she wouldn't try to escape. 'Twas her duty as the Gavin, after all.

When the sun's slender morning rays filtered into the tower chamber, Cambria was hardly able to stir. It seemed winter had visited in the middle of the April night. Tiny crystals of ice frosted the gray stones of the chamber, and her jaw ached from clenching her teeth in the cold. Her fingers and toes were stiff, and the thin fabric she had torn from the pallet did little to insulate her body from the mists outside.

Light footsteps ascended the stairs. They stopped by the door. A key turned in the lock, but she was too frozen to move.

A pretty, doe-eyed maidservant entered with a tray and closed the door. "I'm Gwen, m'lady. I've brought you somethin' to eat," she ventured, her face openly curious.

Cambria slowly sat up on the pallet and gazed at the steaming pot of porridge. Her stomach rumbled. She took the tray from the maid and set it upon her lap. Eyeing Gwen warily, she slipped a small spoonful of the cereal into her mouth and swallowed. 'Twas lumpy, but at least 'twas warm and filling.

Eagerly consuming the porridge, she watched the attendant serving wench with keen interest. Perhaps, she considered, she might escape again after all. The lass was frail, probably no stronger than a sparrow. If she could catch her by surprise . . .

Cambria carefully lowered her scheming eyes and affected her mother's delicate voice. "Please, Gwen," she begged, "you must help me."

Her words obviously made the servant uneasy. The girl started wringing her hands. Cambria fought off a smile. It was going to be devilishly simple to prey upon this one's soft heart.

"I fear I will die if I am left here like this," she continued. "'Tis so cold."

The girl looked upon her with eyes full of pity. "There is to be no escape from the tower, m'lady," she said gently.

"Oh, nay, I could not ask you that," Cambria assured her, shivering, "only could you not bring me clothing to keep me warm? A servant's kirtle, anything."

The maid bit her lip in indecision, then whispered, "Aye, m'lady, seein' as how you're like to freezin' nights and all, but I'd not let the lord catch you with it. He gave orders to bring you naught but meals."

Cambria forced a sweet, thankful smile, even clasping the maid's hand in her own.

The girl blushed. "I'll see what I can do, m'lady." She withdrew her hand and hastily made her way out of the room.

Cambria had to move quickly in spite of her unthawed bones. She gulped down the remaining porridge and tested the strength of her weapon, the clay porridge pot. Twice she looked out the window to check the positions of Holden's men.

'Twas a quarter hour before she heard steps coming up again. She felt an instant of regret for what she was about to do, and she hastily prayed the girl would survive the blow, but she was desperate. With the maid temporarily disposed of and a new set of clothing, Cambria might make an escape.

The key turned in the lock.

Cambria lifted the empty pot high over her head, waiting for the servant to enter. But the door swung open with a force she'd not expected. Startled, she hesitated a moment too long before she brought the heavy vessel down.

To her horror, it wasn't the servant's arm that slammed her body against the wall, causing her to drop the pot, but that of a seething Wolf.

5

G WEN SCURRIED IN BEHIND HIM, GASPING AS SHE REALIZED the shattered pot had been meant for her.

With a snarl, the Wolf seized Cambria roughly about the waist and lugged her past Gwen, who gaped on in astonishment. He hauled her down the steps like a willful child. She fought against him, but all her writhing did naught but raise her kirtle higher and higher up her leg. His great hands seared her like hot iron where they touched her chilled body, and she could feel the tensed muscles of his thighs beneath her as he trudged down the stairs. He held her tightly against a chest that was as unyielding as a tree, and all her struggles only made him pull her closer to that powerful body.

To her amazement, Lord Holden stopped in the hallway, kicking open the door to a richly appointed chamber, and flung her to the great curtained bed in its midst, spilling her limbs haphazardly across the pallet. Before she could recover, he took an iron shackle from his belt and quickly cuffed one of her wrists to the bedpost. Then he stood back, breathing heavily, satisfying himself that she was secure.

"You will *not* escape again!" he shouted, slamming the door closed behind them.

Cambria's fury overrode her fear. She'd had enough of the humiliation of being hauled hither and thither like a sack of laundry. The last threads of her temper frayed.

"I will *not* be your vassal!" she cried, scrambling to her knees, all caution thrown to the wind in the heat of rage. "I will not sit idly by while you slay my people and take my home! I will never pledge fealty to you, you miserable bastard! There is no torture I will not endure for my clan, and no prison of your making will hold me!"

Lord Holden looked incredulous at her audacity. "And you think to replace your father as laird of Gavin." A lock of hair fell over his brow as he railed at her, punctuating each of her faults with an accusing finger. "You cannot control your rampant temper! You greatly overrate your abilities with a sword! And you haven't got a whit of common sense!" He snapped his fingers at her. "Checkmate, my lady! This is the fortress of the enemy. You have no power here. Your very life is in my hands!"

She drilled him with her eyes and tugged violently on the shackle. "I've escaped you before. I *will* have my revenge, I swear it!"

"If you will remember," he bit out, "you have already *taken* your revenge. Roger Fitzroi was my knight."

"'Twas not my hand that ended your knight's life," she hissed, "although I admit if I'd had a dagger, I might well have done the deed myself. He was a bloody, swiving son of a . . ."

"He was the son of a king!" The Wolf burrowed his hand through his mane. "You condone his murder," he barked, "and yet you expect me to believe it wasn't your doing!" He continued sardonically, "It was likewise never your intent to do *me* harm on the battlefield in striking me when I had laid down my arms."

She colored at that remark. She knew there was no excuse for her conduct that day, but she'd be damned if she'd yield the point. "I had the courage to face an adversary twice my size! How many of your knights could say that?"

"None of my knights are that stupid!" he scoffed. "That was not courage. That was foolishness!"

God, she hated the way he stole her words and used them as weapons against her. In frustration, she resorted to hideous name-calling. "You are the vilest baseborn spawn of the devil! I hope to see your black heart torn from you and your putrid remains hung from the foulest tower! You are the very scum of the earth, you filthy, knavish, mud-suckling beast of a . . ."

Somewhere in the midst of her colorful tirade, Holden stopped listening. The absurdity of the situation suddenly struck him. Here he was, the lord of the castle, with the most comely wench he'd ever laid eyes on chained to his bed, and he was exchanging insults with her.

He regarded her with new eyes as she continued her futile raving. Her chestnut tresses cascaded over her shoulders like a waterfall, alternately exposing and concealing her linen-covered breasts with each vehement oath. Her cheeks flushed the color of a ripe peach, and her eyes sparked like two bright crystals flashing fire. Oblivious to her own beauty, unaware of how bewitching she was in her present state, she sat delectably in the midst of his bed like a tempting sweetmeat, ready to be unwrapped and consumed, and that made her all the more attractive. God, she was distracting. He couldn't even remember why he was angry with her. By the saints, it had been too long since he'd had a woman.

". . . and I promise you my revenge will be slow and painful and merciless!" she finished. She'd apparently run out of curses to lay upon him, simply fixing him now with an icy glare.

He responded, not with his previous malice, but with a thickness in his voice that felt as if he'd swallowed honey.

"Revenge?" he asked, moving in on her like his namesake wolf. "What revenge will you take, lady, shackled to my bed?" His eyes flickered over her body, and he only half lied. "Ah, in sooth you wreak your revenge even now."

She might not have understood his words, but the hunger in his regard made her yank the fur coverlet from the bed with her free hand to shield herself. And for the first time, he saw fear in her eyes, genuine, naked fear.

He narrowed his gaze. By Jesu, he'd just stumbled upon the chink in the wench's armor. Violence didn't frighten her—she'd been trained to accept it. But lust she didn't understand, and one always feared what one didn't understand. Perhaps he did have a weapon to use against her after all.

But not now. Too much was at stake. With a rueful smile and enormous effort, he forced himself to back away till she visibly relaxed. It was the most difficult thing he'd done in his life.

"Mark well my words, lady. You are powerless, but you are also safe here. Were you to escape again, there are many men who would not think twice before slitting your pretty throat." He added, "And I'm not certain they would be in the wrong."

"You believe I killed him." It wasn't a question.

"You've done little to prove yourself *in*capable of the deed."

Her frown was thoughtful. "What will you do with me?"

"For the moment, you'll remain here."

Her eyes widened. "You can't mean to leave me chained like this—not to your bed!"

He smirked at her offended propriety and cocked his brow at her, fueling the fire of her temper. "You have a place to sleep. I'll have meals brought to you. And there's a chamberpot beside the bed. You have all the comforts you require."

"Have you no . . . decency?" she sputtered. "I am a lady!"

"No lady curses the way you do, and no lady commits murder."

"I do not curse, you bloody bastard, and I've never killed a man in my life!" she snapped. "How dare you dishonor me by keeping me here. You know well what they will say."

"What will they say?"

She exhaled in a huff of exasperation. "They'll say that you keep me here for . . ." She began to blush. It was most becoming. "That we are . . ."

"Ah, that we are lovers?"

Her face turned crimson.

"They already know you for a murderer," he said. "What consequence they should also believe you a whore?"

The wench lunged against the chain as if she ached to

claw his eyes out. He shook his head at her useless movements.

"I have things to attend to," he told her. "I'll send up bread and wine for you. This time, have a care for Gwen. She is a loyal servant. I'd hate to have to beat her for her assistance in your escape."

She paled at his words, and he suppressed a smile. His threat was ludicrous. He'd never raised his fist to a woman in his life. He pulled a ring of keys from his pouch and dangled it like a bone before a hound.

"I hold the shackle key. It never leaves me." Her face fell as he tucked her only hope back into the pouch. "You'll be isolated here—no one enters my chambers without my permission." He folded his arms across his chest. "It shall prove entertaining, I'm certain, to see just how you plan to make an escape this time."

She glared at him as he inclined his head toward her in farewell, exiting with a flourish out the door.

Cambria, of course, immediately began considering the possibilities for that escape. Unfortunately, with the key in de Ware's possession, freedom was unlikely. How long, she wondered, would he keep her here? He'd said 'twould be breaking a vow to slay her, but wouldn't his knights demand satisfaction? Someone would have to pay for the life of Roger Fitzroi. She crumpled the fur coverlet in her fist. No one would believe the truth. And yet Lord Holden was keeping her alive.

She smiled humorlessly. Perhaps he awaited her confession. After all, an admission of guilt would seal her fate, leaving him blameless. She glanced at the heavy iron band encircling her wrist. He apparently meant to shame her into confessing.

It wouldn't work, of course. She'd learned long ago to put her own pride aside for the needs of her clan. Still, she hoped none of her men would find her in this compromising position. And she prayed Lord Holden would find somewhere else to sleep.

By day's end, it looked as if one prayer had been answered. Gwen had taken away her half-eaten trencher of pottage, the moon had already risen in the black sky, and Lord Holden was nowhere to be seen.

He'd probably found some strumpet's linens to lie between. Well, so much the better, she decided, flouncing over onto her side and punching down the feather bolster. She could have the big, comfortable bed all to herself. She tucked the warm furs about her and, gazing into the dying embers of a fire she couldn't reach to bank, slowly faded off to sleep.

A sparrow trilled enthusiastically from outside the window. Cambria frowned, snuggling more deeply into the furs in protest of the encroaching morn. She sighed at the wonderful enveloping warmth of the big bed. 'Twas almost like being a little girl again, held in her mother's cozy embrace.

The thought brought her fully awake in an instant. She sat up abruptly, pulling free of the arms enclosing her.

The Wolf!

Her motions roused him. Disoriented with panic, she scuffled backwards on the pallet and promptly fell off the bed, landing with a thump on her hindquarters.

Holden lifted himself up on his elbows, his hair askew, and peered down with one sleepy eye, looking completely baffled.

"You . . ." Her voice was scratchy. She felt her cheeks grow hot. "What are you doing here?"

He sighed groggily. "Sleeping. At least I *was.*"

"This is *my* bed!" she gasped.

He took a quick survey of his surroundings. "Nay, it's not. It's *my* bed."

"Then . . ." she sputtered, "then I shouldn't be in it."

He shrugged and gave her a sleepy smile. "That's all right. I forgive you." He settled back onto the bolster and closed his eyes. "It's not the first time I've awakened to find a woman has crawled into my bed."

Her jaw dropped. The man was as vain as Narcissus.

"God's truth, I was going to have you spend the night on the floor," he continued, yawning, "but you'd fallen asleep. I didn't have the heart to push you off the bed. I see you've done that yourself."

"How dare you sleep here with me!" she hissed, tossing her head in what she hoped was righteous condescension.

"How dare I indeed?" he said with a twisted grin. "It shall be the ruin of my reputation. I assure you it's not my usual habit to sleep when there's a woman in my bed."

"You bastard."

"Are you disappointed? I could make amends," he offered, rubbing his sleep-filled eyes.

She shot him a scathing glare. "I'm only disappointed I was unaware of your arrival. I would've tormented you as you slept."

His eyes slowly coursed down her body as if they were melting her garments. "Ah, little wildcat, you *did* torment me."

She felt her mouth go lax. No one had looked at her like that before. No one had said such things to her, and his compelling voice combined with his unashamed countenance completely rattled her.

"Do not call me that," she muttered uncomfortably.

"What am I to call you? You've not yet given me your name," he reminded her, pushing himself up to a sitting position.

Her glance rested overlong on the strong contours of his wide chest, raised boldly above the fur coverlet. 'Twas only curiosity, she told herself, about the faint scar that ran across his ribs. But she had difficulty tearing her eyes away. A few curling dark hairs accented the curve of muscle beside the scar and made a line down his ridged stomach, a line that disappeared thankfully below the coverlet. She raised her eyes again.

He was smiling at her, the knave, an infuriating, all too perceptive smile.

Suddenly, she was disgusted with herself. Damn it, she wasn't some rutting maid. She was here on a mission. He wanted to know who she was. She would tell him.

"I am the Gavin, Cambria, daughter of Angus. I am a lady, and I insist upon my own pallet. I will not share a bed with you. I am not some serving wench who would ease your lusts. . . ."

"Ease my . . . With you?" He chuckled. "I have no need of an unwilling mistress, Cambria, I assure you."

His half-naked presence seemed to fill the room as he rose from the bed, wrapping the coverlet about his waist. Her eyes felt suddenly as overtaxed as a butterfly with a field of daisies all to itself, flitting about madly. He began to pace slowly, and the sensual flex of his torso made things even worse.

"Furthermore, Cambria, you are my prisoner. You may 'insist' on nothing. You will sleep where I command. You will eat what I provide. You will wear what I allow you to wear." He lowered his voice to a soft murmur. "And should it ever be my will that you spread yourself so that I may indeed 'ease my lusts' betwixt your thighs, Cambria, you will do even that."

His words brought her around faster than a hard slap. Her jaw dropped in shock, and her startled head shot up. But before she could deliver a scathing retort, he continued.

"You seem to forget—my sword is at your throat, Cambria. I'd be only too happy to continue reminding you of that fact."

She wished he would stop calling her by name. 'Twas having the most disturbing effect on her.

Without warning, he unwrapped his coverlet and let it drop to the floor.

Appalled at his immodesty, she quickly ducked her head away. What a brash knave he was. No doubt he'd gotten that long scar on his thigh from some hotheaded brawl.

"In any event," he continued, ignoring her discomfiture and donning his chausses, "you'll have the bed to yourself. I'll be away for a few days. It seems there is still a band of renegade Scots roaming the countryside, intent on taking on the entire English army." He shook his head. "Your people's pride will be their undoing."

She lifted her chin defiantly at the sardonic edge in his voice and fixed her eyes on the wall. " 'Tis their pride that has kept them alive."

To her surprise, he nodded in agreement. "Perhaps," he said pensively, "but there are times when pride can be blinding. Your Scots have become fanatics, and fanatics are dangerous, particularly to themselves."

She couldn't think of one suitable argument, so she avoided his gaze. As he dressed, she smoothed the material of her own gown, combed her disheveled hair with her fingers, and primly perched on the edge of the bed.

"You must unchain me," she decided abruptly when he was decent, or at least as decent as he was ever going to be.

"Must I?" He blinked.

"You've said you carry the only shackle key," she began, innocently enough.

"Aye." He folded his arms across his chest.

"Should you by chance be killed by that band of Scots on your little escapade, who would then be left to free me that I may dance on your grave?"

He stared at her in silence a long moment. Then a wry smile curved his lips. "Lady Cambria, I vow your tongue is more poisonous than a viper's."

She had no reply for this that wouldn't merely reinforce his opinion, so she busied herself studying the armor laid out on the pallet. She frowned, scrutinizing a flaw in the mail. The hauberk had obviously weathered many a battle. Its finish was dull, and several of the iron rings were dented from enemy sword.

"The links along the ribs need repair," she muttered, forgetting for the moment that he was the enemy and simply stating the information out of habit.

He looked up, not at the mail, but at her.

She pointed to the place. "Your mail . . . there is damage there, a gap."

He narrowed his eyes at her, but paid little heed to her words. "Tell me, how did a lady come to learn of arms and swordplay?"

"My . . . father taught me." The word was still hard to say. She couldn't believe he was gone.

"Why?"

"Because I am the Gavin."

"You are a woman."

"I can wield a sword," she replied proudly.

"You do have a certain agility and speed," he admitted, pulling a padded gambeson over his head, "but you lack strength, and you've no grasp of chivalry. You cannot continue attacking unarmed opponents. Did your father not teach you that?"

She felt her face flush scarlet. "I know the rules of chivalry," she mumbled.

"Ah, so you chose to ignore them."

She deftly changed the subject. "You must remove the shackle before you go."

He pulled on his soft leather boots and paused in thought. "You expect me to believe I can trust you to stay here?"

"You dare ask me that after *you* betrayed my father's trust?"

"Your father betrayed *my* trust," he insisted.

She could feel the hollow ache of tears gathering in her throat, but she forced them down. "All my father ever cared about were his people and his land. He had no concern for who sat upon the throne." She stabbed him with an icy glare. "He was going to sign your damned documents!"

"He never signed them. He attacked my men."

"He couldn't have!"

"Were you there?" he demanded, his eyes challenging her.

The space of silence grew as her agony of doubt filled the room. She'd cursed herself a thousand times for having slept through the horrible slaughter of her father.

"Nay," she finally admitted, defeat thickening her voice.

His point made, he turned his back on her and slipped his heavy hauberk on. He shrugged the mail over his shoulders and adjusted the length from front to back.

Then he let out a loud sigh and turned to her. "I should not trust you," he murmured.

Nonetheless, he retrieved the ring of keys from the leather pouch lying atop his tabard and jangled it against his palm.

"Your clan is important to you, is it not?"

She lifted her chin, once again as proud as any queen. "'Tis of the highest importance."

"Then will you swear, upon your honor to your clansmen,

that you'll not attempt to escape from this keep while I'm away?"

She gave his words careful consideration. She didn't like making such a promise, but what choice did she have? She slowly nodded her assent. "Aye," she replied, "I swear it."

He bent over her to work the lock, one knee pressing into the pallet beside her. He slipped a finger beneath the shackle band, brushing the delicate skin of the inside of her wrist. She swallowed hard. His hands, though battle-nicked, were long-fingered and nimble, not at all the brutal paws she'd expected. The masculine scent of him—the iron tang of his armor, the musk of leather, some elusive spice, woodruff or cinnamon—seemed to engulf her. His hair curled rebelliously down his neck, and his lips tensed slightly as he tried the various keys. His breath was even and gentle upon her face, and he was close enough for her to see the stubble on his cheek. His lashes were as thick and dark as the trees in a wood, and though they were lowered, she remembered his eyes were the color of Highland pines, deep and wise and mysterious. Odd, she thought, she'd not noticed the gray flecks in them before, but then . . .

Lord, he was staring at her. Flustered, she dropped her gaze. Then she noticed that the shackles were already unlocked. She cleared her throat and rubbed hard at her wrist.

He moved away then, but the air still felt charged around her. She closed her eyes against the sensation. Curse him, this was the man who was responsible for her father's death.

"Thank you," she said frostily.

He winced almost imperceptibly. Then, with a brusque nod, he went to open the door, calling for the squire outside to help him with his armor plate.

"You have leave to wander the castle," he informed her, "but not to go beyond the castle wall. I will issue orders that you are not to be harmed. Even so, were I you, I'd not attract the attention of knights who may have cause to despise you."

He needn't have warned her. She remembered Sir Guy's dark threat vividly.

When the squire finished, his master looked formidable indeed. The chain mail fit over his muscular arms and legs like the scaly plate of a dragon. The rich forest green tabard, emblazoned with the fierce black Wolf of de Ware, draped gracefully over the mail and was caught snugly at his hips with a black leather belt. The gleaming armor plate made his already broad shoulders that much more imposing.

The squire took his leave, handing the lord his gauntlets and great helm as he did so. Lord Holden faced her, pulling the mail gauntlets over his large hands.

"I will return a few days hence, and if you are not here, laird of Gavin," he said ominously, "pray that I never find you."

When he'd left and closed the door behind him, Cambria let out the breath she'd been holding. She stood and flexed her arms like a falcon loosed from its jesses. She was free now.

So why did she still feel imprisoned by the man?

She shivered and looked about her. This chamber was indisputably his domain, or rather he'd *made* it his, from the dark red damask bed curtains and deep blue feather bolsters to the intricate Oriental carpet and the well-ordered quill and parchment set upon the table. Even his scent lingered in the room. He may have gone, but she still belonged to him, just as much as the carpet or the table or the candlesticks. And no matter how magnanimous he'd seemed in granting her her freedom, she was sure he'd left orders for her to be watched closely, just like his other property.

Eventually she drifted over to the arched window. Below, Holden and nine of his men were mounting up to ride off across the flower-studded hills. She prayed they'd not meet Gavin men. Robbie and Graham were so young, like children next to these invaders. The knights made a formidable company, even if they were English, particularly with Lord Holden at their fore.

He must have felt her eyes upon him, for he turned before they rode into the forest and gave her a salute. She stepped back from the window and clapped the shutters close before he could see the pink flush of her cheeks.

A moment later, Gwen timidly crept in with bread and watered wine. She wouldn't meet Cambria's eyes. Cambria imagined she was probably still stung by the near attack of the day before. Her kicked dog expression made Cambria regret her earlier actions, so she broke the loaf of bread and handed the maid a chunk of it in an overture of peace.

As they shared the meal, Cambria casually inquired about de Ware. After all, the first rule of battle was to know the enemy. She'd promised not to attempt escape. She'd said nothing about *planning* to attempt escape.

"Why, the lord's taken all of Bowden under his wing, he has," Gwen told her, warming to the subject. "We were half-starved when he came, but the larders are full now. They call him the Wolf, y'know, but I've not met a kinder master."

This news didn't cheer Cambria. Lord Holden had obviously been bluffing about beating Gwen. Confound it all, she wanted to hear that he was a twisted, malicious beast that fed on the blood of innocents. If he truly had such capacity for kindness, how could she then justify his actions at Blackhaugh? Was it conceivable, as the rest of the Gavin clan seemed to think, that it wasn't Holden de Ware who had conspired to slay her father? She broke off a chunk of the heavy black bread and gnawed at it, considering the possibility.

"Why is he called the Wolf?"

Gwen screwed up her face thoughtfully and answered, "I s'pose it's 'cause he's very brave and cunnin' on the battlefield. Accordin' to all accounts, he's never lost a battle, y'know," she added proudly, sitting a little straighter.

"Never?" She found this difficult to believe, considering the number of dents his armor bore.

"Not a one."

She imagined 'twould be easy to claim such a record if he always caught his enemies unaware the way he had at Blackhaugh. Then she remembered how he'd chided *her* for not following the rules of chivalry. Damn the man! Which was he—slaughterer or saint? Holden de Ware was becoming a frustrating series of contradictions.

"And what did the Wolf do with the knights who opposed him at Bowden?" she asked, sure his cruelty would be demonstrated now.

Gwen shrugged. "None opposed him."

"No one questioned his authority?" she demanded. "They just let him take what he wanted?"

"Why, m'lady," Gwen replied, "if he's never lost a battle, only a fool would challenge him." Then suddenly realizing what she'd said, she gasped and sputtered, "I-I mean . . ."

"He's not yet conquered the Gavin," Cambria stated, her eyes narrowing. She walked to the window of her prison, cocked open the shutter, and gazed out, imagining a time when she'd play the victor, not the captive.

Gwen, seeing that Cambria was preoccupied with her own thoughts, used the moment to mumble an excuse and escape the solar before her tongue could get her into yet another scrape.

"The ashes are warm," Sir Stephen reported, crouching by the makeshift fire and rubbing the gray remains between his fingers.

Holden frowned. He stared at his man without hearing him. A paradox kept biting at his brain with the persistence of a flea. Cambria Gavin, murderess or no, was nonetheless the enemy, and she'd become as troublesome as a thistle beneath a saddle. How could what he felt toward her possibly be called desire? And yet didn't it seem to come with all the symptoms of that primal emotion?

"My lord?" Stephen prompted, scowling back.

Holden blinked. Damn, he thought, he was having trouble concentrating on the task at hand. And by Stephen's expression, his distraction was painfully obvious.

"Warm?" he repeated.

It was that damned sprite. For the first time in his life, he'd met a foe he didn't know how to fight. Never before had he met a woman he couldn't handle. They were usually such pleasant creatures, docile, easy to please, grateful for his sword, even more grateful for his affections. What was wrong with this wench? Part of him wanted to throttle the bloodthirsty Scotswoman, and the other part . . .

The other part he'd sate with the next willing maid he met, he vowed. The Scots lass, after all, held no particular sway over him, no more than any other passing fair female. Why then could he not force her from his mind?

"The ashes, my lord," Stephen said in measured irritation.

Holden clamped his teeth together and willed himself to focus on his duties. He'd be damned if he'd let that little elf bewitch him at this distance.

"How long do you guess, Stephen?"

"No more than an hour."

"We're close then."

"If it's indeed the renegades we're following," Sir Henry piped in from atop his mount.

"Aye, it's them," Sir Myles replied as he knelt in the dust beside the fire. "One of them has orange hair, aye?"

"Aye," Stephen replied.

Myles picked up a single coppery hair between his thumb and finger and held it up for all to see.

"You've the eye of a gerfalcon, Myles," Holden praised. "Good work. We'll separate here. On foot, they can't have gone far." He mounted Ariel and patted her sleek neck. "Stephen, Henry, you come with me. Myles, Owen, and John, travel east. The rest of you head north. We'll meet here again before nightfall. By then, God willing, one of us will have captured the renegades."

Less than an hour later, a rustling in the bushes ahead startled Holden from his troubled thoughts, and the three destriers froze instantly in response to their masters' silent commands. Slowly the men dismounted, the only noises the squeak of shifting saddles and the whisper of drawn blades. Stealthily they crept forward. Holden peered ahead toward the source of the sound, but then his keen ear heard a twig snap in the brush to the left behind them and another rustle of leaves from the right.

He only had time for one thought—they had walked into a trap—before he felt the sharp agony of a blade piercing his flawed mail and sinking deep into his chest.

Cambria watched the day grow rapidly dreary and bleak. Showers were imminent, but the sky aged gracelessly into a vague gray presence that held onto the rain like a miser with his coins. With the knights collected within the keep, she had little desire to leave the security of Holden's chamber. Consequently she grew as restless as the weather. When the clouds finally spilled their harvest, 'twas with a vengeance, and she found herself idly wondering where Holden and his men would find shelter.

She'd been pacing like a lion in a cage, desperately bored, so 'twas with great relief that she welcomed Gwen's arrival with apple coffyns and wine shortly after midday.

The servant proved good enough company. Gleaning news from her was like taking the cork from a keg of ale. Never had she met a maid so eager to wag her tongue on any subject, and since Gwen had struck up a courtship with one of Holden's men, she possessed a wealth of information. Thus Cambria discovered that Holden was one of three sons, the middle one. His older brother Duncan and he shared the same mother, but young Garth was the son of their father's second marriage. Holden had no doubt joined Edward's army in hopes of gaining land for himself. 'Twas one of the only ways a younger son could win property and become a lord in his own right. Still, it chafed at her that one of the properties he'd laid claim to was Gavin land.

Cambria was then forced to listen to Gwen's babbling about the lord's infamous dalliances. According to all reports, there were few maids he'd not bedded, and the de Ware household was constantly enlarging to accommodate a number of green-eyed bastard children whom his older brother Duncan insisted on fostering. Gwen spared no details concerning Holden's alleged prowess and renowned virility, and by the time the supper hour had arrived, Cambria found herself completely irritated by the maid's prattle. Then, as if that weren't enough, as a final insult to Cambria's sensibilities, Gwen coyly informed her that she had plans to meet her own lover, Holden's gaoler, in the dungeon at midnight.

Cambria rolled her eyes. How anyone could focus so much attention on affairs of the heart, or more accurately, the loins, when there were battles to be waged and mouths to be fed, was beyond her ken.

By nightfall, disgusted with Gwen's chatter, weary of confinement, and unable to sleep, Cambria decided to venture forth. Perhaps she could find some tome from Bowden's library in which to bury her nose. To her irritation, she was dogged by a pair of less than discreet squires Lord Holden had no doubt set to shadow her every move.

Tiptoeing down the stairs to the great hall with an illuminated history of Rome, she was displeased to see the spot by the fire already occupied. The ominous Sir Guy half-reclined in a carved chair, his slippered feet up on a stool and his fingers laced peacefully over his large stomach.

Before she could creep back up the steps, he raised his black eyes. "I am under oath to cause you no harm," he grumbled.

No harm indeed, she thought dubiously. Her neck still bore the bruises from the big man's fingers. "I can read elsewhere. I only need—"

"Read?" he interrupted with sudden interest.

"Aye."

"What do you have there?" He nodded toward the book.

Wanting nothing more than to remove herself from the awkward situation, she told him. "'Tis an account of Roman history."

His eyes narrowed suspiciously. "You weren't thinking to steal it?"

"Of course not," she said tightly.

"Bring it here," he commanded, and she thought that while he may be under oath not to harm her, that certainly didn't keep him from ordering her about with his dark scowl and menacing presence. She stifled an oath and took a step toward him. He suddenly seemed larger than she remembered.

"How did you learn to read?" he growled.

"My father taught me."

He smirked. "Swords *and* books, eh?" He sniffed and nodded again at the tome. "What does it say?"

She realized with astonishment that Sir Guy couldn't read. And she could. The idea sent a heady wave of pride surging through her.

Well, she was bored, after all, and the great hall boasted

the brightest fire by which to see. She supposed reading to the enemy was no great crime. She pulled a chair up next to his, wincing at its loud rasp across the stones. Settling onto the seat, she opened the book and pointed to the words as she began reciting them.

The Englishman listened with great fascination, and soon her awkwardness dissolved away. Indeed, in spite of his coarse appearance, Guy was like a little boy enraptured with a new toy. So engrossed did they become with the reading that the harsh scrape of the outer door made them both jump in surprise.

An icy wind blew in angrily through the portal, causing the fire to dance wildly. Cambria shot to her feet. There was a confusion of movement and shouting as several rain-soaked de Ware knights stumbled into the great hall.

One of the men-at-arms called out to whoever was at hand. "Heat water and bring linen!"

Then the wind slammed the door, blocking out the melancholy wailing of the storm.

Two knights struggled toward the fire, carrying something heavy on a big blanket hung between a pair of lances. Cambria gasped as she recognized the silent, pale form stretched out on the makeshift litter.

'Twas Lord Holden, and there was blood everywhere.

SIR GUY TURNED ON HER WITH A FURIOUS GLARE, AS IF SHE were to blame for whatever had transpired.

Somewhere a servant fetched a bucket of water and cloth for bandages, and the physician was roused from his bed. Only after the litter was carefully lowered to the floor did Cambria notice the three men kneeling in cruel chains on the stones beyond the litter, held there by two of Holden's knights. They were bloody and ragged, and it took her a moment to realize who they were.

Robbie's fiery red hair was dulled beneath a crust of filth, but his temper blazed as hot as ever in his angry blue eyes. Beside Robbie was his younger brother, Graham, fourteen summers old, looking suddenly much older in his pain and fear. The third was her older cousin Jamie. 'Twas the first time she'd ever seen him without a smile on his face.

At Guy's harsh command, the two knights dragged the prisoners to their feet and hauled them off to the dungeon. If her clansmen noticed her at all, they showed no sign of it, or perhaps terror blinded them.

Sick in her heart, she retreated from the horrible scene and stole up the stairs. Once returned to the haven of Lord Holden's chamber, she wore a path through the rushes with her pacing.

God, what was she to do? Holden's men were so ferociously protective of him. If the Blackhaugh deserters were responsible for the lord's wounds, she feared they'd not live long. Somehow, she had to help them. Aye, they'd deserted Blackhaugh and joined up with Scots rebels, but they were still Gavins. As her clansmen, she owed them her protection.

Her eyes flickered over the things in the room, *his* things—the tapestry of a boar hunt on the wall, ink and parchment on the table, a whalebone comb, a pair of deerskin boots—and a desperate plan formed in her mind.

She had sworn not to attempt escape while Lord Holden was away, and a vow made in the name of her clan was sacred. But he wasn't away now, was he? So her oath no longer applied. Or so she told herself, though the thought of coming so close to breaking her word left a bitter taste at the back of her throat.

In a matter of moments, the men would bring the lord to his chamber. She used the time to hide, secreting herself behind the long tapestry.

When the knights finally carried in de Ware's unconscious form, so concerned were they with the condition of their lord, they never noticed that the tapestry had grown legs. Blessedly, she seemed to be completely forgotten in the uproar.

She heard a muffled groan as the men eased Holden's body onto the pallet. Strangely, it caused her heart to flutter. It seemed to her that it took an eternity for them to unfasten and remove his mail as she scarcely breathed. From the conversation between de Ware's men and the physician, she learned that they'd been waylaid by a dozen rebels who had somehow been alerted as to their whereabouts. There was talk of a spy. The lord had been wounded by a sword slipped beneath his ribs. One of the three Scots prisoners they managed to capture had done the deed. The blade had cut cleanly, and the flow of blood had been stanched, but he'd lost much, and the travel through the fierce storm had left him weak.

A servant kindled a fire in the fireplace, and everyone but the physician cleared the room to allow the wounded man rest. While the physician rummaged through his chest of cures, Cambria peeped out at Lord Holden.

His hair stuck in damp curls to his forehead, which was

wan and troubled. His nose trembled with each shallow breath. The coppery smell of blood was heavy in the room as the physician bent to inspect the wound. Something deep within her was stirred with pity to see such a fit warrior injured, but of necessity, she swallowed the emotion down like gamey meat. His misfortune was, after all, her good luck.

She waited patiently while the surgeon practiced his arts on the lord, wincing as he stitched up the ugly wound, shutting her ears to Holden's weak groans, sighing out a breath of relief when, near midnight, the physician finally settled down on his own pallet and began to snore at the foot of the bed.

Long before the fingers of dawn stretched over the horizon, she stole from her hiding place. She quickly plaited her loose curls by the dim firelight. Then, casting a cursory glance at the still sleeping lord, she made a hushed exit from his chamber and crept like a mouse through the castle.

As quiet as shadow, she hovered outside the room Gwen shared with several other maidservants. The time seemed to plod by in plowman's shoes as she awaited the hour of the maid's tryst with her lover, the gaoler.

Finally, Gwen emerged from the room, smelling faintly of sweet spice. Cambria followed at a distance, staying close to the shadowy walls of the descending passageways, until she heard the maid speaking concernedly with a young man up around the corner about Lord Holden's condition. He offered her a kiss as consolation, and then Cambria heard the voices recede.

Cautiously, she advanced until she came to the spot where the lovers had met. To her delight, the gaoler's keys still hung from a peg on the wall. She captured them, silencing their jangle in the folds of her kirtle, and peered into the barred peephole of the nearest cell.

The walls were dank and odorous. 'Twas gloomy within, but she could make out three forms huddled in the far corner of the room. When she whistled quietly, the three came instantly to their feet.

"Cambria? What are you doing he—"

"Shh," she whispered. "De Ware's men are everywhere."

As luck would have it, the last of seven keys was the one that fit. Its grating turn in the lock made all four of them freeze in dread, but the sound summoned no guard. After that, their passage was smooth. They wound their way through the halls unseen while most of the castle denizens slept.

Cambria reentered the lord's chamber alone first to be sure that Holden yet slumbered. She woke the physician, sending the groggy man below with a tale of a poisoning from supper. When he'd gone, she motioned her men to come forward.

Once in the chamber, Robbie snarled and briskly pulled a dagger from Holden's discarded belt. Stepping toward the lord, he raised the knife to finish him.

Cambria gasped and caught his wrist, shaking her head firmly. "Nay!" she hissed.

Robbie tried to pull away, his eyes narrowly questioning her, but she gripped him insistently.

"Do you not see? He is our escape!" she whispered. "We wouldn't make it past the curtain wall without a hostage." Dear God, she thought, trying to calm the frantic beating of her heart—Robbie, the boy who had taught her how to gentle a falcon, had nearly killed a man in cold blood.

She took a deep breath and straightened her shoulders. "We'll take him to Blackhaugh. We'll reclaim what is ours."

Robbie's eyes were hooded. "Blackhaugh is no longer . . . ours," he said meaningfully, glancing at the other two rebels.

"My father is gone. Blackhaugh is mine," she said solemnly, "and you are still Gavins."

Robbie stared at her, digesting the words she had spoken, words they both knew her father would never have uttered in his life, then nodded in agreement. The four armed themselves with the weapons in the room and fell silent as they prepared mentally for what they were about to do.

As soon as they began to pull Holden from the pallet, all hell broke loose.

He moaned in agony, and the sound almost gave Cambria a change of heart. From beyond the door, she heard several pairs of footsteps race up the stairs. When the door flew open under Sir Guy's hand, banging against the wall with its force, Robbie, thinking quickly, pressed a dagger to the throat of Lord Holden, who sagged in the arms of the other two Scots.

"We hold your lord!" Cambria shouted to the half-dressed men at the door, surprised at the strength in her voice under the circumstances. "If you would see him live out the day, then heed my words."

Sir Guy's trembling rage made a veritable current in the room. For a moment, it seemed to her that the slender piece of steel held against Holden's neck was too weak a defense against that anger. But Guy made no move toward them.

"We wish only to return to Blackhaugh," she continued. "Your lord will be safe with us as long as we're allowed to travel freely. But if any man should attempt to follow us, de Ware's life is forfeit."

She could tell it cost Sir Guy extreme restraint to allow them to pass. Pure hatred burned in his black eyes as, one by one, the castle folk backed away from the abductors.

The procession downstairs was difficult and slow. Holden moaned in pain with each step, though his eyes never opened. Fresh blood began to seep from his wound. When they reached the great hall, a few of the young maids sobbed in grief for their beloved lord and fled the room. The physician excused himself, returning with an armload of linen rags.

"You must change the bandages," he imparted with grave concern. "Keep the wound clean. There is danger of fever now."

She nodded, then spoke to Sir Guy. "Ready three horses for us with provisions and a litter." As Guy passed the command on to his squire, she added with malicious glee, "And fetch me my father's sword."

Owen purpled and stammered a refusal, but Sir Guy nudged the knight into grudging compliance.

Several tense minutes later, beneath clouds that smothered the distant promise of approaching dawn, Cambria and her small entourage mounted up. With Lord Holden set at knife-point before Robbie in the saddle, they made their escape unhindered. As they sped away, she felt a wave of remorse for betraying Holden's trust. She hadn't truly broken her vow, or so she tried to convince herself, but guilt still pressed heavily upon her.

Behind them, Sir Guy had put a new steward in charge and was already organizing a party to follow the fugitives at a discreet distance. The wench must be mad, he thought, to assume they'd let her escape with their lord.

Only after hours of hard riding through rough-rocked countryside and forests so dense no light passed through did Cambria feel safe enough to rest the mounts and attend to the hostage. They stopped by a narrow stream to let the horses drink and feast on young grass. Cambria helped Robbie ease Holden from the saddle and onto the litter.

The English lord was, if possible, more pale than before. The bandages were soaked with blood. His eyes were sunken and circled with dark rings, and his head lolled backwards. Cambria bit her lip. She couldn't lose him now.

"We have no further need of him," Robbie said with a snort, his blue eyes cool in his ruddy face. "They won't follow us."

"Nay!" she protested, her own vehemence startling her as much as Robbie's new callousness. She blinked up at him. Life among the rebels had altered the boy, she decided, changed him from the gentle youth she'd admired to the hardened, cynical man she now saw before her. She realized with a painful jolt that he'd lost his innocence and, with it, all sense of humanity.

"We need him to gain access to Blackhaugh," she explained, her voice weary with disillusionment. "His half-brother holds the castle, and we don't know how many English are there now."

"He may not live to make the journey," Robbie argued.

Dread washed over her. What if the journey did kill him?

"I'll keep him alive," she said, her words half-promise, half-prayer.

She fetched the linen rags and dampened one in a spring that trickled from the mossy bank. Gently, she sponged Holden's beaded brow and knelt to change his bandage. Some of the blood had dried, sticking the linen to his ribs, so she had to gingerly loosen the edges of the cloth. Holden must have thought she was practicing some form of unspeakable torture, groaning each time she touched him, but, thanks be to God, he was too helpless to defend himself against her necessary ministrations.

As she carefully wrapped new cloth around his ribs, she couldn't help but regard his scarred chest as it rose and fell, the skin flushed with heat. His was a warrior's body, taut and broad, thick with muscle. Dark, curling hairs made a subtle path down his oak-firm stomach, widening below his navel, where her thoughts dared not wander. His pulse swelled the hollow of his throat in a steady rhythm that her own heart was wont to mimic.

Quickly, she averted her eyes. Lord, being so close to him was having a strange effect on her, almost as if his fever were contagious. The sensation was at once disconcerting and compelling. Hastily, she covered him with a blanket from the litter, then busied herself with rinsing out the foul bandages and setting them on rocks to dry.

Night seemed to fall at full-tilt, and Cambria decided they should remain where they were rather than risk traveling in the dark. She agreed 'twould be necessary to secure Holden so he couldn't escape, although secretly she thought 'twas cruel. Jamie hobbled the captive's ankles where he lay on the litter and tied his wrists around a young tree.

She took the first watch of evening, sure that every rustle in the bushes was either Sir Guy or a hungry wolf, and she wasn't certain which she would have preferred to meet. Even afterward, when Robbie took over, she didn't sleep well. Her prisoner, too, seemed to toss and thrash all night at unseen ghosts.

She woke early in the morning, rubbing weary eyes. Pushing herself up on her elbows, she surveyed the small camp. Her eyes alit instantly on Lord Holden. What she found made her wince in shame and anger.

The poor wretch had kicked the blankets from his body, and there was a wet stain on his hose.

Pushing the hair back from her face, she stood and approached him, wrinkling her nose at the odor. His forehead was etched with lines of pain, his cheeks two spots of color in an otherwise wan face. She reached out to touch his stubbled jaw, then pulled her hand back suddenly from the heat. His skin was dry and his lips parched.

Young Graham caught her eye then, entering the clearing with an armful of kindling. He glanced first at her, then Lord Holden, and challenged her with a look that said he had no intention of seeing to the prisoner's comforts.

Muttering a curse, she soaked a clean rag in the spring and brought it, dripping, to Holden's lips. Eagerly as a nursing babe, he sucked at the wet linen, craving the meager moisture even in sleep. Again and again she dampened the cloth and let him gradually slake his thirst in that way. She untied his bonds and noted that his wrists were badly chafed from his fevered stirring in the night.

"Do you think that's wise?" It was Robbie, returning with a brace of coneys he'd snared. Jamie followed at his heels.

"God's blood!" she snapped. "The poor bastard cannot even rouse to relieve himself! Have you lost all sense of honor, Robbie?"

Robbie's eyes grew flat. "He's the enemy, Cambria."

"You wouldn't leave a *dog* in his own piss," she bit out.

Robbie only stared belligerently.

"Jamie," she called, barely controlling her rage, "remove his hose and rinse them. The blanket will have to do for cover now."

Jamie didn't obey at once, but looked to Robbie for approval, which made Cambria livid. At his nod, Jamie gave her a disgusted grimace, but moved to do as he was bid.

She stalked off through the wood before she could lose her temper. Damn them! She was laird now. How dare they question her commands? This had the makings of treason. Her father had been right. She should never have welcomed them back to the clan. They would turn on her as quickly as they had Laird Angus.

Still, for now she needed them. She would just have to proceed carefully then, placate them until she could join with her allies at Blackhaugh.

When she came back to camp, her emotions in check,

Holden was properly covered. She slipped the top of the blanket aside to inspect his wound. Again, she had to sponge the linen bandage loose. This time, beneath the bandage, there was an angry red swelling around the perimeter of the gash. Her heart sank. She recognized the sign of infection, but she had neither the time nor the skills to do anything about it now. Cautiously, she applied a new bandage and rinsed the old one, and although she had strong feelings otherwise, she proclaimed him fit to travel.

The sun had at last appeared through the thick clouds, looking like a grim yellow eye, when the party stopped again to rest. By her calculations, they'd arrive at Blackhaugh the following morning. The weather had been arguably kind to them, waiting in a strange misty limbo between rain and sun.

Their prisoner, however, hadn't fared well. He was too debilitated to eat the food they'd brought with them. The most Cambria could get him to swallow were a few bites of bread soaked in wine. Then, when she inspected his injury, her earlier suspicions were confirmed. A foul smell came from the wound. Hellfire, she thought, she should have abducted the physician, too. What did she know about healing?

She'd have to do something. She couldn't just let him die. Taking a deep breath to steady herself, she gently pressed the edges of the cut. A yellow liquid seeped out, and Holden came alive like a scalded kitchen boy. He cried out and flailed his limbs violently, striking her more than once with a stray fist—on her cheek, on her ear, on her shoulder.

"God's hooks!" Jamie swore, ready to beat their hostage to a bloody pulp.

"It's all right," she groaned, rubbing her cheek where a bruise was no doubt already forming. "He scarcely knows what he does. Hold him still, lads, will you? I'm certain he'll not like what I must do."

The men complied under duress, but only by great effort could they restrain the Englishman. Swallowing down the nausea that crept up the back of her throat, she drained as much of the wound's infection as she could while Holden thrashed wildly. She finished applying the new bandage and, depleted, sat back gracelessly on her haunches to stare hard at the man for whom she was going to so much trouble.

'Twas difficult to believe that she was actually dressing her enemy's wounds. Still, gazing at the sword tucked into her saddle, she knew her father would have been proud of her. She had recovered his weapon, she'd reclaim Blackhaugh, and she had his murderer at her mercy.

What, then, was this underlying shame she felt when she looked at her captive, writhing in torment as he fought unknown demons? Damn it, she shouldn't feel a pittance of remorse for this assassin. He'd come into her life and destroyed all that she held dear! Yet she couldn't look upon his face without her heart reaching out to him in pity.

By nightfall, beside a creek that ran through Gavin land, that pity had turned Cambria into a mass of jangled nerves. Holden hadn't improved. In fact, he'd taken a turn for the worse.

Robbie had left to fetch reinforcements from the Blackhaugh renegades hidden in the hills nearby, and she was again reminding Jamie unnecessarily that the Englishman was of no use to them dead, when Holden began convulsing.

Graham stumbled backward from the litter and crossed himself. "He's possessed by devils!"

Jamie warned, "Aye, he's done for, lass."

Fear stabbed her like a dagger. "Nay!" she denied harshly, threatening with a desperate glare any who would cross her. She forced down the lump in her throat. "Nay! He cannot die! I need him!"

She cast about, looking in vain for some kind of inspiration from the dismal wood. Curse his English hide! She'd be damned if she'd let him die here, not now, not after all the trouble she'd gone to. She sniffed back the stinging in her nose.

Some rash, deep-rooted instinct made her reach down and tear the covers from Holden. His nude body quaked like simmering tallow in the silver-blue moonlight, and he was as hot to the touch as new-forged iron. She had to cool him. Now.

If she could get him to the water . . .

The others gaped on in half-hearted protest while, with a

strength born of necessity, she reached beneath his arms and dragged his heavy, trembling body across the forest floor, toward the gurgling creek.

The cold water stabbed like daggers into her ankles as she pulled him with her into the stream. She shrieked at first with the shock of it, but waded further until the bulk of his body lay submerged. 'Twas pure torture. The icy waves wrapped around her body as if they would freeze her as she stood, and soon she shivered uncontrollably.

But Holden's shuddering eventually ceased. His body began to cool on its own. He would live.

Cambria's own body was suddenly racked with sobs of relief, and she struggled to conceal them from her clansmen as she hauled the Wolf back out of the water and onto the bank. Quivering with cold, she peered down at the man cradled helplessly against her and bit out a self-denigrating oath, forcing herself to admit the sad truth.

She wasn't a killer. While she had the skills, the chivalry, the spirit of a soldier, she wasn't ruthless enough to be a real warrior. She had her enemy in the palm of her hand, and yet she couldn't let harm come to him. She could almost feel the chiding eyes of her father's ghost boring into the back of her.

Her strength spent, she struggled to move Holden off of her. Jamie and Graham, at last snapping out of their amazed stupor, helped her pull him back to the litter. She dried him and wrapped him again in the blanket.

"You saved the bastard's life," Jamie said in wonder.

"Aye," she agreed with a shiver, irony curving her lips. She was exhausted. Her skirts would be icicles by morning. But she'd saved his life. "God grant that he last the night." She added under her breath, "He owes me as much."

A strange bird call woke Cambria. When Jamie mimicked the sound, she realized it was a signal. Shortly after, Robbie returned to camp, announcing that reinforcements were arriving and gloating over the fact that a band of English knights from Bowden Castle had been apprehended by the Scots.

"Good." She'd had an idea that loyal Sir Guy would ignore her warning. "Now we have more hostages to bargain with."

Plans were made to gather at midmorning in the field below Blackhaugh. Robbie, Jamie, and Graham set out to join the rebels in the forest, leaving Cambria to guard the prisoner.

She squinted into the rising sun, ran a grimy hand through her hair, and moved to check on the Englishman. Looking down hopefully at the slumbering knight, she realized that his face was at last peaceful, his brow untroubled, his breathing slow and even. Welcome drops of sweat rolled down his forehead and neck. The fever had broken at last. He was going to live.

An uninvited tear welled in one of her eyes, and she wondered what the devil was wrong with her. Brusquely she wiped the moisture away, glad that her kinsmen weren't near to see it.

She loosed him from the tree, but bound his wrists together before him. There were just the two of them now. She couldn't afford to take chances.

As she began the ritual of changing his bandage, Cambria suddenly felt his regard upon her. She slowly lifted her gaze until their eyes met. All at once, her heart lurched like a whipped ox. His stare was still glazed with pain, but 'twas no longer vacant.

With effort, he parted his lips, croaking a single word. "Thirst."

She dipped a clean rag in the stream and held it to his lips. He chewed on it a few times, then turned away in disgust.

"Thirst," he repeated.

She tossed down the rag, then added water to the bit of wine in her goatskin pouch and crouched behind him. Her heart beating erratically, she gently reached under his heavy head to support it while she helped him drink. He groaned at the pain of movement as he tried to gulp down the sweet refreshment.

"Slowly," she advised.

He clutched the bag with his bound hands, ignoring her words.

"Slowly!"

They battled with the pouch, but in the end, his sapped strength was no match for hers, and he was forced to take the meager sips she allowed.

After he'd drunk, he continued to stare at her with emotionless eyes, eyes that made her feel strangely guilty.

"What's happened?" he asked.

"You were wounded," she replied, lowering her gaze and busying herself with his covers. "From the looks of it, you're lucky to be alive. The blade must have slipped through that flaw in your mail I warned you about."

He was silent for a beat, properly chided. "Where are we?"

"Near Blackhaugh," she said with deliberate pride, expecting an outburst from him. "I go to reclaim it. The renegades fight by my side, and we bargain with your life."

Holden closed his eyes and had surprisingly little to say. "You trust the men who deserted you?"

She felt her cheeks redden. Damn him. He sounded just like her father. How dare he question her judgment?

"Garth will give you Blackhaugh without a fight," he conceded. "But you'll not hold it long."

" 'Tisn't your concern!" she snapped. She didn't want to admit it, but his words seemed eerily prophetic.

Holden said no more, and Cambria, vindictive but not cruel, offered him some cheese and bread. He ate slowly. His mouth was doubtless still dry from the fever.

"Leave me a moment," he abruptly requested.

"Leave you? Are you daft? You'd escape faster than a loosed hare."

"I am scarcely able to move, lady. I merely thought it might offend you to watch my attempts to relieve myself."

The heat that suffused her face was likely a sweet reward for him. Needless to say, she was happy to oblige his wishes.

When she returned, kicking up the forest debris to ensure that he heard her arrival, he was already lying docile upon the litter, his eyes closed in rest.

Shortly afterward, the others joined them, a score or so Scots renegades, roused and hungry for the kill. They held the prisoners from Bowden. At the fore was Sir Guy, his cheek split and his eyes smoldering rage. Hellfire, Cambria realized as he glared at her, even captive as he was, murder infused his black gaze and inspired fear.

She swallowed and glanced away. As she searched the bloodthirsty faces of her countrymen, she saw that Holden had been right about the possible danger of fanatics. But 'twas too late to turn back now. The wheels of revenge had been set in motion.

7

GARTH DE WARE NERVOUSLY STROKED THE SOFT DOWN OF his upper lip. He never should have come, never should have agreed to join his brother's retinue, never should have listened to Holden, who'd refused to believe that his little half-brother had aspirations, not to the battlefield, but to the church. But nay, Holden had insisted he needed to get one final taste of grand adventure before making the decision to take on a monk's robes. And Garth had believed him.

Lo and behold, what had happened?

It was true that things had gone surprisingly well at first. The Scots seemed to appreciate Garth's fairness. He made a point of treating them with respect. He'd even developed a friendship with Malcolm the Steward, who was teaching him a great deal about the fortitude of the Scots. He'd started believing that he could indeed handle the responsibilities of a lordship.

Until now. Now he was convinced he was right in wishing to limit his enterprises to the confines of monastery walls.

Outside the keep, Cambria Gavin held a dagger to his brother's throat. Holden, supported by two men, looked as weak as a maid. A score of savage-looking Scots held hostage a handful of Holden's best knights as well, and they were making outrageous demands. Garth was to surrender himself and the other English within the castle to this girl.

Malcolm, standing beside him atop the wall walk of the castle, swore under his breath. Garth shook his head. How had the maid escaped? How had she acquired a whole company of swordsmen to follow her? And most disturbing of all, how had she brought Holden, his brave, powerful, undefeated brother, to his knees? He pounded his fist upon the stone merlon. Sweet Mary, his brother at the mercy of a woman. It was an abomination.

He knew with a futile certainty that Holden would disapprove of the decision he was about to make, but he had to make it. Garth admittedly had none of the relentlessness for which the older de Wares were famous. His tender heart went out to Holden in his helplessness. He only prayed that his brother would somehow forgive him for that weakness.

Grudgingly, he allowed the Scots to enter the castle.

Holden came in on a litter. Garth fought the almost irresistible instinct to run to his brother. Lord God, he was as pale as parchment. He might be dying.

"Holden," he breathed, his voice breaking.

"He'll heal," the Scots lass said all too optimistically.

He turned his eyes to her then—that smug Gavin vixen who had dared rouse the Wolf—and the de Ware blood in him began to boil. Damn his religious upbringing, it was all he could do to keep from drawing his sword and lopping off the wench's head.

He stretched himself to his full height in an unconscious mimicry of Holden and addressed her directly, his voice unyielding. "What have you done to him?"

The girl blinked, obviously taken aback for a moment by the change in his manner.

"I've brought him back to the living," she replied, rubbing a bruised cheek, "despite his clear determination to avoid my care."

"And what do you intend?" he demanded. From the corner of his eye, he could see that his men itched to take up their surrendered weapons against these barbarians.

"You will either swear fealty to me upon your knighthood," she told him, "or stay below in the dungeon."

Garth didn't bother to seek the counsel of his knights. He

held his arms boldly out before him for the shackles. His men imitated the gesture. They would all die in a damp cell before they would yield to this Scots lass.

Cambria pursed her lips. Stubborn Englishmen, she thought. She could have used those strong arms for the coming battle. Yet she knew full well she would have done the same in their place. With a sigh of exasperation, she ordered the men taken below.

Holden, on the other hand, she secured to the bed in her father's chamber, which adjoined her own. There she could change his bandages and see to his meals. He was too valuable a hostage to be kept in the dungeon where he might fall prey to disease. He was probably a well-loved knight of Edward. 'Twould be stupid to incur the English king's wrath so blatantly by mistreating a favored vassal.

'Twas the excuse she gave the Scots, but it fell far short of the truth. The truth was she couldn't let Holden die. Whether 'twas because of the trouble she'd gone through to save him, or the admiration she bore for his courage, or just the way her heart raced when he caught her in his forthright gaze, she knew she couldn't let harm come to him. She only prayed that when the king of England came to bargain for the Wolf's life, he'd not perceive the emptiness of her threats.

Even after a week, Cambria still didn't feel as if she'd come home. Blackhaugh had changed irrevocably in her absence. To her chagrin, it seemed the Gavins had grown quickly accustomed to living under English rule. Even Malcolm, vexed at her actions, refused to speak with her, only answering her questions with a curt and formal "aye, my lady" or "nay, my lady." He expressed no interest in hearing about her daring escape, and his harsh scrutiny was rife with disapproval, disapproval that many others of the clan shared. She could feel their cool resentment at her interference, as if she were an outsider. It felt like her clan had scattered out of her reach like goatsbeard seeds on an English wind.

She rubbed her eyes and sank down onto the edge of her pallet, pressing her fist into the ache at the small of her back.

She was exhausted. 'Twasn't that she hadn't been trained for leadership. She knew what her duties were. The clan was like a family of children, her father had told her, children who looked to the laird for guidance, discipline, and justice. Still, at the moment, that responsibility seemed overwhelming.

An abrupt knock on her chamber door forced her to square those tired shoulders again. "Come," she called out.

A servant lad plunged into the room. "Milady, you must come! There's a brawl in the tiltyard!"

"Who?" she demanded, coming to her feet.

"Robbie . . ." the servant began. "He said . . ."

"What?"

The boy glanced warily about to make sure they were alone. "He said you spoil the hostage, that you . . ."

"That I what?" she asked, her fury rising.

"That you . . . you wait upon him hand and foot like a . . ." 'Twas obviously too crude a word for the servant to repeat.

Heat flared in Cambria's blood faster than ale tossed on the fire. She snatched her father's sword from the wall and stormed from the room.

The tiltyard was a shambles. Men fought amongst each other, their swords nicking here and there to fleck blood across the polished mail. They hurled insults and kicked up straw and dust as they battled. Without hesitation, she stepped into the fray and confronted Robbie, her sword at the ready. One by one, the others ceased their fighting.

"What nasty rumor would you volley about now, Robbie?" she demanded.

Clearly surprised by the proximity of her blade, Robbie was struck speechless.

Sir Douglas, the man he fought, had no such affliction. "I defend you, my lady, fear not," he said, ready to champion her against Robbie's accusations.

"Defend me against what?" she inquired, her eyes fixed on Robbie.

Douglas would not answer.

But Robbie found his voice. "You keep this English bastard for a pet while all of Scotland prepares for war!" he spat.

She knocked his sword away in one swift movement, catching him off guard, and lifted her own blade to his chest. "I keep him as a hostage," she told him in a deceptively soft voice. "Have you any idea what Edward will do to us if we harm a hair on de Ware's head?"

"Let him come!" Robbie shouted, trying to inspire support in the others. "We'll show him the might of the lion of the north!"

In an instant of awareness, Cambria learned what her father had known all along—Scotland was too weak to win this war by bloodshed. Robbie and the others were so blinded by their fervor that they wouldn't recognize the possibility of defeat. The Gavin—the people, the land—these were what mattered, not the politics of distant London. She suddenly felt a rush of fierce pride and protectiveness that overcame all else.

"I will not allow Gavins to be slaughtered for your cause," she stated.

"Then you would fight alongside the English . . . against us?" Robbie demanded incredulously.

"*I* will not abandon Blackhaugh. Will you . . . again?" she asked, raising a brow.

His face turned a mottled red. "I did *not* abandon—"

"You left my father in his hour of need!" she cried.

Without warning, the torrents of pain she'd subdued from the cruel tragedy of her father's death came unleashed. They overwhelmed her, and her vehemence made Robbie's eyes widen as her blade hovered just inches from his heart.

"You left him to die for the Gavin, you bastard, and yet I welcomed you back to Blackhaugh. I freed you from the hands of the enemy so—"

"Lass! You think to *deliver* me into the hands of the enemy again! I'll not live under the thumb of Edward—"

"Then go!" She pointed harshly with her sword. "Leave Blackhaugh—you and all others who would take up your cause! But take care you do not show your face here again, for if you do, I shall follow my father's advice and name you traitor!"

Robbie swept up his sword with a vengeance and glared

at her. "Lads!" he called. "We are no longer welcome here. Let us join the true Scots in their noble war!"

Although not a man dared reply, all of the renegades followed Robbie as he left the tiltyard.

When they had gone, only a handful of men remained. Cambria addressed the faithful few with a lump in her throat and a confidence she didn't feel.

"My father understood that when all else has been lost, what survives are the people and the land. Rulers will be overthrown, and battles will be fought, but the people and the land will continue. I intend to fight for Blackhaugh, but not by waging war. Lord Holden de Ware is a valuable hostage. We'll keep him as long as 'tis necessary to ensure that we may hold this land in the Gavin name, just as my father intended."

The knights nodded their assent. One by one, they knelt before her to swear their renewed loyalty. She was moved by their gesture, and 'twas with desperate hope that she accepted each one, praying she wasn't dooming them to their death.

Within an hour, as Cambria watched from the wall walk, Robbie and his Gavin followers disappeared from her life and into the dark of the forest. A tear wandered slowly down her cheek as she thought of the men she'd likely never see again—men she'd grown up with, Gavins who had surrendered their clan name for the name of Scotland.

She wouldn't sleep well this night, not with the keep so ill protected. 'Twas near midnight when she climbed the steps to her bedchamber, turning aside briefly to check on her prisoner.

The fire flickered gently in the stillness of the room, adding its soft crackle to the only other sound there, the deep, even breathing of the wounded man lying in the bed.

"Damn you, Robbie," she said under her breath, jabbing at the dozing embers in the fireplace. She put aside the poker, sighing in futility as she eyed Holden's slumbering form. "And you—damn your weak English blood."

For all the care she and Blackhaugh's physician had bestowed upon the hostage—the frequent changing of his bandages, the mopping of his brow, the hearty barley broths she brought daily, even the apparent healing of his wound—he'd seemed to weaken.

Perhaps the waning of his will to live caused him to have fewer stretches of wakefulness. This troubled her deeply. She told herself 'twas because his worsening would destroy their hope of using him as a hostage. But she knew in her heart that 'twas far more than that.

She'd saved his life, forging a bond between them. She felt responsible for him now. And yet, he was her sworn enemy, her father's murderer. How could she justify the way she felt about him—the way her breath quickened even as she imagined the man lying unconscious behind her? Not only the magnificent swell of his warrior's chest, the sensuous movement of his lips when he mumbled in sleep, the inert power of his muscled arms stretched across the pallet, but what resided in his character—the loyalty and trust and esteem he inspired in everyone around him, both his own men and her clan.

God, the conflict wrenched her heart in twain. By some cruel twist of fate her Achilles' heel had become her own admiration for the enemy. More and more, she had difficulty associating the image of her dying father with the noble, tragic face that graced the pillow on this bed.

She sank down upon the foot of the pallet and allowed herself to be hypnotized by the flame fluttering on the hearth.

What was she to do? The rebels had deserted her again. Malcolm wouldn't speak to her. The English lord might not live, and not only did that thought send a ragged twinge across her heart, but it meant the wrath of the king would be visited upon her clan. Never had she needed her father's wisdom so badly.

She sat deep in thought, worrying her fingers in her lap, so preoccupied that she was unaware when the man behind her awakened and lay silently staring at her through slitted eyes.

Holden felt the rough rope around his wrists. His temper immediately flared, until reason reminded him of his predicament. He remained quiet.

There at the foot of the bed was his captor. She looked small to him, vulnerable, haloed there by the firelight, incapable of the treachery she'd dealt him. He remembered only snatches of their journey—the rough trip on the litter, her careful ministrations to his wounds, the cool water that had finally extinguished the fire in his body. He was intrigued by this sweet enemy who cared for him as gently as a nun, even as he knew he had to do everything in his power to escape her.

As he watched her, the young woman's shoulders began to shake. Her head bent in anguish. Lord, she was crying. The sound of her soft sobs tore at his heart.

Of course, she well deserved to weep. Mother of God, in one swift blow of fate, the lady had lost her father, her clan, and her fiefdom. But she'd not wrung her hands and moped like every other wench he'd known. She'd fought back, challenging him, defying his knights, risking her life to save her people. She was an extraordinary woman, this lass who silently bore the burden of her clan as readily as armor on her shoulders and only exorcized her sorrow behind closed doors.

It was a pity she was the enemy.

A quick knock upon the door interrupted Cambria's tears and Holden's musings. He closed his eyes as she rose with a murmured response. When next he opened them, she'd gone.

Before the glow of morning had yet hailed the sun's arrival, Cambria awoke to an ungodly shriek. Her prisoner. Picking up her dagger, she rushed down the hallway, through his door, and to the edge of his bed.

She could see by the torchlight that he seemed to be hallucinating, thrashing madly from side to side to escape some horrible beast. He screamed in terror.

"Cut me free! It comes! It comes for me! In the name of God, cut me free!"

He wrenched wildly at the ropes around his wrists. She

tried to calm him with hushed words, but still he grappled with his bonds. God's blood, his cries would wake the entire castle! She had to do something. A small moan of empathy escaped her as she took up her dagger and sawed rapidly at the bonds.

The moment the last rope frayed apart, his helpless fingers grew suddenly quite capable. He expertly squeezed her wrist, causing her to release the dagger. Before she could understand what was happening, he'd reclaimed the knife, and his other hand tangled viciously in her hair.

His strength had obviously returned. He twisted her body so that she lay defenseless beneath him, the point of the blade pressed to a pulsing vein in her throat. She gasped in pain and surprise and shame as his green eyes flickered victoriously.

"You deceived me," she whispered, stricken. Oh, God, to think that she'd been worried about his health. The wretched beast was as strong as an ox.

"Don't blame me for your folly, madam," he answered calmly. "Where are Garth and the others?"

She narrowed her eyes. "I'd rather die than tell you." Then she regarded him dubiously. "Besides, you'll not slay me."

His anger with her flared briefly in his gaze. "You believe that after the trouble you have caused?"

She flinched as his hold tightened. "You need me alive to . . . to escape."

"Alive, aye, but not necessarily . . . untouched."

Holden let his eyes rake suggestively over her tempting form, intentionally unnerving her. It worked brilliantly. She trembled like a falcon hooded for the first time. He knew where her vulnerability lay now, and although it normally went against his principles to prey on a woman's weaknesses, this woman had proved herself far from weak. He intended to thoroughly disarm her.

Her eyes widened as he drew the dagger slowly, torturously down the front of her bunched shift, between her pale breasts, past her narrow ribs and her hitching abdomen, over her woman's mound. She drew her breath in sharply through her teeth as he pressed the flat of the cold blade suddenly and intimately between her bare thighs.

He spoke evenly despite his inevitable surge of desire, his gaze burning like a steady flame into her frantically darting eyes. "I have another dagger I would gladly sheathe here." He allowed his meaning to sink in. "Now where is Garth?"

This time she didn't hesitate. "In the dungeon."

He slipped the dagger from her, then sat up, planting his knee lightly in the middle of her chest to keep her down. A sharp pain grabbed briefly at his ribs as he snagged the tabard from its perch on the wall and slipped it over his head. He'd been testing his muscles for the last day now. For all his pretense at weakness, all that remained of his injury were a dull ache and that occasional twinge. Within a day or two, his body would return to its former strength.

"Let us go," he told her, placing the blade at her neck once more and prodding her to rise to her feet. He twisted her arm behind her, pushing her toward the door. How frail it felt in his grasp, like the wing of a sparrow. Yet he knew better. This sparrow had flown far with him. He caused her no great pain, but only kept his grip firm, holding her tightly against him so he could control her movements.

She attempted to call out for help just once as they made slow progress down the steps. But so swiftly did his dagger react to her intake of breath, the sound was strangled almost before it was begun. In the great hall, their only company was a groggy serving wench who shuffled about at her labors, taking no notice of them as they skirted the corner of the room and made their way to the dungeon stairs.

Cambria was cooperative as he forced her to traverse the wet, slippery steps in bare feet, leaning upon him for dear life. She likely feared he'd trip on the uneven ground and she'd impale herself on his blade, but he was surefooted enough and managed to keep them both upright. Not a drop of her blood was spilled.

They at last reached the bottom of their descent, where Blackhaugh's gaoler sat snoozing on a three-legged stool. Hearing their approach, the man shot to his feet and gawked stupidly back and forth between the two.

"The keys," Holden said, nodding toward the wall.

"The keys," the gaoler repeated, scratching his head in confusion beneath Cambria's glare.

It was apparent that the slack-jawed servant was weighing the consequences of disobeying each of his superiors. In the end, Holden's wrath evidently overshadowed that of the Gavin wench. Shrugging an apology to his mistress, the gaoler fetched the key ring down from the wall.

Holden nodded toward the long row of cells. "Free my brother and his men."

The gaoler let the breath whistle out through his teeth, but did as he was told. "Aye, my lord."

Garth and his knights emerged from their cramped quarters with delighted grins on their faces. Thank God, they were no worse for wear from their brief stay in the dungeon. They looked at Cambria with undisguised triumph.

"Holden, are you all right?" Garth asked, the hero worship plain in his eyes. "I had thought you were . . . that is, I *knew* they were no match for you."

Cambria squirmed in mute protest at the insult. Holden renewed his grip on her arm and pressed the steel close against her throat as a reminder.

"The armory," he directed his brother.

Garth led them there. The armory was well stocked with claymores and daggers and sundry other weapons, and as the de Ware knights armed themselves generously, Holden addressed them.

"We go not to battle, but to make peace," he said. "The Gavins will not harm us while we hold their laird. Use the weapons only for defense."

He paused a moment, taking Cambria's chin between his thumb and fingers, turning her face up to his. "I have a proposition for the Scots, one that may ensure there is no more bloodshed."

Defiance crackled in her gem-hard eyes, and her delicate nostrils flared in outrage. Her cheeks flushed pink, and her lips compressed into an unyielding line. He looked at her curiously and wondered for a moment if he was doing a wise thing. Then he released her jaw and exhaled a long, decisive breath.

This time the serving wench saw them enter the hall. When the lass beheld her mistress taken captive by a whole assemblage of heavily armed men, she dropped both her jaw and her kettle of water and ran whimpering from the room. In a few moments, the hall was populated by Gavin knights, freshly roused from slumber and meagerly armed. There were less than a score of them.

Holden whispered in Cambria's ear. "These are all the men that remain?"

"Aye," she bit out.

Was it desolation he heard in her voice?

He took his time, studying them, measuring the worth of each of the Gavin men carefully before he spoke. "You," he said to the scowling old, gray-haired gentleman at the fore. "You *must* be the steward."

The man stepped forward with a frown on his face and a hand on his hilt. "I am."

Cambria looked sharply at Holden. He answered her silent question, murmuring, "It's plain. He's the one who looks most eager to kill me."

He regarded the steward with an assessing eye. The surly old bear looked to be a man of his word. His loyalty to his laird, at least, was unquestionable.

"Sir . . . ?"

"Malcolm," was the gruff reply.

"Sir Malcolm," he commanded, "come with me. And you, too, Garth." To the others, he said, "I will not harm your lady if you try no trickery. I wish only to speak in private."

The Scots glanced uneasily at each other, and Malcolm explained. "Speak in private. 'Tis what your man said to Angus Gavin ere he slew our good laird."

Holden frowned. "My man. Roger Fitzroi?" While that revelation in itself did not condemn Roger, it did cast a shadow on the story Roger had told. He nodded in agreement. "Then let us surrender our weapons in good faith."

Garth set aside his blade. Holden dropped his dagger, but replaced it with an arm around Cambria's throat. His message was clear. He could kill her as easily with his bare hands. Of course, he wouldn't harm a woman in a year of fortnights, but the Blackhaugh men didn't know that.

Malcolm looked to his knights to assure their cooperation, unbuckled his sword, then withdrew cautiously with the others to the adjoining chamber.

When they were safely closeted, Holden relaxed his hold on Cambria slightly.

"First, Sir Malcolm, I suspect there may indeed have been foul business afoot for your good laird to have been slain," he confided. "Roger Fitzroi frequently overstepped his authority. For that, I extend my deepest apologies."

Malcolm looked him in the eye for a long while. Then he nodded. "My lord, I think I've known all along that the de Wares are not men to ply such treachery."

Cambria snapped her head around toward the steward in surprise. "What do you—?"

Holden halted her words with a warning squeeze of his forearm. "Secondly, I would have you understand, sir, that it is not my way to hold your lady hostage. I *would* release her and have her swear no treachery, but her word has proved worthless."

"I have never broken my word!" Cambria argued.

He raised his brow dubiously. She would meet no one's eyes.

"I did *not* attempt escape while you were away," she muttered.

He stared at the top of her head in grim amusement. "I shall have to remember to be careful about how I word your promises. Very well, then, will you swear no deceit for the moment, so I may loosen my hold?"

Cambria remained stubbornly silent.

Malcolm tried to calm her. "Come, lass, I would end the bloodshed now. Let us listen to what the Englishman has to say."

Cambria didn't want to listen to what he had to say. 'Twas all lies anyway. But she supposed she couldn't stop the arrogant bastard from speaking.

"Very well," she said sullenly.

He immediately released her. She winced, rubbing her neck from an imaginary injury. Then the Wolf began to pace the small room, weighing some heavy thought, rapping his knuckles occasionally on the oak table.

"There *has* been too much bloodshed. The rebel forces are increasing, but Edward's army is far superior—in number, in battle, in organization. The English *will* win." He turned, flinching as pain lanced across his ribs, but waved Garth's eager attentions away. "You must choose sides. Whatever wrongs have occurred in the past, you must choose sides now. I can retain Blackhaugh for our people, yours and mine, but I must have your cooperation. Neither of us can afford to play this game of chess, taking rooks back and forth until Edward or the rebel Scots arrive. We must prepare for battle now."

Garth seemed to hang on his brother's every word. Malcolm nodded slowly in agreement. Only Cambria stared at him, incredulous. They were lies, she thought, all lies. How could Malcolm be taken in by his deceitful English tongue?

Holden continued, addressing her. "When England subdues the rebellion, Cambria, you will be under English law. A Scotswoman may not hold property under English law. Your father apparently was unaware of this, or he wouldn't have struck such a useless bargain. In essence, he has left you powerless."

"What!" She slitted her eyes at him. "You speak falsely!"

"Nay," Malcolm solemnly interjected. "He is right, lass. Laird Angus had . . . your father had hopes . . . he'd thought that one day . . . that you'd wed before . . ."

"Nay!" she cried.

Her heart twisted with grief. She'd told her father time and time again that she had no intentions of marriage. Had he truly believed she would change her mind?

Malcolm clasped her shoulder. "He'd thought you and Robbie . . . but then Robbie left and . . ."

"Robbie?" Surely not Robbie. He was like a brother. She buried her face in her hands. It couldn't be true. The land that had been her family's for hundreds of years couldn't be snatched from her like this. She shook her head.

"I am sorry," Lord Holden said, "but no matter which side wins, Blackhaugh will not long remain in your hands. The English won't allow you to hold it, and the Scots . . ."

"Have already turned against me," she finished bitterly, jerking her shoulder from Malcolm's grasp.

She closed her eyes against the pain. Little by little, her hopes were being dashed by this imperious invader. Soon she'd be left with nothing.

Holden spoke softly. "I know of only one way to prevent the spilling of more blood, to guarantee peace between our people, and to allow you to keep Blackhaugh."

He waited until she reluctantly returned his gaze.

"Be my wife."

8

THE SILENT MOMENT THAT MET HIS SUGGESTION GREW SO pregnant it was almost comical. Holden supposed it came as a shock to the other three, but he'd given the idea much thought whilst he lay abed over the past few days. He thought it a brilliant solution.

The sacrifice wasn't so great. Although he'd bedded his share of wenches, Holden had never considered himself a romantic, unlike his brother Duncan, who'd pursued women as if they were his Holy Grail. Nay, he was a warrior, a successful one, and his success had come largely by careful strategy and a practical nature. He had no intention of giving up his soldiering, but now he was a lord in his own right. It was time he married and began producing legitimate offspring.

He had what he considered a healthy outlook when it came to taking a wife. A wife was neither a burden nor a blessing. A good wife could be as valuable as a good steward. She represented a man when he went off to war, kept his castle running smoothly, provided him with children. Cambria Gavin could certainly do as much. In sooth, she could be quite helpful, being more familiar than he with the Scots ways. Aye, their union was the perfect answer for peace among their people.

King Edward, too, would likely approve the match, as

long as details of Roger Fitzroi's death remained vague. The monarch had granted Holden permission to use whatever tactics he required to gain the Border alliance, trusting Holden's good judgment.

Of course, the most compelling reason for Holden's decision had nothing to do with good judgment. It was based on neither strategy nor practicality nor honor.

He simply wanted her. In every sense of the word. He wanted her to share his name, his trencher, his bed, his future. He wanted to wake up each morn to the Scots faerie who flavored his dreams.

Oh, she'd fight him. She'd fight him every step of the way. But he'd never failed to tame a wench once he had her between the linens. And he intended to have her there soon and often. His loins stirred just thinking of it. Lord, he found he relished the game to come as much as he did jousting a worthy opponent.

Garth finally broke the long silence, appalled at Cambria's lack of response to the more than generous offer. "There must be another way," he proffered gently. "Any other woman would welcome you, Holden, and be grateful." He shot Cambria a caustic glare.

Cambria wore such a comical look of disbelief that Holden nearly laughed aloud. He'd never been rejected by a female. It was a curious feeling.

"Come now, Garth," he scolded. "Let us not press the lady. The decision is hers to make."

"You bastard!" Cambria finally exploded, making Malcolm and Garth flinch. "Do you imagine I'll let a bloody Englishman wed and bed me? I'd sooner die than—"

"Cambria!" Malcolm interceded, urgently grasping her shoulder. "Listen to me!"

Lord Holden's offer had sparked a fatherly instinct in Malcolm that swelled his heart nigh to bursting. He'd been vexed with Cambria for days now. That cryptic message the squire had delivered when she'd recklessly gone alone to seek revenge on Lord Holden had left him weak with worry.

He was too old to agonize over her every adventure. He'd already lost his best friend. He didn't want to lose Angus's daughter, too. He'd prayed for an answer and saw it in Lord Holden's offer. Already he envisioned Cambria in wedding garb, standing beside this handsome lord, pledging her troth, keeping the castle in Gavin hands to be passed down to the many children they'd have. He could even see Angus smiling down from heaven.

He'd be damned if he'd let the bullheaded wench play games with the future of the clan for her own vanity.

"Cambria," he said gruffly, "your father would be disappointed! He would never have thrown away his life when Blackhaugh was at stake. He gave all he had to ensure that the title would pass to you. Will you now cast it away, make his death in vain, for your pride's sake?"

Cambria clutched her head in her hands. Her thoughts were whirling like a spindle. She could hardly believe that her own man was turning against her, and wondered with what poison the de Wares had infected Malcolm's mind.

Marriage was as appealing to her as jesses were to a falcon. Malcolm knew that. The whole clan knew it. Being a bride to any man, let alone the enemy, was abominable. In sooth, she was better prepared to be executed by the Wolf than wed to him.

Still, a small part of her knew 'twas the only rational thing to do. It *was* the kind of thing the laird of Gavin would have done, sacrifice himself for the good of the clan. She felt her own rebellion slipping away as her options narrowed to the inescapable one Lord Holden presented.

Collecting herself at last, she turned to Holden. "What do you hope to gain by this? I'm no simpleton, de Ware. The fate of my entire clan rests on the decision I make here. I can see how *they* will benefit from this alliance, but what are *your* motives? What do you intend? Will you lure my people into a false security, then slaughter them like sheep? Or will you murder me on our wedding night and claim Blackhaugh for your own?"

"I could claim Blackhaugh now and have you tried for the murder of Sir Roger," he said evenly, giving her pause. "Nay, my motives are simple enough—I need a fortress, supplies, and loyal soldiers to wage this battle, and this is the swiftest, most effective way to achieve that end."

"I see," she murmured.

At least he was honest, she thought. Brutally honest. Though she wouldn't admit it except in the deepest recesses of her heart, his careless words stung her. This wasn't at all what she'd expected in the way of a marriage proposal. She'd had no suitors before, but she'd always imagined that if the time came for courtship, a kind, sweet, gentle Scotsman might come and beg for her hand. She'd refuse, of course, and he'd have to learn to content himself with standing behind her as she commanded the clan, supporting her, admiring her, as faithful to her as a good hound.

That was the dream she'd had before her father's death. Now that dream fled like October leaves in a winter gale. This man had no intention of standing behind her. In fact, he'd probably insist on standing *above* her.

She shuddered with distaste just thinking about it. But what other option did she have? Slowly she paced before him, solemnly weighing her limited choices, considering his offer solely as a political proposal. Then she stopped and lifted a brow. If 'twas only a political matter . . .

"All right," she finally decided, "I'll marry you, but only if . . . certain provisions are made."

"You are hardly in a position to bargain," he reminded her, folding his arms across his oak wall of a chest.

Her gaze strayed to the taut fabric of his tabard, her mind sculpting the perfectly formed chest beneath, the powerful shoulders, the firm stomach. Her heartbeat increased. This, she thought, was going to be difficult.

"'Twill be on my terms," she managed, "or not at all."

He measured her with eyes that seemed to penetrate her garments, her thoughts, her soul. "What 'terms' do you intend?"

She couldn't meet his eyes. "I will wed you . . . provided there be no consummation of the marriage."

Malcolm and Garth gasped simultaneously.

"What?" Holden exploded on a laugh, flinging his arms outward. "You would mock vows given before God? You'd deny me my conjugal rights? That is no marriage, lady—it is a farce!"

"Those are my terms," she affirmed, despite Malcolm's embarrassed squirming. "You need only say aye or nay."

"Nay," Holden replied.

Garth looked well pleased.

She nearly choked in surprise. "What?"

She knew no man relished the idea of chastity, but she never dreamed he'd *insist* upon that aspect of their marriage. Wasn't it, after all, only an alliance for the sake of their countries? "You do not desire the marriage then?"

"Aye, I do," he said, stroking his chin thoughtfully. "Only let the contract read thus: The marriage will remain in name only until such time as the bride *consents* to honor the consummation."

She glanced at Garth, who coughed suddenly. She reviewed Holden's words skeptically, drumming her fingers on the table. "Do you plan to beat me until I consent?"

"There will be no need," he said with irritating smugness.

"You jest," she scoffed, stilling her fingers. "You know I will never come willingly to your bed."

Garth seemed consumed with strangled coughing.

"You *will* come to my bed. It is where a wife sleeps," he informed her, "but while you are there, I'll not take my marriage rights from you until I hear acquiescence from your own lips. And I swear this before your steward."

Malcolm was looking at Holden with amazement, as if he'd promised her the moon. She smirked. How gullible Holden was. He obviously had no idea how strong-willed she could be.

"Done," she agreed.

The marriage contract was drawn up, their marks attached. The wax seals were still warm when Holden took hold of Cambria's arm, speaking for her ears only.

"I'll abide no infidelity on your part."

She cocked him a patronizing smile. "I've no interest in your or any other man's bed."

Holden lifted a sardonic brow. "Well, then, it should prove

interesting to see just how you plan to get heirs for your precious piece of land."

He chuckled, then strode from the hall, leaving her staring after him, dumbfounded.

The fire in the center of the great hall crackled and sparked as the three friends spoke in low tones. Holden's wound ached, and this conversation did nothing to help alleviate the pain.

"Are you mad, Holden?" Sir Guy bit out. "What will the king say? What will your father say?"

He clapped his man on the shoulder. "I assure you, Guy, Edward will think it genius. After all, I've gained him a stronghold in the Borders. And my father?" He lifted the corner of his lip into a rueful grin. "I'm certain he'll be content to have no more of my by-blows running around his castle. Nay, 'tis my mother's wrath I fear most of all, since she'll not get to plan the wedding."

Guy shook his head. "I still say it's sheer lunacy," he muttered under his breath. "The wench is dangerous. She murdered the last man who laid a ha—"

Holden scowled at him, then glanced down at Myles, who shuffled from one foot to the other. The three were alone now, but Holden's men still seemed reluctant to speak their mind.

"The last man who what?" he asked.

"Bah!" Guy snorted. "Can you not see how this looks? 'Tis as if you are . . . submitting to the Scots."

"Cousin, *these* Scots are our allies."

"How can you say that, when that wench has"—Guy counted her sins on his fingers—"taken you hostage, tried to slay you, murdered Sir Roger . . ."

Holden bit the inside of his cheek so he wouldn't lose his temper. "She took me hostage because it was a brilliant tactic. I would have done the same myself. She tried to slay me because she believed I ordered her father's murder under trust. And as far as killing Sir Roger, there are some doubts I have concerning that."

Myles looked up guiltily.

"Perhaps you could clear them up for me?" Holden suggested.

Guy and Myles exchanged glances, reluctant to speak, but Guy finally nodded assent.

Myles cleared his throat nervously. "Sir Guy missed the whole thing, my lord. He was deep in his cups, snoring on the table. He can't be blamed."

Guy colored, ashamed that he'd been less than attentive in his duties.

"For what?" Holden straightened, his interest piqued.

"And I," Myles stammered, "I tried to s-stop him, but he set the h-hound on me."

"Guy?"

"Nay. Roger," Myles gulped. "Roger thought he'd . . . we all . . . he took her upstairs and . . ."

Sir Guy interrupted. "Roger had his way with her, my lord."

Holden felt a chill pass through his heart.

"I tried to stop him, truly I did," Myles chattered. "Owen, he was as drunk as an alewife. I'm sure they meant no harm."

"He raped her?" Holden asked in a calm voice that belied the turmoil he was feeling. No wonder Cambria had asked for that clause in their marriage contract. She'd already been violated once by an English knight.

Guy muttered, "Maybe she had cause to kill him—I know not—but I suspect the king will not take kindly to your making his kinsman's murderer the next Lady de Ware."

"And the Gavins will not take kindly to our executing their laird," Holden snarled.

"Aye," Sir Guy agreed, spitting on the fire. "'Tis a coil, my lord. God's truth, it might have been better had the wench been slain with her father at the first."

He almost didn't finish the sentence, so quickly did Holden go for his throat. Guy gaped like a hooked fish as Holden tightened his grip and burned into him with a black stare.

"Never say that again," Holden whispered. "She is to be my wife, and whether you think her angel or whore, you will speak of her with respect. Do you understand?"

Guy nodded and gave a strangled reply.

Holden released him, then staggered back, stunned. He stared at his own hands as if he couldn't believe what they'd done. Muttering an apology, he strode from the hall out into the courtyard.

Guy fingered his neck to make sure it was in one piece.

Myles stared open-mouthed after Holden. "By the saints' bones, what afflicts him?"

Guy shook his head in disgust. "He is in love with her," he told Myles. "I'd bet my blade on it."

"In love with her?" Myles echoed, still reeling from Holden's display of rage.

"Only love could make him so blind," Guy grumbled, smoothing his beard. "I only pray his wedding night finds him with *his* eight inches sheathed in *her* and not the other way round."

Katie clucked her tongue. The lass refused to don the velvet gown she'd brought to her chamber. And what a shame 'twas, too. The surcoat was a wondrous shade of rich green edged at the neck and sleeves with intricate gold crenelations. The fabric was soft and of rare quality and color, but Cambria had cast it aside like dirty scrap linen.

"I do not go to my love," Cambria insisted. "I have no wish to please him, only to have this thing done with."

Katie wrung her hands and pleaded with her mistress. "My lady, well I know he is English and an enemy, but he means well, and he seems a man of honor." She lowered her voice conspiratorially. "He is quite comely as well, my lady. Ye should make beautiful children."

Cambria shuddered dramatically. "I care not if he has the looks of Adonis and the manner of a saint," she retorted, "I intend to make my protest clear. I'll not garb myself as if I go to a happy event. I'd sooner dress for my execution!"

Katie sighed heavily. There was so much Cambria didn't know. "Lass, 'twill go much better with ye *tonight* if ye're pleasin' to him *today*, if ye get my meanin'," she confided.

Cambria smiled smugly. "I've taken care of that, Katie. You see, the wedding's agreed to, but the bedding is not."

"Oh, aye, so Malcolm's said." She laughed as she thought about the virile beast of a man Cambria was about to wed. "Think ye he'll agree to that?"

"He's *already* agreed to it in the marriage document."

"Ah, Cambria," Katie breathed, shaking her head, "what have ye got yerself into? He's clever, that one. I warrant that promise will last longer on parchment than 'twill in practice."

Cambria frowned at her chiding remark, and Katie at last threw her hands up in surrender. Perhaps she'd send Malcolm up to see if he could talk some sense into the lass.

The steps of the church were strewn with cornflowers, periwinkle, and cowslip, and the air fairly buzzed with a colorful cacophony of voices. Nobles and peasants alike, adorned in their best attire, ranging from the finest burgundy velvet to passably clean sheep's hide, lined the stony road. Every tongue wagged, speculating at the strange event to come. The anticipation rose with the passing minutes.

It was hardly a fit day for a wedding. There had been little time to prepare for either the ceremony or the feast to follow, and the bleak sky threatened to loose its store of rain. The priest, scratching in his woolen frock, looked as if he had been dragged from his bed.

A hush fell gradually over the crowd as Lord Holden at last made his approach from Blackhaugh Castle on his charger, appearing out of the mist like some mythical hero. He had bathed and dressed in a sumptuous black velvet surcoat that matched the trappings of his horse. Detailed silver embroidery was worked into the design of the wolf of de Ware, and the dark color of the background made Holden's eyes a more brilliant green than usual in contrast. His hair, freshly washed, fell in shining mahogany waves to his wide shoulders, and many of the women present would have gladly given up their place in heaven for the chance to hold that head in their lap. Not a lady wasn't envious of Cambria Gavin when Lord Holden halted the steed before the church and dismounted. His bearing exuded his noble birth in spite of the slight favor he was forced to give his wounded side as he walked.

So it was when Cambria finally galloped up, scattering the unfortunate few who stood too close to her path, the priest, the knights, the servants, everyone except Holden, gasped audibly, appalled at her appearance. Sir Guy and Holden's brother Garth looked ready to throttle her, as did Malcolm the Steward. But Holden, to her disappointment, reacted not at all to the fact that she was attired from head to foot in chain mail.

She dismounted and walked toward him, each step of her metal-shod feet ringing clearly on the silent air. But he met her with civility, taking her hand, though 'twas encased in a gauntlet, as if 'twere the most delicate blossom.

It peeved her to see him remain calm, unimpressed with her show of defiance. Surely he was angry with her for her choice of dress. But he didn't blink an eye. 'Twas almost as if he'd expected her to do something like this. And since the impact was lost on him, she almost regretted her rebellious behavior, particularly as the priest stood staring at her with his jaw lax.

Holden cleared his throat, and the priest clumsily began the ceremony. Cambria mumbled her way through the ritual, repeating words she was reluctant to say, while Holden's voice rang strong with conviction. As the priest droned on, she began to feel absolutely slovenly next to Holden, noting his fine garments, his freshly shaved chin, the wonderful, spiced scent of his skin, a pitiful contrast to her unwashed face and tarnished armor.

When the outdoor ritual was complete, the priest held open the door of the church to let all crowd within for the wedding Mass. Beeswax candles filled the shadowy nave, and their light illuminated the jewel-colored glass of the arched windows and danced merrily along the walls in contrast to Cambria's mood. Her mailed footsteps grated with painful starkness over the hallowed stones as they neared the altar.

The ceremony seemed an endless torture. By the conclusion of the rites, Cambria felt like a complete fool. Holden had to repeatedly help her to her feet in the heavy mail after the constant kneeling required in the service, and though he did so without comment, she was sure he was laughing inwardly at her stupidity. Her knees were sore, and she reiterated her vows before God through clenched teeth. What exasperated her more than anything was that Holden seemed to go through the ceremony as if 'twere something he did every day of his life.

Holden knew Cambria was suffering for her folly. He imagined her own pain was punishment enough for her attempted humiliation of him. He would have to make certain that Guy, Garth, and Malcolm in particular did not try to chastise her further. The three of them looked as if they wished to roast her slowly over an open fire.

Already he could see the humor in the situation. He imagined the tales he'd tell his children—*their* children, he amended as he glanced at her beautiful, stubborn profile.

Oh, aye, they'd have children. She obviously had no idea how persuasive he could be. The foolish clause she'd insisted upon in their marriage contract couldn't stop him from seducing her. The most it would do was give her some false impression of immunity to his seduction.

He studied the soft, kissable column of her neck, the tender place beneath her ear. The poor lass didn't know that the art of arousal was a gift with him. His men often teased him about his uncanny ways with the fairer sex, and his skills were a favorite subject of conversation among the ladies. He was very good, a master, and he had no doubt that even this unwilling wench would eventually answer to his touch. And when she finally did, he thought, focusing on her sensual mouth, it would be with a passion as fierce as her temper.

He was brought back to the matter at hand as the priest spoke the final words, blessing their alliance. Holden took the silver de Ware crest ring from his pouch, the one he'd paid a king's ransom to have crafted in time, and faced his bride. He slipped the band onto the tip of his finger and took her hand, turning it palm upward so he could unfasten the gauntlet.

The hush in the nave was the silence of a hundred held breaths as he removed the mail glove. No doubt many in the crowd suspected he'd cast the thing down in challenge. But he only tucked it beneath his arm and slipped the ring from his own finger onto hers. It fit perfectly.

The priest exhaled shakily, then gave permission for the kiss to seal their union. Holden had to admit relief that Cambria had refrained from donning a helm. He handed the gauntlet to the fidgeting priest and turned purposefully to his new wife.

She looked at him guardedly.

He slowly slid the mail coif back from her head, exposing tresses that gleamed in the gold light. Gazing into her liquid eyes with an intensity that he knew shook her to the core, he slipped a hand under the soft curls on one side of her head. With the other hand at her back, he pressed her firmly against him. As he tipped her head back to allow her to receive his kiss, he covertly, languorously traced a finger beneath her ear, eliciting a sharp intake of breath from her. The kiss he gave her was sweet and chaste, but the touch of his hands upon her and the way his body melted into hers were far from innocent.

Suddenly, Cambria felt like the Wolf's victim. Only a moment before, she'd rejoiced at the fact that this farce of a wedding was nearly at an end. Now, she felt herself slipping utterly out of control as Holden touched her. His fingers were unexpectedly gentle, like a falconer's caress, and although she wore a padded gambeson beneath her mail, she could feel the insistent pressure of his hips against her belly. His lips were warm and encouraging on her own trembling mouth, and his breath was pleasantly sweet.

For an instant she panicked, losing her balance. To her chagrin, Holden had to steady her as her legs threatened to buckle under his onslaught.

Then the kiss was over, and she could hear the castle folk cheering. She walked out beside Holden under her own power. But she couldn't bear to lift her flaming face.

For a brief moment they were alone in the adjoining narthex, and Holden caught her by the shoulders.

"Are you all right?" he asked with seemingly genuine care.

"Aye," she croaked, batting his arms away.

"It really is for the best," he said, releasing her. "No doubt our people will soon be exchanging pleasantries, discussing crops, swilling ale," he added with a reassuring grin.

"Aye."

But her mind was not at all on the effect of their marriage on the castle inhabitants. She was still recovering from the effect of his kiss.

In the great hall, fresh rushes and meadowsweet were quickly spread atop the old layer, precious candles brought forth, and the cook scrounged up what simple viands could be found on such short notice for the feast.

Unlike the wedding, which had seemed to Cambria to drone on and on, the meal passed by far too quickly. Due to the haste of the ceremony and the need to prepare for war, Lord Holden had insisted on forgoing the traditional several day feast and opted for a single banquet. The castle folk seemed intent on becoming just as drunk in one night as five, however, and began falling to their ale with enthusiasm.

Serving maids kept busy carrying platters of roast meat and bowls of steaming pottage to and fro, refilling goblets, and avoiding the enthusiastic advances of knights with wandering hands. A lutist played at the front of the hall, but he could scarcely be heard above the commotion in the room. Hounds groveled for bones at the feet of their masters, and children licked their greasy fingers in spite of chiding slaps from their mothers.

Cambria had little appetite. In spite of the assurance of the marriage agreement between them, she dreaded sharing a bed with the English lord. She'd been badly frightened by the strange yearning sensations he'd aroused in her body with a single kiss, and she had no wish to lose her composure again.

She couldn't stomach the roast meats, ruayn cheese, and stewed apples that graced the tables and only nibbled on a crust of fine white bread. She grew weary of being jostled about by well-wishers, and the noise and laughter began to irritate her. In her nervousness, she became unmindful of how many times her cup was filled. She noticed only when she stood suddenly and her eyes seemed to take an extra moment to catch up, that perhaps she'd had a wee bit too much wine.

Holden noticed three cups after that. There was an odd list to Cambria's halting gait, and she actually smiled broadly at him as he came toward her.

"Bride," he admonished softly, amused by her drunkenness, "you will drink yourself into a stupor."

He removed the chalice from her grasp in spite of her objections that that was precisely what she hoped to do.

"Let us leave the feast," he whispered into her ear.

She shivered once uncontrollably, even as she regarded him with obstinate reservation, struggling to focus her eyes.

"Go up. I shall arrive anon," he told her.

She mumbled a good-bye and wandered off through the crowd. He wondered if she'd find her way there. It probably didn't matter anyway, he thought, mentally sighing. She wasn't going to let him between those lovely thighs tonight.

He rose from his chair and announced, "I grow weary from my wound, good people, so I would dispense with the customary wedding night proceedings. My bride and I shall retire now, but we wish the feasting to continue. I give you fair warning, I will be displeased should there be one left standing among you come the morrow."

The castle folk laughed in good humor. Even the most stubborn of the Scots had to grudgingly admit a certain amount of admiration for Lord Holden's civility and warmth.

Only Sir Owen, leaning against the smoky wall in a distant corner, watched the proceedings with hatred twisting his mouth. And no amount of gaiety, not even the company of his favorite whore, could coax the bitter expression from his face.

Holden, only one thing on his mind, stopped briefly to reassure Guy that he'd not let his bride slay him in his sleep.

Then he sipped the last of his wine, giving Cambria a few moments to settle into their chamber.

Finally, glancing impatiently at the door, he set down his empty cup and mounted the stairs amid raucous, heckling cries. He grinned good-naturedly and bid them all good night as he closed the chamber door behind him.

Cambria was perched tautly on the edge of the bed, a strange look of vulnerable defiance in her eyes that he did not at first understand. Damn her, she was still attired in her armor.

Although it vexed him, he spoke calmly. "Lady, I am a man of honor. I intend to keep our agreement. There is no need to wear chain mail in our bed."

She bit her lip in humiliated disgust. "Malcolm is angry with me. He refuses to help me disarm, and I can't find a squire"—she hiccoughed—"sober enough to do it properly."

He bit his cheek to hide a smile. By the saints, she was an engaging sprite. He came toward her, past the popping fire.

"How did you manage to don it?" he asked.

"I told the squire I would wear my armor or nothing."

He smiled devilishly. "Well, would that I had stolen your armor then."

He was sure she wouldn't have gasped so loudly had she not been so drunk.

"Perhaps I *should* let you sleep in it," he said with mock severity. "It would be a fitting punishment for your appearance at our wedding today."

He could see that Cambria wasn't certain whether or not he was jesting, but she sat as straight as a lance, determined to retain her dignity despite her tipsy state.

Finally, chuckling easily, he caught her arm and began unfastening the rivets holding the armor plate together.

"I haven't performed squire's services since I was a boy," he confided, "and I've never performed them for a woman."

Piece by piece, he stripped the armor from her shoulders, elbows, and knees.

Cambria had never felt so relaxed in her life. But then she'd never been so drunk before. As the Englishman unbuckled her plates, she grew keenly aware of his proximity.

She sighed. Everything about Holden exuded masculinity, and yet his touch was as gentle as fleece upon her. His eyes, intent on their task, were a clearer green than she'd remembered. Even the smell of his hair was heavenly. She inclined toward him and breathed deep the dizzying scent. Dear Lord, the wine seemed to have sapped her strength. She could scarcely move. It seemed perfectly natural that he should be undressing her.

Holden was not unaware of the effect he was having on his bride. She was more than appealing, leaning wantonly against him, her eyes heavy-lidded from drink and arousal, but he was determined to adhere to the letter of their agreement. He would make her surrender her heart before he claimed her body.

Finishing with the hauberk and gambeson, he left her to take off her own undergarments beneath the fur coverlet. There was no point in prolonging his agony, after all.

At last, fully cognizant of her curious eyes upon him, he undressed slowly in the golden light.

Cambria was familiar enough with his form. She'd changed his bandages numerous times. But that had been when he was helpless. He was far from helpless now. His body seemed to glow with virility. She turned away when he removed his undergarments, and, although it should have come as no surprise, she was shocked when he suddenly climbed in beside her.

He spoke then, his warm breath teasing her ear, the deep tone calling to primitive urges within her. "Fear not, Cambria."

She responded faintly to his tender use of her name.

"I keep my promises," he said. "I'll not take you against your will." He brushed a lock of hair back from her cheek, and she shivered. "I would ask only one thing of you this night."

"Aye?" she whispered, amazed at the huskiness of her voice.

"A kiss."

'Twas little to ask, she knew, a simple wifely courtesy. Yet she feared 'twould be her undoing. The warrior in her told her to refuse his touch. But the woman wanted it beyond reason. Before a battle between the two could begin, she closed her eyes and lifted her lips for his kiss.

A long, silent moment passed. When she opened her eyes again, Holden was staring down at her with a queer half-smile.

"Nay, love," he admonished, "*I* would have a kiss from *you.*"

The idea of bestowing a kiss upon a near stranger herself was unthinkable. She'd given her father or Malcolm an occasional peck on the cheek, but a lover's kiss? She hardly knew how to begin. Still, he was gazing at her with those deep emerald eyes, waiting expectantly. She wondered how 'twould feel to kiss those curving lips once more.

As he lay back on the pallet, his dark hair falling away from his tan, chiseled face, his sultry eyes never leaving hers, she surrendered to her curiosity. She leaned tentatively over him and pressed shy lips to his.

Holden responded tenderly, drawing her lips subtly between his, carefully controlling her level of arousal. The instant he felt her breathing quicken, he drew back, albeit with great effort on his part, and left her searching for more. There was an ill-concealed expression of longing on her face, one that mirrored the yearnings of his own flesh. But instead of sating it, he only gave her a sweet smile. Ignoring his own hunger as well as hers, he turned away from her to seek sleep.

It was a long while before Cambria could close her eyes. She felt as prickly as a hedgehog. She fidgeted with the heavy silver band that looked so foreign upon her finger. This was the marriage she'd wanted, a political alliance, chaste and simple. But the reality was somehow empty, and 'twould be some time before she would admit the reason for that emptiness.

9

THE PREDAWN MIST SEEPED INTO CAMBRIA'S BRAIN, CREEP-ing through the arched window and summoning her with-out mercy to begin the day as usual, before the sun had even risen. Her mouth was as dry as dust, and her head throbbed. She pressed her fists hard to her temples and looked at the man slumbering in the dim light beside her.

He was Lord Holden de Ware, her husband before God. She shook her head. It was amazing how innocent a man could appear while he lay sleeping. There was no trace either of the scowl he could summon in a moment or the mocking grin he was wont to wear, only the sweet repose of an infant's slumber. She had to remind herself that this man had practi-cally forced her to marry him against her will and that his motives were less than honorable.

Summoning up her resolve to despise him, she stepped from the haven of his bed into the arms of the cold and sul-try morn. She silently pulled on her undergarments, gambe-son, and hose. She'd be damned if this marriage would change anything. She refused to be either placated or tamed. In a familiar routine, she wriggled into her coat of mail and buckled on her broadsword, leaving the impossible armor plate on the chest where Holden had stacked it. Snatching up her gauntlets and shield, she slipped quietly out the door.

• • •

When Holden woke with the sun an hour later, his first response to Cambria's disappearance was fury. The wench must have fled somehow in the night, he decided, preferring the dangers of the forest to that of the Wolf's lair. Finally, forcing himself to calm down, he reasoned that she could be any number of places. He shrugged into a velvet robe, brushed quick fingers through his hair, and went below to look for his bride.

True to his wishes, dozing bodies lay strewn everywhere in the great hall, refuse of the past evening's well-enjoyed feast. He picked his way carefully through the snoozing humanity. The clank of pots came from the kitchen, and he started for the door.

Katie came bustling out, dodging Malcolm's playful swat on her backside, and Holden nearly frightened her witless.

"Oh, milord!" she gasped, turning scarlet. "What are ye doin' up and . . . I mean . . ."

"I have somehow misplaced my wife," he admitted.

"Oh, la!" Katie replied, her hand upon her heart. "Why, my lord, she goes most every mornin' to the—"

"To the garden," Malcolm interjected.

Katie gaped at her husband's blatant lie.

Holden's brow clouded instantly. Malcolm *was* a lousy liar. "To the garden?"

"Well," Malcolm hedged, "some field."

Holden raised himself to his full threatening height. "Where is my wife?"

Malcolm folded his arms and stared at the point of Holden's chin, which was still above his eye level. "I told her not to go below. Her place is with you, I know. I presumed she would remain—"

"You presumed she would stay here obediently?" He looked incredulously at the steward. "Even *I* know her better."

Malcolm's face burned with embarrassment. "I'll show you where she is."

"Do so and quickly! If she's outside the castle wall, she's not safe!"

"I'll carve you to bits like an English roast!"

Holden and Malcolm heard Cambria's colorful threats

long before they saw the sword flash in a downward arc at empty air. Holden watched her from the trees as she turned and struck again at her invisible enemy. He neared stealthily, angered at her brazenness in coming alone, but relieved by her apparent safety. The garden indeed. He motioned for Malcolm to go on back to the castle. He had choice words for Cambria's ears alone.

After Malcolm had gone, he observed his warrior wife for several minutes. She'd foregone a helm, which left her hair loose to dance riotously about her shoulders as she turned and lunged.

The lass was quick. There was a lyrical quality to her movements. But beyond her agility, there was little to recommend her as a fighter. She was recklessly aggressive. Her careless defense left her open so often that in the few minutes he watched her, an enemy could have slain her easily a dozen times.

When she drew near to his place of concealment and he'd seen enough, he stepped suddenly from behind the tall sycamore.

"Well, and what have we here?" he bellowed. "I see I've not taken a wife—I've gained a knight-errant!"

Cambria wheeled in surprise and almost ran him through.

"Put away your sword!" he said sharply. "It is your husband!"

She didn't do so quickly enough for his taste and, incensed at her hesitation, he drew forth his own weapon and knocked her blade aside.

"Whose throat do you plan to slit, my bloodthirsty lady?"

She glared at him. "Any who would come upon my back," she said meaningfully.

He lifted the corner of his lip slightly, then grew serious. "There are renegades about. It's not safe that you should come here alone."

She tossed her head proudly. "I can defend myself."

"So I see," he said, gesturing to the air around them. "Your foe seems to have fled."

She blushed and muttered, "I *can* defend myself."

He stared at her. Someone had obviously disillusioned

Cambria about her abilities. She was overconfident, a dangerous thing in a knight. It was a vital lesson in humility she needed to learn.

"Come, warrior wife, I'll make you a wager," he said.

She eyed him warily.

He tossed his sword to the ground. Then he pulled out a small dagger from his pouch. "I'll wager you cannot defend yourself against me."

"Against that?"

He nodded.

She looked him over. "You have no armor, no shield."

"Even so," he said with a bow.

She pursed her lips, but her eyes flickered eagerly.

"Come," he beckoned. "I'll give you three chances. I'll wager you . . . a kiss. If I win, you must give me a kiss."

Cambria smirked. "And if I win?"

His lip curved up. "You will not."

Cambria's brow clouded with spite. "If I win, I never have to kiss you again."

He shrugged. "All right. Done."

Cambria planted her feet wide, the sword poised before her. Swiftly, with good balance and aim, she came at him. But she let her shield dip, and he used that advantage to dodge the blow and move in close, ending with the point of his dagger at her throat.

"That's one," he told her.

Cambria flinched in embarrassment. How the devil had he seized the advantage so swiftly? Perhaps 'twas only luck. She backed angrily away from him.

"You would do better to defend yourself only," he suggested. "A bad temper is your worst enemy. Losing control of it is a mistake common to novices."

That infuriated her. How dare he call her a novice? She'd held sword in hand since the age of five. She'd show this cocky knight the extent of her abilities. Her speed and agility had always been an amazement to her father. She knew if she could slip under his arm unexpectedly, she could catch him unguarded. She swept up her sword and flexed her knees in preparation.

Holden drew her attack with a threatening jab. She feigned with her shield and came from beneath with her sword, a move that usually surprised her opponents. But he took no apparent notice. His dagger flitted about her like an angry wasp deciding where to sting. She swatted at it a dozen times, but never made contact. Vexed, she lowered her shield and swung recklessly at his head.

One hard blow from the haft of his dagger knocked the sword from her grasp. He crossed his blade against her neck.

"Two," he whispered.

Cambria was fuming now. How could she lose to a man armed with only a dagger? She retrieved her sword and braced herself again. "Come," she snarled. "Come!"

Holden shook his head, but raised the dagger again. She waited for him to make the first move. When he did, 'twas so sudden she had no time to raise her shield. The dagger teased the hem of her tabard, then the buckle of her belt, then the locks of her hair, threatening every part of her.

"Use your shield!" he commanded her.

His criticism infuriated her. She began slicing wildly at him, but to her frustration, not a single stroke landed on anything save the empty air.

Then, to add insult, the rogue tossed the dagger to his left hand, fending off her attack with the dexterity of a juggler.

Holden could have continued, but he was eager for his prize. He unleashed a greater measure of his power, pummeling her from all sides with the flat of the blade. While she was distracted, he wrenched the sword from her with one easy movement, then tore her shield away with a second pass.

Cambria stood with her jaw slack, staring at her hands as if she wondered how they had come to be empty.

"Three," he said, tucking his dagger back into his pouch.

She was gaping at him. He recognized that look. He'd seen it before in the young lads that frequented the tiltyard, lads who worshiped him and would later weave overblown tales for their friends about the great Wolf of de Ware and his mighty sword arm. But by the saints, he'd never thought to see such reverence in the sprite's eyes. It made his heart beat faster.

For a long while, she only gawked at him, awestruck. Then she said, " 'Tis true, isn't it? You've never lost. You've never met your match."

"On the contrary, madam," he said with an entirely different meaning, "I believe I *have* at long last met my match."

His blood was already heated from their skirmish, and to see such naked admiration from his enemy, *this* enemy, fueled the desire within his body. He clenched his teeth to control it.

"Lady," he said in a voice just above a whisper, "beware how you gaze upon me, lest I forget the limits of our wager."

Cambria felt her cheeks pinken. Had she been staring at him? She swiftly glanced away, too late to hide the truth. Nervously, she licked her lips. There was still the wager to pay.

He was standing too close to her. She could hear the gentle rasp of his breath. Did he have to look at her like that, speak to her that way? His eyes were as deep and green as a loch, and his voice was like peasant ale on her ear, rough yet intoxicating.

She steeled herself to pay the wager with as much dignity and as little ado as she could muster. Forcing her gaze to his, she determined he'd not outstare her this time.

'Twas a grave error. Her breath ragged, her blood warm, she was pulled to him like water to a wick. Somehow he moved yet closer, close enough that she could feel the heat emanating from his body, close enough to see the rims of his teeth between his parted lips.

Holden was thrown for an instant by the spark of desire in her eyes. He knew he should cast water on that cinder, douse it while it was yet harmless for both their sakes, but he felt his own passion rising, and he was reluctant to arrest it.

Cambria shivered. She remembered the taste of his mouth, its warmth, its sweetness. That mouth was her undoing. Before she could stop to think of the terrible mistake she was making, she lifted her head, drew near enough to him to feel his breath upon her face, and gave him his due.

Holden returned her kiss, tentatively at first, drawing her out, then with more surety. Her skin was soft and yielding, and she tasted like wild honey.

Cambria felt drawn to him with a curious hunger. His lips were doing things to her—teasing her, beckoning her, feeding voraciously on her, as if he'd consume her soul. She clutched at his shoulders, clinging to him with a fervor she'd never known she possessed, and her own need amazed and frightened her. She was losing control. She could feel passion swirling around her, like a whirlpool tugging her from safe harbor. And she wanted it, wanted his kiss, his touch.

He parted her lips and let the tip of his tongue delve between them to trail fire across her own tongue. She shivered. She wondered how his lips would feel upon her neck, her shoulder, her breast. She wondered how they would feel lower, in the secret spot that swelled and yearned even now. . . .

Nay! With a sudden panicked cry, she shoved him from her, staggering back. She felt her face turn to flame. Sweet Mary, what was she doing? What was he doing to her? He was an Englishman, for God's sake.

But her lips still tingled from his kiss.

The brute had tied her to his bed and practically forced her into marriage.

But his eyes were as dark and smoldering as warm coals.

Damn him, he was responsible for her father's death.

She drew back her fist and plowed it into his face, hard.

Holden caught the blow on his cheek. It knocked his head around, stunning him for a moment. By the time he collected his wits enough to yell after her, she was halfway to the castle, tears streaming down her face, cradling her throbbing hand.

Holden took out his frustrations on the quintain in the tiltyard, macing the straw-stuffed dummy to shreds.

He should have known better. Cambria was nowhere near ready to concede the battle. Lord, what was wrong with him? His own astonishing lack of control left him feeling foolish.

Not since he was a lad had he felt so incapable of subduing that beast in his trews.

And she'd struck him! Not the chiding slap he'd grown used to in his youth when he'd taken a few too many liberties, but a close-fisted, hard-swung punch. God's bones, how was he going to explain a bruised cheek earned the day after his wedding?

He spurred Ariel hard across the field and drove his lance at the quintain so fiercely that it spun like a child's toy and broke.

From the haven of the solar, Cambria shivered as she witnessed Holden's violence in the practice yard. Her knees grew weak. Had she actually dared to strike him, that fierce warrior dispatching knight after knight on the field below?

She swallowed reflexively as he turned his well-muscled destrier, and the two thundered across the field as one beast. How like his steed he was, she thought with a shudder—lean and firm and powerful. She remembered how dangerous those arms were around her. Her heart quickened in her breast at the vivid memory, and a flush stole up her cheek.

As she watched, he swung a blunted mace forward with such force that his Gavin opponent was catapulted backwards from his mount, landing with a deadly thud on the sod. She gasped, digging her fingers into the cold stone of the sill. Lord, had the Wolf killed one of her men? The lad lay silent, still as a winter pond.

Before his destrier had even skidded to a halt, Holden leaped from its back. He dropped the mace, tore the helm from his head, and rushed to the boy, falling to his knees in the dust. Cambria watched as he gingerly lifted the lad's shoulders and removed his helm. The boy's slack face was as pale as cream. She clasped her hand over her mouth in horror.

The Gavin men gathered round, concern etching their brows. Holden ignored them, riveted instead on the lad in his arms. He patted the boy's cheeks and said something to him she couldn't hear. As he lay limp across Holden's knees, the ominous hush stretched like a drawn bow. Cambria held her breath till she grew faint.

Then the boy gasped, filling his lungs with a great rasping sound that reached across the silence all the way up to Cambria's window. The men chuckled in sheepish relief, and Holden tousled the lad's hair as if he were a favorite nephew. Half sick with worry and relief and disgust at men's deadly play, Cambria reeled from the window, collapsing back against the cool rock wall.

When she recovered enough to look again, Holden was sparring afoot with her knights, guiding their sword thrusts, shouting encouragement, blocking their advances with a crossed blade. He'd lined them up in two rows, an arm's width apart, and at Holden's command, they advanced in unison. She narrowed her eyes. Never had her force appeared so well ordered, so formidable.

Now the Wolf tossed aside his sword and threw down his helm, facing them bare-headed and bare-handed but for a shield. She straightened, a queer prickling at the back of her neck. What arrogant game was this?

Six of them attacked at once, and her eyes widened. Was the man mad? Mere weeks ago, they would have called him enemy. Now he dodged their assault single-handedly with naught but a chunk of leather-covered wood, leaving his bare throat as a target for their blades.

She anxiously fingered her own throat. She'd been close enough to the Wolf to see the pulse of his lifeblood. Invincible warrior he might be, but he was as mortal as any man. Why would he leave himself so vulnerable?

The answer came reluctantly to her mind.

He was a man of honor. Only true honor would make a man so foolish. He believed in chivalry, and he expected it from the men he battled, even the Scots.

She picked at a crack in the wall. If honor came so naturally to him, how could he have been a part of her father's betrayal and murder?

The answer was clear. He had not been a part of it.

The Wolf would not scheme to take a castle by wiles—he would storm it by force. The Wolf would not intrigue to gain an alliance—he would command it. And above all, as she'd begun to sense, the Wolf would never have . . .

She closed her heart against the truth, wanting to blame him, needing to hold onto her hatred like a knight needed his sword, but already she felt it slipping inexorably from her grasp, bit by thwarting bit.

Holden hadn't killed her father.

Cambria shut her eyes. In some corner of her mind, a burden lifted, and she no longer felt so torn between vengeance and . . . and that other emotion that tugged at her heart like a puppy on a leash, the one she could not quite define, the one that made her throat go dry when he stood too close, that left her scarcely able to breathe when his lips touched hers and quickened her pulse as she remembered the feel of his strong hands upon her. She had no name for it, this feeling that, cleared of polluting revenge, seemed as new and awkward as a colt on its first legs.

But 'twas there, buried deep within her soul, a queer stirring of pride perhaps, as she looked down again at her brave husband, who had somehow managed to knock every one of her knights to the ground like skittles on a bowling green.

So caught up was she in her reverie that she didn't hear Katie enter the solar.

"Ah, there ye are," the maid trilled.

Cambria started back guiltily from the arrow loop, all too aware of her face's glow.

"Why, lass," Katie began, "whatever . . . ?" The maidservant made her way over to the opening and peered below, a knowing smile curving her lips. "Ah, he is a fine fighter, your lord, is he not?"

Cambria shrugged noncommittally.

"And I'll wager ye might be havin' second thoughts about that bargain ye made."

Flustered, Cambria turned on her, her scarlet skirts twirling about her like storm-tossed roses. "How dare you speak thus to me!"

Katie appeared unruffled by her tone. "I nursed ye when ye were but a bairn, lass. Ye may be the wife of a lord now, but I remember when ye soiled yer linens with the rest o' them. The day I may not speak my mind to ye is the day I'll leave."

Cambria chewed at her lip, duly reprimanded.

"Ah, lass, why do ye torture yerself so? He is a good man and not unpleasant to look upon. I've heard it bandied about that the de Ware brothers are more than capable in—"

"He's an Englishman!" Cambria reminded both Katie and herself. But the words felt strangely flat and meaningless on her tongue. "I'll not suffer him to touch me." She closed her eyes against the clear memory of their kiss only this morning.

"Malcolm is most certain your lord had no part in the deception that killed your father," Katie confided, pulling a rag from the pocket in her surcoat. "I'd wager ye would know the truth as well, if ye'd listen to yer heart. Another of his men, perhaps, a betrayer, but not the lord himself. He's a man of honor. He'd never resort to such treachery. Ye've seen the loyalty he inspires, even in our own folk."

Cambria *had* seen it. The Gavin knights had never fought so well as they did under the lord's painstaking hand.

"But 'tis of little matter now, I suppose." Katie sighed, wiping the dust from the table with her rag. "He's off to the battlefield in two days' time."

Cambria's heart skipped a beat. "The battlefield?"

Katie nodded. "He's commanded a fortnight's provisions for fourscore o' soldiers."

"Where do they go?"

"Oh, la, I know not, just that the lord bid me make preparations."

Cambria's mind raced forward as Katie left the room. Conflicts were numerous along the Borders—cattle raids and the like—but that was too large a company for a mere Border dispute. Nay, this had to be all-out war between the Scots and the English.

She moved toward the arrow loop a last time to peer down at her husband. He sparred viciously now with Sir Guy. His blade sparked against his opponent's, and she shuddered as she thought of Robbie and Graham and Jamie facing the likes of the Wolf on the battlefield.

It didn't take long for word to slip that King Edward himself had called Holden to fight. Cambria heard the servants buzzing about it in the kitchen. This meant that it would be a decisive battle. She dreaded what the outcome would mean for Blackhaugh and her clan.

Listening furtively in the passage beside the knights' quarters, she learned that the men would be traveling north to join the king. As the knights emerged from the room, trudging toward the list for field practice, Cambria hid herself in the stairwell. Finally, thinking all of them had gone, she prepared to step from her place of hiding.

Passing by so closely that she felt the breeze of his movement, Sir Owen swept by her, unseeing, into the knights' quarters and proceeded to sharpen his sword on the grindstone there. She released her captured breath and studied him through the crack of the door.

He was not alone. Emerging from a shadowy corner of the room was an English serving wench. Mousy hair concealed her face as she sauntered up to Owen's side, clinging to him, running brazen hands over his chest as he worked. Cambria nestled back against the wall.

The girl simpered, "I do not wish ye to go to war."

"Don't you fret none about me, Aggie. I'll watch my backside."

"I'd like to watch your backside for ye!" the girl said in a bawdy voice.

"I'll bet you would, Aggie," Owen snickered.

Cambria peeked at them again. She tried to get a good look at Aggie, but the girl had her back to Cambria.

"Why can't I go, too, my love?" she pleaded, moving her hands around to the front of Owen's body, stroking the bulge that was beginning to form beneath the waist of his surcoat.

Cambria was disgusted by both the tawdry display and the fact that she was watching it like a naughty child, but she was afraid to move lest she be discovered.

"Oh, Aggie," Owen moaned, letting the grinding wheel wind down and extracting her hands from his body. "There will be time for this when I come home, and then, my sweet, you and I are going to be wed." He curled a lock of her stringy hair around his finger. "This castle will be ours."

"But 'ow, Owen? I thought ye said the Scots bitch wiggled out of the 'angman's noose and . . ."

The hair stood up on the back of Cambria's neck.

"Shh," Owen soothed. "Never you worry. I've got a plan, I have. Alas, Holden de Ware is not going to survive the battle."

Aggie gasped in unison with Cambria, then giggled conspiratorially, snuggling up against Owen.

"Without him," Owen continued, "she'll be powerless."

"Then ye'll kill 'er?" Aggie asked with sickening zeal.

"There won't be any need. I'm sure King Edward will see everything my way. My brother was to take possession of Blackhaugh. I took care of that obstruction myself, but they all believe the Scotswoman killed him. She'll be hanged for it, and I, my dear, will inherit the castle."

Aggie crowed with glee. Cambria felt ill.

Owen's voice grew bitter. "All those years of submission—'aye, Roger,' 'of course, Roger,' 'as you like, Roger,' listening to my brother boast of his noble blood, taking the rod upon my back for his sins, gobbling up the meager scraps of affection our dear mother threw me—well, they're all finished now." He wheezed a contented sigh. "Soon I'll be the lord of Blackhaugh."

"Say the part about me again, Owen, say it," Aggie begged.

"You, my love, will become Lady Agnes, and you shall wear emeralds about your neck and dine on swan at the high table. You can even take a noblewoman to maid if you like, for your own amusement."

Aggie sighed in contentment. "Oh, Owen, I will count the hours till ye return."

Owen leered at her in what was supposed to be a smile. He set down his sword and pulled Aggie to him, squeezing her affectionately before he began to shove his hand down the bodice of her kirtle with a vulgarity that finally persuaded Cambria to leave, no matter the risk.

She had to find Holden; she had to warn him.

• • • •

Despite the souvenir bruise that colored his cheekbone, reminding him of his wife's earlier unpleasantness, Holden didn't mean to be short with Cambria. He just had a hundred things on his mind.

Tomorrow they would set out to meet with Edward's forces, and it seemed there wasn't enough time to prepare. His own fletcher would have to make arrows all night long to have enough good ones, one of his knights' destriers had twisted a leg, and two of the carts needed their wheels mended. Next to these critical concerns, Cambria's worries seemed insignificant.

"I am *always* cautious in battle," he told her, checking each longbow he packed onto the arms wagon.

The bustle of activity here in the courtyard—knights sparring, servants packing, animals milling about—masked the sound of their conversation, but Cambria still looked nervous.

"You must watch your back," she insisted.

"John!" he called out, tossing a bow to the man. "This one is useless. The recurve is split."

Cambria whispered, "I just heard Owen confess he was responsible for Roger's murder. And now he intends to slay you to inherit Blackhaugh."

"Owen?" He sighed. Why did she protest her innocence now? "Cambria, you needn't worry about your part in Roger's death. It's in the past. I deem it an unfortunate accident. Thomas! Careful with that!"

Cambria grabbed his arm. "Listen! He has already killed one man, his own brother, and gotten away with it. He could do the same to you."

He rolled his eyes. "Cambria, I know what happened at the inn, why you killed Roger—"

"You know nothing!" she burst out. "I did not kill Roger! I tell you, Owen did it, and he'll do it again!"

"Cambria, I've been fighting and killing men since you were a little girl. You'll just have to trust my instincts." He noted the stubborn clench of her jaw. "Did you see to the packing of the kegs of ale?"

Cambria offered no reply. She'd reached the limits of her

patience. She spun on her heel and stalked off, a curse on her lips. The devil take Holden, she thought, for all his blind stupidity. Maybe she should just let fate take its course. The damned fool, he was going to die by his own man's hand, and he was too pigheaded to do anything about it.

Somehow she had to convince him. But not now, not while he was distracted by split recurves and battle provisions. Nay, she'd wait till nightfall, when duty no longer claimed his attentions. She'd wait till they were alone.

The moon gleamed high overhead and the fire burned low by the time Holden came to their chamber. Cambria had trod the rushes to pieces and bitten her nails down to nubs. She'd practiced all the arguments she intended to use on him, honed every weapon in her verbal arsenal. But when he dragged in, wearily running a hand through his hair, his bruise visible evidence of her earlier diplomacy, all her practiced speech deserted her.

He looked up suddenly, as if surprised to find her still awake, and in that instant, all the uncertainty he harbored about the battle to come stood in relief upon his face as clearly as the etched swirls of the moon. For that one brief moment, she longed to comfort him, to smooth the wrinkles from his brow. But as swiftly as they'd appeared, the lines on his face vanished, and he greeted her with the mask of self-assurance he wore for his knights.

"Still awake?" He unbuckled his swordbelt and dropped it beside the bed. "One of us should get some sleep."

"I . . . I could not." She twisted her fingers in her gown.

He nodded. In the waxy moonlight, she could see his bruise, the bruise *she* had put there. It looked like a shadow. She lowered her eyes in shame.

"I . . . I'm sorry I struck you," she blurted. The words sounded strange to her ears. She didn't think she'd ever apologized to anyone before.

He waited for her to look at him, then nodded with that lopsided smile. "When I return from battle, I suppose we'll have to review the code of chivalry."

If you return, she thought, her heart lurching. She wrung her hands as he began undressing. She'd promised herself she'd not lose her temper, that she'd reason with him calmly. But the last thing she felt as he removed his clothing, piece by piece, was calm.

"I need to speak with you." Her voice came out whispery, like the wind through dry leaves.

He had removed his hauberk, and the moon painted the contours of his bare chest with silver. His was a fighter's body, strong and firm, and yet the recent scar just below his ribs reminded her that he was forged of flesh and blood, as vulnerable as any man.

"Is this about Owen?"

"You must believe me," she said, rushing forward to take the hauberk from his hands. "He intends to kill you."

He hooked his thumbs inside his chausses. "As do hundreds of Highlanders. Cambria, you must understand . . ."

"I don't!" She took a deep breath. Already her temper threatened to escape its frail cage. "I *don't* understand. If you die, my clan is defenseless. Why do you not just . . . leave Owen behind?"

His gaze moved from her to the narrow window, where he stared out at the night. He clenched and unclenched his fists once, and when he spoke, his voice was as somber as the gallows. "The Scots forces are vast. In sooth, if we're to win this battle, we need all the men we can take."

He looked back to her then, and the spark of uncertainty she glimpsed in his eyes frightened her. Was there doubt that the English would win?

"Besides," he said with a rueful smile, cupping her chin, "if I left behind every knight who'd ever threatened me, I'd have no army."

Frustrated, she dropped his hauberk to the bed and spoke rashly. "Take me with you."

"What?" He chuckled and frowned all at once.

She placed her palms flat on his chest. "Take me with you. I'll watch your back."

He cradled her head in both his hands. "I cannot take you to battle, Cambria. 'Tis no place for a lady."

"I'll stay behind the lines," she planned. "I'm a keen shot with the bow. If Owen tries anything . . ."

"Cambria." He kissed her forehead. His mouth felt soft, warm, not at all the mouth of a warrior. "It is enough that I risk my men. I'll not risk my wife as well."

"But . . ."

"I swear to you I will take care," he vowed. "I protect my own. I'll do naught to endanger your clan."

But when she felt his heart beating beneath her palm, that heart whose pulse could be ceased by the single lightning slash of a blade, she thought less of her clan than she did of the husband she'd begun reluctantly to admire.

The sound of Holden's soft, soothing snores lulled Cambria to sleep, but at the far end of the night, dark images invaded her dreams, curdling her slumber into a roiling sea of despair.

Bodies were everywhere. Bloody, broken, twisted. Writhing bodies like a vast churning ocean stretching to the far hills. Malcolm. Robbie. Graham. Her clan. They grabbed for her as she waded through them, pleading, screaming, damning her until she clapped her hands to her ears in horror.

Before her was the one she sought, the wolf. His gray fur, tipped by silver, lay matted now with caked blood, and his black lips peeled back in a grimace of pain, exposing long, sharp teeth. His sides heaved as he struggled to draw his dying breath. When she knelt beside him, his nostrils quivered, and he turned to look at her. And then they were *his* eyes, Holden's eyes, green with flecks of gray, gazing at her in one brief flicker of hope, then glazing over with the pale cast of death.

Anguish wrenched her heart. He was gone. The Wolf was gone. She had failed him, failed the Gavins, and now she was utterly alone.

Whether she woke from the trauma of the dream or the sound of Holden rising, she wasn't sure. She feigned sleep, though her heart pounded madly in her breast, and watched him through slitted eyes as he dressed by the gold of the lightening sky. He winced once from his wound as he slipped the hauberk over his head, reminding her again of his mortality. He must not die, she thought. She wouldn't let him.

A moment later, with a whispered farewell and a gentle kiss to her forehead, he left the chamber.

No sooner did Cambria hear the wood of the door meet the wall than she sprang from the bed, fully alert, her heart racing with purpose. She pulled a faded linen kirtle and a rough brown woolen cloak from her chest of clothes. These she quickly donned, pushing her hair back beneath the generous hood of the cloak. She tugged on her oldest leather shoes and tucked her dagger into her belt. Her longbow and arrows she would have to secrete amongst the store of weapons taken along on the journey. She slung them over her shoulder, concealing them beneath a large blanket.

Lord Holden intended to leave his brother Garth and Malcolm behind as stewards for Blackhaugh. Cambria took an extra moment to pen a missive to Malcolm, assuring him she was safe with her husband and that she was acting for the good of the clan. She knew the poor steward would not truly rest easy until she returned home, but she left the note atop her pallet nonetheless.

As she laid her hand across the pillow, she realized she still wore her wedding ring. Peasants didn't own such things. She should slip it off, cache it in her chest of valuables. But somehow it seemed a sacrilege, so she twisted the wolf's head inward and pulled her sleeve low over her hand.

Cautiously, she eased through her chamber door and down the steps. She ambled through the great hall, milling about easily in her rustic garb within the maze of activity.

Knights in full armor strode regally past the scurrying servants, barking out orders for the packing of the wagons outside. Children chased after yelping hounds and were cuffed soundly for their efforts. Hastened along by jostling elbows, Cambria made her way through the courtyard to one of the supply wagons and covertly pushed her bow and quiver into it. Then she stopped by the stables long enough to smudge mud here and there over her arms, legs, and face, gritting her teeth all the while.

"You!" someone called, and she turned with a start, remembering just in time to lower her head.

'Twas young Sir Myles.

"You may fetch me bread and wine," he said. Evidently he hadn't recognized her. She was merely an idle body available to do his bidding. "Bring them to me in the armory."

The young whelp made it sound like an honor, and Cambria had to bite her tongue to restrain a hot retort. Instead, she meekly nodded. Myles rubbed his hands together and smugly strode off.

She shuffled into the kitchen, ducking her head out of sight as Katie brushed past with an armload of cheat bread and oatcakes. She swiped a roll fresh from the table and poured a cup of wine to take to Sir Myles.

As she swung the door to the knights' quarters open with her foot, she almost froze in panic. She could hear the deep tones of her husband addressing a dozen or so knights. Sir Myles was among them, and when he noticed his breakfast, he motioned her over impatiently.

Holden stopped in midsentence. Cambria held her breath. But her husband's eyes held no recognition as he glanced at her cursorily. He resumed speaking when she brought Myles his bread and wine. She briskly excused herself and scurried out the door.

After that, she busied herself loading the wagons with food, cooking vessels, blankets, herbs, and linen for bandages. Within the hour, the knights, well-armed and eager for travel, lined up five abreast before the provision wagons and awaited the command of their lord.

Holden made no speech, but cast a look of longing toward his chamber window that caused Cambria's heart to flutter. Then he turned his mount and took his place at the head of the company.

"Forward," he commanded. The journey had begun.

10

CAMBRIA PAUSED IN THE SHELTERING SHADE OF AN OLD sycamore and wiped the sweat from her brow with the dirty wool sleeve for the hundredth time. The weather had turned uncannily warm over the last few days, but the necessity for secrecy required that she keep the miserably stifling cloak about her. Her feet were blistered from the ill-fitting shoes and the pace Holden insisted on maintaining, and she could hardly stand her own camouflaging odor of stable filth and wet wool. But the worst of it was that it seemed she'd made the trip in vain.

Sir Owen was behaving so damnably nonchalant that she almost believed she'd imagined or misunderstood that whole exchange in the knights' quarters. It looked as if she'd gone to a great deal of trouble for naught. But 'twas too late to turn back. She was committed now to the journey—every sweating, dusty, wretched mile of it.

The de Ware men made the travel particularly nauseating, filling the balmy air with boasts of their feats of prowess in battle and in bed. To her disgust, even her own Gavin knights joined in the melee. According to all accounts, of course, none could hold a candle to the de Ware brothers. When their prattle became too coarse for her blushing ears, she dropped back to join the servants. There, at least, it amused her to hear

the women's versions of the same stories, which were un-
questionably more authentic and less heroic.

They stopped to set up camp as the sun sank low in the
cloudless sky. A nearby stream flowed into a deep pool
shaded by elms where Cambria stole away for a refreshing,
if brief, bath. Afterward, she had no choice but to put on the
same dusty surcoat, and her wet hair clung to her neck beneath her hood. But at least she'd managed to scrub away the
stink of the road.

Upon her return to camp, she set to work digging wild
leeks for the evening pottage. A chatty young girl with
ragged blond hair and sly eyes accompanied her. Cambria
paid little heed to the wench's patter until she chanced to
mention the name of Holden de Ware.

"What's that you say?" Cambria asked, feigning indifference.

"I said, I wonder how long it'll be 'fore the lord picks one
o' us to warm his bed."

"One of us?"

"Aye," she said with a naughty wink. "Annie thinks it'll
be her, and Margaret's been struttin' under his nose like a
lone hen in a coop o' roosters, but I'm thinkin' . . ."

"Is the lord not newly wed?" Cambria asked evenly,
clenching a pair of leeks in her fist.

"Oh, aye," the girl divulged in a whisper, "to a cold bitch,
they say, who don't even let him betwixt her legs." She giggled. "Can you imagine, not sharin' the bed of a de Ware?"

Cambria blinked. Her back stiffened. *Cold bitch*—was
that what they called her? Worse still, was everyone privy to
the sleeping arrangements between Lord Holden and herself?

"Oh, la, if he were mine," the girl continued dreamily,
stroking the long leaves of her leeks, "I'd let him flip me on
my backside any time o' the day, to feel those strong legs o'
his wrapped 'round—"

"Enough!" Cambria commanded sharply.

The girl started at the authority in Cambria's voice.

"Enough . . . leeks, I should think," Cambria continued
lamely, astounded by her own ferocity.

"Oh, aye," the girl replied uneasily, scratching her head.

"I s'pose it were." She shook the dirt from the last few leeks and tucked the lot of them into the front fold of her kirtle.

The servant's words haunted Cambria all afternoon, and by supper, she could only nibble at her food while she watched Holden across the fire.

She could easily see why all the maids were agog over him. Golden flame glowed upon his face, accentuating the fine bones of his cheeks and the strong set of his jaw, while the full moon's light fell across his hair in gentle silver waves. One powerful hand rested across his bent knee, while the other curved around his flagon of wine, and as he drank, his sleeve slipped up to display the flexed muscle of his forearm. His eyes, deep and pensive, revealed none of his thoughts, as he stared into the fire. He raised his cup to his lips, and Cambria remembered his kiss, the way his mouth opened to partake of hers.

An astonishing wave of desire coursed through her.

She turned her back on him abruptly to gather her wits, her fingers twisting at her wedding ring. She cursed under her breath. How soon, she wondered, would he choose someone to "warm his bed"? The women already buzzed about like flies on meat. They could hardly keep their hands and eyes off of him. The serving wenches sidled up to him as closely as they could to refill his cup or offer him another trencher, giggling like half-wits and speaking coy words of flattery. All this he accepted with diplomacy, neither showing particular favor to any one nor discouraging their attentions. Still, it rankled her to watch the vulgar display.

She shouldn't care, she knew. After all, 'twas common enough knowledge that English lords bedded whom they willed, when they willed, married or not. Virility was more highly prized than faithfulness. Besides, their marriage—hers and Holden's—was purely political, wasn't it?

By the end of supper, she was as tense as an oversprung catapult, torn between self-pity and disgust, waiting anxiously for word that some wench had been called to the lord's tent. But at last Holden retired to his pavilion, alone. For tonight, at least, she could rest easy.

She'd just begun to drift off on a threadbare wool blanket

amidst the lull of snoring when an old serving woman came to her. The beldame bore the message that she'd had been summoned to Lord Holden's pavilion. Cambria was certain there had been a mistake—she'd tried to remain all but invisible to the nobles—but the old woman insisted 'twas *her* the lord had called, the wench in the cloak.

Her teeth chattered all the way there. Perhaps 'twas only the cool night air, but something about facing Holden sent a chill up her spine. Had he discovered her identity? Or had he, in some ironic jest of destiny, chosen her as a sweetmeat to end his meal?

She drew the cloak about her face. The servant pulled aside the tent flap and bade her enter.

The pavilion was dark inside. She hesitated, wondering in which corner of his lair the Wolf lurked. The old woman lit a tall candle on a stand beside the pallet with her firebrand before she left, throwing a pool of gold light across the enclosure. It appeared to be empty.

Cambria stood still for several heartbeats, letting her eyes adjust to the candlelight. The tent was modestly furnished. A worn Turkish carpet stretched out across the hard-packed earth. There was a single carved chair and a large locked trunk for clothes and valuables. The thick, fur-covered pallet filled nearly half the space.

Anxiety threatened to destroy her composure, and she fought to keep her expression bland. Her brain buzzed with a hundred different answers she could give should Holden question her presence. But none of them were even remotely convincing.

Outside the pavilion, beneath the watchful moon, Holden paused. He took a deep breath, like a jouster preparing to charge. What would he say to her? What would he do? And most important, why was she here?

If only he'd discovered her earlier. But in sooth, once he believed Cambria safe behind castle walls, he'd focused his mind on naught but the battle ahead, shunning even the maidservants vying so doggedly for his affections. He wished now he hadn't ignored at least one of them in particular.

He'd finally spotted her across this evening's fire. A quick glimpse of the squared curve of her jaw lit by flickering flame had nearly caused him to choke on his wine. And then, watching her, he wondered how he could have been so blind.

There were things about Cambria no cloak could mask. She had a most distinctive walk, for one thing, not a feminine gait, but a warrior's long stride. Then there were the strong, sensuous, familiar curves and planes of her body, revealed when she pushed up her sleeves or hiked her skirts to step over a tree root, when she bent over to serve pottage or leaned far into a cart after a cup.

But now that he'd discovered her, he had to ask himself why she had come.

He wanted to believe she'd followed him, as she'd threatened, in order to protect him from Owen. He wanted to believe her concern for him motivated her decision to rebel against his commands.

But the sad truth was, he could not be entirely sure of her affections. Other than her grudging admiration of his knightly prowess and the suppressed spark of desire he tended to inspire in most women, he had no real proof of her feelings for him.

This alliance with the Border clans was too new, the king's battle too critical, to overlook the possibility, as painful, as improbable as it seemed to him, that Cambria might . . . betray him. He knew she had contacts among the rebels—she had freed the three who'd attacked him, an attack too well arranged for his taste. She was likely sympathetic to the rebels' plight—it seemed all Scots were romantics when it came to futile causes. And she was trying to distract him by casting suspicion upon one of his own men, Sir Owen, coincidentally the one who may have slain her father.

Damn it all, he had to find out where Cambria stood, for the safety of his men. He couldn't afford to allow her time to stir up revolt in the ranks or alert the rebel Scots of their coming.

He sighed heavily and rubbed his hands together. He knew what had to be done. He had to question her. Although he despised the task, he was very good at eliciting information from less than willing individuals. He knew how much force to exert, and where, to get almost any prisoner to sing like a nightingale.

But even as he considered it, he shook his head. He couldn't raise his hand against Cambria. A knight didn't torture a woman. It was unspeakable. Besides, as proud as the little Scots warrior was, he knew threatening her with violence was absolutely useless. She was more than willing to die for her clan.

Nay, he'd have to use a different attack to find the soft spot in her hauberk. He looked up at the dark heavens as if the answer lay there. A soft breeze blew at the nape of his neck, making the hairs there stand on end. And he knew.

He'd use her own vulnerability—her very womanhood, that unexplored passion that lay below the surface of her cool exterior, denied for so long that she wasn't even aware it existed. He'd use it to wring the truth from her.

He drew his knuckles across his mouth as he contemplated the task before him. Summoning a passing squire with a motion of his hand, he quietly bid the lad bring a vessel of wine and two cups. His wife, he decided, was about to experience the touch of a master of seduction.

Cambria heard the rustle of the tent flap, and she held her breath, shielding her face from view. When Holden entered, a dark, large, looming shadow, he breezed past her without acknowledgment. In sooth, Cambria thought he might not have even seen her. Slowly, silently she let the air leak out between her lips.

Without looking up, he poured a measure of wine into two cups.

"Do you not roast, wearing that hood all the time?" he asked.

She didn't dare answer. He might know her voice. But as the silence lengthened, she began to believe his gaze alone could pierce the dim light and her shadowed hood into her very soul. She took the cup he held out for her in trembling fingers, turning aside and sipping at the wine.

After a moment, he tipped back his own cup, finishing it off all at once.

"You're shy," he remarked. "I'd wager you've never lain with a man before now."

She gulped down the strong wine too quickly and was caught up in a spell of coughing. Holden reached out and clapped her a few times on the back, which didn't help in the least.

"Nay!" she croaked.

Holden grimaced. How easy it was for her to lie, he thought ruefully. Sweet Mary, she'd lain with one of his own knights. He hoped to God she wasn't lying about her loyalties as well.

"Then it shall be my pleasure to initiate you in the rites of passion," he said.

"But I do not wish . . ." she blurted out.

"Shh," he soothed, "I am your lord. You are my vassal, I did not ask what you wished. I would bed a woman tonight, and I've chosen you."

Cambria swallowed hard. He certainly was being matter-of-fact about the whole ordeal. He was also not wasting much time. She felt as if she were poised at the edge of a waterfall, about to be pushed over. A torrent of emotions coursed through her—fear, anticipation, indignation, resentment—so rapidly she hardly had time to think.

Holden set his cup down on the chest. Then he leaned aside and blew out the candle, leaving the pavilion in deep shadow disturbed by only the vaguest glow of the moon.

Cambria resisted the urge to slip out the pavilion flap at once into the anonymity of the night. Then she scolded herself for her cowardice. She was on the battlefield now. Running away with no explanation would only postpone the confrontation.

She stood tall. Her eyes had not yet adjusted to the meager light when she heard him circling close about her. She couldn't see him, but she could sense his eyes burning into her, and she couldn't shake the feeling that she was about to be devoured.

He came up behind her, his breath in her ear so sudden she gasped in surprise and dropped her cup. The red wine spilled onto the carpet and was absorbed like a smothered scream. He pulled the hood slowly from her head, twining the fingers of one hand in her hair. The other arm he draped possessively across her collarbone and shoulders. His voice was deceptively gentle.

"Do you know what is to come?"

She remained silent, in spite of the alarm ringing in her head. Without warning, he subtly tightened his hold and clenched his fist in her hair. He wasn't hurting her at all, merely keeping her prisoner in his grasp. She struggled against the confinement nonetheless, her fingers pulling at the taut muscles of his forearm.

"I'm going to kiss you," he whispered. "You've been kissed before, have you not?"

She gave no answer. Her heart thrummed in her throat.

"And I'm going to touch you—your lips, your neck, your breasts . . . in ways no one has ever touched you before."

With that promise, he forced her to endure that touch as he slowly ran the tip of his tongue up the side of her neck. A hot streak of lightning coursed through her body, as if a blade had done the deed. A wounded moan issued from her lips unbidden. She shuddered. Dear God, what was she going to do?

He placed delicate kisses against her throat, and she fought against the dizzying sensation. He breathed against her temple and massaged the back of her head.

"You are so young . . . and soft . . ." He punctuated each of her attributes with a brush of his tongue against the various hollows of her ear. "Supple . . . and warm . . . and beautiful."

She writhed in sensual torment against him. Then he ceased, and she shivered involuntarily.

"Do not . . . do that," she gasped, fighting for a coherent thought.

She should be outraged. After all, her husband was being unfaithful to her with another. Yet that other was none other than herself. 'Twas all too confusing, particularly when he was driving her half-mad with that nuzzling beneath her ear.

"Give me your lips," he murmured against her cheek. "I would have a kiss."

Her heart plunged fearfully. Jesu, he might recognize her kiss. But before she could duck away, he turned her head to his and ran his broad tongue boldly across her lips. When she opened her mouth in surprise, he closed his lips over hers.

Never had she been kissed like this. The timid bussing she'd given him was as nothing compared to this. He sucked gently on each lip, nipped at them as if he were tasting her. Then he deepened the kiss, drank her very soul from her and poured it back into her again. Even the passion of their wedding kiss paled against the purely erotic mating of their mouths now as his tongue tickled across, then moved languorously between her lips, parting them easily.

She felt as if she were under an enchantment. Her limbs remained rigid in their posture of resistance, but her mouth acted with a will of its own. His kiss demanded an answer, and she gave it as her lips sought his with an age-old hunger.

"Easy, my little nymph," he coaxed, though there was strain in his voice. "We have all night. There will be more pleasure for you if we take our time."

With great dexterity, no doubt from practice, he parted her cloak and quickly loosened the laced front of her kirtle. The cool night air filtering over her bared skin startled her for a moment. Then, before she could guess his intent, he slid a hand beneath her gown and traced the outline of the top of her breast with schooled fingers. She trembled beneath his touch.

Holden groaned. Her skin felt like silk beneath the pads of his fingers. What a fool he'd been to agree to that damned marriage document. He brushed a thumb across the fabric still covering her taut nipple, and she drew in a sharp breath. He tried, but could not ignore the yearnings of his own flesh.

"Stop that! You must not . . ." Cambria began in a curiously thick voice, attempting to sound authoritative and failing miserably.

"Shh," he said, stroking her again, absorbing her shiver with his own body. He could feel her resolve beginning to melt. Soon, like all the prisoners he'd ever tortured, she would be like molten iron on the forge, compliant to his will. That was if his own resistance held out, he thought wryly as a wave of desire flooded his loins.

When he moved his hand to seek her other breast, she moaned softly against his cheek. He placed tiny kisses along the line of her jaw, continuing to caress and tease her with his fingers. Then, sensing her imminent surrender, he gently dragged her back against his body, gritting his teeth as her buttocks pressed against the throbbing column of his manhood. Taking a step backwards, he pulled her down with him onto his chair, settling her across his knees.

"Now," he told her in a voice he fought to keep steady as he twisted the wedding ring on her finger aright, "you will tell me, wife, why you are here."

11

I T TOOK CAMBRIA A MOMENT, REELING IN A FOG OF OVER-whelming sensations, to realize what he'd said. Even then, she couldn't for the life of her frame an appropriate reply.

"What?" she whispered at last. "You know? How did you know?"

He answered with more raw desire than he'd intended. "Did you think I hadn't memorized every inch of you, watching you sleep beside me?"

The mist began to clear from Cambria's mind. She drew a ragged breath. Part of her wanted to collapse in relief—Holden hadn't been unfaithful after all—but that emotion was soon squelched beneath a landslide of other, far more powerful ones.

"You let me make a fool of myself," she said as the truth dawned. Then anger ignited in her faster than a spark on a thatched roof. "You made me suffer in this damnably hot cloak . . . forced me to wait on your knights hand and foot when . . . You commanded me to your pavilion like a common . . ."

"Enough!" He halted her with a shake, realizing too late that he should never have stopped seducing her. He'd had her in the palm of his hand. Now, she was slipping from his grasp. "The fact remains that you are here, garbed as a peasant, and I need to know why."

Cambria fumed, struggling against his renewed grip. She felt utterly humiliated. She wished to God she'd never come. She should have just let him march off to his death.

"I don't have to account for my comings and goings!" she snapped, tears of shame gathering in her eyes. "I am the laird of Gavin!"

"Laird you may be," he countered firmly, "but you've wed me, and now *I* am your overlord."

She jerked against him. "Am I a prisoner?"

"Until you comply with my command and tell me why you are here, aye."

She clamped her jaw shut, aghast at its trembling, and gave him her most withering glare, even though 'twas wasted in the darkness. She'd be damned if she'd tell him why she'd come. By God, she'd not hear him laugh now at her misplaced concern.

Holden whispered against her cheek. "Perhaps you came because you missed my kisses."

Before she could retort with some cutting remark, Holden took her jaw firmly in one hand and pressed his lips hard against hers. Predictably, she squealed in outrage, kicking and batting at him. He knew now how it would feel to wrestle a wildcat. When he released her abruptly, she was forced to grab onto him to keep from toppling from his lap.

"Let me go!" she hissed even as she clutched at him for balance.

"Not until you answer me."

She refused.

"Why have you followed me, Cambria?" Threat tainted his murmur as he trailed one finger down her throat, dangerously close to her breast.

"We had a bargain, *husband*," she, protested, batting at his roving hand, "or is your word worthless?"

"I have never broken my word," he answered calmly, capturing her wrist. "Rest assured I've no intention of bedding you."

Holden wished his body would believe that. The truth was it was taking every ounce of discipline he possessed to hide his increasing ardor. Wincing as Cambria squirmed against his loins, he trapped her other wrist and held both arms down with one of his hands.

Then, as swiftly as a falcon swooping down on its prey, he captured her by the hair, drawing her head back to press his voracious mouth against her neck.

For one crazed moment, as his teeth raked her fragile skin, Cambria thought he meant to bite her. Then his mouth slipped upwards, and she whimpered in dread as he neared her sensitive ear.

"This is a battle you cannot win, Cambria," he breathed gently. "I've far more experience on this battleground. Sooner or later, your body will end up fighting for my side."

Cambria shivered. God help her, he was right. His voice was as seductive as honey, and already her blood warmed to his touch.

She should never have come to his pavilion. She had to get away. Yet he held her immobile, like a fly in a spider's web. The most she could do was wiggle in his lap, and she blushed to think what she'd feel against her bottom if she did that.

He kept her head still as his tongue began to lave her ear tenderly, and instantly, all thought of escape spun away like maple seeds in the wind. She could neither stop her moan of sweet agony nor resist when he released her to slide his fingers under the neck of her kirtle and along the valley of her bosom.

He cupped one of her breasts beneath the linen, squeezing gently, slowly circling the nipple with his thumb. She protested faintly, a protest he silenced with soft words—words of encouragement, words of praise, words that left her breathless.

"I want to suckle there," he whispered.

Her face grew hot as the blood surged in her veins. No one had ever said such a thing to her. "Nay!" she hissed. 'Twas unthinkable. Yet she quivered, imagining the subtle strain of his lips and tongue upon her breast. A shaft of desire as sharp as an arrow shot through her. She offered small resistance as he tipped her back against one arm, sliding his other hand across her ribs and drawing back the kirtle to bare her.

She felt the tickle of his rich mane upon her breast a moment before his mouth came down upon her nipple. He tugged gently at first, then drew her firmly between his lips until she felt his power all the way to her toes. Nothing could have prepared her for the ecstasy of his tongue as it moistened her flesh and seemed to suck her will from her. To her utter horror, she actually groaned in complaint when he stopped to speak again. She was appalled to discover she'd tangled her own desperate fingers in his hair.

"Tell me, Cambria," he murmured, nuzzling her neck, "why did you follow me? Did you think to betray me to your Scots?"

Cambria froze. His words struck like a clear bolt of lightning on a black night. She suddenly realized what he was doing. The bastard was torturing her for information. He was not here as her husband tonight. He was on a soldier's mission.

She felt as if she'd been kicked in the stomach. Her own husband didn't trust her.

Cursing herself for believing he could possibly be overcome with lust for her, she growled with the fury of a trapped animal and thrashed upon his lap. Although the pain of this rack had been sweet, it had obviously been contrived to elicit a confession from her, and that she'd not forgive. Now she had no intention of *ever* revealing why she'd come. He could rot in hell, as far as she was concerned. Somehow she had to steel herself against his persuasion. Somehow she had to resist him and maintain control of her body.

That control lasted a good dozen heartbeats after Holden reached down determinedly and lifted one of her legs over the far side of his own, inching her kirtle up over her spread knees.

Cambria knew she was in danger. She began struggling anew, trying to bring her legs back together, but Holden's held them apart. When he pulled her back full against him, she was immobilized more from the shock of the iron-hard evidence of his desire beneath her than the bands of his arms around her.

Holden felt her stiffen. He'd hoped she wouldn't notice

the effect she was having on him. After all, a woman could have an aroused man at her mercy in a matter of moments. Lord, he thought as he boldly stroked his fingers along her inner thigh, closer and closer to the soft down between her legs, perhaps he wouldn't win this fight after all. It felt as if the seams of his hose were about to burst.

"Why," he murmured raggedly. "Why have you come?"

Cambria arched away from his seductive touch and clamped her mouth and her eyes shut. God, his hand hovered but inches from her nest of woman's curls.

"Answer me."

Cambria's pride screamed at her to resist. She opened her mouth to protest, but when his warm palm pressed down against her loins, the words that came out were not what she intended. "Ah, God," she moaned, despising her own weak will. "Will you cease if I tell you?"

Holden bit the inside of his cheek. God, she was so hot and wet and tempting, he wondered who was the more tortured. He spoke with difficulty. "Tell me," he replied, keeping his hand firm against her.

"I came, as I said, to watch your back," she whispered hastily, eager for release.

He did not release her. "At one time, you wanted a dagger in my back," he reminded her, easing up slightly on the pressure. "You are certain you didn't come to aid the rebels?"

She frowned, only half capable of coherent thought. Was that what he thought? She was laird of her clan. Why would she aid the rebels? "'Tis a stupid question," she told him.

"Answer it."

She balked, but when Holden let one finger delve momentarily between the folds of her womanhood, she smothered a shriek and could not reply quickly enough. "I did not come to aid the rebels!" She wished she *had* betrayed him, and, God, she wished he wouldn't touch her there.

"So you truly came to protect me?"

"Yes, damn you!" God's bones—she wished he would remove his hand.

Holden was silent for a long while, digesting what Cambria had said. If she was this adamant about Owen's guilt, about his threats, if she was so sure of it she'd left her precious Blackhaugh to follow her husband into battle, could there be some truth to her fears? He needed to find out what had transpired during her capture.

"Tell me everything about that night at the inn," he said at last.

"You didn't listen before," she said, scowling. "Why would you listen now? Why should I waste my time?"

He curled his fingers down over her nest of curls again. God, she was a stubborn woman. "Because if you don't, I'll do wonderful, terrible things to you till you beg for my caresses. You don't want that, do you?" Lord, what was he saying? This was the strangest interrogation he'd ever conducted.

Cambria didn't doubt his threat. She'd already had a taste of his warfare. "All right, then. Let me go," she sulked.

Holden tossed her skirt back over her knees and helped her up, still clutching to one of her wrists so she wouldn't flee.

She told him what she knew, naturally omitting details that might incriminate her, or embarrass her, or make her seem the least bit less than perfectly innocent. And for once he listened. At least, she supposed he listened. In the dark, he might have been dozing off to her discourse, for all she knew.

When she'd finished, Holden spoke quietly, like the calm before a maelstrom. "Sir Guy and Sir Myles told the story somewhat differently. They heard you threaten to kill Roger."

She cleared her throat awkwardly. "Kill Roger?" she squeaked. "I suppose . . . that is, I *may* have said . . ."

Unprepared for the growl of anger from Lord Holden, she was even more unprepared for the move to come. In one moment she was standing beside her husband, and in the next, he had picked her up off her feet and tossed her onto her back across the fur-covered pallet. His palms pressed her shoulders hard into the mattress.

"You little liar," he said tightly. "I'll have the truth from you, the entire truth, if I have to torment you half the night!"

Holden felt furious with her now, enraged with her deceiving tongue, hurt by her betrayal. He dropped his hands to the neckline of her threadbare kirtle and tore the frail garment asunder, baring her for his onslaught. He wouldn't hurt her, of course—he never let his temper interfere with his control—but he'd wring the facts from her if it was the last thing he did.

Cambria thrashed on the pallet. She could feel Holden's rage. What was wrong with him? She'd told him the truth about the inn . . . well, most of it. What more did he want? God, she felt completely vulnerable now, lying there half-naked, her heart beating a rapid cadence against her ribs.

She swung at him with her fists. A few of her punches landed on firm flesh before his arms snaked around her wrists. Then he settled his formidable weight upon her hips, and she found herself pinned to the pallet. Damn him, he straddled her like she was some palfrey.

What he did next astonished her. Slowly, deliberately, he raised one of her fists and pried it open with his strong fingers. He nipped the palm of her hand with his teeth, then let his tongue trail across her skin until he was licking at the webbing between her fingers. She gasped at the current that rushed through her as he grazed the length of each of her fingers with his teeth.

"You threatened to kill him, didn't you?" His voice was dangerously soft.

Holden clenched his teeth. His body was becoming dangerously hard. He used all his power of concentration to ignore the lusty womanflesh so warm beneath his loins as Cambria squirmed, trying to snatch back her hand. He joined her wrists above her head with one of his arms, freeing the other to do as he pleased. Wary of her sharp teeth, he caught her jaw firmly in his hand and turned her head to the side.

Cambria stiffened as she felt his warm breath upon her cheek. Then, without warning, his tongue delved deep into the hollow of her ear. She nearly bucked off the bed.

"Did you threaten to kill Roger?" he whispered.

"Aye!" she hissed, angry at the way her body was responding, the way it actually craved his touch. God, she'd tell him anything if she could just have her control back.

"Good," he said smugly. "At last you're speaking truth."

"You bastard," she muttered, trying to shake her head free.

He impertinently licked her eyelids with the tip of his tongue as he turned her head to the other side.

"Myles and Guy told me they heard sounds from the room," Holden breathed, making her cringe in anticipation, "sounds of heavy objects striking the wall."

Cambria clenched her teeth together so tightly she thought they would crack. She wished she had a heavy object right now.

"Did you throw anything at Roger?"

His words tickled her neck, but in spite of bracing herself for what she knew was to come, her body still betrayed her, writhing in delicious agony when his mouth closed over her ear.

"Nay!" she sobbed.

"Nay? You didn't throw anything?"

"Aye!" she said fiercely. "Aye, I threw anything I could find . . . a candlestick, a pot . . ."

"A dagger?" he asked carefully, releasing her jaw. "Hmm?"

He moved the fingers of his free hand along her collarbone, then lower, brushing the crest of one nipple with his palm. She winced at her body's eager response. He lowered his head to the other breast and impudently licked across the nipple, blowing a cool breath upon it that stiffened it instantly. She moaned.

"Damn you, what do you want from me?"

He shut his eyes tightly. He knew what he wanted from her. Her uneven breathing and involuntary groans incited him almost beyond his control. Aye, he knew exactly what he wanted.

"I want the truth," he said instead.

"I didn't kill your knight."

Holden's voice grew deathly quiet. "Did Roger touch you?"

She hesitated, then chose to deliberately misunderstand him. "Of course he touched me," she muttered. "I've told you he dragged me up to the room of the inn."

"Cambria," Holden growled in warning.

He slid his hand down her belly. She tried to roll over onto her stomach, but his thighs trapped her. He buried his fingers boldly in her curling thatch of hair and pressed firmly against her. Unwittingly, her hips answered him, pushing upward of their own accord.

"Did he touch you like this?"

"Damn you to hell!" she groaned.

"Did he touch you like this?"

Cambria wanted to hurt him. "Nay!" she shouted. "His touch was much more pleasing!"

He seemed unaffected by the lie. "Then thank God I don't please you so well, else I might find a dagger buried in *my* chest."

Then he began moving his fingers, sliding across the moist folds of her skin. She thought she'd die of mortification, yet didn't want him to stop. Surely he possessed some secret power, the ability to leave her helpless with the gentle touch of a single fingertip.

"Did you kill Roger because he . . . raped you?" he murmured.

"He didn't rape me," she breathed, surrendering at last, adrift on an erotic sea beneath his touch. "He tried, but he was too sotted for it. And on the grave of my father," she sighed, her voice gone soft and womanly, "I swear I didn't kill your knight."

Holden closed his eyes and nodded slowly in the darkness, relieved. She was telling the truth. He could hear the resignation in her voice.

"You believe Owen killed his brother?"

"Aye," she said thickly.

"And that he intends to kill me?"

"Aye." She sucked in a breath as Holden's thumb moved over her in lazy circles. Dear God, it felt as if her mind was not her own. She wanted him to cease, yet she wanted something more. "Please," she sighed.

"Please?" Holden's breath caught in his throat. He halted his movements. Surely his stubborn Cambria was not ready to surrender . . . everything. "Please stop or please go on?"

Her long moment of indecision evoked a chuckle of irony from him that ended in a frustrated groan, "Oh, lady, there is nothing I'd like better than to take you here and now."

A surge of desire swept through his loins as if to lend credence to his words. It took every bit of his willpower not to tear the trews away and drive that aching part of him deep into her soft, wet sheath. He shut his eyes, tight.

"I am a man of my word. I must hear it from your own lips."

Please, God, he begged inwardly, *deliver me from this torment.* But God paid no heed, and the silence dragged on as Cambria battled her own desires. It wasn't to be, he decided, not tonight. He drew his hand from her and released her wrists.

"I regret I must leave you so unsatisfied," he said tautly, "but it's an oath you yourself have bound me to."

He wondered if she ached half as much as he did. He swore he was throbbing from his waist to his knees. Never had a woman aroused him so completely nor left him so shaken. He let out a ragged breath, his body exhausted from long denial, and cursed the wretched honor that kept him from bedding his own wife.

Cambria buried her face in the crook of her arm. Never had she known such torment, such confusion. Her body was suffused with a nameless longing, every fiber of her being stretched taut as a bowstring. The Wolf had brought her, trembling, to the border of an undiscovered country, and now he was abandoning her there. He'd humiliated her, conquered her, disgraced her. He'd beaten her soundly in this battle, as he'd promised he would.

But she'd be damned if she'd admit it. Better that she endure the fires of unrequited passion than surrender to her foe in a moment of weakness.

Clenching her teeth, she turned to her side and curled up into a ball. 'Twould be a long, sleepless night.

Somehow she managed to get some little rest, but 'twas far from peaceful. A moment past sunrise, she awoke with a gasp. The same terrible, dark dream of suffering and death had invaded her slumber. She felt like she was choking on the stench of the grave. Her heart pounded as if it longed to escape her breast.

Then the nightmare that had been so real fled like an insubstantial puff of smoke. For a moment, she couldn't recall where she was. She shook her head, and then her memory came flooding back in a painful rush as she gathered the rags of her torn kirtle about her.

She was alone in his bed, left there by her brute of a husband. He had tortured her—there was no other word for it. He'd used her own passions against her, seduced her mercilessly, and then deserted her, left her alone to face the scorn of everyone in the camp. She was surprised he hadn't just stolen her virginity and been done with it. But then he'd said it himself. As much as she despised him at this moment, he was a man of his word. He'd left her intact.

She pushed the hair back from her face and looked hopelessly at her ruined clothing. Damn the bastard, he'd hardly left her a scrap to wear. Well, she decided, compressing her lips and pulling the coverlet from the bed, she'd show him a thing or two about Scots pride. She'd wrap furs about her as her ancestors had and walk out of the pavilion with her head held high.

Suddenly, the tent flap snapped open, and Holden was there at the entry, haloed by morning sunlight. She quickly averted her eyes. The last thing she wanted to see was the Wolf gloating over his easy victory of the night before. She supposed she'd never hear the end of it. He had won. He had taken her will from her, fairly and without a struggle.

Eventually, curiosity outweighed obstinance, and she finally scowled up at him. She was startled by his expression. No smugness molded his features, only something akin to regret. In fact, he looked rather like a wayward child come to ask forgiveness as he offered her a bundle of new clothing.

"I'd prefer to keep your identity secret," he ventured, tossing the garments to the pallet when she didn't reach for them, "for your safety."

She only stared mutely, pleasantly astonished that he made no mention of the previous night. At her silence, he cleared his throat and slipped into his more natural tone of command.

"You'll stay well away from the fighting when it begins. I know not what weapons you have secreted away for yourself, but they'll remain where they are. Do you understand?"

She gave him a sidelong glance. How did he know her so well? "You fear I will turn my weapons on you?"

"Nay, I think not," he assured her, his eyes flickering with mild amusement, "since your own life would be forfeit were you to raise a hand against me. I don't think you would be so foolish as to intentionally deprive your clan of their laird."

With that, he turned and left, leaving her to sort out her own dilemma as she carelessly rent the kirtle from her body and slipped the new gown over her head. 'Twas of blue woad, a peasant's shade, and it clung annoyingly to her every curve, but at least 'twas whole. She donned her cloak, took a deep breath, and stepped out of the pavilion.

To her relief, everyone seemed much too busy to notice her. The servants were breaking camp, and the air vibrated with the sounds of rattling cookpots and swishing skirts, the clank of armor plate, the squeak of harness and cart, and snatches of conversation about the impending battle.

Gone was the levity of the previous day. In accordance with the king's plan, war would begin on the morrow. The knights mounted up and rode in silence, the only herald of their passing the creak of rolling wagons and the constant drumming of horses' hooves on the hard-packed earth. Deep into the land of the Scots they rode, and with each passing hour, the silence grew more complete, until by nightfall, with a single small fire and a supper of cold salted meat and bread, the only noises in the camp were the soft snores of foot soldiers and the nervous snuffling of horses.

Holden, unable to sleep, polished his sword by the light of the stars. Tonight his blade gleamed. On the morrow, it would be stained with Scots blood. And God willing, he'd live to polish it again by nightfall.

He'd met briefly with Edward. The king, after heartily toasting Holden for his strategic acquisition of a Scots bride, had divulged his strategy for acquiring Berwick.

The reports of the enemy's strength gave Holden pause. Strategically, all was in the Scots' favor. They vastly outnumbered the English. This was their soil, and 'twas a well-known fact that soldiers fought better in defense of their own land. To add to the challenge, Holden had to watch for betrayal in his own ranks.

Holden turned his sword's hilt until it shone a band of reflected moonlight onto a spider's web stretched between blades of grass. So precariously the thing hung, frail and fleeting, an intricate work of weaving suspended by a single thread.

Thus was Holden's world.

He believed Cambria now, or at least believed that she believed. But he could do nothing about it. He could not openly accuse his own knight . . . yet. Holden dared not burden the king on the eve of a great battle with trivial wrongs he could right himself at a more suitable time. He did intend to right them. But in sooth, at present there was no substantial proof of Owen's crime other than Cambria's word, and Holden had to be absolutely certain of his man's guilt before he raised the hand of justice. It could be that Owen's actions today might serve to tighten the noose around his own neck. After all, the best way to catch a fox with blood on its paws, to make sure it would never kill again, was to keep a close watch on the dovecote.

In the meantime, he had to keep Owen away from the king. One rumor from the bastard's lying lips accusing Holden's new bride of Roger's murder could destroy everything he'd labored for at Blackhaugh.

So Holden walked that fragile web and, like the vigilant spider sitting in its midst, acted as the keeper of the delicate balance.

The night had ripened to the color of a plump fig by the time Holden sheathed his sword and sought out his pallet with a branch lit by the last coals of the fire. Cambria had gone to bed hours before, and when he heard her slow, even breathing beneath the coverlet, he felt a twinge of regret that she wasn't awake. He'd treated her callously the past night, and he wished to make amends. He would have liked to speak to her about the battle to come or have her fuss over his chain mail. He would have liked to give her a chaste kiss good night. He smiled ruefully. It was not so bad, he decided, possessing a wife.

As he began to undress, he heard her breathing change. She whimpered softly, twitching in her sleep with some fearful dream. He held his makeshift candle close. Her brow was troubled, and she murmured in the cryptic language only dreamers can decipher. He wondered if he should wake her.

Cambria still saw them, even when she buried her head in her hands. Their anguish seeped through her fingers, through her eyelids, infesting her mind. The dying, too numerous to count, covered the hills, pleading in agony, their stiffening limbs reaching hopefully for death's claw, their glazed eyes staring, staring. . . .

Someone called her name. She turned toward the voice. Before her stood her father—living, breathing, a paradox amidst the expanse of spreading death. With a cry of joy, she stepped forward to go to him. But before she could take a second step, a great wolf appeared at Laird Angus's flank, a wolf with paws as large as a man's head and green eyes as chilling as a winter loch.

Without a second thought, she swung her bow from off her shoulder and nocked an arrow into place, aiming for the beast's heart. But her father held up his hand to ward her off, and she hesitated. In that instant, a shrouded figure like an enormous dark raven swooped between them, and before she could cry out, drove a bladed talon into the laird's breast. He fell silently to the ground.

The wolf ambled to the laird's side, sniffed at the motionless body, then raised his head and let out a mournful cry. Cambria clapped her hands to her ears and began to tremble uncontrollably. Soon her own piteous cry joined the call of the wolf, rising on the air like a bagpipe's lament.

Suddenly, someone was shaking her, shouting at her, words muffled and distant to her stoppered ears. The thick fog of dreams dispersed only gradually, and she flinched as the light of a single flame burned away the last vestiges of the nightmare.

The Wolf looked down upon her, his face clouded with concern. He turned her chin toward him, commanding her attention.

"What is it, Cambria?" he demanded. "Are you in pain?"

She stared up at her husband, his face made demonic by the shifting shadows.

"Blood," she breathed. "So much blood. My father . . ."

"Shh. It's all right. You've only had . . ."

"And the screams . . ."

"Cambria," he whispered, brushing a lock of hair back from her brow.

"There was a wolf . . . fierce . . . terrible . . ." She shuddered. The wolf had had Holden's eyes, and yet . . .

"Shh. You're safe now."

She frowned. "It wasn't the wolf."

"It was a dream, Cambria."

"No. No." She searched his eyes, seeking some glimmer of treachery, some trace of the evil that must reside in him, but finding only the truth. "It wasn't the wolf who killed my father. He meant to *save* him."

Holden stroked her forehead, his callused fingers a curious comfort. She looked at him through new eyes, at last completely absolved of the guilt with which she'd veiled him since the beginning.

"You meant to *save* him," she said, and the words acted like an enchantment, dispelling the last threads of the dark shroud surrounding her husband, revealing a man who seemed a stranger to her, a man who was at once both thrilling and terrifying.

Holden stuck the point of his sword into the ground to make the shape of the cross. He knelt in the dust, clasping his hands before him, and watched for a moment as the sun struggled up over the distant hill. His knights were up early as well, honing swords, donning armor, and quietly reviewing siege formations.

Holden had never felt so reluctant to fight.

He wasn't afraid, never that. Though the Scots outnumbered them, he was confident the English would win. But this morning, when all the world blossomed before him in ignorant splendor, he was concerned with the price of the battle.

Contrary to what most believed of the Wolf, as much as he loved fighting, he had little affection for war. War cut down too many youths scarcely grown into their mail and too many old warriors with strong arms but failing sight. He was weary of killing. And, for the first time in his life, he was lucidly cognizant of his own mortality.

That awareness startled him. He'd never valued his life all that much. He was a second son. War was his occupation. He'd thought little of his fate, only bedded whomever was convenient, ate the meat of fresh kill, and battled another man's enemies when he was told.

Now he was a lord in his own right. He had a wife. And the promise of a future. He needed to survive this battle and all the battles to come, not for Edward's sake, not even for the illustrious name of de Ware, but for the sake of the irritating little Scots sprite he couldn't banish from his thoughts.

Damn it all, he wanted to make love to Cambria, true love. What he'd seen in her eyes last night after the dream—the softening, the acceptance—he wanted to see that again. He'd melted inside when she'd looked at him like that. Winning her heart had felt more glorious than any victory he'd won on the battlefield.

Now he needed to make restitution for the wretched way he'd courted her, to show her the chivalrous side of the Wolf, to woo her gently, as she deserved. And, with a fervor that made him tremble, he realized he wanted to make children with her. How his brother Duncan would laugh at that, the idea that the Wolf might wish to be tethered by a family.

But it was true, and by God, he couldn't let Edward's skirmish take that opportunity away from him.

He closed his eyes, praying for a quick end to the battle. Then he made the sign of the cross and kissed the pommel of his sword. The sun was up. It was time to face the enemy.

• • •

Cambria checked the dagger tucked into her belt for the tenth time. She supposed her bow and arrows would have to wait until they grew nearer to the battlefield. After all, she couldn't let Holden catch her with weapons.

Sweet Mary, he'd clap her in irons if he knew how she disobeyed him. But she had to do everything in her power to protect him, even if 'twas against his will. After all, he was the overlord of Blackhaugh. He was the guardian of her clan. And, she thought, her heart skipping a beat as she recalled the tenderness and comfort he'd shown her last night, he was her husband.

For a long while she'd fought a growing admiration for the Wolf, for his strength, his fairness, his diplomacy. Further, she'd denied an increasing attraction to the man who could put a catch in her breath with a coy wink, a crooked smile, or the nervous clench of his fist, all because she believed him guilty of her father's murder. Now, relieved of that shadow, her spirit felt as light as thistledown.

There was no question of loyalty now. She would do everything in her power to preserve the life of Holden de Ware.

She'd never seen him so serious, so focused as he looked now. 'Twas no wonder the man had never lost a battle. He exuded and inspired confidence in his knights, organizing them skillfully into an efficient, precise fighting force. However, she also knew this single-minded drive might well be his undoing. His quest for victory in battle might well leave him inattentive to dangers from within the ranks. She had warned him, but she suspected he'd taken the warning lightly, for Owen still moved freely about. And now the mad, distracted gaze in Owen's eyes had returned, boding ill for Holden.

Somewhere up ahead Halidon Hill, the rise before Berwick, awaited in dew-covered innocence, and as the company rode forward a thrumming began in Cambria's body, that thrill of eager restlessness that always preceded a fight. She'd never witnessed a full-scale siege, only those matches arranged at tournaments as entertainments and the frequent cattle raids that were more mischief than bloodsport. Her stomach churned with nervous excitement.

At long last, near the edge of the dense forest, Holden raised a hand to stop their progress. In the distance, crossing the field like a wash of wind rustling the heather, waved the plaids of a thousand Scotsmen.

The Scots had not waited at Berwick for the invaders to lay siege. Nay, they surprised their attackers, marching boldly across Halidon Hill to greet the English with swords.

Holden cursed, then began shouting urgent commands, rousing his men to action. Swiftly, they lined up along the rise, archers at the fore, foot soldiers following, mounted knights behind. Between the opposing hillsides dipped a marshy grassland. Cambria doubted the horses would be of much use on the slippery ground.

While the servants retreated to the woods to prepare litters for the wounded, Cambria retrieved her weapons and furtively followed the men-at-arms. A surge of nervous energy coursed through her veins, like the tingling she felt before she couched her lance to charge. She crept to a place amid the pines where the oxen were tethered. This position gave her a clear view of the battlefield, as well as concealing her. From the trees, she could see the distant Scots forming a schiltron upon the opposing hill, the oval ring of spears looking impenetrable. Fear dried her mouth. There were clearly far more of them than English soldiers.

Holden clucked to his steed, reining her to the fore of his knights. Settling his helm into place over his head, he turned about and waited for the king's sign.

Cambria shivered. An eery silence fell over the land. Only an occasional sparrow's chirp or the buzz of an insect intruded upon the stillness. A lone bagpipe from the opposite hill began its mournful wail, a Siren to be resisted as her heart was drawn to its familiar call. In unison, the Scots rebels began to advance, their subdued plaids flapping like a single flag of heather patchwork. The English, less eager to leave their high vantage point, held their place with the archers at the fore.

All the pride of Robert the Bruce and all the pain of long-suffered oppression echoed in the plaintive cry of the pipes as the schiltron approached like a great spiny beast. The boasting voices of Scots soldiers could be heard as they neared, goading one another to a quicker pace, a fiercer aggression, growing louder and louder until they were a rumbling across the field. Then, incited by zealous chieftains into recklessness, the beast rushed headlong onto the marshland.

Cambria gasped. 'Twas a foolhardy advance. Anyone could see that. The Scots had made themselves easy targets for the English archers, who fired over the front line of their schiltron and rained shafts down onto the men behind. One by one, the Scots fell under the storm of arrows, writhing and screaming with pain as they were struck. Still the beast relentlessly, futilely, advanced.

Cambria felt sick as she watched the inevitable slaughter of her countrymen. Nothing could have prepared her for the horrifying spectacle. Hundreds of fine young Scots were slain in the first terrible moments, while there seemed to be no casualties at all among the English.

Holden scowled in disbelief, unable to fathom what he was seeing. If he'd thought the Scots' first move was foolhardy, their second strategy he considered sheer lunacy. The remaining rebels began to ascend the hill held by the English. They apparently thought to intimidate the English with their bravado, but they did nothing other than walk into the weapons of the enemy. He was disgusted by their rashness, aghast at the needless sacrifice of human flesh.

The Scots who managed to survive the archers were easily dispatched by the foot soldiers and men-at-arms wielding axe, mace, and sword. In fact, Holden did little actual fighting himself, as the mounted knights were the last line of defense.

The battle was a massacre. The proud Scots would not surrender. Within moments there were less than half of them left fighting the English.

Cambria dug her fingernails into the pine bark, so overwhelmed with shock at the dreadful carnage that she almost missed Owen's furtive movement toward Lord Holden.

Holden and Guy had dismounted and were embroiled in combat with two desperate rebels. Sir Guy had slain one of them and wounded the other mortally, but the Scotsman continued to fight against the very forces of nature. Just as Holden claimed the soldier's life with a merciful blow of his broadsword, Sir Owen moved forward, dagger drawn. In that instant, Cambria stepped from the shelter of the trees and fitted an arrow to her bow.

She held her breath. She'd never slain a man, but she couldn't stand by and watch Holden fall to this traitor's blade. As Owen drew back his arm to strike, she aimed for his evil heart, pulled the bowstring back hard, and sent the shaft flying.

12

THE POORLY FLETCHED ARROW DROPPED IN MIDFLIGHT, MISS-
ing its mark by nearly half a yard and lodging in Owen's
thigh. The shot had some effect—he screamed in pain and
was felled, glaring at her in furious disbelief—but he remained very much alive.

Sir Guy's eyes widened as he beheld his fallen country-
man. That arrow had come from *behind* the lines. He tore the
helm from his head, then sought and found the culprit—a
peasant woman. With a snarl, he charged the small, shrouded
female, knocked the bow from her grasp, and threw her, facedown, to the ground. Anchoring her with his knee, he pulled
her head back by the hair. The oxen nearby squealed and
stamped, upset by the smell of battle. He held his dagger to
the woman's throat, sorely tempted to slit it immediately, too
enraged to question whose worthless life he held in his
hands.

But Holden was calling him, waving wildly with his
sword. Guy hesitated, and in that instant, Holden paid for his
inattention to the battle, falling prey to a young Scotsman
who had come upon him unawares. Guy cursed as the boy's
sword took a bite out of Holden's shoulder.

The wench beneath him sobbed in protest. "The arrow
missed its mark! Someone must stop him!"

Sir Guy growled harshly. "Rebel spy! Thank *God* your

arrow missed its mark! Had you slain my lord, I would have delivered you to hell by now upon my blade!"

Looking up again, Guy saw that most of the Scots had been routed. Holden had almost finished off the one faltering youth, despite his wound, and Owen had vanished, probably to tend to his injury. With the war essentially ended, Guy could leave the battlefield to take the handling of this traitor upon himself.

He pinioned one of his captive's arms, bringing her brusquely to her feet. Then he pushed her roughly along before him toward the haven of the trees, pressing his blade as a reminder against her throat. His blood was hot from war, his ire aroused, his purpose honed to a fine point. Thus, it was several moments before he realized there was something familiar about his quarry and the chestnut tresses spilling over onto his hands. He relaxed his grip fractionally as doubt flitted through his mind.

Suddenly, he seized his captive by the shoulders and wheeled her around to face him. The lass was quaking, but she nonetheless met the challenge in his eyes. He stumbled back awkwardly, dumbfounded.

"My lady . . ." he began in confusion, responding instinctively to her rank.

Cambria thought quickly. Perhaps she could take advantage of Guy's doubt and play upon his indecision. She brought herself up to her full height, which was unfortunately still well below his.

"How dare you lay hands upon me!" she chided imperiously, trying to intimidate him. She saw with regret that her moment of victory was to be short-lived.

Guy recovered quickly from the shock. He evaluated the situation only briefly before advancing on her.

"Lady you may be, but I serve my lord first and foremost," he informed her.

Cambria backed away as he came close, but not in fear. She'd been trained to resist, not to surrender. Besides, Owen was still loose. Someone had to stop him. Perhaps, she thought recklessly, there was yet time to finish the job she'd begun. She turned and fled in the direction of the war.

She hadn't counted on traffic coming from the battlefield. She whipped her head around in time to glimpse the broad ebony chest of Holden's steed coming straight for her.

Holden swore. He was able to rein in soon enough to avoid a collision, just barely. Cambria skidded on the wet leaves and fell beneath Ariel's hooves. He spoke sharply to the mare, effectively stilling her movements so the lass wouldn't be trampled. Then he reached down a mailed hand to assist Cambria.

There was a rebellious look in her flashing eyes he didn't like. Not now, he thought testily. He could ill afford to have the king witness this willfulness on the part of his wife.

"Do not make a spectacle of yourself," he hissed, towering over her atop his mount, for by now a few of the other knights had begun to take an interest in this woman who had so brazenly appeared on the field of battle.

"Spectacle?" she breathed, her mouth round with shock and hurt. In the next moment, her short temper charged in to rescue her. "You ungrateful cur!" she cried, coming to her feet. "I saved your life." Then she made the deadly mistake of spitting at his bloody gauntleted hand, turning her back on him and walking away.

A few foot soldiers chuckled. Holden swore under his breath, and before Cambria could reach the shelter of the trees, he kicked his steed into pursuit. In a cloud of dust, the destrier skidded to her side, and he scooped Cambria up unceremoniously to deposit her facedown across his lap.

Cambria screamed in outrage. How dare he humiliate her? She bucked in a frenzy to be free of him, nearly losing her balance and tumbling to the ground below. Then suddenly, beneath her kirtle, she felt the hard steel of his mail-covered hand against her naked bottom. Stunned, she ceased her movements.

"Wife, I should thrash you for your disobedience," Holden bit out for her ears alone. "Would you like it done publicly or privately?"

Her ears burned, but she acquiesced and was still. The gauntlet sliding back down her thigh made her shiver.

"Guy!" Holden called.

"My lord," Guy boomed smugly. "I regret I am the one to bring news of your wife's treachery to your notice."

Holden lifted a brow. Guy didn't sound sorry in the least. In fact, Sir Guy hadn't trusted Cambria Gavin since the day she'd allied herself with those Scots rebels to take him hostage. "She admitted she missed her mark when she hit Owen," Guy added. "I believe, my lord, she was aiming for you."

"She did miss her mark." He grimly nodded his head. "But her arrow wasn't meant for me." Cambria stilled on his lap.

"She was aiming for Owen. She intended, I am sure, to pierce the bastard's black heart."

Sir Guy sputtered like a sail with the wind knocked out of it. "Owen?"

"Aye. He is your traitor."

"The one who had you waylaid in the forest?"

"No doubt. Since that failed, he was apparently trying to kill me on the battlefield."

The others who heard began to mutter amongst themselves.

"Then she shot to save your life, not take it?" Guy scowled, as if he'd been told he'd just swallowed a bug.

"Aye," Holden answered, loud enough for all to hear.

For the sake of the Gavin name and the name of de Ware, he had to assure the accuracy of the account for the gossips who were even now wagging their tongues in the king's ear. He pulled Cambria up to sit before him, while his steed danced in protest at the movement.

"My loyal wife acted to save my life just now," he announced. "The Gavins have truly shown their bravery this day." A cheer arose from the soldiers. In the uproar, he leaned down to Guy and gave a quick command. "Take two others and see if you can find Owen. He cannot have gone far with that wound. And someone alert the king."

Guy nodded and, drawing his blade, left to comply.

Saluting, Holden wheeled his destrier to duck into a more private section of the wood. He spoke not a word as they traveled the winding path, too wounded by his wife's disobedience—nay, not only her disobedience, but her mistrust. Did she not think he could defend himself against one attacker? He flinched as his new injury gave him a stinging reminder of what a single attacker had just cost him. Damn the wench, she unmanned him with her lack of faith.

He reined in abruptly, and Cambria nearly fell against Ariel's neck. This spot seemed secluded enough, he thought sardonically, far from the eyes and ears of those who might object to him thrashing his wife.

Then he sighed. He wearily slid the mail coif back from his head. He was fooling himself. He'd never lay a hand on Cambria. True, the short ride hadn't cooled his temper much, but he was capable of confining his violence to his own imagination.

"I commanded you to stay in camp," he said, turning her face toward him.

"You would be dead now if I had," she argued, jerking away.

He swore. "Have you no belief in my competence? I knew Owen was there. I've fought him a hundred times. I know his weaknesses. I saw the blow ere it was struck," he defended. "In sooth, had you left it to me, lady, I would have easily turned the blade aside. And the quarry would not have escaped."

"You allowed him to escape?" she demanded, ignoring the other matter.

His eyes narrowed as quickly as clouds gathering for a storm. "In my concern for *you*, milady," he bit out, insulted, "I did perhaps let my attention slip."

After a moment of fuming silence, she grumbled, "The arrow *was* meant for his heart."

"You missed by more than a foot," he replied, raising a brow. "I suppose I should be thankful to be alive myself."

"My *aim* is true. 'Twas but a faulty shaft. The fletcher at Blackhaugh is lazy and careless."

He refused to be distracted from his purpose by her flimsy

excuses. "Your fletcher is not the only careless one. You've committed a serious offense . . . and you've disobeyed your lord once too often, wife."

"But I saved your life!" she cried. "You said it yourself."

"You *endangered* my life!" he roared back, and Ariel bristled at the sudden noise.

Only then did Cambria glance at the blood upon his shoulder where the mail had been severed. He was satisfied by a sharp intake of breath from her.

"Aye, 'tis the price I paid for worrying about your hide instead of mine." He winced as his mail rubbed against the slash. "You've done a foolish thing, Cambria."

"Foolish!"

"Aye. Did you not think how it might look to have two brothers dead by your hand?"

"But I didn't kill—"

"There is no proof you didn't kill Roger, other than your word," he said frankly. "There may never be enough proof." He rubbed a weary hand over his chin. "You're making it difficult for me to protect you. I want you to stay away from Owen."

She folded her arms across her bosom. "And you are making it difficult for me to protect my clan. I want *you* to stay away from Owen."

He felt his anger dissolve like salt in water as she stared up at him with her elfin eyes. She was a stubborn witch, but what she did, she did out of loyalty. After a moment, a smile tugged at the corner of his mouth. "Agreed."

When he took Cambria back to his pavilion, he set a guard at the entrance. He let her believe he didn't trust her to stay inside, but in truth, the guard was there to keep intruders out. He'd not rest easy until Owen was captured.

In the meantime, he had to seek attention for his shoulder. And it was imperative that he speak with the king before rumors could wreak their damage.

As expected, the gossip reached the king before he did, and Holden was subjected to Edward's interest in the intriguing, romantic tale of his Scots wife defending him against her own people. Holden didn't have the heart to cor-

rect the stóry's inaccuracies, argue about Cambria's less than
pure motives, or mention that it was a Fitzroi she had shot.
The king, delighted by what sounded like the basis for a jon-
gleur's ballad, made him promise to bring the "Heroine of
Halidon" into his presence on the morrow.

Cambria paced back and forth inside Holden's pavilion, wearing down the nap of his rug. In the silence of solitude, images
of Halidon returned to haunt her, too like the nightmares slith-
ering through her sleep of late. She murmured psalms to herself all afternoon, trying to keep her mind busy, attempting to
distract herself from too much introspection. God, she would
have given anything for a book or a game of chess, even with
Sir Guy, something to take her mind off what she'd seen
today.

She flopped down onto the pallet and closed her eyes. Still
she saw the gaping wounds of beardless boys. She sat up
again, rubbed the anxious wrinkles from her forehead, and
began to study the madder-dyed design worked into the carpet.

'Twas the color of blood.

When a servant entered with food for her, she refused it.
Even the wine in her cup reminded her of blood pooling beneath slain knights.

At long last, with the dropping of night's hood, she was
mercifully blinded from the horrors of the day. She lit no
candle, lest it encroach on her hard-earned peace, and soon
repose found her in the formless country between thought
and dreams.

The rise of Halidon lay before her again. Cambria moved
her mouth in the soundless protest of nightmares as her feet
were drawn inexorably toward it. She shut her eyes against
the sight, but the vision remained.

The dream was the same as before, but starker, clearer,
rendered with details gleaned from the actual skirmish. The
refuse of mass slaughter stretched as far as she could see,
thousands of bodies strewn about as carelessly as rags, the
once fine wool plaids stained with blood and mire. Far off,
the high keening of widows rose on the air, at odds with the

pleased chuckles from English knights nearby. The coppery smell of fresh wounds was strong in her nostrils, and her stomach lurched dangerously. She glanced down at her hands. They were drenched with blood. Frantically, she wiped them on her skirts, to no avail. The widows' song blew through her soul like melancholy wind, and the English laughter grew louder. She rubbed and rubbed her hands, but the blood wouldn't come off, and the Englishmen kept laughing and laughing. . . .

"Murderers!" she screamed.

Cambria's moan brought Holden instantly to her side. He hadn't wanted to disturb her, coming to bed so late, but it appeared her dreams had done that already. His candle cast a halo of golden light around her as he jostled her arm, trying to waken her.

Her eyes flew wide, and she drew back as if he'd burned her. "Murder!" she hissed in horror. "What the English did—'twas murder!"

He gripped her shoulder to try to calm her, but she flung her arm wide, knocking the candle from his grasp. It guttered and extinguished itself, plunging the pavilion into darkness.

Then Cambria began to curse like a squire. She pummeled his bare chest, hard. He pressed his palm carefully over her mouth to muffle her cries and, guarding his injured shoulder as best he could, let her strike him at will.

He knew what she was doing. He'd seen it in green knights before, knights exposed to the horrors of war for the first time. All the fury, fear, and despair of battle stayed bottled up inside until it could find an appropriate outlet. For some, it was the lists, the tourneys, the harmless duels fought for honor and a lady's favor. For others, it was found at the bottom of a jack of ale or in the arms of a whore. But Cambria had no such outlet. So he let her vent her anguish and helplessness on his own body.

After several moments, when her blows subsided and he could feel wet, warm tears on his hand, he leaned over her, speaking in gentle, controlled tones.

"It is done, Cambria," he said softly. "Their souls are at peace." He squeezed her shoulder. "The Scots knew the cost.

All men know the price of battle. It's not pretty. At times, it's not even noble. But it is the way of war." He enclosed her hand in his own. Her fingers were callused, the nails bitten to the quick, but her hand was much smaller than one would expect, just as her heart was much softer. "Did you dream of the battle?"

She nodded. He could feel the tension in her, her brave attempts to stop the telltale hitching in her chest, and it clutched at his heart. He longed to take her into his arms, the way he'd wanted to comfort that wretched wildcat. But she was the Gavin. She was the laird. And lairds did not cry. For her pride's sake, he would ignore her tears.

He reached out and absently rubbed a lock of her hair between his thumb and finger. "Tell me about your father."

She was silent so long that he thought she'd drifted off to sleep. When she spoke at last, her voice was quiet, tentative.

"He was a great laird. He loved Blackhaugh. He loved the land, and he loved the clan. He loved my mother so well that he never took another to wife . . . even though it left me as sole heir. He taught me everything—hunting, hawking, and ha— . . ." She sniffed. "Swordfighting. He bought me a destrier when I was three years old and taught me to lead cattle raids when I was eleven." She gave a little laugh. "I remember my first raid. I was so excited and proud riding up to Blackhaugh with a dozen stolen cows that my father hadn't the heart to tell me they were Gavin cattle."

He chuckled. He'd never led a cattle raid, but he'd gotten into plenty of mischief as a boy. "Your father must have been a great man."

She sniffled. "I miss him," she murmured. "I miss him." And then she dissolved into tears.

A deep sigh emptied Holden's chest. With one hand, he reached out and caressed the back of her head, and with the other, he pulled her slowly up to him in a gentle embrace. He murmured assurances to her as he placed her head against his good shoulder, rocking her back and forth a long while.

At what point the change happened, he wasn't sure. Gradually Cambria's sobbing at his throat turned to kisses she bestowed there. His stroking of her hair took on a sensuous design. He took her chin in his hand and kissed the salty tears from her face. She touched her mouth to his with the delicacy of mist kissing the surface of a loch.

And then, emboldened, Cambria took his face in both her hands and kissed him full on the mouth. It was a kiss of absolution, he sensed, a bittersweet attempt to eradicate the nightmare of Halidon and her father's loss. A tortured groan slipped from his throat.

His will was too weak. If she continued, he'd do things she would regret on the morrow. He couldn't let her go on. He couldn't endure another night like the last one, fanning the flames of her lust while denying his own. He put a painful end to the kiss by covering her eager lips with his fingers.

His gesture did nothing to dim her smoldering desire. She ran her palms across his chest as if she sought a way to his heart. He caught her stray hands and pushed them away.

"Nay," he said thickly. "I . . . want you too much." A wave of desire coursed through his loins, lending proof to his words. "I won't be able to stop myself this time. I am sorry."

Cambria swallowed hard. By all the saints, she wanted him. In spite of her promise, in spite of her pride, she wanted Holden. And, she decided, calling upon her renowned Gavin stubbornness, she'd be damned if she would let him refuse her. Before she could think further and possibly change her mind, she shook loose Holden's hands and began to push down the coverlet between them.

Holden sucked in a quick breath when he realized what her overture meant. God, he hoped she realized what she was doing. He rolled back slowly while she moved the furs out of the way, as if moving too fast might give her second thoughts. He didn't want to frighten her. Sweet Lord, he prayed he had the control not to hurt her. Suddenly, absurdly, he felt like an untried youth.

Cambria's hands found him in the dark. His body was magnificent, proud, lean, contoured as flawlessly as a fine blade. She shivered as her forearm brushed the bold manifestation of his desire that seemed to her a brazen lance. The implication gave her pause, but she was committed now, and she'd not retreat from the challenge she'd issued. With clumsy fingers, she began to pick at the back laces of her kirtle.

Holden retrieved his dagger from the swordbelt beside the pallet and sliced the laces neatly. The garment dropped from her shoulders like a dying rose, and she willingly, breathlessly removed her linen underclothing, baring her body for him.

Holden cradled her face in his hands. He kissed her deeply, hungrily, and she responded with a ferocity that nearly unleashed his own tempered passions. She was like soft, warm velvet against his body, and the sweet, smoky smell of her hair and the weak moans in the back of her throat were calling him to answer. He knew the answer, longed to give it, but couldn't, not yet.

"I've given you my word," he murmured against her cheek. "I won't consummate this marriage until you wish it so."

Cambria trembled in his arms. The silence between them grew as taut as the long, last moment before the release of an arrow from a bow.

"I wish it," she finally whispered. "I wish it so."

Holden wiped the sweat from his lip, then lowered her to the pallet. Dear God, he thought as he remembered the lovely, soft nest of her curls, it was going to cost him much to subdue his own desires as he worked to satisfy hers. Her responsiveness had the power to intoxicate them both. He had to bear in mind that this wanton vixen was still a virgin. She'd require patience.

He hovered over her, kissed her eyes, her hair, her fingertips, shuddered when her hands unabashedly reached up to explore his body. Groaning helplessly, he bent and captured a succulent nipple in his mouth. She moaned beneath him, brazenly lifting her hips to contact his. He gasped, then stifled the sound, suckling at her breast like a starving man. His fingers traced a leisurely path up to the juncture of her thighs, and he pulled gently at the hair there. Moving upward again, he kissed her open mouth, letting his tongue dance with hers and graze the edges of her teeth. At last he eased his large body down over hers, covering her completely.

Cambria strained instinctively upward against him, burying her head in the crook of his neck, overcome by the sensation of the powerful muscles enveloping her, the full, warm shaft brushing her skin. His hands found hers, locking her fingers in a gentle bondage.

"Easy, little sprite," he said huskily against her ear as he bent his head to kiss between her breasts and lower to her navel.

She stiffened with a faint protest and tried in vain to extract her fingers from his. Surely he did not mean to . . . Ah, God, she could feel his breath upon her woman's curls. His mouth nuzzled her, and she cried out, squeezing his fingers. He moved between her thighs, and when his tongue grazed her flesh, she turned her head onto her shoulder, squirming in sweet distress. Again and again his tongue lapped at her, savoring her like honey from the comb. She could feel her face turn to flame, but not for the world did she wish him to stop.

Holden had to stop. He was in danger of losing control. Breathing raggedly, he placed a single, final kiss upon the soft, dark flower of her blossoming womanhood, and then kissed his way to her mouth.

Cambria was astonished by her own pleasant, musky taste on his lips, and she let her tongue venture into his mouth, trailing across the rims of his teeth and lapping at his tongue. As she explored, he released her hands and placed his palm against the wet curls between her legs. She writhed against it, wanting more, aching with a hunger she didn't understand. He stroked her with a moist finger, edging more and more deeply into her while his thumb stroked delicately above. She rocked her hips in a steady rhythm, counter to his movements, moaning at the feel of his finger inside her. The pressure was exhilarating, and she couldn't stop the cries that came to her lips.

The sounds she made almost drove Holden over the edge of desire. While one hand continued to pleasure her, he tenderly wiped the beads of perspiration from her brow with the other.

"Cambria," he said hoarsely, "I must cause you . . .

pain . . . this first time. I do not wish it, but 'tis so. 'Twill be brief, I promise, and then you shall never endure it again."

Cambria scarcely paid heed to his words. She was a Gavin. She feared no pain. Every nerve in her body was awake and crying out for succor.

"I'm ready, Englishman," she said in a voice that was half plea, half demand.

Holden wasted no time. He coaxed her thighs apart and entered her fully, groaning as her warm sheath surrounded him like a blanket.

Cambria was stunned by the burning that knifed through her loins. But she was a warrior, she reminded herself. She had never cried out in pain. She would not do so now. Clenching her teeth as he waited for her to adjust to his invasion, she willed the sting to recede, and it did.

When her hands relaxed upon his shoulders, Holden began to move, very slowly at first, letting her grow accustomed to the feel of him.

Cambria learned quickly. Once the pain had vanished, she could not get close enough to him. She pressed upwards against the bones of his hip, and he squeezed her buttocks, urging her higher. She wrapped her long legs around him, and Holden gasped at her welcome boldness. He'd never experienced such ferocity in a woman before, and it excited him beyond control.

They strove together like well-matched champions, meeting blow for blow, straining in ecstatic battle, attacking and retreating, only to advance again. Before long, they were mating in a frenzy of passion and instinct. Holden pounded into her like the surf of the North Sea. She clawed at his back as if he would save her from drowning in the sensation. With each thrust, she felt herself being purged of the horrifying images at Halidon, and she clung fiercely to him, willing him to stay with her forever.

They rode passion's wave together, and just as they reached the crest, Cambria looked impossibly through the darkness into Holden's eyes, blue crystal shooting fire into green, green smoldering back into blue. At that instant of vulnerability, she felt their souls meet, and she knew that neither time nor distance nor death itself could ever part them. Then the wave crashed thunderously, and with a primal cry of relief, they fell to the earth to lay like castaways on a forbidden shore.

13

THE PAIN WAS EXCRUCIATING. OWEN SHIVERED WITH NEARLY uncontrollable panic and dread as he groped for the edge of the lichen-covered boulder. With a grunt, he fell against it, bruising his shoulder. Then he lay back, rolling his eyes skyward to the shifting pine boughs, catching his breath. Every limp had been an agony. He'd cursed the name of Cambria Gavin at every step, but when he finally reached the cover of the wood, he was certain he'd lost his pursuer.

He wanted to sleep now, to close his watering eyes and drift off to oblivion. But then she wouldn't be punished. She'd go on living. And more than sleep, he longed to see her suffer.

He knew what he must do, even as he whimpered against the thought. With trembling fingers, he ripped the bottom two inches from his blood-stained tabard. As he hitched air into his lungs, he balled the cloth and shoved it solidly between his teeth.

The arrow had surprised him—it had been loosed not from enemy hands, but from behind their own English lines. Incapacitated by the pain, he had nonetheless instinctively sought out his attacker. How unmanning it had been to find the culprit was a peasant woman. Then he'd seen her face, and in that brief moment of recognition, he'd known a hatred beyond all reason. Only his desperation to survive had prevented him from crossing the space between them and tearing that Scots bitch limb from limb with his bare hands.

For now, he told himself, his nostrils flaring with the effort to breathe, he would retreat. He'd withdraw like an injured animal, lick his wounds, and curl up within himself to heal. There would be time later to kill her, her and her lover. He giggled nervously in anticipation. He wanted to take his time with her, and for that he would need his strength.

Sweat beading his clammy face, he shuddered and put both hands to the arrow protruding from his thigh. His eyes bulged from their sockets as he exerted steadily with almost inhuman might. At last, the point budged, and he pulled the shaft slowly from his muscle. The balled cloth muffled his screams of torment as the point tore backwards through his flesh till it was free.

The ragged wound bled furiously. He nearly fainted from the loss. He tore the rag from his mouth to stanch the flow, certain he'd live now. He fell back against the boulder, swatting clumsily at insistent flies, drifting into a long-awaited, troubled sleep. The midday sun pierced through the forest canopy and cooked him in his armor.

Hours later, with the sun well into its downward climb, the point of a sword jostled him awake. For a moment he was disoriented. Then the throbbing in his leg brought everything back.

A dozen savages surrounded him, their grimy faces peering down at him with contempt. They were Scots, their diverse somber plaids draped haphazardly across their shoulders, and the lot of them looked eager to spill English blood.

"Owen?" the one with the sword asked.

Owen recognized the lilting accent and red hair, even if his vision was too blurred to see clearly. It was the Gavin rebel. Damn his luck, he'd have to think quickly. And it was so hard to think when one was in pain.

"Is it you, Robbie?" he wheezed at last. "Thank God!"

The rebels eyed him warily.

"On your feet!" Robbie commanded, prodding him with a sword.

Owen's voice was but a weak croak. "I've been sorely wounded, Robbie."

Robbie glanced cursorily at Owen's bloody leg. "You've given us no new information since the attempt on de Ware's life. Have your loyalties shifted then?"

"I still bear messages for the rebels," Owen lied. "I was sent by them to find you. Why were you not at Halidon?"

Robbie's eyes flared at the slight, and he puffed up his chest. "'Twas my men who were the eyes and ears of the Scots. We weren't at Halidon, because we traveled with the English, under their noses. We knew their number and strength days ago."

Owen sighed dramatically, "Alas, I fear 'tis too late."

"Too late?"

"Aye," he reported grimly. "By now we've lost the battle."

Robbie regarded him incredulously. "Lost the battle at Halidon? But our numbers were vast. 'Tisn't possible."

The Scots gripped their weapons as if they'd march to war even now. Owen suppressed a smirk at their impotent ambition.

"Nonetheless, 'tis true," he said, shaking his head.

Robbie cursed and kicked at the hard ground. Then he wheeled toward Owen and regarded him slyly. "How did you come to be wounded?"

Owen didn't have to feign his wrath. He answered through tightly gritted teeth. "An enemy arrow pierced me."

"The English discovered your treason?" Robbie guessed.

"Aye," he replied, thinking how ridiculously gullible these Scots were. "If only I'd found you sooner . . ."

Robbie gazed down at him, and Owen could almost see the scale tipping back and forth on his face. Then he motioned to one of his men. "See that his wound is tended properly. If the battle at Halidon has been lost, 'twill only be a matter of time until the English return."

Owen nodded in agreement.

"We must leave this place," Robbie continued.

"If I may be so bold," Owen began, barely able to contain his sudden glee at this turn of events, "I believe I may have a plan worth considering."

He hardly felt the pain as Robbie's man changed his dressing, only wincing occasionally as he described his daring proposal to the eager Scots.

The warmth of the sun seeping into the serge tent woke Cambria. She was shocked to find herself sprawled shamelessly next to the sleeping bulk of Lord Holden, her legs dangling out from under the fur coverlet. Beneath her, spots of maiden's blood flecked the cream-colored linens. Good Lord, she prayed no meddling servant had peeked in on them.

She reached for her rumpled kirtle, pulling it inch by inch from beneath the weight of Holden's hindquarters, and slipped it over her head for modesty, in spite of the fact that the laces were completely severed. She wondered idly how many of her gowns Holden would destroy in his haste to bed her. Then a flush stole up her cheeks as she remembered it had been *she* who had been so impatient for their joining.

She lay back on the pallet once more and peered at the man who was her husband. He lay flat on his back. From the look of his bandages, his shoulder hadn't worsened, and his face was clear and untroubled by fever. In sooth, he looked like a sweet angel as he slept.

Holden had given her far more than absolution last night. He'd made her feel alive. She'd experienced immense power beyond her wildest imaginings, hand in hand with a vulnerability so dangerous it had made her tremble. In one exhilarating, terrifying moment she had conquered him and been conquered. Had she betrayed her clan by bedding the enemy? Or had she emerged victorious? Her mind was a blur of contradictions.

She had to get out, to be alone for a while, to sort out her thoughts in the open cathedral of a Scots forest. She stood for a moment in the leaf-dappled shade of the tent, attempting to rub the swelling from her eyes, raking her hair into some semblance of order. Then she stole across the spongy carpet. Just as she lifted the pavilion flap, Holden called to her.

"Do not go yet."

Damn! She'd hoped to escape his notice. She wasn't ready to talk to him or even look him in the eye. But when she turned resignedly, her reluctance melted like butter on hot bread.

Holden sat up on his elbows, leaving the glorious breadth of his chest exposed. Damp curls clung to his neck, and there was a shadow of masculine stubble on his cheeks. His eyes were yet heavy-lidded from slumber, his lips were parted hopefully. Her heart caught in her throat as she fought the urge to gulp. How much easier it was to look upon him as he slept. Awake, he was too vital, too magnetic, too unpredictable.

Holden cleared his throat. "We must talk, you and I," he said in his most solemn voice, pulling his discarded tabard modestly across his lap. It would not do to let her see how much her tempestuous beauty affected him as he watched the warm light bathe the exposed skin of her shoulders.

Her smoky eyes were as captivating as the fog above a loch, and her swollen lips gave her a sultry, sensual mien. Her hair was snarled hopelessly, but it only served to remind him of her passion. God, he thought, if he continued his thoughts in that direction, he'd be pushing her onto her back again within moments. And something in her manner told him that would be a mistake just now.

"Come," he told her, patting the mattress beside him.

Indecision flickered in her eyes, but finally she joined him on the pallet, sitting stiffly on the edge. He half-smiled at her sudden shyness, particularly since the entire back of her kirtle gaped open, revealing that arrow-straight back.

"There will be a feast this evening," he told her simply. "Edward wishes to meet the lady I have wed without his consent."

Cambria whirled toward him, her awkwardness forgotten in her surprise. "Meet . . . your king?"

"*Our* king," he corrected casually. "He wishes to see for himself the Scotswoman who would follow her English husband to war and protect him with bow and arrow."

Her face grew warm. "You told him?" She suddenly longed to pummel her husband.

"The tale reached his ears long before I got to him,"

Holden said. "'Tis well. Now there is no questioning your loyalty."

"But I didn't do it for the English. I did it for my clan," she told him bluntly.

He winced. "A fact best left unmentioned where Edward is concerned. In sooth, I'd rather you said as little as possible."

I'm sure you would, she thought rebelliously. There was much she wanted to say to the king—protest the appointment of Balliol, argue about the unification of Scotland and England, rage over the atrocity committed against her father.

"I will be obeyed in this, Cambria. It will serve no purpose for you to act the shrew," he assured her, his eyes issuing a warning. "I've wagered much in marrying you without the king's blessing. I must prove that I've made a prudent decision. If you attempt to disgrace me with that sharp tongue of yours before Edward—"

"My tongue is not sharp!" she huffed.

"Lady," he said, laughing, "were it any sharper, you'd not need a dagger to cut your meat."

She shot him her most scathing look. Whatever she had expected this morning, it certainly wasn't insults.

"Remember that any shame you bring upon me shames your clan as well," he reminded her.

She considered his words. 'Twas difficult for her to imagine playing the docile wife. But if 'twould save the Gavin, she'd do it. She dropped her shoulders and extinguished the fire in her eyes. She supposed he was right. The clan came first.

Then, in a flash, the reality of her situation hit her with full force. "I cannot meet the king!" she hissed.

Holden looked at her grimly.

"I have nothing to wear, not even my chain mail!" she cried. "He will not believe me a laird when I am garbed like a peasant! Look at me!"

He did, every delicious inch of her, and he wished wryly that she truly did have nothing to wear. Clearing his throat, he replied. "'Tis no matter . . ."

"No matter to *you* . . . you have clothing as befits a lord, but I . . ."

Holden had little patience for the whims of fashion. "You *will* meet Edward, if I have to drag you naked before him."

Cambria hardly heard him. Already her mind was trying to think of ways to repair her kirtle, to make herself presentable. God, if she'd only brought her armor—at least *that* she knew how to polish to a silvery sheen. She jumped up from the pallet, and Holden caught her arm.

"Thank you," he said gently, sincerely, "for last night, for your precious gift."

His clear, penetrating gaze made her heart flutter like a pennon. She dropped her eyes and mumbled something in reply that made him smile. Then, snatching up her cloak, she rushed awkwardly from the pavilion. A moment later, when she realized she'd told him it had been her pleasure, her face grew hot.

She pulled the cowl close about her head and walked briskly past the curious faces, taking a well-worn path to the nearby stream. She couldn't afford to think about last night—how she had lost control so utterly and let passion cloud her judgment, how the mere sight of the Wolf had sent her heart racing.

Nay, she scolded herself, she had to think like a laird now. There was much planning to do concerning her meeting with the king. She promised herself she'd not disgrace her husband, nor would she call the king's wrath down upon the Gavin, but she had to use the encounter to her best advantage. She had to find a way to dissuade Edward from granting Balliol the Scots throne.

Deep in thought, she picked her way through the lush fern and past sleek elm saplings toward the rushing stream. As she neared the bank, she was disappointed to hear the voices of a trio of men conversing quietly over the sound of the water. It seemed she would have no solitude after all. Her foot snapped a crisp twig, and two of the men jumped to their feet to glare at her.

"Forgive me," she said, hiding her amusement at their exaggerated reaction. "I didn't mean to frighten you."

The two men grew wary, puzzled by her accent, she presumed, but the third motioned them to silence.

"Come, good woman," he said warmly. "There is plenty of water for all."

The friendly one was handsome and as golden as summer. He was quite young, but his calm disposition made him seem older. The other two appeared annoyed by his overtures. She supposed that was because she sounded Scots and looked to be below their station. They were obviously English nobility. Even without their jeweled belts and fur-lined garments, she could tell by their manner and bearing that they were of high rank.

"You are from King Edward's army?" she inquired, dropping to the water's muddy edge to wash her hands.

The two men looked at each other in chagrin, and the third again bade them be still.

"Aye," he said with a nod. "We have come from Halidon. 'Twas a promising victory."

Her stomach turned, but she continued to smile sweetly. " 'Twas hardly a victory."

The Englishmen's eyes widened at the audacity of her comment.

"Your sympathies lie with the rebel Scots then?" the young one asked, narrowing his eyes in scrutiny.

She rinsed her hands and thought for a moment. "My *sympathies* lie there, but my *loyalty* I give to my lord who fights for your king."

The man smiled. "Well spoken. Perhaps you are well advised to pity these disorderly rebels. They certainly do not know how to fight. It is only by appointing them their own king that the savages will be tamed."

"Aye, their own king, but certainly not Balliol!" she pronounced, taking umbrage. "The Scots do not respect him!"

The man ignored the agitated protests of his companions. "And who do they respect?" he asked with interest.

She frowned. "I know not, but he'd at least have to be a true Scot himself, born *and* raised in the mother country."

"If your lord heard you speak this way," the man cautioned, "he'd likely beat you."

Her eyes glittered. "He would not dare." With that, she plunged both hands into the water and sluiced it up over her face, scrubbing the sleep from her eyes.

The man lifted his brows at her impetuosity, then crouched to dabble his fingers in the stream. "Who *is* your lord, lass?"

She patted her face dry on a clean corner of her kirtle. "Holden de Ware, sir."

The man's eyes flitted up to her suddenly, and he seemed to be studying every inch of her face. Then an amused grin settled onto his lips. "Ah, I have heard tell of him. Is he not called the Wolf? 'Tis said he has never lost a battle."

"Aye." She drew herself up proudly to her full height.

"But if your sympathies lie with the Scots, why would you wish to ally yourself with a man who will surely crush them?"

"Because," she revealed, "I am his wife."

Somehow the man did not look surprised, although his companions made remarks of outrage at what they assumed an obvious lie. The golden man began to chuckle deep in his chest. "And *I,*" he said with a hearty laugh, coming to his feet and making a half-bow, "am the king of England."

Her temper flared. "Do not mock me!" The two nobles recoiled, obviously shocked by her outspokenness, but she continued in a scathing voice. "Else I will set my great Wolf of a husband on you, and he will take the leer from your face!"

The two gentlemen actually looked as if they would choke on their astonishment. She wondered if they were ill. But the third man continued to be highly amused by her threats, even wiping a tear of laughter from his eye.

"I've heard tell of this new wife of de Ware's. 'Tis said she is so ugly that she must hide beneath a cloak," he teased.

She bridled, but wouldn't take the bait. "You may judge for yourself whether that be true."

"That she abducted her husband at the point of a dagger?"

"An act of desperation," she assured him.

"'Tis also rumored that she wore chain mail to her own wedding and that she fights like a man."

"'Tis true that I know the use of the sword," she answered.

The man's eyes gleamed. "Perhaps you'll do me the honor of a friendly duel then. It would be refreshing for a change to fight a woman in an arena where I have half a chance of winning."

She met his stare. "As you see, I am unarmed."

"John," the man directed, gesturing to one of the knights, "lend the lass your sword." The man sputtered, appalled at the suggestion. "Come, come," he insisted with a good-natured frown.

"Perhaps he is afraid his sword will be loath to return to him after it has tasted my grip," she taunted.

The one called John looked like he might burst as his face blackened with outrage, but she didn't fear him. He was obviously beholden to the younger man. He unsheathed his sword and threw it at her, pommel first, with enough force to knock a person down, but she managed to catch it squarely in both hands. Shrugging her shoulders, she let the cloak fall to the ground and kicked it out of the way. Too late, she remembered her kirtle was slit down the back. But there would be time for modesty later. Now, she was defending her honor.

The man ambled forward, and she could see that he was quite tall and long of limb. A superior reach, however, did not necessarily a victor make. In fact, if one was swift, and she was, speed could have a clear advantage over size. His eyes danced with merriment, and he drew his blade eagerly, a noble sword, true and shining, with some kind of intricate carving and jewels upon the hilt. He struck first, a gentle tap, to test her mettle. She knocked the blow away effortlessly, smirking impatiently at him. He sliced again, and she easily tossed his attack aside and advanced. Taken by surprise, he retreated a few paces, and his companions growled their disapproval.

"It seems," she told him as she fought, "that your friends have little faith in your swordplay."

The man happily blocked her blows. "Nay, 'tis only that they are amazed by yours!"

Cambria liked this man. His honesty was refreshing. He

complimented her even as they battled. Of course, as timid and tentative as his blows were, he would naturally be impressed by her technique. In sooth, he seemed to have no qualms about her swordfighting and did not appear to be offended in the least by her skills, as others inevitably were. As much as she'd sought seclusion this morning, it felt good to focus her scattered energies on a tangible opponent. This encounter was rather enjoyable, she realized as she took a downward slice at his head.

A quarter mile away, within the walls of his tent, Holden cursed himself for letting Cambria go off alone. Sir Guy had just returned to the encampment in disappointment. His prey had slipped through his fingers like an eel. Owen was still about, and if there was trouble, Cambria's stubborn head would no doubt lead her directly into it. He dressed quickly and began searching the camp for his wife.

When he heard the clang of sword upon sword coming from the wood, he drew his own blade and crept soundlessly through the trees. Peering through the low branches of a willow, he saw his worst nightmare realized. Before his very eyes, their swords clashing with fervent purpose, fought his wife and his king.

14

CAMBRIA CHUCKLED IN TRIUMPH AS HER GRINNING OPPO-nent retreated toward the stream. They'd been sparring happily for only a few minutes, and already she'd won the advantage. She raised her blade for the symbolic kill.

Suddenly she found herself grabbed from behind. One thick arm wrapped around her waist, and another tore the sword from her grasp, flinging it across the clearing. Before she could even lay eyes on her captor's face, she knew 'twas Holden—something about his scent or the familiar heat of his fury—and she grew enraged that he should have interfered with her sport. She opened her mouth to curse him when, to her amazement, he wound a cruel fist in her hair. Pressing her roughly down to her knees on the damp forest floor, he forced her to bow her head.

"I beg you to forgive her, Your Majesty," he said all too clearly.

Her bones turned to jelly. She didn't dare move. She didn't dare speak. She didn't dare lift her eyes. Dear God, she'd been fighting the king.

It all made sense now. 'Twas no wonder the man's companions were nearly apoplectic with concern. Everything she'd heard about the ruthless English monarch came rushing into her head. Holy Mary, she wondered if she'd live out the day. She racked her brain. What in God's name had she said to him? What unadulterated opinions had she dared to espouse to the king of England? Screwing up her courage, she peeked at him from beneath worried brows.

Edward took one glimpse of her, cowering like a kicked hound, and fell into robust gales of laughter. "Perhaps," he roared, "perhaps I shall forgive *you*, Holden, for interrupting my play! In sooth, I have not been so entertained in a long while!"

As she knelt before the king, her heart rattling rapidly in her chest, the pressure of Holden's hand lessened slightly, and she began to see the humor of the situation. Good Lord, the king of England had challenged her to a duel, goaded her into it with his teasing, and she had fallen neatly into his trap! She wondered what her father would have said to that. The idea made her lips twitch, and soon her shoulders started to shake with repressed laughter. Much to Holden's chagrin, she was sure, before long she was sobbing with mirth.

Holden finally released his grip and shook his head in wonder. "My wife is gone from me but a few moments, and I arrive to find my lady and my liege engaged in mortal combat," he said in mock disgust, "and now you tell me it is play!"

The golden king chuckled. "You were right, de Ware. Your lady is a rare gem. I wholly approve of your choice."

Holden bowed with an elaborate flourish. "My thanks, Your Majesty."

"Although, were I you," Edward said with a twinkle in his eye, "I think I'd prefer a little more honey and a little less mustard with my game!"

Holden smiled at the king's pun. "Ah, but you are a gentleman, Majesty. I am a soldier. I've always loved a good battle."

"Was it one of your 'battles' then that cost your lady her gown?" the king commented with amusement.

Cambria flushed at the reminder, reaching behind her to hold the edges of the garment together. Edward bid her rise with a gesture, then winked conspiratorially at Holden. "Do learn to untie the laces, de Ware, or you'll deplete your wealth purchasing new gowns."

Holden managed to chuckle politely at the jest, but his mind was fixed on the disobedient vixen rising to her feet before him. He was furious with Cambria, despite the fact that the soft scent of her hair beneath his chin was driving him to distraction.

When the king dismissed them, Cambria curtseyed demurely, returned the borrowed sword, then retrieved her cloak, leaving the forest with nary a glance toward her lord and master.

Holden caught up with her moments later in his pavilion, throwing back the flap with a vengeance. He startled her, and Cambria, clad only in a sleeveless linen shift, clutched her torn kirtle protectively to her chest. In two long strides, he closed the space between them. His fingers clenched and bit into her bare upper arm, and she winced in surprise.

"Do not let me see you raise your sword against another again, do you hear me?" he snapped.

She tore her arm from his grasp. "You would *not* have seen me had you kept to your own affairs."

"You *are* my affair!" he shouted. "We are wed, madam."

He rubbed his brow in frustration and began to pace like a cornered wolf. "I cannot believe you dared confront the king," he muttered.

"I knew him not," she shrugged. "He was as any other man."

Cambria's own words gave her pause. She realized the truth of them. Edward wasn't the monster she'd once imagined, the demon Robbie would have had her believe. He was merely a mortal, a simple man clothed in the robes of royalty. She wondered why the Scots were so opposed to the leadership of this young, fair-haired, laughing sovereign.

"Had you let your loyalties be known," Holden assured her, "you would have found he is *not* like any other man. He has limitless power." A shudder betrayed his emotions. "He could have had you executed on the spot!"

"I *did* tell him of my loyalties," she said, unable to understand Holden's concern. The golden knight seemed harmless enough, and he seemed to like her.

"You told Edward . . ." Holden sunk dismally into his chair, his eyes flat and his mouth agape.

"I didn't know him," she explained with another shrug.

"Perhaps that is God's mercy," he said weakly. "Had you known him, I'm certain you would have tried to run him through!"

"Run him through? Do you truly believe I have no honor? 'Twas a friendly match!"

Holden turned his back on Cambria and swallowed uncomfortably as he visualized again the duel in the woods. "Your honor certainly would have been in question had you injured the king or—or slain him, now wouldn't it?" he asked hoarsely.

But that wasn't his real fear. He wasn't worried in the least about the king. He'd seen the fight. Edward had easily blocked her blows, merely goaded Cambria into attacking him. Besides, the king's guard would have intervened had she so much as sliced a thread from his surcoat. But Cambria was so reckless and aggressive and impetuous that Edward might have harmed her unintentionally. She might have slipped onto his blade. God, he didn't want to think about it.

"I would not slay or even wound a man in a friendly battle!" Cambria stated, clearly offended. "Not even an Englishman."

He turned and looked at her for a long while, wavering in indecision, then sighed resignedly. "Promise me you won't raise your sword against Edward again, even in sport." He slumped down onto his chair. "I don't believe my heart could endure it."

A small smile touched the corners of her lips. "I swear, my lord," she complied, but then the light of mischief danced in her eyes. "However, if the king should *command* it, I don't—"

"Cambria," he warned her, "do not attempt to make me completely mad. I am halfway there already."

She grinned, instantly enchanting him out of his ire. God's bones, it was a cruel jest of fate that she should cause him as much trouble as she did joy, but how could he stay angry at her when she looked at him like that? His fears soothed for the moment, he saw his wife now as if for the first time. Her threadbare shift did little to hide her soft, sweet curves, particularly where the muted gold sunlight pierced the sheer linen. Lord, she was lovely. Her skin glowed from the morning's duel, and her cheeks wore the flush of health. Her eyes sparkled like a bubbling spring, and when she blushed at his forthright appraisal, her gaze softened receptively. And best of all, she was his. He felt a powerful surge of need arise in him, his body remembering well last night's coupling.

Cambria felt the breath quicken in her breast as Holden's warm gaze slowly raked down her body. Sweet Mary—his thoughts were as transparent as rainwater. He wanted her. Now.

She should resist him, she knew. 'Twas midmorn, bright daylight. Outside, the encampment was fully awake. She could hear servants hurrying to and fro, knights barking out commands, pages grumbling at their duties. Anyone could walk in upon them. Anyone could overhear the sounds of their lovemaking. 'Twasn't decent.

Still, the intensity of his vibrant stare sent a shiver of delight up her spine, reminding her of the unspeakable pleasures he could bring her. Her knees quivered, her lips parted, and an aching need blossomed between her thighs.

Without a word, he came to her. Their lips met first, caressing slowly, their lingering pace denying the urgency of their desire. Holden's fingers filtered through her hair as if touching it for the first time. Cambria's hands fluttered over each rippling muscle through his linen shirt with complete fascination. They sampled each other as if savoring a rare dessert of spun sugar.

Holden knew from the first taste that he was ensnared. Never had he been so besotted with one woman. It was dangerous, this obsession. But his mind did not long dwell on such fears, for when her hands slipped beneath his tunic to seek their pleasure, all rational thought left him. Her fingers burned fire as they traced the line of his collarbone and grazed his ribs. When her hands dared to creep lower, he groaned and took her by the wrists, shaking his head.

Cambria was thoroughly intoxicated by the feel of him.

She wanted to touch him all over. Each plane of his body had a different, wonderful texture. His cheek was rough with stubble, his breast wide and firm, his stomach flat and softly furred.

Giving no more thought to the time of day and the possibility of discovery, they separated long enough to undress, their eyes never breaking contact. Wool garments were discarded, and linen soughed to the carpet like cherry blossoms in summer. At last, they stood naked together in the pale light of morning, an arm's length away, regarding one another with limpid eyes of desire.

Holden thought he'd never beheld such a beautifully sculpted body, supple and strong, yet still so womanly, every inch of flesh made for his embrace. Already he longed to kiss the spot where her shoulder curved into the hollow above her breast, to pillow his head against the soft cushion of her bosom.

Cambria felt a strange lethargy creep over her. Her eyelids grew heavy, her movements slow, as if she'd taken a draught of opium wine. Her breath dropped deep in her chest, and her knees grew weak as she saw that the Wolf was quite ready for her.

They approached with almost painful stealth. Holden felt as if he would burst. Cambria was near faint with longing. The air rippled with current, and when their bodies finally touched, it was as if they were irrevocably joined by the forces of nature.

Cambria was nearly overcome by the warmth of Holden's skin as his massive arms enfolded her with quiet strength.

Holden was astonished by his own instinctive gentleness as her nipples brushed his ribs and her soft woman's curls tickled his thigh. He kneaded the muscles of her buttocks, reveling in her sleek curves.

She licked and bit tenderly at his breast, fascinated by the taste of him. Slowly, he moved his hands down to clasp her behind the thighs, then effortlessly lifted her and laid her back onto his pallet. She trembled beneath him in expectation. Pure lust burned in his gaze, and she knew that emerald

fire reflected in her own eyes as she regarded him shamelessly.

Suddenly, with delicious savagery, Holden's mouth
swooped down upon hers in a kiss that claimed her for his.
When she embraced him with all the strength of her need, he
made a low growl in his throat, lifted her knees back against
her chest, and pushed deeply into her.

She gasped in pleased surprise as he filled her completely.
She wrapped her legs possessively around him and pressed
her heels into his back, beckoning him ever closer.

Their mating was silent then, but for their labored breathing and the rustling of the bed linen. 'Twas as if they were
afraid to speak, afraid to rend the fragile fabric of their new
love with careless words. They only stared at one another,
watching a wondrous palette of emotions color their eyes—
lust, hope, fear, surrender—as their bodies became caught up
in the restless rhythm of desire.

When Cambria thought she could bear no more, that she
must turn away from his searing gaze, Holden's breath
caught and his face glowed with the glory of release. Shud-
ders racked his body with the power of a galloping steed as
he cried out his triumph. The sweet agony in his eyes was so
moving that her own body swelled with a vibrant warmth,
and she moved toward and found her own victorious relief.
Waves of pleasure sluiced over her again and again until passion's tide slowly ebbed into a lulling wash, cleansing her
very soul.

Long afterward, when her heart had evened and her breath
had slowed, he slid deliciously against her with his wet,
warm skin, licking her shoulder, tickling her neck with his
hair.

"You are magnificent," he murmured.

Her lips curved into a satisfied smile, but she had no
strength to make reply. She only sighed contentedly and
snuggled deeper into his arms, into the slumber of the re-
plete, into the land of dreams.

The golden monarch visited her again in that world,
wielding his jeweled sword. Again they battled, but together

this time, he in royal robes, she in her Gavin tabard. And she was leading the charge.

She awoke with a luxurious yawn in Holden's embrace. The dream must be her destiny, she decided. 'Twas the reason fate had brought her here—to this husband, to this battle, to this king. She would be the instrument of peace. There was no doubt in her mind now.

'Twas her destiny to make Edward see his folly.

Owen looked up through the clearing beyond the elms at the impressive, impenetrable stones of the castle. He felt it again—that secure knowledge that Blackhaugh would shortly be his. The dozen ragged Scotsmen behind him had less confidence, of course. They kept their hooded cloaks well around them, their hands close to their weapons. Their eyes flitted nervously about. But then they knew nothing about the determination of a desperate man.

Even now, Owen knew that the sentry he'd spotted on the parapet would be scurrying through the passages to alert Holden's brother of their presence. Owen grinned. His leg pained him, but he paid it little heed, so overcome was he with the power he was about to wield.

As they approached the oak portal, it slowly creaked open, as if he'd willed it so. That pleased him greatly.

"Owen," Garth said by way of greeting.

Owen grinned in friendship, the expression forced and oddly foreign. He shrugged. "I caught a Scots arrow."

Garth glanced briefly at the bandaged leg. He was obviously not much concerned with Owen's injuries.

"And Holden?" Garth asked, worry etched into his face.

Owen nodded. "He is well. He sent us to let you know the battle was a success. He'll return shortly. In the meantime, we could use a bath and . . ."

"Of course." Now that Garth's fears were relieved, he remembered his courtesy and invited them within the walls.

No sooner had the doors thundered shut than the Scots drew their blades. Garth gasped as cold steel from more than one sword pressed suddenly and surely against his throat.

"I told you it'd be simple," Owen chuckled to his cohorts.

"What is the mean— . . . ?" Garth began, but the nick of Robbie's sword stopped him short.

Owen rubbed his hands together with glee. "Now we have only to wait for Lord Holden de Ware to fall into the trap." At his command, the rebels pushed their quarry roughly into the great hall. "Not cut from the same cloth as your brother, are you?" Owen taunted. He hit his mark—Garth's face reddened in shame. "No need to explain. I know all about that."

Within the hour, Garth, Malcolm, and all of Blackhaugh's men-at-arms were safe under lock and key. Owen would just as soon have slain them all, for he was sure they could never be trusted to serve him, but he still needed to ally himself with Robbie's men. In spite of their new loyalty to him, he suspected they'd not look kindly upon the mass slaughter of their clansmen.

Robbie leaned back against the curtain wall, picking meat from his teeth with his fingernail. The once busy courtyard was now ominously still. Only occasionally, a hawk would swoop down at the castle, or a woman would skitter fearfully along a wall to pass by the rebels. His men strutted about, planning the overthrow with loud enthusiasm and punctuating their boasts with hearty slaps upon the back.

But from what Robbie could tell, Owen did not appear overly concerned with the needs of the Scots rebels. Instead, he seemed more preoccupied with the fates of Holden and Cambria. That did not sit well with Robbie. More than once, Owen had slipped and referred to Blackhaugh as *his* castle. To make matters worse, the man was becoming more and more obsessive, possibly in part from the fever he suffered from his suppurating wound. The stupid man, Robbie thought—he'd lose that leg if he didn't seek help for it. Still, there was something unsettling about the way Owen's eyes gleamed with febrile light, something that seemed more lunatic than sickly.

In the end, Robbie decided there was naught to be done for it. He and his men had passed the point of redemption. Their brash capture of Blackhaugh was a fait accompli, and, right or wrong, they would have to live with that deed.

• • • •

The campfire popped as King Edward tossed a stripped boar's rib onto it, prompting a maidservant to fetch another. Holden looked down at his own half-eaten portion, unable to stomach another bite. The air was redolent with the scents of roast boar, pungent evergreens, and something else, something that made him seethe with silent rage—the stink of court intrigue.

His wife was embroiled in it now, the little fool, and she hadn't the vaguest notion of what she was doing. She was like a tiny water bug caught in an enormous whirlpool.

Cambria laughed again from across the fire. The sound was as dissonant to his ears as the grating of rusty mail.

At least, he had to concede, she hadn't shamed him by her appearance. She looked absolutely radiant by the waning fire's glow. The imp had stolen one of his own green velvet surcoats, cleverly slipped it over a borrowed kirtle, and girded it with his best silver chain. His wife was resourceful, he had to admit, if somewhat less than scrupulous.

As he peered at her over his cup of ale, she smiled coyly at the king, playfully catching the sleeve of his garment. Holden ground his teeth together and clenched his fists against the urge to grab her and drag her forcibly from the monarch's side.

Guy leaned close to Holden. "She plays with fire, your wife," he murmured.

"Aye."

Holden's fingers threatened to crush his silver goblet. Cambria was indeed playing a dangerous game for one who had never been to court, never encountered the intrigues and nuances of political conversation. The meddling wench thought to manipulate Edward with flirtation, to move him to empathy for the Scots. She had no idea what she was doing.

Of course, Edward lapped up the attention she paid him. He even appeared to consider her so carefully couched suggestions. But Holden knew Edward. Once the king's mind was made up, nothing would cause him to swerve from his purpose.

"What will you do?" Guy muttered.

Holden bit the inside of his cheek. He didn't have an answer.

Guy took a large swig of ale, then set his cup down with a decisive thump. "She'll brand herself a conspirator against the Crown," he grumbled, "and take the house of de Ware down with her."

Holden nodded. Those had been his exact thoughts. He finished off his own ale in a single gulp and rose to approach the king. If he couldn't silence his meddling wife, then he'd just have to remove her.

He greeted Edward with a bow and his most charming smile. "Majesty, your hospitality has been most warm and welcome. But I fear my old warrior's bones grow weary. By your leave, I would take my lady and retire for the evening."

Cambria stiffened as he dug his fingers pointedly into her shoulder.

Edward pouted. "Would you take the spark from our fire, then?" he asked, pretending offense.

"I fear it is so, Majesty," he glibly replied, "for the fires at home need tending."

Cambria bristled frostily at his frank remark, but held her tongue. She was clever enough not to taint the progress she believed she'd made with the king by a display of temper.

Edward smiled winningly. "Well, my dear, your Wolf awaits impatiently. Take care he does not devour you."

The folk around the dying embers chuckled politely at the king's wit. Cambria coyly lowered her eyes as she rose and curtseyed to Edward. But when she turned toward Holden, a hundred unspoken threats smoldered in her eyes.

The tension was like a stifled scream as they walked in stony silence through the shifting shadows of the firelit pines. He guided her with an iron fist around her elbow. She railed against the contact, but at least she was wise enough not to raise her voice while they were yet in hearing range.

Then he pushed her through the opening of his pavilion. She sputtered as the material flapped about her face, and as soon as he released her arm, she spun around, facing him with all the fight of a spitting kitten.

"What do you mean by this?" she demanded, placing her hands squarely on her hips.

"What do *I* . . ." he began incredulously. "Madam, you have played your last game of intrigue."

"Intrigue? I befriend *your* king, and you call it intrigue?"

"You are a novice," he told her, his voice dripping with scorn. "Your ploys are so transparent, I wonder that the king didn't tire of them sooner."

Her lips formed a silent, mortified "oh."

"You will return to Blackhaugh on the morrow," he informed her, dipping his hands into the basin of water by the entrance.

"You cannot command me—"

"I can and I do!" he thundered, his anger descending like a storm cloud over a valley. "Pack what you like this eve, for you leave at first light."

"Nay. I have influence over the king. . . ."

"The only influence you have over the king, my lady, is concerning his opinion about the loyalty of de Ware!" His voice had risen to a shout, but he'd effectively silenced her. He continued in controlled tones, drying his hands on a linen towel. "Now, pack your things, and do not think to defy me in this. I will not allow you to put the name of de Ware at risk. My king and my country are foremost in my heart."

He felt a twinge of guilt at that confession. It was not at all true. As any wise lord, he put his family and vassals foremost, knowing that king and country often bent under the thumb of ridicule and public opinion. He naturally played the game of confidant, but a part of him was always guarded, ready to set sail with the change of the political winds.

Wedding Cambria, Holden had assumed responsibility for her and her clan as well—they were now part of his circle of protection—but, damn the wench, she was jeopardizing his ability to provide that protection. If she proved dangerous to the fragile threads of the de Ware reputation, she endangered his family and her own. Mayhap if he tried to explain . . .

Curse her willfulness, he decided. He owed her no explanation for his actions. He was her lord and master. On the morrow, he'd send her away with two of his best men, and that would be that.

"I suggest you be about your labors," he said coolly, undressing and stretching himself out across the pallet, "then get what rest you can."

Despite his properly admonished wife's pacing and flouncing and the hurling of her possessions into a pile, it wasn't long before he was taking in the deep, relieved breaths of slumber.

Cambria slammed her boots onto the floor in rage. How dare he dismiss her so easily! So king and country came first to him, did they? Well, two could play at that game, and she planned to let him know in no uncertain terms that for her, her clan came first. In fact, with the great responsibilities her clan entailed, she doubted she would have much time, if any, left over for wifely duties once he returned to Blackhaugh.

Raising her chin defiantly, she shuffled out of her kirtle and under the covers, facing the future with new determination. She was careful not to let any part of her body touch the Englishman's as they slept side by side through the longest night she'd ever endured.

The sun had no mercy on Cambria's gritty eyes. She blinked them several times as she plodded along on the palfrey, but they still stung from lack of sleep and the dirt of the road.

One knight rode before her, one behind, and from their silence, she could tell they resented being sent upon this nursemaid's mission.

Sir Guy led the way, still wallowing in the shame of having lost Sir Owen. He likely felt suitably punished, riding solemnly before her, wearing his duty like an ascetic's hair shirt. Close behind her was Sir Myles, as sullen as a summer squall. This had been his first campaign. She'd doubtless ruined it, forcing him to abandon his place of glory to accompany her home.

Needless to say, there was little conversation between the three as they rode down the dusty road, which suited Cambria perfectly. She had no desire to defend her actions, actions she felt were completely justified.

She was glad she'd spoken with the king. 'Twas important that she convey the thoughts of her people to this English monarch. In that, she felt she'd succeeded.

She couldn't have been further from the truth.

Even as she rode proudly off across the countryside, Holden was attempting to repair the damage she had done. He smiled as winningly as he could at Edward, considering the embarrassing circumstances.

"She *is* outspoken, Majesty," he agreed, trying to appear casual as he sipped his morning wine, "but I assure you, she merely wags her tongue about fanciful notions, as a woman will, and calls them fact."

The king nodded, but didn't look entirely convinced.

Holden hated lying to him. In sooth, he believed nothing of the sort. Cambria's opinions were as valid as any. It was true that for the Scots, putting Balliol on the throne was an abomination. But telling Edward so would profit nothing. And now he had to persuade the king that such notions were simply idle chatter on her part.

"She battled with the sword forthrightly enough," Edward challenged, his eyes never leaving his own goblet.

"She has some background in warfare," he countered, "but I fear her father was neglectful of her studies in diplomacy and courtesy."

Edward pursed his lips thoughtfully. "I trust, then, you will endeavor to educate her in the subtleties of court behavior, the dangers of wagging tongues, and so forth?"

Holden restrained a sigh of relief. "Aye, Majesty. Already I've sent her home, and she no doubt stings from that rebuff."

A smile teased the corners of Edward's lip. "No doubt." He stood and turned to go, then caught himself. "Have you found the traitor yet, de Ware?"

"Not yet," Holden answered tightly. "We think he may have joined the Scots rebels."

"Hmm, slippery eel." The king's eyes glittered with a trace of mockery. "Do you need . . . help, Wolf? I can lend you some of my men if you . . ."

Holden straightened. "Nay, Majesty."

"Well, when you do find him, bring him to me, will you?"

He drained the last of his cup. " 'Tis always best to make an example of traitors." Bitter pain flickered briefly in Edward's eyes, and Holden wondered if the king was remembering Roger Mortimer, his mother's lover, whom he'd executed but a few years past for treason.

"Aye, Majesty." He inclined his head in farewell as the king prepared to leave.

"By the way, I'm glad 'tis you who will tame the Scots wench," the king said over his shoulder, surprising him. "She's a spirited mare. You'll calm her spirit without breaking it. Good luck, de Ware."

Holden looked after the king in wonder. Sometimes His Majesty could be too all-knowing. Then again, hadn't Edward just said he was pleased that Holden would be the one to . . . *tame* her? He barked once in laughter at that thought. Edward was mistaken there. Cambria Gavin would never be tamed.

For three days following Edward's departure, Holden's men maintained a watch over the land in the event renegade Scots again made attempts to challenge the English occupation. For Holden, time dragged its feet as it did for a boy hauled to Mass. He was bored by the inactivity, curiously restless. And his relentless pacing through the camp annoyed his fellow knights, who claimed they knew the name of his torment better than he did.

It was her, he finally admitted. It was that stubborn, soft, raging, gentle, reckless, beautiful Scots witch. And he was little better than a yoked ox wearing a rut around a mill wheel as he lumbered helplessly around her memory. She antagonized him, certainly, drove him half-mad with her intrigues and insults. But he'd begun to grow accustomed to this new field of battle. His mind was primed for the fight. He missed her, his little warrior, and although the thought was selfish, he began to regret sending Cambria away.

It was while he was idly grooming Ariel, dreaming in too vivid detail of his return to his wife's side, that a young messenger arrived, agitated and out of breath.

"My lord, " the boy gasped.

Holden turned. The message in the lad's eyes was unmistakable. For a moment, his heart stopped. Every sense was suddenly as keen as a new-honed knife.

"Cambria," Holden breathed.

It was a statement, not a question, and the messenger looked puzzled for a moment. "Aye, my lord. How did you know . . . ?"

Dread stabbed its icy blade into Holden's chest, twisting mercilessly at his heart.

"She is with Sir Owen, my lord," the boy told him, "at Blackhaugh."

"Owen is at Blackhaugh?"

"He's taken the castle. He said I was to tell you . . ."

Holden heard nothing else. Dear God, he had sent his wife into the arms of the enemy,

"My lord?" The boy was looking up at him expectantly.

Instantly, Holden clenched his jaw, and he became a cold-blooded warrior. His eyes grew alert, resolute, and as dispassionate as the wolf's on the hunt.

The messenger drew back a pace and made the sign of the cross. Holden armed himself, filled a satchel with meager provisions, and mounted his stamping charger. Then, leaving instructions with his men to follow as soon as they could, he rode off in a spray of dirt and pebbles that sounded eerily like the rattling of dry bones in a grave.

15

A FAINT BREEZE BLEW IN THE WINDOW OF BLACKHAUGH'S
tower, lifting tendrils of Cambria's hair about her battered face. Bracing her back against the rough stone, she shivered in her torn shift despite the warmth of the day. She cursed herself for the stubborn pride that kept her from eating the food Owen brought, pride that had gained her naught but weakened muscles.

Not that strength would serve her much. Her hands were bound in iron above her head, and all of her attempts to free herself had earned her only pain each time the shackles bit into her injured wrists. Long ago she'd given up trying to work the heavy ring over her head loose from the wall. Her arms were gloved in blood from the effort.

She wondered what game Owen played and what in God's name was happening beyond the tower walls.

Without preamble, the door of the chamber flew open, banging back against the wall. Owen entered briskly, his unkempt hair hanging down over his eyes like a frayed tapestry, and limped past her to the window. Peering below, his face was transformed by an ugly grin, and he rubbed his hands together like a hungry fly. Cambria could only muse at the source of his glee.

With the blissful sigh of a lizard spotting a bug, Owen approached her. Almost lovingly, he caressed her cheek. She could feel her flesh crawl. The shackles pinning her wrists to the wall afforded her no room to strike him, and he'd bound her legs with heavy chains after she'd landed a healthy kick to his belly. Still she managed to whip her head around in time to bite into the meaty part of his palm, hard enough to draw blood.

He yelped in pain and drew back his mangled hand. With the back of his other fist, he cracked her hard across the cheek, splintering her vision in an explosion of sparks. She slumped weakly against the wall, stifling a moan.

It wasn't the first bruise she'd earned since her unfortunate arrival at Blackhaugh. Curse her luck, she'd walked straight into a trap. The shame of it was almost worse than the beating she'd endured at Owen's hands.

They'd all been waiting for her—Robbie, Graham, Jamie, the remnants of the Gavin rebels—and they'd already imprisoned her loyal clansmen. God only knew what they'd done with Garth.

It had taken six men to subdue and haul Guy and Myles off to the dungeon while Cambria awaited her fate.

Angry and foolhardy, she'd spit on Owen, showing no fear of the bastard, despite Robbie's anxious warnings. And both she and the Gavin rebels had paid for her audacity. With a dagger at their laird's throat, Robbie and his men, still Gavins at heart, had no choice but to surrender to Owen's will. He'd locked them all up and carted her off to the tower.

By the time the brute tired of using his fists, there wasn't an inch of her that didn't ache. The taste of blood was still heavy in her mouth.

But she hadn't surrendered. Even now, half-conscious, her belly empty and fresh blood trickling down her cheek, she would not cower before him as he wished.

Owen sucked at his wounded hand and spit the salty blood onto the rushes. He'd had almost all he could bear of Lady Cambria de Ware and her unflappable insolence. She was surely the offspring of the devil and a she-cat, with her raking claws and dagger-sharp teeth. It was hard to believe at one time he'd wanted to poke his piece in her. He thought less often of bedding her now, prickly as she was, and more of torturing the Wolf with her slow murder. If he couldn't bring the bitch to her knees, he would at least see de Ware humbled before him.

With a decisive grunt, he reached for an urn of water on the table. He flung its contents at the wench to jar her from her stupor.

Cambria sucked in a startled breath as the water slapped her face. She sniffled and choked as it burned high inside her nose, making her eyes tear.

"Wake up, wench!" Owen snarled from above her, a peculiar grimace of both loathing and arousal on his face. "Your lord husband has arrived."

Cambria came fully alert at his words. Holden! Relief and dread warred within her, churning her stomach. Had he come alone? Would he fall into the same trap she had? She had to warn him. She opened her mouth to scream, but her cry ended in a gurgle when Owen's strangling fingers closed about her throat.

His breath reeked of onions. "Scream," he hissed, "and I'll slay every one of your clan—men, women, and children."

Dark spots floated before her eyes before he released her. She slumped against the stones, gasping for air.

Not that, she thought, anything but that. He could take Blackhaugh. He could beat her into oblivion. But to touch her clan . . . Fear became a waking nightmare, worse than any to ever invade her slumber. She saw them in her mind's eye, her ancestors, her family, thousands of Gavins—men, women, and children, specters cursed and wandering the earth for all eternity, blaming her with their ghostly eyes, moaning her name.

She couldn't let it come to pass, couldn't let this monster destroy the Gavins. She was her father's daughter. She was the laird. She had to protect her clan.

Even if to remain silent was to betray her husband.

"Cooperate," Owen mused, "and mayhap I'll spare your life, take you on as my own personal servant."

Owen glanced down at her and clucked his tongue. He doubted that. The wench was a mess, a dripping, bruised, swollen-faced, tangle-haired mess. Still, that didn't stop his ballocks from bulging in his trews at the idea of swiving her before the high and mighty Holden de Ware, just for spite.

He exhaled a contented breath. Fate had smiled on Owen the Bastard at last. The wench's timely arrival at Blackhaugh couldn't have been more perfect if it had been served up on a gold platter. She'd been practically alone, the Wolf nowhere in sight. She'd ridden through the front gates and straight into Owen's hands.

Now she was about to become the perfect hostage.

"Come, let us greet your noble hero, shall we?" he sneered. He picked up the shackle key from the table, swinging it tauntingly before her. "I'll loose you now, but there will be a dagger at your throat," he cautioned. "I suggest you move with care. I'd hate to damage the Wolf's precious bitch . . . too soon."

Snickering, he carefully freed her from the wall ring, leaving her hands in the shackles. With the blade pressed close against her throat, he prodded her up, and she shuffled awkwardly over to the window.

Cambria peered down anxiously, faint with hunger, fainter at the sight of her husband, who looked to her like a bright angel with the sun sparkling on his chain mail and flashing off of the helm in the crook of his arm. Now that he was here, all the horrors of the past days knotted in her throat, threatening to burst forth in sobs of relief.

But she couldn't afford to give rein to her emotions. She had to think.

He had come, not alone, but with a vast company of his knights. He intended to do battle then. Cambria bit her lip. If he brazenly assailed the keep, the Wolf might indeed ride victorious into Blackhaugh, but only to find that Owen had killed all of its inhabitants.

She had to keep him from attacking, but how?

Holden clenched his fists in the reins, and Ariel tossed her mane in protest. He immediately tugged the horse's head back around, fighting to restrain himself, too, as he beheld Cambria in Owen's clutches at the tower window.

Her face was discolored with bruises. Blood stained her cheek and arms. Heavy chains crossed her body.

His heart plunged to the depths of his gut. Beside him, his men gasped in outrage. It was only by great dint of will that he controlled a trembling of fury and bloodlust.

"De Ware," Owen called out, "my thanks for the use of your wife. She's proved a welcome . . . amusement."

Holden kept his face a mask of grim control as he stared at the bastard, whom he now despised with all his soul.

"In sooth," Owen taunted, "I may just have to keep her to warm my bed."

Holden stilled his eager mount. By Christ, if that fiend had bedded Cambria, he'd string the devil up by his ballocks.

"What do you want, Fitzroi?" he said, amazed at the levelness of his voice.

"Oh, I already have what I want," he sneered. Then the churl reached brazenly across Cambria's shoulder and thrust a hand into the top of her shift, fondling her breast.

Holden heard the soft curses of his men about him, but he only set his teeth, silently swearing he would chop that insolent hand off before the sun set. Ariel stomped at the sod, expressing the rage Holden felt.

Then Cambria locked gazes with him, and the anger froze in his veins. Any other woman would have turned away in shame at what Owen forced her to bear, but his Cambria stood bravely, unflinching, the same way Holden had, taking that beating long ago for killing the hound. Her eyes communicated what she could not—that her will was strong, that while Owen touched her body, he did not touch her spirit, and that she would endure anything, *anything* for her clan. And in that moment, while the Scots breeze snarled his courageous wife's hair and the sun shone down on her like an angel's blessing, a clot of tears choked him, and he knew *he* would endure anything for *her*.

She sent him a message then, not with words, not with gestures. He was too far from her for any kind of real exchange. But somehow she spoke to him. *Let Owen do to me what he will,* she said, *but save my clan.*

He nodded infinitesimally. He understood her silent plea.

But he did not intend to surrender Cambria, no matter what she expected. He intended to save them all.

He tore his gaze away. If he wanted to rescue his bride, he'd have to take desperate action soon. Wheeling Ariel about, he conferred with his men.

"We have to assume that Garth, Guy, and Miles are either imprisoned or dead." The thought shook him to the core. He couldn't afford to dwell on it. "I'm certain the same is true of the rebel Gavins. Surely none of them would stand for such . . . degradation of their laird."

Stephen reined forward. "Can he be reasoned with? The king knows of his perfidy now. His life is already forfeit. Perhaps he will surrender."

"Nay!" Holden said, more harshly than he intended. "Nay, there's no telling what the traitor will do. He might seek vengeance, slaughter whoever remains inside the castle walls. Or he might panic, flee with . . . a hostage."

Though no one voiced it, every man knew who that hostage would be.

"Do we lay siege then, my lord?" Stephen asked.

"And starve our own people?" Holden shook his head. A siege would take far too long anyway. He didn't want Owen alive one more day. "Nay, I'll nibble at his bait, see what he intends."

'Twas wiser to stalk Owen with stealth, to let him believe he had the Wolf on a short leash. But first, he had to get Cambria out of danger. He turned Ariel about and faced his foe.

"Fitzroi!" he called out. "If the wench has bedded you, then she's spoiled goods." Even at this distance, he could see Cambria flinch. God, he hated to hurt her, but it was the only way. "She's served her purpose already. You can keep the whore."

To Holden's relief, his loyal men remained stolid on their mounts. They knew their lord well, that he would never speak ill of a woman. They recognized his words for what they were—a blatant piece of deception.

Owen, however, sputtered in surprise. He'd obviously expected jealous rage, not dismissal. His hand jerked ever so slightly with the knife, nicking Cambria's throat. Holden's heart leaped into his mouth.

But Cambria didn't wince from the cut. She stared woodenly, as if the knife prick was nothing atop the deep wound Holden had just dealt her. Lord, he had to get her away from that monster.

"What have you done with my men?" he bellowed. "Garth, Sir Guy, and Myles?"

Owen snatched up the suggestion as eagerly as a child after sweetmeats. "Your men? If you would see them alive again, de Ware," he said, shoving his now useless prisoner aside, "there is a demand I would make of you."

Holden breathed an invisible sigh of relief as Cambria slipped from Owen's grasp like a too-small mouse through a hawk's talons.

"Make it," he commanded Owen.

"By rights, Blackhaugh should have belonged to my brother, God rest his soul. I am the next in line. The keep is rightfully mine. Surrender it," Owen dared him.

Holden smirked elaborately. Sarcasm dripped from his lips. "Anything else?"

Owen trembled with anger, and spittle flew out of his mouth as he spoke. "Do not mock me! I have allies here! Give me Blackhaugh willingly, or I shall inform the king that your wife is a murderess, that she has royal blood on her hands."

Holden sucked in a quick breath. Could Owen make Edward believe that? Logic told him nay. After all, the de Wares had been loyal vassals to the king for generations. But if Edward suspected Holden's judgment was clouded by love . . . God's bones. Myles and Guy, Cambria's sole defense, the only witnesses to what truly happened at the inn, might already be dead. Without them, there was no proof she *hadn't* slain Edward's uncle.

Holden shuddered. Edward was unbending when it came to matters of justice. He'd arranged the execution of his mother's beloved Roger Mortimer easily enough. If the king believed Owen, he wouldn't hesitate to exact as harsh a judgment against Cambria.

He couldn't let that happen. No matter that he'd promised to deliver the traitor to Edward, he couldn't give Owen the chance to bend the king's ear. Nay, he'd see the bastard dead before the sun kissed the horizon.

Somehow he had to goad Owen into fighting. And to do that, he must gull the churl into thinking he had half a chance of winning.

With a cluck to Ariel, he began to rein her back and forth in a clear display of anger.

"You would turn against the very household that fostered you?"

"I have no great affection for the house of de Ware!" Owen shouted. "Your father only took me in because I was Roger's brother!"

Holden threw his helm to the ground in pretended frustration.

Owen seemed satisfied by this response and began to grow smug. "You still have Bowden Castle, de Ware," he sang out. "Be content with that."

"I will not let what is rightfully mine be taken from me!" Holden thundered, raising his fist to the sky.

Owen chortled. "This keep is not rightfully yours!"

Holden punched his fist into his palm. He didn't want to lay siege, and he wouldn't pitch an outright battle against his own vassals. But if he could needle Owen into waging war with champions . . .

"If I lay siege, you won't last a month. There are not enough stores in Blackhaugh." 'Twas a lie, but he gambled that Owen had neglected to check the castle's provisions. "Let us choose champions to battle for possession of the keep. A fight to the death."

Holden knew his foe was not stupid. Owen would never send a single champion against a man of Holden's reputation. But if the odds were evened, if he tempted Owen with the possibility of conquering the unconquerable Wolf . . .

"The Wolf of de Ware," he said, "against ten of your best men!"

•   •   •

Owen scratched at his beard, mulling over Holden's words. Damn! He wished he had ten knights. He would have liked to see the Wolf's thus far undefeated face ground into the dust. Besides, earning the reputation as the man who'd conquered England's greatest warrior would be as effective a defense as an extra curtain wall around the castle. But, sadly, he didn't have even one ally left to do battle.

Still, if what Holden said about Blackhaugh's stores was true, he had to take a more timely course of action. He no longer had the resources or the constitution to endure a long siege. His leg was worsening. For days he'd denied it, but already he suffered bouts of fever. If he didn't get to a physician, it wouldn't be long before he succumbed to complete delirium.

He spat on the sill in disgust, sick with the irony that, though he held Blackhaugh and all its inhabitants hostage, he was still powerless against the Wolf.

Then, in a dark corner of his brain, a single thought crawled forth like a glistening pink worm from beneath moldy mulch, a notion so delectably twisted, so diabolically clever that he nearly choked on his glee.

"All right, de Ware," he called down. "I accept your challenge. Prepare to meet your end."

Holden didn't have time to wonder at Owen's ready agreement. The knave spun quickly away from the window, disappearing from sight. Then a shriek echoed from within the tower.

Cambria.

Holden felt her scream like a blade drawn swiftly across his heart. Holy Mother, if that pox-ridden swine had hurt her . . . His throat closed painfully. God, he couldn't bear the thought of losing Cambria.

He loved her.

Damn his soul, in his entire life he'd never been able to say those words before. He'd scarcely admitted, even to himself, that the feeling existed. He'd lusted after women, and he'd adored them from afar. But now he knew. Now he realized, with an almost physical ache, that he loved the Scots wench, loved her beyond reason, beyond understanding, and more than life itself. The king be damned, his country be damned, if he came through this and was able to hold her in his arms again, he would tell her he loved her until she grew sick from the hearing of it.

He'd believed he possessed Cambria. She was his vassal, after all, to command as he did his knights. He was the lord of Blackhaugh, and her world should rightly center on serving him.

But that was not the truth of it at all. His lip curled in irony as he dismounted to retrieve his helm. *His* world was the one turned all awry. Cambria could lead him a chase, pricking him like an irremovable thorn and attacking him with the most irreverent tirades, and yet he never felt more alive than when she was working her wiles on him, grappling with him over the Scots' cause, challenging him with her dagger-sharp wit, taunting him with her glorious woman's body.

The past few days had been pure hell without her. Lord, merely gazing upon her made his heart quicken in his breast. Every turn of her head, every spark in her eye, each gesture that was unique to her captivated him. Nay, he admitted, clutching his helm beneath his arm, he was no lord and master to Cambria Gavin. He was the willing prisoner of her heart.

And, by God's grace, when he had pummeled Owen's men into the dust, he'd sweep her into his arms, surrender the key to his soul, and hold on to her forever.

The cruel syllables echoed over and over in the empty shell of Cambria's heart—*spoiled goods . . . keep the whore . . .*

He couldn't have meant it, not the man who'd melted her with a kiss, who'd chased away her nightmares in his arms, who'd vowed before God to keep her and honor her. Yet his heartless words bruised her far worse than any blows from Owen's fists.

Had she mistaken their silent exchange? She'd sworn in that one moment when they locked gazes that they'd understood one another, that together, somehow, some way, they would overthrow Owen.

Perhaps she'd been wrong. He'd been so angry with her the last time they spoke. Perhaps the Wolf *had* only used her to gain control of Blackhaugh. Perhaps she *had* "served her purpose." It was too awful, too painful to consider.

Besides, a greater challenge awaited her.

Owen had unlocked her shackles and cast her chains to the floor, replacing them with a coat of mail, gauntlets, and a surcoat.

Half-hysterical laughter threatened to issue from her mouth as she realized Owen's intent, but in the next heartbeat, the brute stifled it with a wad of cloth stuffed between her lips. Her eyes watered as he shoved the rag deep into her mouth, making her gag. Then he tied it in place with a strip of linen, pulling it so tight that she imagined her lips would crack. Over it all, he plunged a heavy steel helm, and Cambria battled panic as she strove to breathe in the suffocating bascinet.

From the shade of the dovecote, Katie watched, her chin a-tremble, as the bastard Englishman dragged Cambria to the middle of the courtyard. The old servant chewed on her fist to stop the foolish tears that would do the girl no good, fighting back the urge to rush to her mistress's aid. She hadn't laid eyes on Cambria since the lass's untimely arrival, but by the girl's staggering gait and the droop of her shoulders, Katie knew she'd been mistreated.

It vexed her to be so free, yet so helpless. Aye, Owen had given the women run of the keep, but he'd threatened to slay Cambria if any of them left. The bastard needed their service, and he knew they were powerless against him since he held their laird. Katie had made frequent visits to Malcolm below, but likewise, he'd told her that even if the servants were able to steal the dungeon keys from Owen, which was impossible, since he slept locked in the tower, there was naught any of them dared do while he held the laird.

And now the monster was sending the poor lass out to battle her husband, the Wolf, who would likely cut her down in the wink of an eye before he even knew who it was he attacked.

Katie couldn't bear it. She'd already witnessed the deaths of Cambria's mother and father. She could not stand idly by while Owen destroyed what little was left of the Gavin clan.

As Owen tried to maneuver the unwieldy destrier in the midst of the courtyard, the sun caught on the dull iron ring of castle keys dangling from his belt by a leather thong. They jangled against his thigh, taunting her. She gnawed at her lip. If she could only get to them, somehow cut that tie . . .

Her heart fluttering against her ribs like a sparrow trapped in pavilion walls, she stepped from hiding and crossed determinedly to where Owen battled to control the nervous steed.

Sweat beaded the man's brow, and his face bore a deathly pallor. He reeked of the infection in his leg and the wine he constantly consumed to dull its ache. He was not long for this world, and with a vengeance that surely damned her soul, Katie wished the man would die on the spot. But he only limped forward, jerking hard on the horse's lead.

She came up behind him, her heart pounding so fiercely she feared he might hear it. Biting her lip to stop its quivering, she slipped an embroidery needle from her pouch. Before she had time to regret her actions, she jammed it hard into the steed's flank.

The horse screamed, rearing in protest, and Katie was nearly trampled. In the confusion, Owen staggered back with a curse. Swiftly, before he could regain his presence of mind, Katie drew her eating dagger and sliced forward.

The knife grazed his side, scarcely breaking the skin, and he snarled more in fury than pain. But he wheeled on her with eyes as black as the devil's. The last thing she remembered was the crack of his fist exploding against her chin and splinters of light like a chapel window bursting in her face.

Cambria's eyes flooded with tears of anguish and rage. Her poor beloved Katie. The old maid lay still as death on the sward, her russet skirts sprawled on the ground like a withered rose.

Owen grabbed Cambria's arm, and she tried to wrench away, wanting nothing more than to beat him to a bloody pulp. But she knew she hadn't the strength to finish him off, and she couldn't afford to rile him. He'd only take his anger out on her clan anyway, as he'd already done with Katie.

So she cast one last despondent look at the servant who had raised her, the dear woman who had sacrificed herself for the laird.

Then a dark glimmer within the folds of Katie's skirt caught her eye. Cradled in the servant's still palm were the castle keys.

"Mount!" Owen growled.

Hope pierced her bleak despair like a slender blade of sunshine. But there was no time now, no chance to take advantage of her discovery. She wasn't even sure if Katie lived or died.

"Mount!"

Cambria swallowed the impulse to stand her ground and did as she was told. The sooner she was out of the keep, the sooner her clan would be safe. Still, her limbs felt leaden as she climbed into the saddle, albeit more from the burden of duty than from the weight of the armor plate Owen had forced her to wear.

Owen seized the reins of the destrier so she couldn't possibly spur the horse to trample him. Then he issued a dire threat.

"If you reveal yourself to de Ware or make any attempt to avoid this battle, do not doubt that I will take yon torch and light the dungeon on fire. You'll hear your clansmen scream your name in agony as they burn alive."

Her heart tolling like a burial bell, Cambria rode slowly toward the front gate. 'Twas likely she rode to her death. Holden would never guess it was her. He'd probably slay her in a few calculated strokes, never suspecting until he tore the helm away and beheld her sightless eyes that Owen had sent his own wife to fight him.

But fight him she would, for her clan's sake. She was a laird now, she thought, lifting her chin. Her life belonged to the Gavins. If she didn't do everything in her power to protect them, then she was as worthless as an arrow with no point. Nay, she would die for them if need be. She only prayed that if Holden killed her, the Gavins would forgive

him, and that he would stay to protect the clan, no matter
how easily he could toss her aside.

At the very least, she consoled herself, 'twas a noble way
to die—in the defense of the Gavins. Holden would slay her,
and Blackhaugh would revert to his hands, his and the clan
who had grown to respect him—Malcolm and Katie and . . .

She sniffed back the tears that threatened to undermine
her control and kicked once at the destrier. It was best this
way, she decided, swift and with honor.

Slowly, Owen cranked the outer gates open. The hinges
creaked heavily on the tense and silent air. Cambria tossed
her head and sat erect. She would fight proudly for the
Gavin. Her father would smile down on her from heaven.
Taking a deep breath through quivering nostrils, she let her
steed canter down the incline to her waiting husband.

Holden wasn't deceived for an instant. He knew from the size
and the carriage of the knight exactly who it was. What
bloody trickery was this? Did Owen truly imagine he
wouldn't know his own wife?

The men around him began to converse in curious whis-
pers as she approached. When she was but twenty feet distant, they fell silent. Their scowls clearly showed they
disapproved of the disparity in size between him and the unknown warrior.

Owen had returned to the tower window, and Holden
saluted the knight for his benefit. "Hola!"

Cambria made no answer. Holden frowned. So she didn't
wish to be known. Why? Was it possible she'd taken his
reckless words to heart? Did she believe she'd been used?
Had she come willingly to do battle with him? Nay, it could
not be. Surely she'd not champion a monster such as Owen.

"Have you made your peace with God, sirrah?" he said
loudly, buying time so he could nudge Ariel closer to her
dappled steed.

Her nod was barely discernible.

"In the name of sweet Christ," he murmured just loudly
enough for her to hear, "I swear to you I meant none of
the . . ."

"Get on with it!" Owen yelled, waving a flaming brand menacingly from the tower window.

Cambria suddenly reined her mount back in panic, trying to maintain distance between them. Clearly she intended to avoid discourse with him at all costs. Mayhap Owen had threatened her then. Her or her clan.

He cursed softly, wishing he could look her in the eye and know the truth of her silence.

It appeared battle was unavoidable. He took his time, covering his head with his helm and tugging on his gauntlets. He cast a glance at his weapons. He wouldn't use the lance—Cambria had little skill with it. Better to use arms for close combat.

"Swords?" he suggested, as Ariel pawed at the ground and tossed her head impatiently.

Cambria nodded ever so slightly, then dismounted, catching at the stirrup for balance as her legs tried to buckle beneath her.

He climbed down from his steed, playing for time to think—bending to adjust a rivet here, examining the surface of his shield. All the while, Cambria stood absolutely still, one mailed hand resting on the pommel of her sheathed sword.

He flexed his sword arm, thinking.

Of course. 'Twas a ruse Owen played, sending Cambria out as his champion. The bastard knew Holden would easily dispatch her, then be devastated by the act he'd committed. Murdering his wife would ruin Holden in the eyes of the Gavin clan, as well as destroy his de Ware reputation. Then, while Holden wallowed in shame, Owen could perpetrate a more permanent claim to Blackhaugh.

If such were indeed Owen's purpose, it followed then that he had no intention of honoring his word whatsoever. He intended neither to release the captives nor to surrender the castle.

Surely Cambria knew Owen sent her to her death. But perhaps 'twas what she wanted. Perhaps she sacrificed herself to save her clan.

Mother of God, he wished Cambria would speak to him—

a whisper, a curse, anything. He needed to know what was transpiring in that brain of hers.

Unable to stall any longer, he moved forward and slowly unsheathed. The whisper of steel on leather seemed deafening on the pregnant air. Cambria drew forth her own blade, holding it before her with both hands. For a moment, she stood frozen, like a hart held captive in a great wolf's soothing stare before the kill. Then he brought his blade around easily, slowly, to test her response.

Her block was sluggish. As he'd suspected, captivity had made her weak, and this enraged him. How he wished it was Owen before him now. He would cut the savage to ribbons.

Cambria frowned, disgusted by her pathetic block of his blow. Her arm throbbed faintly. The last few days had drained her strength till she was like a doddering newborn foal. Damn it, she had to do better than this. What if, by some miracle, Katie revived to make use of those keys? Cambria had to summon up the strength to fend off Holden, at least long enough to see her clansmen freed. But how could she draw her blade against him when her heart was not in it?

Spoiled goods, she thought. *Keep the whore.* She let his brutal words fuel her power and lashed out at him with awakened fire.

Holden easily dodged the attack, turning her blade gently aside. She was going to tire herself too soon, before he had time to come up with a plan. He had to think quickly.

A small, subtle movement upon the rise of Blackhaugh Castle distracted him for a moment. Perhaps it was his imagination, he thought, and yet . . .

He maneuvered the battle so he could watch over Cambria's head through the narrow slit of his helm. Aye, there had been movement! The great iron-bound gates of the castle were gradually opening.

He batted at Cambria's shoulder with the flat of his blade. Blinking his eyes to make sure he'd seen correctly, he looked again. A thatch of recognizably red hair poked through the crack of the gates. Robbie.

Holden blocked Cambria's sideswipe with his shield. Fury bubbled up in him like boiling oil. So Owen did not intend to even fight chivalrously. He was sending the Gavin rebels out to slaughter him. Did the fool not know the de Ware knights would make minced meat out of the Scots lads? Or was that what he had in mind?

Cambria stumbled forward, and he caught her against his shield so she would not fall. Then he glanced again at the gates. Cambria's maidservant, Katie, widened the breach of the door, and a second, third, and fourth face joined Robbie's. They were unmistakably Garth, Guy, and Myles, looking none the worse for wear. A sudden rush of joy coursed through Holden's veins. Bless the clever Gavins; while Owen was chortling gleefully above, someone had loosed his men.

Holden turned his victorious shout into a counterfeit snarl of rage and pressed his attack in order to distract any onlookers from what was afoot. Winning the hostages back, of course, did not in itself guarantee taking Blackhaugh without bloodshed, and he refused to spill the blood of innocent victims within the castle walls. Nay, he needed to send in a small party of men to help take the keep peacefully while Owen was distracted.

Cambria slashed wildly at his neck, and he deflected the blade. The solution came to him all at once. It called for a great deal of drama and illusion on his part, playacting more suited to his brother Duncan. But such an unexpected twist might effectively draw Owen's attention away. It might allow him to get instructions to his knights.

Cambria's arm flagged again. He had to revive her spirits. His ruse depended upon her strength.

"Cambria," he said softly, "I love you. More than life. But I want you to fight with me now. Fight with me as you've never fought before. Fight for the Gavin, and I swear I'll help you save them."

For a moment she stood stunned. He feared she'd not lift her blade again. Then she seemed to grow light, as if a burden had dropped from her shoulders. With renewed vigor, she lashed out at him like a sudden storm, her blade flashing like lightning as it attempted to strike anywhere it could. She advanced on him for the first time, and he retreated a few paces.

Cambria had prepared herself for Holden's death blow. Scarcely able to gasp enough air in the close helm, her muscles reduced to disobedient jelly, she'd had neither the will nor the power to continue fighting. But when Holden spoke to her, calling her by name, confessing his love, vowing to save her people, sweet hope filled her like a reviving nectar flooding her veins.

Suddenly the words that had seemed so brutal before rang hollow in her ear. Of course. He'd used them as weapons to protect her. She understood that now. His offhand dismissal of her had served to pluck her from Owen's grasp.

Now he wanted her to fight him. Why, she couldn't fathom. But she trusted him. When it came to warfare, she'd never seen a warrior with better instincts.

So she renewed her attack, and for a strange moment, seemed to take the upper hand. He cowered back. Then, in the blink of an eye, he lost his footing on the slick, dew-washed grass. By some horrible accident, he slipped onto her outstretched sword.

The blade severed the mail and slid over his ribs at the side. The sensation made Cambria suddenly nauseous. She couldn't tell how deeply she had cut him, but when she quickly pulled back her blade, it was stained with his blood.

The cut hurt, much more than Holden had anticipated. He let out a cry of pain that was only half-feigned. But then he knew that believability was essential. The sting was a small price to pay for the safety of those he loved. He groaned again in pretended agony, stumbled, and fell heavily. He could hear the astonished squalling from Owen as the bastard's plans were foiled.

Cambria faltered back, shocked. Dear God, what had she done? Surely the turn of an ankle couldn't have upset Holden's keen sense of balance so completely. God's wounds, he had virtually fallen on her sword. The thought made her stomach lurch dangerously. With the exception of

Owen, she'd never seriously wounded anyone, and the sight of a man crashing to the earth by her hand caused her to stumble, dazed. That her victim was her beloved husband made her sink to her knees, unable to tear her eyes away from the sight of Holden's blood smeared on her sword.

He was so still. Surely she could not have slain him—the Wolf of de Ware, who had never been defeated in battle. Yet there he was, horribly silent on the damp ground.

In the next breath, her view of Holden was blocked by his knights, who crowded around him in amazement and concern. Between their bodies, she could catch glimpses of his limp form as someone loosened and removed his helm. He looked groggy and weak, his lips trembling with each breath that rattled between them. Dear God, he must be hurt badly.

Sir Stephen couldn't understand at first what it was Lord Holden was saying as he bent his head close. He drew his brows together into a grim frown.

"Do not harm Owen's champion," Holden repeated tightly. Then, noting Stephen's confusion, he said more distinctly, "Owen's champion—protect Owen's champion."

Stephen wondered greatly at the lord's words. Perhaps Holden was delirious from his wound. He cocked his head to look at Owen's warrior, who knelt motionless on the sod. Then, turning back to Holden, he cradled his lord's head in his arms and bent low to hear the balance of his instructions.

"'Tis but a needle prick," Holden whispered, "but you must let it be believed I am grievously wounded, near death."

Stephen glanced at the slowly widening spot of blood staining Lord Holden's tabard. He prayed the Wolf was right.

"The Gavins have breached the gates from the inside," Holden continued. "Six of you steal into the castle and find Fitzroi. I'll fight until you signal from the parapet." He paused, gasping as a spasm of pain gripped him. "To Owen, I shall seem to lose the battle. Stephen, afterward you must take his champion into the forest, safe, away from the fighting."

Stephen nodded, then helped the fallen lord to his feet, fetched his sword, and replaced his helm. As soon as Holden steadied himself enough to face his adversary, Stephen began to pass a surreptitious message through the ranks, outlining the lord's plans.

Holden took a shuffling step toward Cambria. "Arise, foe!" he called weakly. "I am not yet finished with you."

Cambria felt sick as she slowly got to her feet, as if she had swallowed a great sack of sand. 'Twas not the way it should happen. Once, what seemed like a lifetime ago, she would have been glad of the opportunity to skewer the Wolf and hang him from the highest tower of Blackhaugh, but now she had no stomach for his blood. Marking his flesh with her blade was like cutting out a piece of her own heart. She couldn't do it. She dropped her sword.

"'Tis naught, Cambria," he whispered, "only a scratch I suffer gladly for the Gavin. We are honor bound to fight. We cannot disappoint the bastard."

Though she was sick at heart, she lifted her blade with leaden arms, shuddering as she saw the crimson lacing its edge.

Holden wondered how much longer she could last. He poked at her a few times with his sword and kept his shield low, drawing her hesitant attack further and further afield, until Owen's eye was drawn well away from the main gate.

High above the field, peering down at the scene that was like the unfolding of an unfamiliar play, Owen cackled with merriment. This was even better than he'd anticipated. True, his original plans had been turned awry, but this development was quite provocative. It seemed he would win all around.

By some miracle, Cambria was about to slay her husband. Owen prayed she'd unmask as he was dying, so Lord Holden would go to his grave in eternal shame. If Cambria was victorious, Owen could rightfully claim Blackhaugh. Best of all, he'd still have that ballock-swelling wench to do with as he wished.

The thought made him quiver. Once she was healed of those bruises and properly muzzled, the Scots wench was comely enough to stretch a man's chausses to bursting. Of course, he would have to keep her hidden from Aggie. Christ's wounds, if he liked, he could lock de Ware's bitch away indefinitely to use at his pleasure. He rubbed his groin absently with the thought of such absolute power.

While Owen watched, embroiled in his own fantasies and the curious battle below, beneath his notice, one by one, a half dozen de Ware knights stole off toward the main gate and amassed there.

Cambria swallowed back the bitter bile rising in her throat. Something must be terribly wrong with Holden, she thought. This predicament seemed impossible. For the love of Mary, he was the Wolf of de Ware. No one could defeat him, least of all her. He limped badly, but still he fought, a ribbon of blood trickling down his side. Her arm was jarred by a swipe of his shield, and she labored to steady her blade, but she had no desire to return the blow.

"Just a moment more, Cambria," Holden rasped, leaning heavily on his shield. "Come on. Where's that hot Gavin temper?"

Cambria blinked back the moisture blurring her vision. Her poor husband could scarcely stand.

"Fight me," he insisted. "Fight me for the generations of your clan who warred, sweated, bled for this corner of the earth. Fight me for your father's sake, for the sake of the Gavin."

His words at last stirred her heart. Lifting her chin, she faced him squarely, dredging up her Gavin pride for one last assault.

Sparks shot out from her blade as it met his, and the clang of steel on steel rang on the air like bells tolling a violent Mass. She attacked him with all the might of her wronged ancestors, the blood rising in her like a vengeful sea.

Holden let her come, holding off her vicious onslaught with his shield, until he saw his man wave from the curtain wall. Now he could finish the masquerade.

He launched a final furious attack, his blade flashing like lightning all about Cambria, but never touching her. Then, when he seemed to have gained the upper hand, he let his sword slip from his fingers. It sank in a hopelessly slow arc to the earth.

Too late, Cambria glimpsed the falling blade. There was naught she could do. Her own blow was already struck. There was no way to stop the descent of her sword toward his body. No time to turn the weapon aside.

16

TIME DRAGGED TO A SHRIEKING HALT IN CAMBRIA'S MIND. Her blade seemed almost to caress Holden as it sliced through his hauberk and across his ribs. She stared, aghast, as he slowly staggered back, the front of his armor defiled by a broadening stain of hideous red. He reached up to stanch the flow of blood with a single mailed fist, then stood for an awful, eternal, pained moment before succumbing to the forces of the earth's pull.

When he fell, she relinquished her sword to the earth as if it were some vile snake. She had been prepared to die, but she'd not been prepared to kill. Her heart wrenched painfully, coldly enveloped in a cloud of profound emptiness and silent despair, until a cry broke through the mists.

It was Sir Stephen, bent over his lord in anguish. "Nay!" the knight raged, his fist accusing the very heavens.

Then he turned to her, resting his full gaze, icy and damning, upon the foe who had felled his beloved lord. She never cowered from his regard, bearing her guilt with numb acquiescence. She didn't flinch when his murderous sword pricked at her throat and his steely fist roughly seized her arm. Her spirit was sick, her will to live vanished. Her soul grew cold as the grave and as silent.

And then a horrible sound rose within her steel helm, a soft keening that blossomed into a wail so deeply despondent that all who were near crossed themselves superstitiously. She wondered vaguely who made such an anguished noise, wishing it would stop.

Stephen whipped his head around sharply. That voice! He stared at his captive, trying in vain to see through the shadowed slit of the knight's helm. But even blind, he would have known the voice of a woman. The blood stilled in his veins. Suddenly it was clear to him—who the champion must be and why Holden had given those orders.

Before anyone else could catch on to the deception, he had to stop her wailing. With a grimace of regret, he cuffed her, just hard enough to startle the sound from her. Then he hurried to do his lord's bidding, picking up her sword, leading her away from the field of battle and toward the wood.

From his perch, Owen whined in protest as his Scots prize was abducted under his nose. "Nay!" he shrieked. "You cannot take my . . . my knight!"

"You have the castle!" her captor roared back. "You have won Blackhaugh! The knight is ours!"

"But . . ." Owen began, and then he decided it was no use. He'd been confounded on two counts—de Ware had never discovered his slayer, and now the wench was lost to the both of them. At least, he consoled himself, he'd won Blackhaugh. He also held the hostages, and while Holden de Ware was no longer alive to demand them, someone would pay dearly to see them come to no harm. His mouth watered as he thought about the vast wealth of the de Ware family that had fostered him.

Stephen knew, cleaving to Lady Cambria's side as she stumbled along, that if he didn't guide her, she'd wander aimlessly off, so deep was her despair. He pushed aside saplings crowding the path so the branches wouldn't slap her, though from her eery, detached silence, he doubted she'd even feel them. They waded through the brambles to a stand of maples whose bright-leaved limbs made a thick canopy overhead.

Stephen cast a wary eye behind him to assure himself that no one followed. Then he sheathed his sword and led her gently along the overgrown trail. As they progressed through the densest part of the forest, past groves of massive oaks and ancient conifers, he periodically stopped to bend the branches of the trees into the letter *H,* the discreet mark Stephen and Holden had used since they were children. Holden would find them easily.

At last, they entered a clearing in the wood where an old, diseased pine had toppled amidst a circle of its companions and a little light filtered down through the interwoven branches. He halted Cambria, grasping her shoulders in concern.

"Lady Cambria?" he asked rhetorically.

She gave no response, her arms limp under his fingers. He longed to reassure her—what hell she must be suffering to believe she'd slain her husband—and yet she had willingly engaged in the fight. Besides, it was not for him to conjecture or elaborate upon the succinct instructions Lord Holden had given him. He was to keep her safe and secret, no more. He moved away, kicking in frustration at a tuft of dead moss clinging to the decaying log, then cleared his throat.

"He must love you well," he murmured, watching a trail of ants traverse the worm-eaten bark. "A man would *have* to love a woman to let her wound him thus."

His words appeared to fall on deaf ears. Damn it, something should be done for her. "Do but have faith, my lady," he blurted out, "and all will be set aright, I swear it."

The lady's silence was unnerving. Perhaps if he could see her face, her eyes . . . "You must be sweltering in there," he said with false levity. "Allow me, I pray you."

He tentatively reached forward to take her helm between his palms. His hands trembled oddly, as if they feared what they would discover. Then he grumbled at his own hesitance, and with great care, he loosened the helm, lifting it gingerly from her shoulders.

What he found beneath made his trembling increase, not with fear, but with rage. He flung the helm to the forest floor with a violent oath.

The gentle lady was gagged cruelly, the rag about her mouth so tight that it nearly cut into her cheeks. One eye was purple and swollen, and her brow was split, leaving a crusted trail of blood. Her hair was a hopeless tangle, and sweat trickled in dirty rivulets down her face. She drew in labored, whistling breaths through her quivering nose. Worse than all these atrocities, however, was the vacant stare of her eyes, the emotionless glaze that told him she'd abandoned all hope. He'd seen that look a hundred times on widows' faces.

Tenderly, he loosed the knot in the gag. He swallowed anxiously, anticipating Holden's wrath when he discovered Cambria's injuries, wondering with a shudder what would become of the one who had caused them. For the moment, at least, in the undisturbed peace of the deep wood, he would offer the lady what meager succor was possible.

Owen's triumphant grin grew tight on his face. Something was wrong. He couldn't quite grasp the elusive reason for his sense of discord, but something was very definitely wrong. Why was the courtyard below so quiet? Usually at least a score of maidservants flitted about, tending to the animals, drawing water from the well, preparing food. A stealthy foreboding crept up on him like a storm cloud preparing to loose its burden of bad tidings.

"The keys!" he hissed, patting his thigh where they used to hang, searching his memory, and finally recalling the old woman with the dagger.

He spun so quickly away from the window that he tripped over the pile of Cambria's chains and dropped the fiery brand he'd used to threaten the girl. Before he could move away, the flame of the fallen torch licked at the hem of his surcoat, finding nourishment.

He had no time for this, he thought absurdly, batting at the fabric. But his motions only fanned the flame. The material smoked and curled, singed black by its fiery predator. He slapped frantically at the smoldering garment, finally unbuckling his swordbelt and flinging the tabard off over his head, hurling it into the corner where it continued to happily devour itself.

Owen ran a shaky hand over his face. He had to think. The prisoners ran loose within the walls. He knew that now. The brief, sweet victory he'd enjoyed curdled on his tongue. He should have slain them all when he had the chance. The Gavins were probably marshaling their men even now to gain command of the castle. And, he thought, watching the tiny flames lose interest in his surcoat to leap playfully toward the tapestry, they would eventually come for him.

Unless . . .

Holden wasn't about to let his knights go in after Owen alone. He'd given his sweat and blood to win the castle back, and he wanted to see Owen's miserable face when Lord Holden de Ware rose as if from the dead to claim Blackhaugh. So, despite his men's protests, he cast off his hauberk, hastily bandaged the worst of his injuries, and limped through the gates to the courtyard under his own power. The servants seemed only too glad to see him, and while the rebel Scots obviously didn't relish allying themselves with the English, Robbie had learned the lesser of evils. Full of remorse, he led Holden to the tower himself.

The situation was still precarious—Holden dared not endanger any hostage Owen might yet have with him. He drew his sword, remaining at the foot of the stairs while two of his men stealthily climbed the spiraling steps, their boots making muffled scrapes on the stones as they ascended.

The door to the tower room was closed, but not bolted. The first knight heaved it open with his shoulder while the other slipped his sword through the opening. But a blast of heat and orange flame sent them staggering back. Thick smoke billowed out around them like a frothing ocean wave.

"Careful!" Holden shouted, afraid Owen had set some diabolical trap.

The men waved the noxious fumes away and squinted through the fire.

"No one's here, my lord!"

"Wait!" coughed the second, pointing. "In the corner. A knight's tabard, burning. It's a bar sinister!"

"And the man?" Holden asked.

The first man peered closer. "It's . . . it would have been . . . Owen, my lord."

Holden scowled. Owen? Burned to death? How?

"Fitting end for the devil," Guy muttered beside him.

The surrounding knights murmured in agreement as the two men retreated swiftly down the stairs. Holden sheathed his sword, baffled. How could Owen be dead? Without a fight? Without a last stand? His demise came too swiftly, too . . . conveniently. Or perhaps, he thought grimly, he was only feeling cheated of his vengeance. He'd wanted to tear the monster limb from limb for what he'd done to Cambria. But whatever his doubts, they'd have to wait. The castle was in danger of incinerating.

"Garth, assemble teams to fight the blaze!" he commanded.

The castle denizens sprang to life under Garth's charge, evacuating the other chambers, moving trunks and livestock and food, fetching water in wooden buckets.

Holden scanned the tower. What he looked for, he wasn't sure. But something unsettled him. All Owen's careful plotting, his narrow escapes, his twisted schemes . . . destroyed in the blink of an eye. By fire. Why fire?

He knew the answer at once. Fire left no footprint, no evidence.

So who had set the blaze?

"God's teeth!"

Ignoring the sharp pain that lanced across his bandaged chest, he wheeled and hobbled through the scurrying servants and soldiers toward the gate as fast as he could.

Just in time. As he rounded the curtain wall, Owen dropped to the ground from a long iron chain suspended from the tower embrasure. The released chain buckled and banged against the stones like a deranged black snake as Owen stumbled forward on his injured leg.

Holden clenched his teeth and unsheathed. "Turn and fight, coward!"

Astounded, Owen staggered. His eyes widened in disbelief. "How . . . ?"

"Draw your weapon!"

Owen gaped on, his jaw loose. "But you should be dead."

"As should you, for what you did to my wife," Holden

replied, steeling his jaw. "I've come to remedy that state of affairs."

Owen's eyes flitted wildly about, weighing the possibility of escape and coming up short.

"Prepare to die," Holden ground out.

Owen nervously licked his lips. "I'm wounded."

"We're both wounded. Draw your blade, and die like a man."

Biting out a foul oath, Owen reluctantly pulled forth his sword and crouched for combat.

Holden was at a disadvantage. He still wore his mail chausses, but his upper body was defenseless, naked but for the blood-soaked bandage. He had to depend wholly on the fact that he was the better swordsman.

Owen circled away, his eyes gleaming maliciously. "She'll never forgive you, you know," he sneered. "Those things you said."

Owen was obviously trying to rattle him. It wouldn't work. Holden advanced, slowly turning his blade in his grip.

"And then where will your precious Scots alliance be?"

The man didn't know what he was talking about. Of course Cambria would forgive him. She was his wife, wasn't she? As for the alliance . . .

Owen struck once, hard, against Holden's injured side. Holden cursed under his breath. He should have seen that one coming.

"You've lost her," Owen continued, creeping like a crab at the verge of Holden's reach, "just like you'll lose Blackhaugh."

Holden slashed forward, slicing Owen's arm, but not as deeply as he wanted to. Owen backed away, wheezing in pain.

"You may kill me," Owen gasped, "but it won't solve anything. She'll never trust you again. The Scots will never trust you. You'll lose the keep, and I'll still win."

Holden didn't believe that for a moment. Cambria knew about the strategies of war. Why he'd done what he'd done. What he'd been forced to say. He wiped his sweaty palm absently across his chest. It came back drenched in scarlet.

God, he was dripping blood again. That last maneuver had torn open the gash.

"And you'll always wonder," Owen said, panting with malevolent cheer, "about the babe."

Holden stumbled. Owen's grinning face began to swim in his vision, doubling, tripling. A soft, soothing, dark cloud flirted at the edges of his sight. Lord, he couldn't faint. Not now.

Desperate, he doubled his left fist, lifting it high. With sheer determination and force, he brought it down, pounding it as hard as he could against his wounded ribs. Pain burst through the fog of unconsciousness, wrenching a groan from him, but bringing him instantly awake.

"You'll never know," Owen taunted, nibbling at Holden's soul like a crow after carrion, "if the child is yours or mine."

Child? What child? What was Owen talking about? He swung his blade about, but Owen danced out of the way.

"You see," Owen continued, huffing now, his eyes mad with his story, "I bedded the bitch."

Holden couldn't blot out the image that sprang to his mind—the repulsive, monstrous Owen sprawled atop Cambria. He slashed out again, but he could feel his strength ebbing. Owen dodged the blow.

"Oh, she wasn't willing. You have *that* right." He swung at Holden's head and missed. "But it's amazing what one can do with the proper restraints."

Holden's mouth twisted into a snarl. Owen had raped Cambria. He began to tremble with rage as he envisioned it: Owen's filthy claws gripping her soft flesh, his foul mouth staining her skin with slavering kisses, his pathetic bird's cock savaging her tender body.

"Oh, aye," Owen crowed, limping out of Holden's reach, "I pumped her quite full of my bastard seed, de Ware."

A growl started low in Holden's throat.

"So you'll wonder yourself several months from now . . ." Owen leered, his eyes yellow with madness. He chopped forward twice, but Holden blocked his blows. "When she spews out that mewling babe . . ."

Holden tightened both hands around the hilt of his sword and hung on to consciousness by pure will.

Owen grinned in ugly triumph. "Whose is it?"

Volcanic wrath boiled up in Holden. All Owen's evil, all his own pain, all Cambria's suffering welled into a fount of fury, enraging and empowering him. He raised his sword high. The reflection of flames from the tower flashed gold along its sharp edge. And then he slashed downward.

The last thing he saw before the dark waters of unconsciousness closed over his eyes was Owen's leering head tumbling from his shoulders.

"Cambria."

Fine hairs rose on the back of Cambria's neck, like the brush of a spider's web. She thought for a moment she'd heard . . . but nay—'twas only the wind soughing through the trees. The sun had shifted the lacy shadows of the forest canopy to the far side of the clearing now, and the kind knight who'd accompanied her here was gone. She shivered once and withdrew again into her silent vigil.

"Cambria."

She froze. 'Twas not the wind then. The air around her suddenly felt charged, and the skin of her back tingled as if she were about to be struck by lightning. She ventured a glance toward the heavens, but the visible patches of sky were unblemished by cloud.

Dear God, she was losing her mind, hearing things. 'Twas the horrible thing she'd done that was making her hear his voice, making her flesh crawl with electric fear.

"Cambria."

Nay, she thought, nay! She must numb herself to what had happened, lock it all away into the darkest alcove of her mind. If she could only stop her ears against the echo of his voice. . . .

"Cambria." The voice was louder this time, closer.

With the wariness of a cat, she straightened slowly, repulsed and yet compelled to seek out the source of her torment. She rose on quaking limbs and turned to face what horrible apparition awaited.

• • •

Holden held his breath. He'd stood behind her a long while after he'd sent Stephen along, trying to piece together the right words, words even the long trek through the forest had done nothing to inspire. How small she'd seemed sitting upon the stump, despair clear in the forlorn slope of her shoulders.

He couldn't expect her trust. He'd given her little reason to trust him. He'd called her whore and cast her aside like offal. He'd even deceived her into believing she'd slain him. He wouldn't blame her if she acted to rectify that deception now with a quick thrust of her sword.

But he had to try.

Now she turned slowly to face him, fear paling her to the color of the moon. When he saw what damage had been done to her, rage rose in him, a rage so black he had to force his eyes away lest he frighten her further with his fury.

God's wounds, he wanted to kill Owen all over again. Her face was riddled with dark bruises, her cheek cut, one eye blackened and swollen. He ground his teeth together. Silently, he cursed fate for cheating him of the pleasure of murdering Owen by slow torture. He squeezed his fists hard until his nails dug into his palms, remaining quiet only by great dint of will.

He glanced up again at the poor girl staring at him, wild-eyed and shivering as with the ague. She was crossing herself, murmuring prayers under her breath. Her action drained the tension from his body.

"Don't be afraid," he told her, taking a step forward.

Cambria felt, beneath the scream of fear rising in her throat, a shout of joy begging for release. She stumbled back against the log.

He frowned. "I won't harm you."

She shook her head in terrified bewilderment. "But I killed you. Your blood is on my s—" She gagged with the sickening memory.

"Nay, I am not dead." He took another step toward her.

She pressed her hands to her head, trying to stop the array of contradictory images streaking through her brain. Holden had to be dead. She'd felt the blade sink into his flesh. She'd seen the blood. She'd suffered the harsh accusation in his men's eyes. He *had* to be dead.

And yet she so longed for him to be alive, to look once more into his stormy eyes, to hear the deep roll of his voice, to touch his warm flesh. Perhaps her desperate mind had conjured his image.

"Cambria, I swear I am as alive as you." He held an upturned hand toward her. "Come. See for yourself."

She narrowed her eyes at his outstretched arm and bit her trembling lip. He was dead. She knew that as surely as she knew her own lineage. Yet he stood before her, speaking to her—half-naked, his chest swathed in bandages—but here, looking as alive as flesh and blood could be. Could a phantom seem so real?

A tiny blossom of hope lifted its head for one moment as she felt herself drawn to his beckoning hand. She'd never slain a man before. Could it be her aim was not so true? That she'd not dealt him a mortal wound? Perhaps, she dared to believe, he *was* alive.

The breath stilled in her breast. A thankful sob welled up inside her. Her nose stung as she fought to control the sea of emotions threatening to drown her. God had had mercy upon her after all. Sweet Jesu, Holden was not dead. She reached out tremulously for him, stretching her fingers out to touch the warm tips of his.

With a soft cry, she lunged forward, dissolving into his embrace. Nothing had ever felt more solid, more real than his fierce arms about her, his warm chest against her cheek, his love wrapped around her heart.

"Your wounds . . . how can you ever forgive . . ." she began before tears choked her.

Her words caught Holden like a boot in the stomach. Forgive her? He prayed she would forgive *him*. He had vowed to protect her, and yet she bore the marks of his failure to do that— one eye swollen almost shut, bruises coloring her cheeks, red abrasions at the sides of . . . He reached out so suddenly for her that it made her flinch. His fingers touched the corner of her mouth. She'd been gagged, he realized, and it all became instantly clear—why she'd gone willingly to battle, why she'd remained silent. A muscle in his cheek began to twitch with anger, and his jaw tightened to rock hardness.

"I *am* sorry," Cambria breathed, misunderstanding his dark looks.

Holden shook his head and, despite the rage at Owen that surged in his blood, he forced his teeth apart in a reassuring grin.

"For these nicks? I've lost more blood shaving. Lady, if the day ever comes that I am defeated, I assure you it will not be at the hands of a runty Scots sprite."

She let the insult go, but his boast gave her pause, and she remembered Stephen's words: *He must love you well to let you wound him thus.* "Are you saying you *let* me wound you?"

He shrugged.

She searched his eyes as if she wondered at his sanity. "Why?"

"To distract Owen. While he was drooling over the sight of his wee Scots champion quelling the Wolf, my men were able to steal into the castle."

"Blackhaugh?"

He grinned. "Is secure."

Cambria felt her heart flutter in her breast. Could it possibly be true? Sweet Lord, she'd not thought to walk the parapet of Blackhaugh again, and now . . . She felt her eyes soften in gratitude. The Wolf had said he would hold the castle for her clan. It appeared he'd already made good on his promise.

Only one black shadow yet hung to mar the glorious triumph.

"What of . . . Owen?" She whispered the question, fearing that uttering his name might summon him.

"Dead." Holden's voice was flat, ominous, final. He left no room for questions, and Cambria wasn't sure she wanted to hear the answers anyway. She nodded, wrapping her arms around herself as if to ward off Owen's chill shade.

When she looked up at Holden again, his eyes grew very

serious, their gray-green depths as foreboding as the North Sea. He struggled for words.

"Did Owen . . . " he asked. "Did he . . ." Holden shut his eyes for a moment, then searched her face, unable to finish the question. Her expression closed before his eyes. He wanted to curse, but didn't. She had obviously read his meaning, but he could see she didn't want to answer him. God, his heart pained him that a knight of his own company should have wrought so much damage upon her. "Tell me," he coaxed.

"Do you suspect I am 'spoiled goods'?" she asked carefully. "Is that what you want to know?"

"Cambria," he said in a hushed voice, "it was never my intent to hurt you." He clenched his jaw, and his voice cracked. "But when I saw you up there in the claws of that beast, I would have sold my soul to have you returned safely to me. All those things I said, I said only to protect you."

"Aye," she admitted, lowering her eyes. "I know."

"I wouldn't hurt you for the world, Cambria."

She turned aside and gazed thoughtfully off into the dense nest of trees. "What if I told you," she murmured, "that Owen had forced himself upon me, that I may now carry his seed?"

Holden swallowed the acid rising in his gorge. The picture of Owen pawing his precious Cambria was too awful to bear, but he'd already lived that possibility.

He answered raggedly. "The child would be half yours. I would care for it as my own."

"And me? Would you still share my bed?"

He nodded solemnly and whispered, "I'd want to take you back so completely that it would wash away any memory of that bastard."

He'd spoken more vehemently than he'd intended, yet Cambria's eyes gentled as she cocked them up at him.

"What if I told you instead," she said evenly, "that I fought him at every turn, bit and scratched and scorned him until he beat me and called me witch and could not even think of bedding me?"

He looked sharply at her, searching her battered face for

the truth. It was there, in the stubborn tilt of her chin, the flashing defiance of her eyes, the set of her jaw.

"*That* I would sooner believe," he admitted, letting out a grateful rush of air. "You are ever wont to be a thistle under a man's saddle." His relief soured, however, as he saw again how that thistle had been trod underfoot. "Ah, Cambria . . ."

Words could not serve to tell her how he felt. He moved forward, wrapping one arm about her neck, placing his hand gingerly upon her face, removing all doubt from her with a kiss.

Cambria gave a small moan. He was crushing her bruised lips, and his hand upon her jaw pained her, but she welcomed his embrace. The stubble of his chin was rough on her face, his skin warm and alive against hers. She had no strength to answer his ardor, but neither did she resist his arms, and 'twas a long while before she could speak around the lump in her throat.

"When I thought I'd slain you . . ." she began.

"Shh," he soothed, stroking her cheek with the back of his finger. "Ah, God, Cambria, when I discovered that devil's spawn had sent you for his champion, that he wanted me to . . . kill . . ." The words stuck in his throat.

She closed her eyes for a moment, as if to blot out the memory. Then a glimmer of irony crept into her voice. "I do believe he was glad of an excuse to be rid of me."

"He was a fool," Holden told her passionately, gathering a handful of her hair between his fingers and thinking it was more precious than spun gold.

Then he kissed her again, a tender kiss this time, like the flicker of a moth on the evening wind. Cambria closed her eyes and shivered against him, lifting her lips for more. But Holden knew he could not give more and keep from succumbing to that beast of desire that already tugged at its leash. She had been through much, he told himself. She needed rest.

So he let her recline in the cradle of his arms, and before long, she was drawing in the deep air of sleep. He listened to her soft breathing as if it were a consort playing for his benefit. All around them in the filtered light of the forest, the peaceful sounds of airborne insects and fat squirrels spiraling up oak trees made a lulling music in the Gavin wood.

This was ecstasy, he decided, snuggling closer—a beautiful woman in his embrace, a magnificent castle to command, loyal vassals at his side. There was naught more a man could ask. And he owed it all to her.

"Ah, Cambria, Lady de Ware, laird of Gavin," he murmured against her hair, "how I love you." The words came easily to his lips now. Later, when she was awake, he'd say them again, say them a thousand times. "I swear to protect you and your clan with my life. Never again need you fight your battles alone. I am henceforth your knight, my lady. 'Tis I who will wield the Gavin blade and vanquish your enemies. Now and forevermore."

A sweet smile graced Cambria's face, and he pressed a kiss upon her forehead. Soon, he vowed, he intended to see that his sweet wife would have no greater troubles than deciding whether to have capon or quail for supper. She had put the clan first for most of her life. It was time someone put *her* first.

17

HOLDEN BEAMED WITH PRIDE AS HE SCANNED BLACK-
haugh's courtyard. Over the past several weeks, he'd demanded a great deal from the castle denizens, yet there
wasn't a shiftless or unwilling soul among them. A man
couldn't wish for more loyal vassals than these Scots, and he
was proud he'd won them with honor rather than force of
will.

The work on the castle proceeded with even greater effi-
ciency than he'd thought possible. Brawny workers sweated
over the stones and mortar they hauled up the stairs for the
new tower. Woodworkers kept up a steady rhythm of pounding as they skillfully selected and dovetailed long planks together for the flooring. Sir Guy repaired the quintain,
replacing it with a figure of uncanny likeness to Duncan de
Ware, gleefully informing him that it might be the only way
he could hope to defeat his older brother.

Thanks to capable Katie, young maids ran hither and
thither most of the day, sweeping out the musty rushes from
the great hall and replacing them with fragrant grasses,
heather, and thyme gathered from the fields, laundering bed
linens till they snapped white as sails in the summer breeze,
mending plaids and wattle fences and scraped knees.

This morn, two little boys with sun-freckled faces crossed
the courtyard with a platter of cheeses and salted meats for

the workers, and the scent of fresh bread wafted from the bakehouse. A pair of waddling old women chased a fugitive pig back into its newly swept pen.

Holden felt as content as a hound with a full belly.

Summer found love blossoming everywhere. Blackhaugh had never seen so many weddings in a single season. Young Gwen snared a reformed Robbie for her own. Jamie found a pale milkmaid from Bowden to warm his heart and his bed. Even Sir Guy was pestered by a bonnie bit of a Scots temptress from the Campbell clan, eliciting wagers as to how long the siege would last. And shining down over everyone was the glow of affection between the Wolf and his mate.

Only Holden's brother Garth seemed immune to the fever. Deciding he'd had quite enough adventure for one lifetime, he left to return home to his ecclesiastical studies. Holden agreed, on the condition that Garth break the news of his wedding to the rest of the de Ware household.

Holden intended to bring his Scots bride to England one day, but he couldn't leave just now, not while there was so much work to be done. He belonged to Blackhaugh as much as it belonged to him. To gain the full respect of the Gavins and to firmly establish the alliance, he had to earn it, and part of the price was hard work. The other part was compromise. Though 'twas essential to impose some kind of English order upon the Scots' wild mode of warfare, he had to concede there were some things he could learn from their rough-hewn ways. He'd no wish to conquer this proud people. Nay, he desired to join them.

To that end, he labored harder than he'd ever labored in his life. Yet it was good work, honest work. And all his efforts, all the long hours, the back-breaking toil—everything—he did to impress the woman he'd come to cherish, that little Scots elf who yet slumbered in their bed above-stairs like a naughty layabed.

He grinned, then winced at what a lovesick pup he'd become. Once he'd believed a wife of little import, less import than a good steward or a trusty squire. But not even for the king had he toiled so tirelessly as he did for his precious lady laird. In sooth, he'd pushed himself so arduously, laboring ceaselessly from dawn to well after dusk, that night after night, he'd fallen into bed and instant sleep, exhausted.

Sweet Mary, he suddenly realized, had it truly been a week since he'd lain with his wife? He glanced up toward the window where Cambria still lay abed, remembering the tantalizing way her breast had slipped out from beneath the linens this morn as she lay sleeping, the enticing pout of her dream-kissed lips, the sweet fragrance of her womanly body. His blood warmed like mulled wine.

It *had* been a week. Well, then, it was time to make amends.

Cambria stretched luxuriously across the thyme-scented pillow, then grimaced as a twinge lanced through her shoulder. Her arms ached from the rigorous training Sir Guy had put her through yesterday. She supposed she shouldn't have worked so hard. But after such a long absence from the tiltyard while her body healed, it felt marvelous to have the blood surging through her veins again, to feel the healthy sweat of battle on her brow. It felt almost as good as . . .

Coupling with Holden. Flame flooded her cheeks. Again. By the saints—every time she thought of him, molten heat blossomed in her belly and coursed relentlessly down her limbs, setting her flesh afire.

Ah, she thought, no woman could love a man so well. Her heart swelled with pride when he sat beside her at supper. She blushed when he winked suggestively at her from across the great hall. She never let him get within arm's reach without reaching her arms out for him.

She felt alive. Part of it was the sultry warmth of summer and the peace the land enjoyed. Part of it was her healing and return to the tiltyard. And part of it was the sense of wholeness Holden brought to her.

His green eyes reflected her own pride now when they gazed toward the Gavin wood. His feet no longer stumbled upon the uneven step at the bottom of Blackhaugh's larder. Even his speech had altered ever so slightly, taking on the subtle lilt of the Borders. He belonged to Blackhaugh now, and to the Gavins. He belonged to her. He completed her.

But there was another reason she felt so vital, so full of life, a reason she'd discovered only recently. And if she didn't speak to Holden soon about it, she thought she might well burst with the news.

Holden had been too busy in the last several days to do more than murmur good day as they passed in the hallways. Now, in the delicious languor of the morning, her body remembered all too vividly everything about him—the hushed whisper of his breath beneath her ear, the soft brush of his lips upon her skin, the feel of his rough-haired thigh slung over hers, claiming her.

She flopped restlessly onto her back, kicking off the covers, and stared up at the ceiling, where sunlight stretched across the thick beams. Lord—how she missed him, craved him with all of her being. Lying in bed alone the past week, without his caresses, without his warmth, was slow torture. She'd never have believed it possible, but more than she'd missed her destrier, more than she'd missed her sword, she missed the touch of the Wolf.

She closed her eyes and tried to imagine his face above her—his smoky green gaze, the subtle curve of his mouth, the spicy scent of his hair, the taste of wine on his tongue. She let one hand trace the neglected contours of her body, move over the places he hadn't touched in days—the hollow of her throat where her pulse raced, the curve of her shoulder where he oft nestled his head, the crest of her breast that even now stiffened as she slid a thumb across the aching nubbin. She sighed and moved her hand lower, across the flat plane of her belly, toward the nest of crisp curls below, to the place where desire simmered like liquid fire. . . .

Suddenly the latch of the door rattled from its bed. Her eyes popped open. She stiffened.

Holden! Her cheeks flamed. With a sound that was half-gasp and half-giggle, she yanked the coverlet up under her chin and slammed her eyes shut, feigning sleep.

The oak panel creaked open. His presence intruded into the darkened room like a burning brand. Her heart hammered at her ribs. But she didn't dare open her eyes. If she looked at him, he'd know—know what she'd been thinking. That she was wanton. That she was weak.

Holden took a deep, measured breath as he ran his gaze along the length of the woman in his bed. She was naked beneath that coverlet. He knew it. And knowing made his task all that much more difficult.

Seven days had been too long. They were strangers again. Here he stood with a platter of sweetmeats like a squire come to beg the affections of a maid. It was like starting over. And the last thing his raging, snarling hound of a body wanted was to start over. Not when she was his wife. Not when she lay naked under there.

The telltale flutterings of Cambria's eyelids belied her pathetic attempt at pretending sleep.

"You're awake," he accused, reining in the beast of his lust and easing the door shut behind him.

Her eyelids twitched, their lashes brushing soft and thick upon her pink cheek.

"I've brought sweetmeats," he crooned, unpinning his cloak with one hand and draping it across the chest at the foot of the bed. It was almost laughable, he thought. The Wolf of de Ware reduced to courting his own wife with sweets.

And still Cambria pretended to doze. She was holding her breath, but a rapid heartbeat pulsed in her neck. God—that slim, smooth column begged for a kiss.

"Well then," he softly announced, creeping close, "since you are not awake to protest . . ." He lowered his head to hers until he could see the nervous quiver of her nostrils. "Perhaps I shall steal a kiss from you now, and . . ."

Her eyes snapped open.

"Ah," he breathed, mildly disappointed. "You *are* awake. Have a sweetmeat then."

He popped a honeyed walnut between her astonished lips and stuffed another into his own mouth. Sweet syrup bathed his tongue. But even as the honey swirled around his palate, he was certain the flavor paled in comparison to the sweetness of Cambria's kiss.

As if she knew his thoughts, Cambria flicked out her

tongue to lap up a stray drop of honey from her lower lip. And then he saw it in her eyes. Lord—she could hide nothing from him. Desire. Naked, pure, powerful desire.

Instantly, all the molten lust bottled up for seven lonely days surged within him. He ached to press his lips to hers, to hold her against his hungry flesh, to couple with her. And she wanted it as well. Her gaze was hot and liquescent, her skin flushed with longing. Her eyelids dropped infinitesimally as she stared at his mouth. . . .

He sighed her name. She closed her eyes. He let the platter of walnuts clatter to the floor and lowered his mouth to hers. It was as sweet as coming home. Her lips softened at once in eager welcome. Her arms pulled him close, and he caught the curious, wonderful fragrance of her hair—a blending of thyme and leather and the sweet woodruff of her bath. He tangled his hand in the thick tresses, deepening the kiss, grazing the tips of her teeth with his tongue, then plunging into the honey-sweet recesses of her mouth. She tasted of heaven and summer and the wild hills of Scotland, of freedom and youth and desire.

With trembling fingers, he snagged the upper edge of the coverlet and slowly drew it back to her waist, feasting on her at first with his eyes and then his lips, until he'd baptized every inch of bared skin. His heart pounded in his chest as he hastily removed his surcoat and tunic. His trews near split their seam with the swell of arousal before he could take them off.

And then, sliding the coverlet down, he lay upon her, flesh to fevered flesh. He groaned with the pleasured pain of it. She was perfection—warm, yielding, and female. Her body cleaved to his like fine chain mail, caressing his shoulders, enveloping his chest, molding to his thighs. He shivered as delicious, fiery waves of desire rocked him.

Cambria moaned breathlessly. What she'd imagined before was nothing compared to the reality of Holden's touch. Where his fingers lingered there was fire. Where his lips brushed . . .

She drew in great draughts of his male scent—smoke and leather and spice. She tasted the salty tang of his muscles as she feverishly kissed his shoulder and lapped at the pillar of his neck. And she knew she was hopelessly drunk with desire. It mattered not whether he thought her wanton or witch. She only knew she wanted this. Needed it. This closeness, this soul-forging intimacy. Now.

Her heart hammered insistently at her breast, urging her on, compelling her to quench her growing thirst. Her body strove upward against his hot flesh, as if with a will of its own, arching her toward her destiny, toward what must be.

And then he sank into her, hot and strong and true as a lance, filling the hungry place inside her, and the breath was raked from her throat. This was the melding she'd desired, the joining of their bodies until there was not a whisper's breadth between them, the summoning of her heart by his until they beat in tandem.

He drew back then, prolonging the agony of separation as his flesh pulled slowly from hers. And just before she could sob in protest, he sheathed himself once more. Firmly. Deeply.

A low cry of passion was wrung from her lips. Every inch of her body felt charged with lightning. She peered through lead-heavy lashes at the forest-dark eyes above her. They were half closed, glazed with need, shadowed with purpose. They told her he knew exactly what he was doing, and nothing on heaven or earth would stop him. She closed her eyes and surrendered to him.

Holden feared it would be over far too soon. Never had he felt so aroused. But the woman beneath him deserved more. She deserved his patience. She deserved his restraint. He tried to think of her desires, lapping delicately at the shell of her ear, tracing the curve of her breast, grazing slowly across the nubbin of flesh that was the center of her need. But the more she responded, the more demanding his own body became, like a runaway warhorse charging to its natural rhythm.

And then they were galloping together. She clutched to his mane, and he whispered meaningless commands against her hair. Faster and harder they rode, climbing the mountain of desire, striving upward with muscle and sinew and quivering flesh until the pinnacle was in sight.

Cambria gasped as she crested the top of the hill. A lush, fertile valley seemed to stretch out before her, taking her breath away, promising its bounty, filling her with awe. Holden must have felt it, too, for he paused on the precipice. And then they were racing down the hill together, bounding, falling, tumbling—wild and free and alive with joy.

Cambria didn't remember drifting off. But the next thing she knew, she was drowsily rousing to find Holden easing his weight from her, tucking the coverlet in around her, and moving toward the window to gaze at the countryside beyond. Sunlight burnished the contours of his body, accentuating the wide curve of his breast, the casual sling of his hip, the rounded swell of his shoulder. Every inch of him exuded power.

And yet he was capable of infinite tenderness. His touch could be iron firm or as delicate as the wing of a butterfly, and the way he caressed her breast . . . Jesu—already her woman's mound throbbed again hopefully.

Holden turned from the fire and dusted his hands. He glanced toward the pallet. Cambria was awake. Lord, she was beautiful. Her hair was artfully tousled. Her skin glowed like a pale candle. Her eyes glimmered behind sultry lashes. And she was looking at him *that* way again. By the saints, she tempted him. She'd felt like an angel in his arms—warm and soft and sweet.

But he couldn't let her distract him again. He had building to supervise. The new floor had to be . . .

She pushed herself up onto an elbow. One coy pink nipple peeped innocently out from beneath the fur coverlet.

He cleared his throat. There were important matters waiting. It was imperative that . . .

She ran her tongue quickly over her lips. And Holden's good intentions fled quicker than a baker caught with short loaves.

Twice more she drained him of his strength and all sense, until he lay limp as custard across the pallet.

"Laird Gavin," Holden murmured wearily, "are you quite finished with me?"

She giggled low, cuddling into the crook of his arm. "There is one other favor I would ask of you, Lord Holden."

"Ask," he sighed, "and it shall be yours."

She grinned and drew a circle on his chest with her finger. "Do you think you could spare a carpenter to build a special piece for me?"

"What do you require?" he asked, closing his eyes to soak up the wonderful warmth of her body. "A wooden chest? A cupboard? A pedestal to set me upon?"

She took a playful swat at him. "Nay, you vain oaf. A cradle."

"A cradle? But why . . ."

The breath froze inside him. It seemed the whole world ground to a wrenching halt, and the room suddenly darkened, as if a black cloud covered the sun. Her words and his thoughts hung in the air, like lethal arrows caught in mid-flight, and for a blessed space of time, he was unable to make sense of what he'd heard. His eyes fixated on the ceiling, but saw naught.

And then the earth stirred, slowly resuming its turn, only now his breath felt oddly altered, dense, unrecognizable, as if he'd somehow crossed into a foreign clime where the air was thicker, perhaps poisoned. His heart beat like a leaden tambour in his chest, and his throat was too clogged to speak.

Surely she wasn't . . . He swallowed hard, afraid to look at her, afraid he'd find what he feared most in her eyes.

"Holden?"

"A cradle," he repeated.

"Mm-hmm."

Cambria grinned wide. Sometimes men could be so blind. "Do you not want to know why?"

"You're . . ."

"I'm with child, Holden." Just saying it aloud made her feel aglow with happiness.

But Holden offered no reply; He only stiffened against her.

"Holden?" Sudden misgiving threatened to sour her joy. "Did you hear me?"

"Aye, you're with child." His voice was gruff, cold, distant. Sweet Christ—what was wrong with him?

"Holden, is something . . . ?" A moment ago, she'd floated on an angel's wings. Now she was Icarus, careening toward the earth. "You know . . . you know the child is yours?"

"Oh, aye," he said, his tone as bitter as rue. " 'Twas I who did the deed."

Tears welled in her eyes, and she bit her lip to still its tremor. "Are you not happy?" she whispered.

He disengaged himself from her then, sparing her not a glance, and got up from the bed, the bed where they had made love only moments before. He dressed with careless haste.

She felt her heart crumble like a castle wall under siege.

"Oh, God!" she cried, not caring that he heard her weep. "Do you not . . . love me?"

He rounded on her then, his eyes fierce with pain and rage and something else she could not name. "I love you more than life itself! More than . . ." His voice broke, and with a curse, he stormed from the room.

Stunned and hurt and utterly bewildered, she clapped a hand over her mouth, muffling the sobs that racked her body, sobs that refused to subside until it was far past morning and Holden was far past forgiveness.

The season ripened, and summer-burnished leaves began to litter the forest floor. Heather splashed across the hill in muted golds and crimsons and purples. Berries swelled round and red in the wood, and the world glowed with the mellow light of autumn.

Cambria should have been happy. After all, she grew new life in her body. But Holden's inexplicable withdrawal diminished her joy like dense fog clouding the sun. He avoided her eyes. His touches became less frequent. And once Blackhaugh's new tower was completed, he decided to take up residence there. Alone.

The worst of it was he'd not tell her what troubled him. Everything else they could discuss. They argued at length about the virtues of acquiring cattle by payment instead of by stealth. They spoke together about the purchase of land and the fortification of the castle. They conferred about the idea of holding a tournament come spring. But whenever she mentioned his heir, 'twas as if a helm closed over his face, and he'd offer no explanation for his cool detachment.

A million ridiculous possibilities crossed her mind. She was too fat. He found her ugly. He didn't love her anymore. He regretted marrying her. And in her condition, foolish tears came as readily to her eyes as dew on a spider web.

But Holden was seldom around to witness them. He used every excuse to distance himself from her—practicing till dark in the lists, fishing half the morning, hunting with falcon most of the afternoon.

He was already risen this morn, well before the sun. She could barely make out the company through the narrow window, the dozen night-shrouded figures below, stamping their feet on the frozen ground and hoisting long poles over their shoulders. But she could hear them—Malcolm's soft chuckle rising on the mist, Guy's grumbling, their shivers as they blew into their cold hands, and above it all, the gentle commanding tone of the Wolf as the men set off to try their luck in the nearby snow-fed stream that ran through the Gavin holding.

She backed away from the window and pulled the coverlet closer about her. Ordinarily she'd balk at the thought of donning cold chain mail on a morning like this. God's wounds—'twas still mostly night. But she had demons to battle, fiends for which she had no name, and if Holden would not stay to help her vanquish them with words, then she'd slay them the only way she could—with the sword.

If Holden had cared to notice, he would have discovered that she'd never stopped her swordplay, despite her condition. Though he'd likely have forbidden it because of the babe, she felt as hale as ever, and she intended to spar until she no longer fit into her hauberk.

No one seemed to miss her anyway. The servants assumed

she lay abed, and the squires she sparred with she swore to silence. She always stole back in at midmorning, and by then the castle was buzzing with activity. Aye, she was as free as a meadowlark. She should have been happy.

But she wiped a tear away as she dragged her chausses up over her gently rounded belly. She wouldn't cry, she told herself. She must be strong now. After all, she carried the laird of Gavin in her womb. She must be strong for herself and the babe who would one day rule the clan land, with or without his father's blessing.

18

"AND *I* TELL *YOU* MY EYES ARE *NOT* THE COLOR OF EMER-alds," the lady argued, although a pleased twinkle crept into those eyes. "They are more the hue of pond frogs."

The handsome giant beside her grinned and swept her up off her feet in a swish of russet skirts, eliciting a gasp from her.

"Duncan de Ware!" she scolded, her eyes sparkling in mock disapproval. "Put me down this instant!"

Duncan ignored her light struggles, and with a wicked grin, perused her boldly until a blush stained her cheeks. How beautiful she was, he thought. Her eyes were indeed as clear and green as emeralds, her skin milky and soft, and her cheeks like twin roses. But her hair—ah, her hair was perhaps her best feature. It was the colors of wheat and sunshine and moonlight all blended, and at his pleading, she wore it in loose curls to her waist. He tangled a hand in it, reveling in its silkiness.

"Put you down? On the forest floor?" he teased. "Nay, good lady. It's not fit soil for your dainty feet."

Linet rolled her eyes heavenward for what seemed the hundredth time that day. Her husband could be a buffoon at times, but she couldn't help but love him. He lightened her spirit with a wit and charm that had been absent from her dreary life of looms and ledgers before she met him. She still found it hard to believe that the tall, striking, azure-eyed heir of the de Ware family had married *her,* a wool merchant's daughter with little patience for his frivolity. Of course, that was the case no longer, she reflected. Now she had trouble keeping a lovesick grin off of her face.

"My dainty feet have served me well for the past ten miles, I daresay," she answered.

It had been her husband's idea to abandon his retinue this morning. He was anxious to surprise his brother and this new Scots wife of his, the inimitable lady of whom Garth told the most amazing tales. So the two of them had stolen off without the others, in peasant's garb and on foot. What Duncan had assured her was a few miles had turned into a very long walk indeed, but she'd certainly not been bored on the journey. He regaled her constantly with tales of heroism, snatches of bawdy songs, and shameless flattery.

As her champion carried her through the temperate wood, nestled against his broad chest, gazing down at her as if she were some treasure he'd discovered, she found herself wishing there were always only the two of them in the world.

Suddenly, the sound of distant swordplay caught their attention. Duncan's manner changed abruptly. He let her slip gracefully to the ground and set her behind him as he reached under his cloak and pulled forth his sword.

They crept forward, their eyes alert, until they topped the crest of a rolling, sycamore-covered hill. Above the leafy limbs of the forest stretched the tower of a great castle of blue-gray stone, perhaps three hundred yards hence. But before the fortress grew a dense stand of elms, and it was in a large circular clearing of that wood that a small group of warriors exchanged blows.

"Blackhaugh," Duncan whispered, standing upright and gesturing grandly, as if he owned the castle himself.

They skirted the edge of the clearing, watching unobtrusively as a half-dozen armed lads surrounded a single fighter who assaulted them savagely. After a moment, Duncan sheathed his sword. Theirs was obviously a friendly exercise.

Linet continued to watch. There was something about that fighter . . .

"That knight in the midst is not a man," she murmured abruptly.

"What?" Duncan whispered back, lifting a brow. "Do you think it's a ghost?"

"Nay," she hissed, annoyed at his levity, "the knight is real enough, but . . . 'tisn't a man. 'Tis a woman."

He sighed good-naturedly. "Linet, my dear, you find intrigue in the simplest things. I suppose it comes from living such a drab life before you met me."

She chided him with a glare.

"That," he added, folding his arms across his chest, "could not possibly be a woman."

"You stubborn dolt," she said affectionately.

His mouth quirked in a half-smile that made him look as if she'd just given him a compliment.

"That is no woman," he assured her. "No woman could fight like that." Duncan knew an instant after the words left his mouth that he was in trouble. Linet's eyes had taken on the dangerous gleam of challenge, and he feared he was about to enter a verbal battle he'd surely lose. "All right," he decided. "Shall we ask . . . that person what manner of being it is?"

She crossed her arms expectantly.

"Very well. I suppose I shall have to issue a challenge to yon knight, then," he said with mock reluctance, although he itched to do just that. He affected a heavy sigh. "When I've won, I'll force him to remove his helm."

"Nay," Linet protested, "you cannot fight her!" She didn't even want to think about what her bear of a husband could do to a maiden on the field of battle. "You may harm her!"

"*He* seems to be fending off six knights as it is," Duncan murmured sarcastically, "and I thank you, dear lady, for showing concern for *my* welfare."

"After this, Duncan de Ware," she warned, "I'll not bring you compliments again on a silver platter, but you know very well you are probably the best swordsman in England, far better than those six knights put together."

"Aye." He grinned. "But it *is* good to hear it from your lips."

Linet couldn't stay irritated with him for long when he looked at her with those sparkling, dark-lashed eyes. She supposed she'd just have to trust him to be careful.

He shook his head in amusement, cleared his throat, and stepped forward to gain the warriors' attention.

Cambria heard the intruder call out and ceased fighting. For one awful moment, she was sure 'twas Holden, returning early from fishing, and her heart slammed against her ribs.

Then she turned and saw that this man was a stranger with hair of ebony. When she peered at him more closely through the slit of her visor, she felt her knees go weak. Before her was the face on the quintain—a taller, darker version of Holden de Ware with mischievous blue eyes and the attire of a peasant. It could be none other than Duncan, Holden's brother.

And the small woman behind him—that must be his wife. She too was garbed in the modest russet gown of a peasant, but her skin gleamed like pale samite, her eyes were the color of new grass, her hair a mane of glorious, noble blonde.

Cambria grew painfully aware of her own disheveled state. Thank God she'd not removed her helm. A hundred thoughts raced through her mind, chiefly how she could extricate herself from this situation with as little ado as possible.

"Sir Knight," Duncan called out formally, "you fight bravely against so many. Will you honor me by doing battle against *my* blade?"

One of the squires stepped forward in Cambria's defense with gentle Scots diplomacy. " 'Twould hardly be a sporting match, sir. You are not at all well armed. Perhaps you'd rather . . ."

"No matter," Duncan insisted. "Your knight is better armed, but I admittedly have the advantage of size over . . ."

"Nay, good sir," the squire followed up. "Choose one of us others. You can see this one's exhausted."

Cambria was far from exhausted. Her blood had just begun to pump warmly in her veins. A tiny voice in the back of her mind told her she should decline the challenge. But the squires she practiced with were so skittish of her, tempering their blows as if they thought she were made of glass. 'Twould be heaven to face a real opponent. Holden wouldn't find out. She could trust the Squires to remain silent. When the battle was over, she'd leave the clearing with her helm on and no one the wiser.

Before common sense could change her mind, she shook her shoulders to loosen them up, faced Holden's brother, and made ready to strike.

Scarcely had the squire jumped from between them when Duncan whipped his blade out, letting it hover restlessly before him. As was his habit, Duncan let his opponent attack first. The sword flashed and clanged loudly as it contacted his blade several times. The knight's blows were not particularly powerful nor were they very accurate, so he had little trouble lunging out of the way, but that didn't diminish his enjoyment. He always preferred style to brute force anyway. And never had he seen such style, such brash confidence, nimbleness, and aggression in an opponent so obviously overmatched. When fully grown, and with the proper discipline and humility, he thought, this youth might make an extraordinary warrior.

He fought, fascinated, as the knight kept up a rapid barrage of attacks. Still, he wasn't so enthralled that he didn't notice one of the squires slipping away from the others to lope off across the countryside.

Holden froze at the top of the rise. His chest constricted painfully as he peered down from the slope before Blackhaugh. He could scarcely draw breath for the terror that choked him. Just as the squire reported, there was Cambria, in all her glory and armor, slashing and leaping in mortal combat. And towering over her, a great beast bent on her destruction, was his unconquerable brother, Duncan. His heart pounding wildly, he unsheathed and charged at the warriors.

"Cease!" he thundered.

Cambria gasped, her sword arm frozen in the air.

Duncan was delighted with Holden's timing. With the

other knight's attention drawn away, he executed a quick flick of his wrist and, with a ready grin, sent his opponent's blade sailing across the clearing.

"Ah, *there* is my advantage at last!" he crowed. "What kept you, brother?"

To his surprise, the dark look didn't lift from Holden's face. In fact, Holden seemed almost oblivious to his presence. Even more astonishing, however, Holden's rage seemed to be directed not at him, but at his opponent. He looked fit to kill the young knight.

"Is this how you greet my kin?" Holden bellowed, fear cracking his voice. "With the point of a blade?"

The squires hung their heads, as if they were to blame.

"In sooth," Duncan admitted, "it was *my* challenge."

Holden's eyes locked on Cambria. "You didn't bother to tell him, did you?" Holden knew by her silence that he was right. She hadn't told Duncan who she was nor her condition. Still, he had the irrational urge to knock his brother alongside the head. Why could no one else see that Cambria was a woman?

Linet frowned from the sidelines, sizing up this brother of Duncan's. She could see the similarities at once between the two—their stature, their good looks—but there the resemblance ended. Where Duncan was spirited and engaging, Holden was as surly as a bear. She hated him at once. In fact, if he weren't so beloved of her husband, she would have marched up to him and told him in no uncertain terms just what she thought of his yelling at a woman like that.

Duncan set the point of his sword in the dirt and rested his free fist on his hip. He was unaccustomed to being ignored, especially by his own long-absent brother. It seemed Holden had become rather heavy-handed with his vassals. Still, he knew better than to interfere. His brother was a lord in his own right now. Linet, however, Duncan noticed from the corner of his eye, had no such qualms about intruding. She looked ready to jump into the fray.

•   •   •

Holden couldn't take a proper breath. He trembled like a skittish colt. Reaching out, he hauled Cambria to him by the front of her tabard, more to assure himself she was whole than to intimidate her.

"What do you think you're doing?" he spat to cover his fear. He twisted his fist in her garment and swore. Jesu, his heart wouldn't stop pounding. He'd sparred with his brother since they were children. No one was such a formidable warrior. Duncan could have sliced Cambria's head from her shoulders in the blink of an eye. He shuddered at the thought.

"You little fool!" he shouted hoarsely, then flung his sword arm out to point at Duncan. "You are looking at the finest swordsman alive! He's battled four at a time and conquered men twice his size! He won his spurs before he'd even grown his first beard!"

Duncan kicked at the ground, clearly embarrassed by the praise.

Linet watched the exchange with growing amazement, her mind working as swiftly as a well-strung loom. She was beginning to understand who the young warrior was and why Holden was so agitated. Perhaps, she allowed, Duncan's brother was not such an ogre after all.

Meanwhile, Holden continued with his tirade. "I've watched Duncan mow down an entire line of knights in a melee, single-handedly."

"Now, brother, there I must beg the truth," Duncan intervened. He was growing somewhat uncomfortable with the lengthy recounting of his feats of prowess. He feared the gaping Scots squires might try to kiss the hem of his garment sometime soon if Holden continued. "A full three-quarters of those knights were so drunk they could hardly sit their mounts."

Holden's eyes darted over to him, their fury undimmed yet colored by something foreign, something akin to sheer terror. "And you! Don't you have enough men your own size to fight?"

Duncan shrugged off the hostility. "Holden, calm yourself. It was only a friendly match. Can you not leave this vassal's scolding for a later time? My wife and I have yet to be properly greeted. She'll think you a mannerless boor."".

Holden let his shoulders drop a notch. For the first time, he noticed the blonde woman standing behind Duncan. She regarded him with a curiously tender expression he couldn't fathom.

After a lengthy pause, Duncan rolled his eyes. "All right then. Lady Linet, I would like you to meet my mannerless boor of a brother, Lord Holden de Ware."

Linet moved to Duncan's side and offered a dazzling smile, but Holden stood silent, befuddled, unable to contend with the horror that still raged within him.

Duncan shook his head. "So, where are you keeping your Scots hellion of a wife, Holden? Is she so ugly you must hide her away?" He grunted suddenly, unprepared for Linet's elbow jab to his ribs.

"Dolt!" she called him under her breath.

Holden's mouth compressed into a grim line, and he sheathed his sword. Then he caught Cambria's helm in the crook of one arm and pulled it upwards and off. Her long chestnut hair tumbled forth over her shoulders, and her eyes flashed rebelliously.

Duncan literally staggered from the impact. Linet had been right. The knight was a woman. He fumbled and dropped his precious sword, for once in his life at a loss for words.

"This," Holden snarled, "is my wife."

19

LINET'S TRIUMPHANT SMILE DIMMED WHEN SHE SAW THE look in Cambria's eyes. The poor girl was mortified, her face crimson. She would meet no one's eyes, but only stared at the ground with a fierce and silent pride. Something about her made a surge of protectiveness well up in Linet. She liked the lass immediately. True, Cambria hardly looked like the lady of the castle. Her hair was drenched in sweat. Her face was no stranger to dirt. But there was substance to her—spirit. She seemed to embody the wild soul of Scotland itself.

Unfortunately, Linet couldn't know how much her close scrutiny disturbed Cambria.

Never had Cambria glimpsed such a pale and fragile creature as Linet. An angel stood before her, a lily-white angel with frail features and flowing blonde hair, the one jongleurs always sang about. She was perfect—well-mannered, beautiful, serene. Cambria lowered her eyes. All at once, she felt keenly the drop of sweat sliding down her own temple, the dust around her neck, the weight of the mail flattening her breasts, her burgeoning stomach. Jesu, she wished she'd stayed abed this morning. The taste of shame was like metal on her tongue as her glance flickered over to the young woman again. The angel's delicate hands had probably never touched the edge of a blade, let alone wielded one in battle.

And the woman's husband still gaped at Cambria like a hooked flounder.

Why had Holden unmasked her? She could have left the field untarnished. He could have salvaged their honor. Damn him! She could have met his kin later. But now there was little she could do to make restitution for his humiliating introduction. Still, she'd not be daunted. Blackhaugh was *her* home, and no matter what hostile tone Holden took, she'd at least welcome his kin with courtesy, the Scots' hallmark for centuries.

Calling on the strength and pride of generations of Gavins to sustain her, she announced, "I am Cambria Gavin, the laird of Blackhaugh, and I wel—"

"You are Lady Cambria *de Ware*," Holden gritted out. His brows lowered in a mixture of displeasure and disappointment.

Cambria's cheeks burned. The speech stuck in her throat. Of course she was Lady Cambria de Ware. 'Twas only force of habit and nervousness that made her forget. But Holden no doubt thought she intended the slight. There was no noble way to extricate herself from the embarrassing situation. And to her horror, a painful knot had risen in her throat. So for the benefit of the frail angel who looked as if she would faint at any moment, Cambria gathered what dignity she could scrape up, gave the visitors a brief nod, and swung around toward Blackhaugh.

Ignoring her gathering tears, she stiffly walked up the hill, her fists clamped at her sides, and tried not to think about what Lady Linet was whispering behind her delicate hand. All the way up the incline she felt Holden's eyes upon her—cursing her, condemning her, but worst of all, ashamed of her.

It didn't matter, she told herself. He was only an Englishman, after all. What he thought of her had no bearing on who she truly was. Damn his disappointed scowl—she *was* the Gavin! Marriage didn't change that.

As for meeting his kin with a sword, even Duncan had explained 'twas *his* challenge. Why then did Holden insist on humiliating her? Unless he thought she had humiliated *him.* . . .

She pictured again the blonde angel hanging on Duncan's arm. Perhaps Linet was more of what Holden desired in a wife. Perhaps he preferred a woman to be quiet and docile and frail, none of which described Cambria. Perhaps Holden was ashamed of her. And that was the reason he'd become so distant with her of late.

Pah! She dashed away a tear. If she didn't possess Linet's delicate countenance or sweet mien or pretty speech, 'twas only because she wasn't properly trained to be any man's wife. Holden should have known that, she thought, sniffling. Or else he should never have married her.

Somehow her leaden feet managed to carry her up the sward, and her head was still held high when at last she passed through the barbican. Stumbling only once, she almost reached the haven of the keep and the promise of solitude.

But Holden had followed her, and before she could reach safe harbor, he swung her about by the shoulders. For one fleeting moment, she thought she glimpsed care and concern in his eyes. But then they flattened, and his mouth turned down at the corners.

"You will not endanger the babe you carry in this way. You are not to spar again."

Tears welled in her eyes, but she refused to let them escape. "And what do you care of the babe?" she choked out. "All these weeks you have not made one mention of it. 'Tis as if it docs not exist."

All the color vanished from his face. "Is that what you think?"

"What am I to think?" she muttered, mindful of the scattering of servants that passed nearby in the courtyard. Then the pain that she'd kept carefully in check burst forth in a bitter hiss. "You do not speak of it. You do not ask after me. You do not touch me, hold me, kiss me. Christ's bones—we do not even share a bed anymore."

He only stared at her. She couldn't read his thoughts. Her

heart was breaking, and all he offered was silence. She cursed him on a sob.

"'Tis well you killed your mother ere she could see what a cold-hearted bastard you would become!"

Holden's eyes grew instantly flat and chill. He released her like a poisonous spider. Anger ticced in the muscle of his cheek, and his fists opened and closed. For a terrible moment, she wondered if he would strike her. But then, she looked into his eyes and glimpsed evidence of another emotion beneath his tightly checked wrath—raw, profound hurt.

As quickly as she made that discovery, he shut her out, and she wasn't certain that she hadn't merely imagined his look of pain. And then he was gone with a whirl of his cloak before she could steal another glance or even draw another breath.

Holden braced himself against the cold stones of Blackhaugh's stairwell, where he'd hidden for most of the afternoon. It felt as if a great weight had been dropped on his chest. This woman to whom he'd pledged his undying devotion, for whom he'd put his own body at risk, for whom he'd sacrificed the familiarity of his homeland for a wild and savage country, had crushed him with a single blow. She'd cut him to the quick.

But he couldn't hide away for the rest of his life. Nor could he remain here until she birthed the babe. Duncan would wonder where he'd gone, and those nosy Scots would come sniffing around soon.

His heart heavy, he trudged downstairs, ignoring the curious glances of the supper guests. Duncan and Linet sat at the high table, but he didn't spare them a word. Cambria was conspicuously missing. He grabbed up two leather jacks full of ale from a table, then escaped through the main door of the great hall into the night.

The cool air was bracing, and he took a long pull of ale, attempting to warm his heart. He wandered aimlessly, cursing the full moon and kicking at the damp sod of the courtyard, stopping only when he reached the stables. He shuffled in through the double door, past the quietly nickering horses, swilling ale with a vengeance. The warm, familiar smells of the stable—the fresh hay, the sweat of the horses, the pungent leather tack—were some comfort at least. Clutching his drink to his breast, he settled down into a moonlit corner.

Duncan recognized all too well the emotion on Holden's face as he swept through the hall. It was the expression of a dog kicked once too many times, the countenance of a man haunted by his past.

After the supper tables were cleared and the guests assigned their pallets for the night, Duncan bid Linet a sweet good night and set out to hunt for his brother.

It didn't take long to find him. Holden was muttering loudly and incoherently to the stabled horses. When Duncan moved to stand in the doorway, blocking the light of the moon, Holden looked up from his dark corner with fluttering eyelids and beckoned him nearer. Duncan shook his head in pity, crouching down beside him.

Holden was drunk. As far as Duncan knew, he only got that way under one condition—when someone indiscreetly mentioned the death of their birth mother.

Duncan sighed and took hold of Holden's forearm. He'd gone over the facts a hundred times, though not in a long while. And he'd willingly go over them a hundred more. He'd assure Holden their mother's death wasn't his doing, that she'd been weak from the beginning, that with so much blood lost, nothing could have saved her.

Holden mumbled, "Never fall in love, Duncan."

Duncan screwed up his forehead. Love? What was he muttering? Wasn't he upset about his birthing having killed their mother? Perhaps he was too drunk for conversation. He tugged on Holden's arm. "Holden, come back inside. It grows late."

"Aye," Holden agreed. "Far too late. The deed is done. I've destroyed her."

Duncan ran a weary hand over his face. "Who?" he asked, although he suspected he knew.

"The Scots wench," Holden slurred. "I've ruined her."

"How have you ruined her?"

Holden smacked his fist into the wall of the stable. Duncan winced. He'd have bruised knuckles on the morrow.

"Damn it! I bedded her. I bedded my wife."

Duncan frowned. Holden might as well have said he'd *beaten* his wife for all the despair that lined his face. He wrapped a companionable arm around his brother. "Holden, that's what one *does* with a wife. You see, that's the beauty of it. You find yourself—"

"But now she's with . . ." Holden shook off his brother's arm. "Hellfire, Duncan! She's with child."

"With child?" Duncan's heart tripped as he relived in memory one of the fierce swipes he'd taken at Holden's bride with his sword. Dear God—he'd not only battled with a woman. He'd battled with a *pregnant* woman! The thought made him feel ill.

But it was Holden's eyes that were shadowed with misery, haunted with pain. "It's my child, Duncan."

"But that's marvelous!" He extended his hand. "Come. Let's tell Linet. She'll be delighted to hear she's—"

"Nay!" Holden argued, drunkenly batting away Duncan's gesture. "Do you not see?" He seized the front of Duncan's surcoat in desperate fists. "I've murdered her. I've murdered my wife."

"But Holden . . ."

"Leave me . . . alone," Holden croaked, his hands losing their grasp. Then he promptly slumped over onto the fodder.

Duncan shook his head. Holden never could abide much drink. And what was he ranting on about? Murdering his wife? How could he possibly think . . .

Died in childbirth. It hit him like a sack of chain mail. Their mother had died in childbirth. And now Holden feared Cambria would do the same. Never mind that he'd already fathered half a dozen by-blows off other wenches, all hale and hearty. This one was different. This one was his wife. This one he loved.

Duncan looked down at the great, iron-hard knight slumped on the stable floor, laid low not by the steel weapons that were as much a part of his life as the air he breathed, but by the fragile strings of his heart. This was the man who had once sworn his soul to battle, the little boy who had revered the sword above all.

Duncan smiled. How the mighty warrior had fallen. And he knew all too well the name of Holden's conqueror, for he'd faced that assailant himself. Its name was woman.

With a sigh, he bent to pick up Holden. Only by sheer stubbornness was he able to sling his heavy brother across his shoulders to carry him. Then, opting for a resting place far away from the wife who caused Holden so much torment, Duncan hauled him off to an empty storage room over the armory.

There was no cure for what Holden was suffering. Until Cambria delivered the babe, screeching and bellowing and cursing his name, and living to tell the tale, he'd not rest easy. The best that Duncan could do for his brother was distract him. And, he thought, rubbing his hands together, the best way to do that was to keep him busy with his sword.

Holden sat up with a start in the dark, wakened by a familiar scraping shriek. A loud oath sprang to his lips, one he instantly regretted. He clapped his palms to his throbbing temples. Sainted Mary, his head ached! And his wits felt as thick as his tongue. Good God, what addlebrain was sharpening a sword in the middle of the night in the middle of his chamber? No, he amended, the middle of *this* chamber. Where was he? He remembered being in the stables. He couldn't recall coming here.

Slowly, he struggled to his knees in the makeshift pallet of bunched straw. He winced, holding his head in his hands to stop its spinning. From the sound of it, he was in the room directly above the armory, and although his bones protested every movement, he knew he had to go down the steps to investigate. The horrible grating was nigh as painful and inescapable as a honeybee in a close helm.

Groaning as he came to his feet, he shuffled to the door, combing his hair with his fingers. He mumbled curses every step of the way until he stood before the door of the armory. There was a respite in the grating, then it resumed, and he shivered in revulsion as the sound seemed to slither up his spine.

He flung open the door. "What in the name . . . !" he tried to bellow, although it came out as more of a whine.

His brother Duncan looked up from the wheel, his grin wide and irritating.

"Must you?" Holden muttered icily, nodding to the whetstone.

"Ah, Holden," Duncan said cheerily, letting the wheel wind itself down to a slow creak, "paying the price for those two jacks of ale last night, are you?"

Holden grumbled.

"Well, little brother, I warn you, 'twill be a stiff price indeed you'll pay at the next tournament if you insist on keeping such demanding bedfellows." He sheathed his sword and stood with his fists on his hips, regarding Holden from head to toe, clucking his tongue all the while. "Even so, 'tis poor competition you'll be," he said with mock sorrow, "if you've been practicing with that ugly, sluggish quintain of yours. Why, I can hit that lout smack in the eye and swive my wife ere it comes round again."

Holden cracked a weary smile at that. "Mayhap that says more about your swiving than my quintain."

Duncan gasped in dramatic effrontery and drew his sword again. "Sir, I believe I'll have to challenge you for that!"

Holden shook his head. He had no desire to exert his aching bones in pointless swordplay.

"What! You refuse me?" Duncan set the point of his sword on the ground and sniffed, clearly goading him. "Have you grown lazy then, Sir Lord-of-Your-Own-Castle? Do these Scots fight all your battles now?"

Holden grimaced. He could not long resist a challenge from his older brother, and Duncan knew it. "Very well," he agreed. "I'll fetch my squire and meet you in the lists within the hour." He added with heavy sarcasm, "Perhaps by then the sun will have come up, and we'll actually be able to see one another."

• • •

The battle dragged through half the morning, but was not yet won when a royal messenger arrived at Blackhaugh. Calling a stalemate, the brothers adjourned from the field to take refreshment in the great hall and to hear news of Edward.

Cambria reluctantly joined the men below. She would have preferred to sleep the winter through than to face Holden's indifference. But a royal messenger was her concern as laird of Blackhaugh. She clasped sweaty palms together as her husband mulled over the parchment bearing the king's seal. She could guess what it said. Edward needed the de Ware sword arm again.

Cambria swallowed. She shouldn't have cared. Even when Holden was at Blackhaugh, he wasn't . . . present. Still, the thought of not seeing her husband for weeks or months, of giving birth to the babe without him near . . .

"It is rumored France, my lord," the messenger was saying. "There is asylum for him there. As for the declaration, the king believes the Scots will readily assent."

"Then Edward doesn't know the Scots," Holden murmured.

Cambria's curiosity got the best of her. "Assent to what?"

Duncan told her. "Edward has declared much of the south of Scotland to be under his own rule now."

Cambria planted her fists on her hips, forgetting her despondence in her outrage. "That is preposterous! Does he think to eat up Scotland piece by piece like some hungry beast? Robert the Bruce's supporters have not forgotten. Even now, his son David——"

"Has fled," Holden finished. "To France."

She was struck numb. David fled? The son of Robert the Bruce turned tail? How could he desert his own country? His father had never done so, even when it meant his death.

'Twas as if Holden had heard her thoughts. "The boy is likely pursuing French support for his claim to the throne."

Perhaps, she thought, perhaps that was it. Still, she'd not condone David's actions. "So who will keep the French from acquiring Scotland in turn?" she muttered in disgust.

Holden let out a sigh, fully aware she was right.

"You go to battle?" Cambria asked, a catch in her voice.

"Nay," Holden assured her, but his voice was grim. He spoke as if to himself. "Nay, we must not use the sword. It's a poor diplomat. It should be only a messenger's mission, pointing out the lesser evil. We must convince them there will be a greater harmony under Edward's own reign than that of Balliol."

She agreed with him. But she doubted the loyalist Scots would embrace English rule as readily as Holden believed. There would be fighting. And Holden's life would be at risk.

"Where do you go? When do you leave?" she asked, trying to keep the tremor from her words.

"To Edinburgh," Holden told her.

"The king bids us make all haste," Duncan said.

Holden's eyes met Cambria's, and she almost imagined she saw a trace of regret there. "We should leave on the morrow."

She scarcely heeded the rest of what he said, how many carts and what provisions he'd require, who'd stay behind, all the details of the journey. All she could think about was how unfair it was. She was going to have his child, damn it all, and once again they were about to be torn apart by the ravages of politics.

Ariel lifted a restless hoof, stirring the fog in swirls upon the sod. Like her master, she could scarcely wait to leave.

Holden was sure the castle would be safe in his absence. Malcolm was more than trustworthy. Blackhaugh's larder was well stocked. The keep was secure. There was naught to worry about, as long as he didn't think of . . . He shook his head, as impatient as his mount. The sooner he left, the better.

It wasn't that he'd tired of his new role as lord. Aye, the title came with a great deal of responsibility, but it was just the sort of challenge he welcomed. Blackhaugh was magnificent. The countryside was breathtaking, the people fast feeling like family. He couldn't even imagine going back to England.

And it wasn't that he thirsted for war. God knew he'd had

enough of spilling blood. In his youth he'd battled anything on two legs, but now with a holding, with a wife . . .

Cambria. She was the reason. He closed his eyes and pounded a fist on the bed of the arms wagon. If he let them, the images would overwhelm him again, cloud his vision and turn him into a quivering mass of fear. He couldn't let them do that. He was off to war. He'd need all the steel nerve he possessed to keep himself and his men alive.

The arms wagon was loaded now. All the provisions had been packed. The knights, his brother's and his own, were mounted. Horses snorted and chuffed out white feathers of breath on the damp air. Wives and mistresses winked or sobbed or kissed their men farewell. Their subdued voices floated over the pervasive creak of leather like doves' calls in the cote. He could feel her behind him, yards away, but there, staring at his back, beckoning him wordlessly to turn toward her. He cursed under his breath. If he turned, he'd be lost. But if he didn't . . .

He slowly pivoted to face her. She was the most beautiful thing on the face of the earth. Her soft gray underkirtle seemed part of the mists. Her unbound hair cascaded over her shoulders like the winding roots of a Gavin oak. Her eyes, illuminated by the dark blue of her sideless surcoat, shone with wisdom and pride. And bewilderment as he continued to stare at her, motionless.

How could he live without her? he mourned. What in God's name had he done? Cambria was the most precious part of his life, yet he'd put her in danger. He'd filled her womb with a child, and because of it she might die. Like his mother. His throat tightened painfully as he traced her altered silhouette with his eyes—the full breasts, the subtly widened hips, the gently rounded bulge of her belly.

His feet moved of their own accord, bringing him closer, quickening his step until he was running toward her. She reached forward for him until, with a cry of relief and fear and desperation, he took her in his arms.

She felt like home. Her warmth permeated fog and chain mail and the armored recesses of his heart. Her body cleaved to him perfectly, though she was fat with child, as if it had been made for just that. Her hair curled against his cheek, filling him with her scent—the scent of heather and moss and wood smoke and all things fresh and green. God, if anything happened to her . . . He took her head in rough hands and with his thumbs brushed away the tears marring her cheeks. He searched her eyes, looking for . . . what? Reassurance? Forgiveness? Compassion? He found only sorrow.

Heedless of the crowd about them, he tilted his head and captured her lips with his own. She tasted as sweet as love itself, as sweet as heaven. He poured his own bittersweet emotions into the kiss, pledging her his soul, giving her the one promise he hadn't the power to keep—the promise of life. And then he tore himself away.

If he lingered one moment longer, he knew he'd not go to fight for any man. And yet if he remained, he'd shortly drive himself mad with worry. It was best this way, he told himself, striding across the courtyard with nary a backward glance. A hasty farewell. Blunt and brief. Like the merciful blow given a mortally wounded knight. Why then, he wondered, did his heart languish in pain for weeks afterward?

20

BEYOND THE SHUTTERED WINDOWS OF THE SOLAR, AUTUMN-grayed leaves twisted in death throes and floated to the earth. Frost laced the hard ground. Breath came out in steamy curls. The morning mists lengthened with the season, and the shroud of night, too, stretched out its cool hand until they met across days that were gray and unchanging. Only the black skeletons of trees marred the soft, hovering fog, like dark lightning against a pale sky, and the crunch of autumn leaves grew muffled in the damp caress of winter.

All Saint's Day passed, and Christmas. Cambria grew round and unwieldy, waddling from room to room, snuggling up to the fire one moment, then asking Katie to throw open a shutter the next. And soon, as if nature winked in mockery at the de Wares, one day Linet discovered that she, too, carried a babe. Every morn, as regular as the bells of Mass, pale and quivering, the poor woman emptied her belly of whatever she'd eaten the night before.

Behind the confining walls of Blackhaugh, the ladies of de Ware grew restless.

A log popped and shifted on the fire. Cambria spread a parchment out across the table. Scrutinizing the drawing, she ran a hand over her huge stomach and pressed back the tiny foot that always managed to wedge itself beneath her ribs.

Linet looked up briefly from her spot by the hearth, where she bent over a lapful of needlework, and chuckled.

Cambria frowned. "Robbie suggested wings on the poleyns. Although Malcolm thinks less weight is better." The babe must have been in accord. It aimed a particularly hearty kick at her rib. She winced. "Still, against those new Italian thunder tubes . . ."

"By the saints' bones, Cambria!" Linet laughed. "The babe won't go to war till he's at least . . . six! Italian thunder tubes indeed."

Cambria's temper simmered beneath the surface. "Mayhap English babes are coddled till they're half-grown," she bit out, "but in Scotland, if you remember, we wield a sword as soon as we can walk."

"Oh, la!" Katie crooned, sweeping into the solar. "Would ye wield a sword e'en now in the solar, m'lady? And against your poor sister?" She clucked her tongue and squinted down at Linet's handiwork. "Ah, never ye mind, lass. Ye must be near yer time. Yer mother was the same way, all waspy-tongued and thistly."

"I am not thistl—" Cambria began. Then she glanced down at the corner of the parchment. 'Twas wadded in her fist. Sheepishly, she released it. Katie was right. She hadn't been herself lately. So far, she'd designed a half dozen variations on poleyns, several gauntlets with padded woolen wrist guards, and two different coats of plates, all for the tiny knight who wasn't even born yet. Maybe 'twas ridiculous. She picked up a sliver of charred wood from the table, made a few subtle changes to the sketch, then tossed the parchment aside.

"I'm sorry," she murmured.

Linet smiled engagingly, quick to forgive. "I spoke to the armorer this morn. He's already stamped the de Ware crest on all the plates. All it wants is for a seamstress to stitch them to the gambeson. If you can settle on the finishing touches soon, 'twill be completed in time for the babe's arrival."

Cambria nodded, but she knew her polite smile didn't quite reach her eyes. She was weary. Weary of being sequestered indoors. Weary of the burden in her womb. Weary of worrying about her husband. The last word from Holden had come weeks ago. The missive had been succinct and careful. After all, treason could be construed from less than enthusiastic reports. But Cambria could tell he was frustrated. His "messenger's mission" had stretched into an absence of months.

At times it seemed to her that Holden de Ware must have been a dream she'd had long ago, that she'd imagined his deep, compelling eyes, his warm, insistent kiss, the comforting sweep of his arms around her. And yet the evidence of their intimacy stirred within her, substantial, alive, real. She ran her palm over her swollen belly for the hundredth time.

Katie patted her hand. "Why don't ye take a wee nap in your chamber, m'lady? Ye must be worn out. Ye've been workin' on those designs o' yours all mornin'. I'll come up with a warm posset later."

A nap did sound good. She'd slept badly the last night. The babe had kicked and struggled in her womb like a bagged kitten. If she slept, perhaps she could find some peace. Perhaps she could forget her melancholy.

She bade Linet a good day, and Katie steered Cambria to her chamber. She saw her settled comfortably in the plump bed, stirring the banked fire to life and placing a motherly kiss on her forehead. Before Katie reached the door, Cambria sank toward slumber, unable to summon the energy even to bid the maid farewell.

It seemed hours later that the serenity of her dreamless sleep was shattered as a servant burst into the room.

"M'lady!" the woman cried breathlessly.

Disoriented and drowsy, Cambria struggled to sit up in the tangle of the bedclothes and her wits. The woman looked vaguely familiar, but Cambria couldn't quite place the strange hazel eyes and thin lips.

"What is it?"

The maid nervously secured the door behind her. "I was told to come straightaway to you," she whispered hastily.

Cambria rubbed the fog from her eyes.

" 'Tis about yer 'usband."

The blood drained from her face.

" 'E's wounded, m'lady, somethin' fierce." The maid worked her fingers together. " 'E's been askin' for ye, but 'e's too far gone to move."

Cambria's eyes flattened. Her heart thudded woodenly against her chest.

"I can take ye to 'im," the maid offered. Then she glanced suspiciously around the chamber. "If ye think yer nurse-maid'll let ye go."

There was no question. Cambria *had* to go to him. No matter what the risk, she had to go to him. Malcolm and Katie would never allow it, she knew, nor would any of the clan. But she had to see her husband. She'd saved him from the ravages of fever once before, saved his life. Perhaps she could do it again.

With quivering hands, she gathered linen for bandages, a dagger, and what healing herbs she kept on her table. Then she donned beggar's rags. If fortune favored her, no one would notice the plump, shambling peasant making her way through the front gate.

With the maidservant trailing behind, she managed to clear Blackhaugh's wall unremarked. But padding along the stretch of the main road, intent upon her grave mission, she let her guard slip.

The attack took her completely by surprise. The maidservant grabbed her roughly and shoved her into the thicket before she could resist or draw her dagger. And just as a chunk of rock slammed against Cambria's temple, sending her to a land of no thoughts, she remembered who the woman was. Owen's whore.

Linet rubbed the small of her back with one hand and her gritty, sleep-starved eyes with the other. Never had she felt so helpless, so useless.

Cambria had vanished. No one could find her. They'd searched for two days and nights now. They'd tried the hounds. They'd tried hunting parties. They'd even ventured into the camps of long-time foes to ask if the laird of Gavin had been seen.

A tear slipped from Linet's eye. Damn that foolhardy

Cambria! If this was all some adventure she'd embarked upon to assuage her boredom . . . But even as she thought the words, she knew they weren't true. Alone, Cambria might have indulged in such mischief, but she carried a babe now. She wouldn't dream of putting that life at risk. So where was she?

Linet stared out the solar window into the black, clear sky peppered with a thousand stars, and the great expanse of the heavens made her shiver. Cambria could be anywhere in the vast world, anywhere at all. It would take a miracle to find her. It would take the eyes of the falcon and the instincts of . . .

A Wolf. The hair prickled at the back of her neck. It wasn't the first time she'd thought of Duncan. A dozen times she'd considered sending someone to him. Surely he'd know what to do. He'd be easy to locate. He was no doubt fighting in the front lines of the war near Edinburgh. But she couldn't send someone into that peril—to bear the brunt of both the battle and Holden's fury when he learned his wife was missing.

She sighed resignedly. Holden must be told. Maybe there was naught he could do. Maybe it was too late to save Cambria. But Holden would never forgive Linet if she didn't give him the chance to try.

She swallowed hard. She'd go herself. It couldn't be far. She'd be safe enough. Surely no one, Scots or English, would attack a pregnant woman. She'd find Duncan. And, God willing, he'd find Cambria.

"Missing!"

Duncan scowled, recovered at last from the shock of discovering his newly pregnant wife in the war camp with naught but a scrawny squire for escort.

Holden focused on Linet's face as intently as a falcon on prey, making the poor lady cringe. "What do you mean, 'missing'?"

Linet shook her grief-weary head. "She's nowhere to be found, Holden."

Holden's anger turned instantly to breathless fear. He searched Linet's eyes. "You're serious."

Linet's face dissolved into a mask of such hopelessness that he didn't need to answer the question.

Holden's heart tumbled inside his chest. He suddenly couldn't draw breath. "What . . . how . . ."

"No one knows," Linet said, her voice breaking. "We've looked everywhere. Malcolm's beside himself. I thought if I came . . ."

Holden had to master his heart before panic claimed him. There was still hope. There was always hope.

"How long have you been traveling?"

"Two days," the squire reported.

Holden bit back a curse.

Duncan voiced one.

"And how long has she been missing?" he asked.

"Five days, all told," she choked out.

Holden nodded, controlling keen despair only by clenching his jaw and looking past Linet's crumbling countenance. Five days. Sweet Christ. Much could happen in five days.

He swallowed down the terror that rose up to claim him, blew out a thin breath, and steeled his shoulders. "I'll leave at once."

"I'll come with you," Duncan said.

"And the king?" Linet said, glancing nervously at the soldiers encamped nearby.

"The de Wares have given more than their share of service," Duncan assured her.

"I've long since proven my loyalty to the king," Holden murmured. "It's time I proved my loyalty to my wife."

Holden raked his hands through his hair as he searched feverishly through the Gavin woods. He'd sent his men back to Blackhaugh at sunset. But he couldn't cease his own searching, no matter that his eyes could barely pierce the deep shade of the forest. He never doubted for a moment he'd find Cambria. He couldn't afford to doubt it. He only hoped he'd find her in time. For more than an hour, he stomped through the underbrush, trampling bushes, searching for a sign—a scrap of cloth, a footprint . . . a drop of blood. He swayed on his feet. *God,* he prayed, *let her be safe.*

Then, as he mouthed that silent plea, his attention was caught by an unnatural break in the branches ahead. He rubbed his forehead, afraid weariness may have made him imagine what he'd seen. But when he looked again, it was still there—the unmistakable shape of an *H* made from the bent branches of an oak. Faint hope sprang to his breast. Sweet Jesu! Someone had left him a trail.

A hard slap startled Cambria awake. Her head rocked over the splintery floor with the impact.

"Wake up, bitch!"

'Twas Aggie's strident screeching. Cambria caught an unpleasant whiff of her own unwashed body and started to gag. The events of the past days crashed down on her like a cartload of armor. A hundred times she'd wished she were not so unwieldy, a thousand times that she had her sword. She was useless like this, she thought, lying on her side, gagged, bound hand and foot, fat and slow and vulnerable.

She was ashamed she'd been so easily fooled. Holden would be disappointed at her gullibility, but she'd gladly endure a scolding from him just to see his face again. Aggie had threatened harm to her babe, to Holden's heir, if she fought her. She'd had no choice but to follow the maid, half-conscious, to this sagging, deserted cottage like a docile sheep. Still, at every opportunity she could, Cambria had feigned fatigue, leaning up against a tree, and while Aggie's attention was elsewhere, she'd bent branches into the *H* Sir Stephen had taught her, leaving behind a trail. Now it seemed as though that trail would never be discovered.

"'Aven't ye birthed that whelp yet?" Aggie whined. "It's been nigh a week now, and I'm growin' weary o' this hovel." She scratched her nose and bent down to stare into Cambria's face. "Be a good lass, now, an' I'll give ye aught to eat. We can't 'ave the heir o' Blackhaugh goin' 'ungry, now, can we?" She cackled and roughly loosed the gag from around Cambria's jaw.

"Wa . . . ter . . ." Cambria's voice was little more than a

croak, and she hated to beg so pitifully, but her throat was parched, and her thirst that of two.

"Oh, aye, aye, ye'll 'ave yer water," Aggie grumbled, snatching up a skin from the battered oak table and sloshing its contents into Cambria's mouth.

Cambria welcomed the precious liquid and the bits of bread Aggie hand-fed her afterward, though they were tough to chew and difficult to swallow.

"'Tisn't easy, is it, chokin' down peasant bread?" Aggie sneered. "'At's all I've 'ad to eat my 'ole life—the leavin's." She wadded another piece and stuck it carefully between Cambria's teeth. "But no more," she said, her feline eyes gleaming. "I'm goin' to be a lady now. I'm goin' to live in 'at big castle o' yers."

"Blackhaugh?" Cambria managed to rasp out around the bit of bread.

"Wi' servants o' my own to feed me an' dress me . . ."

"You?"

Aggie glared sharply down at her. "Aye. Me." She set aside the chunk of bread. "Just as soon as ye see fit to birth 'at babe."

Cambria choked down the last piece of bread. She was afraid to ask, but she had to know. "What are you planning?"

Aggie ran her finger idly along the edge of the table. "I'm goin' to save yer babe, lassie, don't ye fret. And Lord 'olden, when 'e sees 'ow pitiful sorry I am 'at I couldn't save the both o' ye . . ." She sighed and drew her thin lips into a trembling pout. "'E'll keep me in the best chamber o'Blackhaugh fer savin' 'is heir, 'e will, so proper grateful 'e'll be."

Cambria's heart fluttered. Aggie's plan was diabolical. Ruthless. And worst of all, she was right. It would work. Holden would take the woman at her word. Dear God, she couldn't leave her babe in this madwoman's charge. It was unthinkable. She had to say something, anything, to change Aggie's mind.

Summoning up all her powers of deception, Cambria managed to force a peal of derisive laughter from her throat.

Aggie turned on her with the fury of a vexed cat. "'Ow

dare ye!" she spat. "Ye won't be laughin' long after I yank 'at whelp from ye!"

Cambria continued to rock with laughter.

Aggie stamped her foot. "Damn yer eyes! What ails ye?"

Cambria shook her head. "Holden's heir, is it?" She fought to contain her mirth. "You foolish woman!"

Aggie was beside herself now with anger. "'Ow *dare* ye!"

"Holden won't be grateful in the least," Cambria chuckled. "The babe isn't his."

Aggie sucked in a shocked breath. "What do ye mean?"

"The babe isn't his, and he knows it." Cambria let melancholy color her words, a melancholy only half-feigned. "Why do you think he so willingly left for war?"

Aggie chewed at her lip. "Then whose babe is it?"

Cambria took a deep lungful of air. She'd have to be prepared for anything now. "I think you know the answer to that."

A panoply of emotions coursed across Aggie's face—confusion, fury, hurt, disbelief—before she said his name. "Owen."

Cambria held her breath. Perhaps Aggie would let her go now. There was no point in keeping her. Owen was dead. Holden was removed from the game. As far as Aggie was concerned, Cambria was no longer a pawn.

The corners of Aggie's mouth turned down, and her eyes grew ugly. "Poor Owen. 'E never could resist a twitchin' skirt," she muttered. "And I'll wager ye strutted yer backside by 'im every chance ye 'ad. If it weren't fer ye, 'e'd never 'ave strayed. If it weren't fer ye, 'e might still be alive. An' I'd be packin' to move into Blackhaugh. Ye bitch."

Aggie's gaze fell on Cambria's knife, embedded in the table, and a sly smile distorted her features.

Cambria squirmed in her bonds.

Aggie seesawed the blade out of the oak and turned it over in her fingers. The burnished dagger hovered inches from Cambria's face.

"'Tis yer fault," Aggie whispered, leaning close, her eyes glassy.

Cambria winced as a drop of Aggie's sweat dripped onto her cheek. God, no, she thought. She couldn't die like this. Not bound and helpless. Not by her own knife.

"'Twill be a pleasure to slay ye, ye and yer spawn," Aggie hissed. She raised the dagger high, coupling her hands on the haft.

Cambria had no time. No leverage. No momentum. The blade dropped. She ducked her head and rolled onto her back, toward the attack. The movement surprised Aggie enough to ruin her aim. The tip of the blade only grazed Cambria's shoulder. But now Cambria's arms were pinned beneath her, and her stomach was fully exposed.

Leering down, Aggie recovered her balance and raised the weapon again. The blade gleamed as it split the air. This time there was nowhere to go. Screaming as she strained the muscles of her stomach, Cambria shot her ankles upward like a loosed catapult. She caught Aggie alongside the head, knocking her sideways. Cambria groaned. Her stomach felt afire. But she'd gained a few precious seconds. While Aggie recovered her wits, Cambria got her legs under her enough to kneel.

Then Aggie slashed out in wild fury. Cambria bent forward to shield her vulnerable belly. The knife gashed her forehead. Once. Twice. Grazed her cheek. Aggie's mad spittle sprayed her face.

Cambria couldn't last much longer. Not with her hands bound behind her. Not without a weapon of any kind. She waited for Aggie to draw back for another strike. She gritted her teeth. Then she swung forward with her head as hard as she could, cracking it against Aggie's. Pain flashed through her temples and down her neck. Her ears buzzed. Her vision fractured into a million fragments. But the knife whistled past her, harmless.

When her sight returned, Aggie lay limp on the floor, the dagger deposited like an offering between them. Cambria had to work fast. Ignoring the complaints of her stomach, the sting of her shoulder, and the blood that threatened to seep into her eyes, she inched backward on her knees toward the knife.

The haft was slippery with blood and sweat. It kept sliding out of Cambria's fingers as she awkwardly sawed at the ropes binding her wrists behind her. She dropped it. Cursing under her breath, she groped blindly for it. She pricked her finger on the point. Then her left hand closed about it. Carefully she tried to transfer the dagger to her right hand. But it dropped again. Frantic now, she scrabbled her fingertips along the splintery floor, shoving a sliver under one of her nails.

A small moan sounded behind her. Aggie was rousing. Cambria had to get the knife. A sob of panic built in her throat. Her fingers grazed metal, drove it away, caught it again. She had the dagger in her hand.

Then Aggie collided with her, pushing her forward, hard. The cornerstone of the hearth rose up to pound against her forehead. The floor slammed into her, shoving her firm womb against her soft organs with the force of a huge iron ball shot from a thunder tube. She couldn't move. She couldn't breathe. But she still clenched the dagger tightly in her bound fists, holding on to it for dear life.

A strange squeal came from behind her. Aggie. Stretched out gracelessly atop Cambria's back, her bony frame trembling. Her fingers clawed at Cambria's shoulders, digging in a hopeless struggle. Her voice sounded parchment-thin as she gasped against the shell of Cambria's ear.

"Nay . . . nay."

Cambria shuddered. A thin stream of pink saliva hung from Aggie's lips, dropped to the floor. She closed her eyes against the sight. 'Twas too late. Cambria's dagger had found anchor. She loosened her fingers around the weapon. Aggie rolled weakly from her, sobbing once in bewilderment when she saw the blade buried deep in her breast and the spreading scarlet staining her kirtle.

Then, with pathetic determination, scraping and clawing her way, Aggie crawled forward, as if she could escape death's reach. 'Twas a painful eternity before the last rasping breath of life wheezed out from between her lips. When Cambria found the nerve to look, Aggie lay collapsed at her feet.

At last, as if Aggie's passing left room for a new soul on the earth, with a rush of warm liquid, Cambria felt the babe within her demand to be born.

Holden plunged forward, fording streams, whipping away branches, searching for the signs of the *H,* backtracking when they became too sparse. At last the marks led him to an overgrown hovel, a squalid, deserted place made nearly invisible with heavy vines.

Slowly he crept forward. Strange sounds came from the cottage, pathetic sounds that turned his brave soul to custard, sounds like an animal in heat—groaning, tortured noises. His heart pulsed in his throat as he slipped his sword from its sheath and neared the open door.

In the dim light, it was difficult to see what lay within. There was a shifting lump near the stone hearth that looked like a moving pile of laundry. It was from there that the noises came. Cautiously, he inched through the doorway. He could hear a panting, like the rough breathing of a wounded creature.

It was Cambria's familiar moan that pulled at his very soul, that human sound that rent his heart and made him drop his sword and his guard to go to her. Fear slammed into his chest. There was blood everywhere. Her whimpers were piteous, gut-wrenching. Dear God, he prayed, let her be unhurt! Let her live!

"Cambria," he called hoarsely, kneeling beside her.

The moaning ceased.

"Cambria!" he cried, reaching his hands out, yet afraid to make contact.

Her head whipped around, and he could see the shine of her wide eyes.

"Holden?" Her voice was weak.

Tears filled his eyes. He let them fall. "I am here now. You'll be safe. I swear it."

She groaned again.

He touched her cheek tentatively. "Oh, God, Cambria, what's been done to you?"

A sound eerily like a chuckle escaped Cambria, but it was

immediately wrenched from her mouth as another wave of pain seemed to overpower her. When she could speak again, she said rapidly, "Fetch a clean blanket, Holden, hurry."

Dear God, she was dying, he thought. But he didn't question her command. He would've brought her the moon. The best he could offer was his cloak.

"Now cut me loose," she gasped before pain rendered her speechless once more.

He swiped at his tear-blinded eyes and carefully severed the cords about her wrists and ankles. It was all his fault. If only he'd stayed with her . . .

Cambria chuffed breaths of air into the dark room, and Holden closed his eyes. Tears squeezed between his lashes and left burning trails down his cheeks. *Please, God,* he prayed, *don't let her die.* He was afraid to touch her, afraid of what mortal wound he would find. He cast his gaze away in despair, and it was then that he divined what the lump beside him was. He nearly fell back on his haunches as he recognized the ashen face of Sir Owen's slut, Agnes.

"She's dead," Cambria whispered. Then she moaned loud.

Christ's blood, her cries were driving him mad. He must do something. He wiped at his trembling mouth with the back of his hand.

"Cambria, we must get you home, to Blackhaugh, to the physician."

"Not . . . now."

"I'll carry you," he pleaded, reaching beneath her. God, her garments were drenched. "Cambria, if you lose any more blood . . ."

She barked out a little laugh. "'Tis not . . . blood."

Ah, God, Holden thought, she was delirious. He tried to move her.

"Nay!" she cried. "It comes! It comes!"

She clenched her fists and lifted her head from the floor. For an awful moment, he thought she'd seen the specter of death coming for her, that she was about to breathe her last. Her features contorted in a rictus that seemed part anguish and part ecstasy. Then his eyes adjusted to the low light of the room. He could make out Cambria's profile. She was as round as an overstuffed goose.

"You are not having . . . Holy Mother of God," he breathed, and for an irrational instant wondered how it could have happened. "You are not . . ."

"Not . . . for . . . long," she panted.

Reality hit him like a mallet. Cambria was not wounded. She was in the throes of labor.

Any other man would have been relieved. But dread ran icy fingers along Holden's spine. Nightmares of his own mother, screaming and writhing in agony as she succumbed to a bloody death, racked his mind. Cambria bore down, her body heaving with effort, and an overwhelming urge to flee consumed him. But he was immobilized by panic.

"You must . . . help . . ." she gasped.

Holden turned his head away in terror. He had done this to her. He had gotten her with child. He was fated to kill another kinswoman. "Ah, Christ!"

Suddenly Cambria's fists tangled in his tabard, and she yanked him down to her. "Listen, Englishman!" she hissed like an angry cat between gulps of air. "If you do not help me . . . I will tell your son . . . his father is an English coward."

Her threat brought him around faster than a hard slap. It wasn't what she said. It was the determination with which she said it. She had faith, even if he didn't. Together they would get through this. Sweet Mary, had he been gone so long he'd forgotten Cambria's stubbornness, her will, her tenacity? She was nothing like his pale, delicate mother. She was a Scotswoman, by God, a laird, a warrior. Cambria would battle heaven and hell to survive, if only to scoff at the weakness an Englishman had shown her. She would live, if only to boast about how she'd birthed her firstborn by herself in a humble cottage. And she'd gloat about the fact that he'd sat helplessly by.

Holden swallowed hard and pushed back the sleeves of his hauberk. He murmured a prayer and moved between Cambria's knees. If she could fight the battle, so could he.

He looked into her pain-glazed eyes and saw no fear, no

hesitation, only challenge and determination. God, the way he felt . . . He had to tell her. "I love you." His voice broke, and his hands trembled as he placed them upon her bloody thighs. But he told her.

"And I love you," she said between ragged gasps, giving him a brilliant smile.

The heir of de Ware and the next laird of Gavin was about to enter the world. He'd be damned if he'd desert his wife on the battlefield. And he'd be damned if he'd be excluded from this legendary birth.

epilogue

"Mama!"

Cambria could hear the wailing of her four-year-old nephew all the way across Blackhaugh's rise. She looked up from her sketches of armor designs and raised an inquisitive brow.

Linet clucked her tongue and tossed her long golden braid over her shoulder. She set aside the swatches of wool she'd been showing to Cambria and waited for her son to come crying into her skirts.

"Mama!" he called, his hand clenched to his eye and his chubby legs pumping through the grass. "Skye did it again!"

Cambria brought her hand up to her mouth, half in horror and half to cover her amusement. 'Twas good to have Holden's kin at Blackhaugh. But they'd been in Scotland a mere two days, and already it appeared Cambria's daughter had bested her cousin in a brawl for the third time. She looked to Linet in apology and set off to seek out her wayward child.

Skye was a handful, that was sure, as wild and unbiddable as . . . well, as *she* had once been. At least, so Malcolm the Steward oft complained. Still, Cambria frequently discovered the grumbling steward and his ubiquitous companion, Sir Guy, arguing the nuances of a certain maneuver of the sword while Skye aped them brilliantly.

Holden didn't seem to mind. Her abduction had convinced him of the merits of arming his women. In sooth, he'd taken to teaching them himself the finer points of defense.

He also had great plans for their two-year-old son, Angus, who was further up the hill at present, sleeping off a meal of porridge in his father's arms. Holden had already begun the little lad's training, giving him a wooden sword and carrying him proudly upon his destrier as he pointed out the best warriors in his company.

Ah, there was one of his best now, Cambria thought with a smile as she spied Skye leaping over a boulder to battle an oak stump. The wee brawler was certainly good for one thing, she had to admit—Skye tested Cambria's armor designs before they were forged for the knights. No warrior could have put chain mail and plate through a more thorough trial.

"Mama!" Skye cried as she spotted her mother. "I defeated that varlet, Sir Roland de Ware! I am the champion!"

Cambria forced her features into a frown, which was no easy feat. "And why were you battling your cousin?"

Skye pouted. "He said his papa could best my papa." She screwed up her forehead. "'Tisn't true, is it?"

Cambria let a grin slip onto her face. "Well, that will be determined on the morrow in the great tournament, Skye. But 'tis naught for the two of you to battle over. You know, not all disagreements need be settled with the fists and sword." She settled down onto the boulder and wrapped an arm around her mail-clad daughter. "Have I ever told you the story of how your father asked me to marry him?"

Holden shifted his sleepy son in his arms and examined more closely the monk's missive.

"I'll be damned," he whispered.

The monk flinched visibly at the oath.

"Well, well," his brother Duncan chimed in over his shoulder, his blue eyes sparkling as he perused the note. "It's high time, is it not?"

Then Duncan peered past him, and Holden followed his

gaze. Linet was waddling up the hill toward them, her flaxen-haired son clinging to her swollen belly.

"Ah, Linet, my love, there you are," Duncan beamed, holding his hand out to assist her. "I fear, my lady, I may have to delay besting this brother of mine in the lists. It seems we're needed back in England."

Linet absently stroked her belly, her soft green eyes dimming sadly. Holden knew she wanted Cambria by her side for the birth.

"We'll come along as well," Holden assured her.

"Roland!" Duncan shouted suddenly at the sight of his son, whose eye appeared to be turning an ugly shade of purple. "How came you by this, lad?"

"Skye did it!" the little boy cried in barely discernible words. "Skye said she was a knight and we were having a battle!"

Holden rolled his eyes and clenched his jaw. He had been hearing tales similar to this one for some six months now. More than half the castle children had injuries somehow related to Skye. It was beginning to be an embarrassment.

Duncan, however, only laughed and tapped at the document in his hand. "Well, it seems our littlest brother is in for a bit of fatherly woes himself!"

"Garth?" Linet asked.

"He's taking a wife. A matter of honor, it says here," Duncan said with a grin, gesturing to the missive.

"He is to be a father himself shortly," Holden said, running a sweaty hand through his hair. "And it appears he does not mean a *holy* father. He has summoned our entire retinue to come in all haste to his wedding."

"Garth?" Linet asked. "Married?"

She swatted little Roland on the bottom and sent him racing off into the arms of his favorite new friend, Sir Guy, who had appeared on the field.

"But Garth has been living in a monastery . . ." she argued.

Holden and Duncan exchanged knowing grins.

"He *is* a de Ware," Duncan explained.

Holden chuckled, disturbing his slumbering son, then jiggled the boy back to sleep. He was delighted that Garth was going to have a family. There was nothing quite so rewarding as a cherished wife and nothing as balancing as fatherhood. No glorious campaign, no accumulation of wealth, no victory in the tournament could please him so well as the piece of heaven he'd found in his family's embrace.

A silver flash across the field caught his eye. There were his precious jewels now—Cambria and Skye—bounding across the grass in twin coats of sparkling mail. His heart swelled at the sight of them. They were his beloved ladies, both as beautiful as Highland lochs, as bewitching as woodland sprites, as abandoned and carefree as Scotland herself.

He took a deep breath of fresh Gavin air and strode toward them to share the good news.

SEDUCTION ROMANCE

Prepare to be seduced…by the sexy new romance series from Jove!

Brand-new, full-length, one-night-stand-alone novels featuring the most seductive heroes in the history of love….

❑ **A HINT OF HEATHER**

by Rebecca Hagan Lee   0-515-12905-4

❑ **A ROGUE'S PLEASURE**

by Hope Tarr   0-515-12951-8

❑ **MY LORD PIRATE**

by Laura Renken   0-515-12984-4

All books $5.99